NOT FLESH NOR FEATHERS

CHERIE
PRIEST

NOT FLESH
NOR FEATHERS

❧

AN EDEN MOORE STORY

❧

TITAN BOOKS

NOT FLESH NOR FEATHERS
Print edition ISBN: 9780857687746
E-book edition ISBN: 9780857687890

Published by Titan Books
A division of Titan Publishing Group Ltd
144 Southwark Street, London SE1 0UP

First edition: October 2012
1 3 5 7 9 10 8 6 4 2
© 2007, 2012 by Cherie Priest. All rights reserved.

This edition published by arrangement with Tor Books,
an imprint of Tom Doherty Associates, LLC.

A CIP catalogue record for this title is available from the British Library.

Printed and bound in Great Britain by CPI Group Ltd.

What did you think of this book? We love to hear from our readers.
Please email us at: readerfeedback@titanemail.com,
or write to us at the above address.

To receive advance information, news, competitions, and exclusive offers online,
please sign up for the Titan newsletter on our website.

WWW.TITANBOOKS.COM

THIS ONE'S FOR MY HUSBAND, ARIC—BECAUSE THE
FLAMING ZOMBIES WERE HIS IDEA

1

WATER, WATER EVERYWHERE

The Tennessee River has swollen again, and nothing stops it. Not the locks or the dams. Not the TVA. I know that it was different once—that Chattanooga was a crossroads, alive and healthy; a place of promise and opportunity. But like all things left wet for too long, it warps. It rots. And now it would drown us all to keep us.

The great gorge fills, and the city sinks behind me.

In 1973 when the river last rose like this, my aunt Louise was fourteen years old and my mother Leslie was eleven. They lived on the north shore of the city, but this was back before the neighborhoods were renovated into quirky suburbia. There was no sprawling green park or blue-topped carousel with vintage-look horses.

On the very spot where the lion fountains spit water streams in the summer, there once was a closed-up armory. Like all things utilitarian and military, it was gray and smooth with no hint of ornamentation. It was a work building—a barn for the army's cast-off supplies, surrounded by a chain-link fence.

Lu said she never saw anyone come in or out of the place, and so far as the neighborhood kids knew, it was deserted—and therefore a target. This is a story I had to drag out of her throat, word by word.

She's never liked to talk about my mother.

By the time the girls reached the armory, it had stopped raining and the river lapped up against the rocky bank at the bottom of the short hill. The chain-link fence was twisted open in more than one place, and any of those holes was big enough to fit a teenaged girl through.

It was a neighborhood game: who could get inside fastest, who could find the coolest souvenir. Who could stay inside the longest without getting scared.

"It's empty," Lu assured her little sister. "There's nothing in there but a bunch of old equipment, and most of it's covered up. I don't know why you're so keen to get inside."

"Because you and Shelly went without me last week." Leslie sulked, peeling the fence back and holding it tight. "That's why."

Lu ducked underneath and took Leslie's hand to bring her through the hole. "If I'd known you'd make such a stink about it, I'd've brought you sooner. Now's not a good time. It could start raining again any minute, and things are flooding up."

"It's got to be now, while Momma's asleep. You were the dummy who got caught. If you hadn't got caught, we could go on Sunday."

"We could still go on Sunday if you really want."

Leslie sniffed. "Can *not*. You're grounded."

"Only so long as she knows where I'm at." Lu pointed up at a broken window. "That's the best way in. There's—" She cut herself off. A fat raindrop splashed down onto her cheek. "Jeez. Hurry up. It's starting again."

Though the girls looked much alike, Lu was the older, taller, and stronger of the pair. Her hair was knotted into black braids and her jeans were ratty around the knees, showing brown skin and scabs where she'd fallen one time too many. She put her shoulder against a sopping wet crate and shoved it hard. It inched its way to a spot beneath the window. "Hang on, it's high. I'll get another one so you can step up."

"No, I got it." Leslie hoisted herself onto the crate and poked at the broken bits of glass. She glanced down at her cut-off shorts and wished they reached farther down her legs.

"Don't touch those. Look. Someone reached inside and unlocked it." Lu pushed the frame and it scraped against the sill. "Hurry up and get inside. Aw, shit."

"That's a quarter for the swears jar."

"Not unless Momma hears me, it's not. Get in, and get your look around. We've got to be fast."

"Why?"

"Look at the river."

Leslie glanced over her shoulder, out to the south and to the bridges. "Wow. I've never seen it like that before. It's right at the edge of the building. Usually it stays down by the rocks."

"Yeah, it does. This is way too high, and I think it's getting higher. Look at that boat over there. It used to be tied down at the dock. Look where it is now."

"Whoa."

Lu shoved at her sister's bottom. "Go on. For real."

"I'm going. What are you, scared?"

"Not of anything inside, no. But I don't like the look of that water. It shouldn't be so high." Even as she spoke, gray waves knocked themselves against the south end of the old armory. They beat a slapdash time there, creeping up along the cinderblock walls.

Leslie's legs popped over the windowsill and she dropped herself down onto something below. "What's this?" Her voice echoed loud against the high, corrugated metal ceiling.

"I don't know. Something to step on. Climb on down, if you're going to. It's raining again out here, and I'm getting soaked. And the river… I don't like the look of it. It's too *full*. And…"

"And what?"

Lu murmured the rest. "And I don't think it's supposed to be that *color*."

"What?"

"It's always sort of gray and blue. Maybe it's just the clouds or something." Lu slung her leg past the broken glass and climbed inside to stand beside Leslie. Together they were perched atop another set of boxes, or possibly a large piece of machinery—it was something covered with a khaki-colored canvas that was thick like a tent.

Leslie stamped her feet. "It feels solid."

"It *is* solid. Look at all the footprints on this thing. We do this all the time. Come on down then, if you're coming. Let's get this over with. The river's rising, and Momma won't sleep forever."

"Shelly will cover for us."

"She'll try." Lu hopped down to the cement floor and brushed her hands off on her jeans. "But there's no telling if it'll work or not. I'm grounded, remember?"

"Forever and a day. Do you think she meant it?" Leslie stepped down beside her, and copied Lu's hand-wiping gesture.

Lu shrugged. "Probably. But that don't mean she can make it stick. Well, this is it. You happy now?"

"Yeah," she breathed. "I guess. It's dark in here. Did you bring a light?"

"No. It's still daytime. We don't need a light. Your eyes'll get used to it. Come on. I'll walk you through and then we'll leave and you won't make a big stink about it anymore. Deal?"

"The whole thing. I want to see everything you got to see with Shelly."

"Fine, yeah. The whole thing. But we're going to do it fast."

By then the rain was not so much falling as plummeting. Louder and louder it came down, and Leslie was right—it was dark inside, despite the afternoon hour. Within the disused armory, all the space was filled with veiled gear and shrouded military tackle. From floor to ceiling the ghostly monsters stood still and silent, lumpy and lame.

"What's underneath the sheets?" Leslie wanted to know, but Lu didn't know and nobody else did either.

"Stuff. Army stuff. Big machines and trucks. Boxes of junk. Most of those sheets are tied down, and it's too hard to pull them up."

"What? I can't hear you."

The rain was too much, the echo was too hearty. Water poured onto the old metal roof as if the river had overturned to empty itself. It drove so steady that the sound fuzzed out to a harsh white noise.

"Hurry up," Lu said, ignoring Leslie's request to repeat herself.

"We're going to have to ride our bikes home in this, aren't we?"

"It's only getting worse. This is stupid. Les, this is stupid."

"Not getting scared, are you?"

Lu looked back up at the window, and down at the floor.

"Les, the water's coming in. We've got to go."

"Shit," the younger girl whistled, lifting her sneaker up and splashing it back down.

"Quarter for the swears jar."

"Not if Momma doesn't hear it, right?"

They stared back and forth at each other, and held their breath while the sky dropped down outside. "Les. Let's go. It's not letting up. It's just getting worse."

"Can't get much worse."

Lu took Leslie's wrist and tugged her back towards the window. Leslie's token resistance was feeble. "We can't ride in this weather. Maybe if we wait it'll let up," she protested, but the water was climbing up her ankles, and the fight was leaving her.

The older girl reached the makeshift exit first and scaled the now-soaked tarp with a couple of well-placed footholds. She used her arm to shield her eyes from the blowing rain that gushed through the broken window.

Leslie prattled on below. "We're going to have to run for it. We'll have to walk the bikes and we're going to get wet in the rain."

"Jesus, Les," Lu said. "We're going to have to swim for it."

"What? Don't say that. It's just rain."

"No, it's not just rain."

"It *is* rain—I'm standing in it right now!"

"No, Les. It's the *river*."

More water squeezed through the cracks beneath the doors, and the tide crawled up past nervous ankles, past the hems of jeans, up along skinny shins. "Lu? Lu, I don't like this. Lu?"

"I don't like it either. Get out of that water. Get up here, now. Come on. You'll catch cold." She sent down one hand and Leslie grabbed it, pulling herself up.

"Let me see out the window."

"No. It's just water, but it's coming up fast and I bet we don't have bikes anymore anyway. They probably washed away by now."

"You're just trying to scare me," Leslie accused, but she didn't push past Lu to look outside. She reached down to her feet and squished her shoes to let out some of the water. She twisted the bottom of her jeans and wrung out more. "It's getting cold in here. And the water—where's it all coming from, *Lu*?"

"What? Be quiet, I'm trying to think."

"Lu, look at the floor. Lu, *look at the floor.*"

"I'm looking! I see it, okay? I see how the water's coming up."

A loud creak popped through the hideous white noise of the hammering rain.

Leslie jumped and scrambled higher, to stand just below her sister. "What was that?"

"How should I know? Stop it, you're panicking. Don't panic. It's just water. It's just water."

"It's a lot of water."

"But we're on top of all this stuff. We're real high up. It won't reach us. When it stops raining, it'll all run back down to the river, that's what it'll do. It can't rain forever. Maybe we'll even find our bikes. Maybe Momma won't kill us."

"You're going to be grounded until you're dead."

"Get on up here."

Leslie squeaked with alarm, and pointed back at the ground. "It's still getting higher!"

"Well it's not going to get as high as the roof or anything. There's—there's an attic, Shelly said. She went up there with a boy once, but don't tell her I told you about it."

"Which boy?"

"I don't know. One of 'em. Just, come on. We can climb across these, over to the other side—I think that's it, that's the attic door in the ceiling, see it?" They were both getting drenched, standing beside the open window. Lu took Leslie's face in her hand and directed it to a handle above them, across the armory space.

"I see it. Yeah. We can make that, can't we?"

"We can make it." But the water was rising still, filling up the spaces between the cloaked machines. A foot at a time it crawled the walls, so fast that if Lu picked a spot on the wall to stare at, she could count to ten and watch it disappear. At the window the rain was finding easy entry, and the river was waiting its turn.

"This is bad, isn't it?" Leslie fretted. She stood close to her sister and shivered.

"It's not *that* bad. Here. Stretch your legs, you can make that next stack—see? Just crawl and be careful. You won't fall. You go first. I'll help you."

"You go first."

"All right. We'll do it that way, then." Lu reached out one long arm and snagged the tightly fitted tarp on the next pile of junk over. By shifting her weight she closed the distance and grabbed a handful of canvas, using it to haul herself over. She extended her hand back to Leslie. "Here—come on. I'll pull you."

Leslie nodded and held out her hand. She let her sister heave her across, and when she arrived on the new spot, she clung to the heap and dug her fingers into its bulk. "Only one more, right?"

"Just one more. Then we'll be right under the attic, and I'll pull the door down so we can go up inside. It'll be drier there. We'll be safe for a long time. Long enough for the rain to stop and the water to go down, anyhow."

"Okay. Okay. Don't let go of my hand."

"I've got to for a second. The next one's closer, see?" Lu only leaned to reach the second stack of covered military detritus. She could span the gap between them if she stretched her legs apart, so she made herself a bridge and let the smaller girl scramble across her body. "Now give me your hand again."

She didn't need to ask twice. Leslie thrust her fingers into Lu's. "I'm getting scared."

"That's okay. This is kind of scary. But don't freak out on me. Freaking out only makes it worse." Lu reached for the metal latch above her head and gave it a good yank. The ceiling held, and groaned.

"You'll have to—Les, put your arms around my waist. Pick your feet up, yeah. Like that. I'm not heavy enough. Pick up your feet. There, that's it." Combined, their weight pulled against the springs and coils above, and the hatch reluctantly slumped down with a jerky flop. A ladder on a set of rollers followed it. Lu grabbed the bottom rung and pulled.

"It's dirty up there."

"It's dirty and *wet* down here. Go on. I'll hold the door down, you go up the steps."

"You go first."

"I can't. You're not heavy enough to hold the door down. Just go. I'm right behind you."

"You better not be fooling me."

"I'm not fooling you." Lu's arms shook as she held the door low enough for Leslie to scale. Beneath them, the water soaked its way up the veiled machines, rising foot by frightening foot. By Lu's estimation, if they'd stayed on the floor it would have been up to her little sister's waist; but she also knew that on the other side of the window, more water waited. The whole river was knocking, asking to come inside—and it had shown up quick on the doorstep. She'd sworn the flood wouldn't make it to the armory's old roof, but she wasn't as sure as she pretended.

Later she would learn that a dam somewhere up river had failed, and that's why the water had come so high, so fast. And later, it was easy to say that if she'd only known, she never would have brought her sister out to explore.

But back then, as the afternoon grew late and the sky went dark and the Tennessee River oozed up out of its bed, Lu could only work with the decisions she'd already made. She pushed at Leslie's feet, then scurried up after her.

With the weight of the girls removed, the door clapped itself shut into the floor behind them.

"It's dark up here," Leslie whispered, because big, dark places made her think of church.

"You said it was dark down *there*."

"Well, it's even *darker* up here."

"You'll get used to it."

The attic was as dirty as Leslie had declared, and darker than Lu was willing to admit. Rain noise was louder there too, since nothing but the thin metal roof separated the girls from the sky. Lu peeled off her sweater and wrapped it around Leslie, who was wetter and colder, or so it seemed. "Don't touch the pink stuff in the floor," she said, pointing to the half-finished floors. "It'll make you itch, or that's what Shelly said. It's insulation. Walk on the boards in between them, if you can."

"Okay." On shaky legs Leslie did as she was told, struggling to stand astride the beams that would hold her. "This sucks. We can balance up here above the itchy pink stuff, or balance down there above the water."

16

Lu lifted her voice to be heard above the battering rain. "The pink stuff is warm, at least, and it won't drown you if you sit in it too long. So I'll take the pink stuff, if it's all the same to you. Let's go back there—the floor's more covered. Less pink stuff to worry about."

Together they tiptoed across the wood planks and dodged curtains of cobwebs, Leslie going first with Lu's hands on her shoulders. If either of them had been any taller, they would've had to crouch. But as it was, both of them could lift their hands and brace themselves on the underside of the roof.

Leslie coughed and wiped at her face. "It smells gross up here."

Down by one of Lu's feet, curled in a pink, fluffy bed, the remains of a rat lay decomposing. "It's just… old stuff. Old places. They smell like this, after a while. Don't worry about it. Keep going."

When they reached the back corner they sat down, curling their arms and legs until they folded around themselves, and around each other. "I'm cold," Leslie complained, but Lu knew she was mostly just afraid and didn't want to say so.

"Yeah, it's chilly in here. But you'll warm up as you dry off."

Down came the rain and washed out all the other sounds except for the occasional cracking, creaking complaint of the old armory. But the armory was built to last. It would not fall, it would only fill.

Night settled in early because of the weather, and the rain kept coming.

Antsy and damp, the girls huddled close without speaking much. Once it was dark there was no sense in speaking. There was no reason to talk about heading home; the only real question was when to start shouting for help. The time hadn't come quite yet—there was a balance that must be tipped. Their fear of their mother had to be outweighed by their fear of being trapped, and for a long time the fear of their mother won out.

Lu also thought that if they stayed missing long enough, there might be a chance that parental relief would be great enough to overrule parental retribution. Her hopes weren't high, but she was running low on hope as the night dragged on, so she clung to what she could get.

Lulled by the violent downpour and its insistent beat on the metal roof, eventually the sisters dozed.

But they awoke with a jolt and grasped at each other's arms.

"What was that noise?" Leslie demanded, though she knew her sister didn't know any better than she did.

The noise sounded again and they were both awake enough to hear it clearly. It was something hard and knocking. Something dense and thick, with deliberate intent.

"Somebody's there?" Lu guessed. "I don't know. It sounds like…" She hesitated, listening hard.

There, again. Another blow. This one made their bottoms jump.

Leslie breathed faster. "Somebody's right underneath us. I think."

"Not somebody? Maybe something floating." Lu knew as soon as she said it that she shouldn't have.

"What? You think the water's got that high?" There was the panic again. "Floating up so high that it hits against the ceiling underneath us? You don't really think—"

Lu thought of the river outside the window, and how it boiled at the walls of the armory. She believed yes, that the water could get that high; and she figured that yes, something must be floating up to the ceiling in the hollow space below. But to say so meant that her sister must know it too; and though she was not such a nervous little sister as little sisters went, ten or twelve feet of water underfoot might be enough to send anybody into a fit.

But there wasn't much point in denying it. The banging continued faster, or maybe only in more places. Maybe it came from more than one—crate? Machine? At least that's what it sounded like to the girls, who crushed their bodies against each other, trying to be small, and trying to be blind.

Lu said she didn't really want to know. Leslie didn't either, and that was why she let Lu cover her eyes with a sleeve, even though there wasn't anything to see.

There was plenty to hear, from every direction all at once.

"What is that?" Leslie groaned again, her head buried in the crook of her sister's neck. It did not occur to either of them to call out for help. Whatever was bungling and bumping its way along the ceiling was not friendly, and it was not helpful.

"*Shhh*—" Lu told her, and she rocked her back and forth.

Pound, pound, pound went the noise until it was louder than the rain had ever gotten, though less rhythmic.

"Oh shit, Lu. You know what they are."

"Be *quiet*."

"They're *hands*, aren't they? Listen, do you hear them? Listen, Lu. They're hands. But they ain't alive anymore."

"Shush up. Stop talking."

Leslie lifted her head and narrowed her eyes. "I can hear them. Can't you? Don't you hear what they're trying to say?"

"No, and you can't either. Hush it, would you?" Lu tried to force her sister's head back down but Leslie wouldn't let it go.

"But that door is really heavy, ain't it? They won't be able to

AN EDEN MOORE STORY

pull it down, I don't think. Not unless the water gets higher, and, listen, it's stopped raining."

She was right. The sudden quiet threw into sharp relief the dull staccato beneath the floor where they sat.

"Be quiet, Les. For Jesus' sake, shut up. You want them to hear you?"

"Who cares?" she said, and the eerie, knowing glare she gave to Lu made her stomach knot and sink. "Can't you tell? They already know we're here."

But the door was heavy, and it held. And by the time the first hint of dawn came creeping down the Tennessee River gorge, the water was retreating its way back to the river's bed. Though they wouldn't open the attic door, the girls shouted out to police when they heard the sirens, and when the man with a megaphone called to them from a small, flat boat.

They were home by breakfast, but all of their mother's worry didn't keep the pair of them from being grounded indefinitely.

And late at night, while her little sister slept, Lu listened for the hammering of the searching hands. She never heard it again, but Leslie dreamed of it for weeks—whispering frantic prayers into her pillow between twilight and dawn.

Tell the burned-up man it was all a mistake. Tell him it was all a mistake.

2

OUR LORD AND SAVIOR

Christ Adams has a typo on his social security card. I've seen it, because he likes to flash it around, in case anyone disbelieves him—and a lot of people do. He's the most entertaining liar in town.

He slipped another cigarette out of the pack and pushed a lock of Day-Glo orange hair out of his face while he sucked the thing alight. We were sitting together down by the river, on the cement curbs that pass for seating along Ross's Landing. The pier's polished metal architecture gleamed in the sharp winter sun, but Christ wouldn't go near it. He wouldn't get any closer than the bank, where the terraced steps offered a fine view of the river.

"I'm taking a chance coming this close. We both are. And so are those idiots over there, pushing strollers and fishing. I'd rather scoop my eyes out with a grapefruit spoon than sit so close to the water."

"It's a nice day to walk around down there," I sort of argued. "It's only a little chilly."

"It isn't chilly for January."

"It's chilly for *me*."

"Whatever, Eden." He chewed the filter end of his cigarette until it fit the yellowed groove between his teeth. He shook his head and pulled his jacket tighter around his shoulders. Christ was about my height, maybe five foot ten, but I probably outweighed him by twenty or thirty pounds. He had that lean, starved look to him that comes from lots of physical activity and not enough nutrition. His was a body built by nicotine, Waffle House, and artificial sweetener.

"Where's your skateboard?" I asked, only because I'd never before seen him without it.

He shrugged and twitched, as if the question annoyed him. "Busted. Same night as Pat went missing. I told you that part."

"No. You haven't told me anything yet. Since when is Pat missing?"

"Since the same night my board got busted. Besides, if I had it, the cops would've thrown me out as soon as we sat down. Some bullshit about defacing the steps. But it's not our boards that tear up the steps. I don't care what they say."

I stretched out and crossed my feet, leaning back and pulling my sunglasses down off the top of my head. "There's not much arguing about the graffiti, though."

"That's just protest. Freedom of speech. If the cops at the landing would leave us alone—"

"Then you'd find some other place to make trouble. Look, man—not today. Just say your piece and let me move along. I've made nice. I put down my paper and left my window seat because you *had* to have a word. Well, have it."

"All right. You want the fifty-cent version? Here it is: you'd be a goddamn madwoman to move into those apartments over there." Christ pointed across the river to the north shore, where a low-cut skyline was developing beside the river.

"What the hell? First Lu, now you. What's wrong with them? They're beautiful, they're almost finished, and I've already put down my deposit, thank you very much. I'm moving in on the first of next month."

He cocked his head and took a long drag. "Lu—that's your aunt? Hell, if I were her I'd be damned happy to have you out of the house at long last."

"She and Dave have been hinting hard for a couple of years now, nudging me towards getting my own place. But now that I've finally taken them up on it, all they do is argue with me about the location."

"What's their problem with it?"

"Lu says it's too close to the river—that when the river floods it'll be a muddy mess down there. But hell, the whole city clusters up against the river, or at least all the good stuff. You'd have to go all the way back to the ridges to get away from it, and that's probably a couple of miles. Anyway, that's what TVA is for, isn't it? To keep the river where it's supposed to be? And I'll get renter's insurance. I'll be fine."

He waved the cigarette at me with one hand and buttoned his jacket shut with the other. "She's right. It's too close to the river. I'd be worried about that too, if I were you."

"Why? What's so scary about the river?"

With a deep breath and a pensive squint, he answered, "It's like being afraid of the dark, I think. I mean, you're not really afraid of the *dark*—you're afraid of the things *in* the dark. That's what being afraid of the river is like. That's what I'm trying to say."

I whacked him with my sunglasses. "So you're afraid of driftwood and fish, pretty much?"

"The fish in this river? Hell, yeah, they scare me. Haven't you seen the signs?"

"I've seen them." I nodded. They're posted at regular intervals along the banks, warning people who fish there not to eat more than one of their catch a week because of the pollution levels.

He dropped his voice and crawled to a crouch in order to bring his face closer to mine. "You know it's not the fish, Eden. You know it isn't, as sure as I do. You've *got* to know it too."

"Jesus, Christ. Settle down." I pushed him back to a seated position and withdrew, trying to re-establish some personal space. He's not a scary guy, not really—not for someone thirty years old who still wears anarchy symbols stitched to his clothes. But I'd never seen him quite so agitated. "What's going on out here that's got you so wound up?"

"It's not on the news—not yet—but it will be, soon. The wrong people have been going missing, so no, it's not on the news yet. But one of these days, one way or another, the right people are going to disappear. And then those fascist media overlords will stand up and take notice."

"Backtrack for me, please. What are we talking about?"

"People are *dying*, Eden. Down by the river. Something is taking them, one at a time, here and there. Two skater kids last week. A couple of bums this week. So far, it's just nobodies like me. But the things in the river are getting bolder, or stronger. They're coming out earlier and earlier, not just in the middle of the night anymore."

"All right, I'll bite—'they' *who*?"

He picked at his shoe, the one held together with duct tape.

"Don't know. If you see them, it's too late. But they come up out of the water, I know that much. And don't let the cops tell you that their stupid little community service campaigns are what's keeping the kids off the landing. That's bullshit. They're staying away because their friends are dying."

"Man, maybe they're just… leaving. People leave here in droves. Hell, you've left more times than I can count. Where was it last time, California?"

"San Francisco. But I came *back*. These guys won't be back. And it doesn't matter. Not yet. Nobody important enough has been taken for the city to stand up and wonder what's going on."

His pack of cigarettes slid off his knee and I picked it up, tapping one loose and feeding it to him as if it might calm him down. He lit it off the edge of the one that was nearly smoked down to nothing and gulped down a chest full of tobacco, but it didn't soothe him any.

"It won't be me, either," he grumbled, tweaking his lips around the Camel. "Even if they get me, it won't be *my* mangled corpse that raises the alarm. Nobody cares if I go. It'll have to be someone else."

"Okay, I think that's just about all the cryptic I've got patience for today, and I'm already full-up on crazy." I stood and dusted off the seat of my jeans.

He reached out to grab my arm. I thought I ducked fast enough, but he caught my wrist. "Don't move in there. People are dying, Eden. Not people you'd know, but one of these days a body's going to float up that no one can zip into a bag and forget."

"Let go of me, Christ, for real. I don't know what you're trying to do here—"

He did as I told him, and put his hands on his head as if it

25

hurt him. "I don't either. I just wanted to tell you, and see if you got it. I wanted to see if you understood, but I guess you don't, or you don't care."

"Don't be like that."

"Fuck you," he said, but I didn't hear any real malice in it. He only sounded tired. "Maybe it'll be *you* they pull out of the water. Maybe you'll be the one who makes it an issue. Everybody knows who *you* are."

I picked up my bag and the to-go cup of coffee I'd brought from Greyfriar's. "Don't remind me."

"You're famous. You're *famous*," he chanted in an annoying sing-song. "You're famous, you bitch. You can wear all the thrift store shirts you can buy, but you're not like us. Go find somewhere *else* to hang out if you're not going to notice."

I turned away.

It was just Christ. He pulled tantrums like that all the time, like a giant overgrown kid. If he couldn't get the attention he wanted, then any attention would do. "Switch to decaf, Christ. Come back when you want to talk like a civilized grown-up."

"Is that all you've got? Hey—" He stopped short, like he'd thought of something important. He scrambled up to me and held out his hands. "Hey, okay—try this, then. You know that homeless guy, everyone called him Catfood Dude because he smelled like cat food?"

I thought about it for a second, then nodded. "Hangs around at the food court at the mall, and at the bus stop by the ChooChoo. Always wears that jumpsuit, even in the dead of summer."

"You won't be seeing him anymore. He's gone now, and I don't mean he hopped a Greyhound for Atlanta. He's dead. *Taken*, like the rest of them."

"I saw him just the other day, in front of the pizza place by Greyfriar's—on that bench where he always is. I don't believe for a second that he's really gone anywhere. Tell me something useful, or let me go. I've got things to do today other than hang around and listen to you spinning yarn."

"He went down by the river, walking last night. One of my boys saw him there, and heard some commotion. Heard some splashing. And this morning? Freddie found that cap that he wears, washed up by the fountains at the bridge. There was blood on it."

"Oh good *grief*, there's no way for you to know that any of that's true. It washed up? With blood still on it? I don't buy that for a second."

"There was hair stuck in it too—and gray shit that looked like fish meat, but was probably brains!"

"And… I think we're done here." Next he'd tell me about a still-beating heart found at the bottom of the wading pool at the aquarium fountain next door. I didn't believe him because I had no reason to. He'd say anything at all if it'd lift your eyebrows.

"Benny's wrong about you," he shouted behind me. "You're not cool. You're just another self-centered, trust-fund hippie-tart from the mountain!"

I glanced over my shoulder. "Write that one into your next slam poem. It's not bad."

He dropped his outdoor voice immediately. "Hey thanks, I will. And if you see Jamie, tell him I'm looking for him."

"I'll do that," I promised.

I climbed up the grassy hill past the stairs and stepped into the street. You can't get mad at Christ, because that means he wins. You can only beat him by absorbing it all and telling him he's doing a good job. That's how deep his insecurity goes—all the way to the bottom. The worst thing you can do to throw him off is to pay him a compliment.

That afternoon was the second time he'd tried to sit me down and tell me something, but there's only so much rope you can give him before he tries to hang you with it.

I'd learned—partly from experience, and partly from our mutual pal Benny Scott—that it was best to treat him like a kid who refuses to eat. Leave him alone. When he gets hungry enough, he'll eat. If Christ wasn't full of it and he really had something to tell me, he'd get around to it eventually, and if I waited him out long enough he'd strip away all the crazy stuff first.

This was just build-up. Foreplay. Or, as I was coming to think of it—time wasting.

True, I hadn't seen Pat skating around lately and I hadn't seen Catfood Dude since the day before last, but that wasn't so unusual. The skater crowd is nomadic and fluid at best, transient at worst. Every now and again someone will vanish for a year or two, and no one will notice until he shows back up again with stories about having moved to New Jersey. Or Boston. Or Atlanta. Or wherever.

In the wake of those who leave, an elaborate mythos might rise up. Stories leak out like fairy tales, as if every place else is some weird, faraway fantasy land. Some of them are kidnapped, some begin flash-in-the-pan music careers, some turn to crime. Some of them go on to have great adventures, a few of which might even be true.

But the point is, they always come back. They all do, whether they want to or not.

3

THE WHITE LADY

I walked towards the coffeehouse but changed my mind halfway there and went back to my car instead. The Death Nugget was parked on the street in front of a fast-food Mexican chain. I climbed inside and checked my cell phone, which I'd left in the glove box.

No surprises there. Harry, my old friend and partner in crime, had called, but I knew what that was about, so I didn't check the voicemail right away. He'd be in town next week, and if all went according to plan, he'd have my half-brother Malachi with him. This was possibly one of my dumber plans, but now that I had put it into motion I was a little anxious about how it was all going to go down—which was the real reason I didn't check the voicemail. I didn't want to deal with it.

It's been almost three years since I first met Harry, and a bit less than that since I came to know Malachi as someone other than "that guy who tries to kill me every ten years or so." It would take ages to explain how I've come to terms with such bizarreness, but it's worked itself out to a balance.

The question was, would my beloved aunt and uncle see it that way? Could they get past the fact that he had tried to kill me and get used to the idea that we were trying to be friends?

I doubted it, but in the interest of growing up, moving out, and becoming a proper adult before my twenties were completely behind me, it was time for me to let them know what was going on. I was still working out the finer details of how I was going to break it to them, but that was half the fun of procrastinating and denial.

Unfortunately, this would be an especially tough sell when they were already pissed at me about the apartment. What I really didn't understand—and couldn't figure out—was what everyone thought was so wrong with the North Shore Apartments. I'd been inside them, and I could say firsthand that they were *fabulous*.

They weren't very big, but that meant they were surprisingly affordable for such prime real estate. And they were gorgeous, with high ceilings, bright white walls, lots of windows and a neat little bar area off the kitchen. Best of all, they were just over the river and down the hill from UTC, where I'd freshly re-enrolled. Come summer, I would begin my quest to finish at least one of my incomplete college degrees.

The apartments were down the street from Coolidge Park, with its lion fountains and its big carousel. They weren't far from the mountain, and they weren't in the ghetto. And on a nice day, I could walk to class if I wanted to. What's not to like?

Of course, none of these selling points had made a dent in Lu's displeasure. She wouldn't say why, other than that she thought the location was horrible and that I should move up farther away from the river. Even Dave was surprised by her reaction, so I didn't feel quite so crazy. He agreed that they seemed ideal, and when he sided with me, it only made Lu more flustered.

I'd ended up leaving the house and heading downtown just to get away from the whole situation. Maybe Dave could talk some sense into her, or at least drag some sense out of her. I couldn't imagine what had made her so crazy when I mentioned the north shore. You would've thought I'd told her I was bringing Malachi over for dinner.

The thought made my head hurt, but it was hard to get away from. The big meeting was only a few days away. I still hadn't decided whether or not to surprise them outright or warn them beforehand. I was leaning towards an advance warning, for Malachi's personal safety.

But it didn't have to be a lot of advance notice, I didn't think. It could be put for off a little while yet.

My phone began to ring again, and upon checking the display I answered it.

"You coming?" Nick Alders asked, without offering any introductory pleasantries.

"I'll be there in a few minutes."

"You're late already."

"I got sidetracked," I said, starting my car and pulling into traffic. "I'm on my way now, so don't get fussy. This probably won't work anyway, so I hope you aren't hanging your entire journalistic career on it."

The reporter didn't sound too concerned. "It's just a filler piece, but it might make a good one."

"It would've been better around Halloween, don't you think?"

"Yeah, well. The Read House wasn't having problems back around Halloween. You've said it before yourself—the dead don't give a shit about the calendar or the clock."

"They certainly don't seem to," I agreed. "I wonder what's got the Lady in White's panties in a bunch."

"It would be nice if you could shed some light on the subject. Soon. Because I haven't got all day. Which is why I said three o'clock, and not three thirty."

"Knock it off, Nick. I'm practically there already. If you're really pressed for time, you ought to pick another day to do this. There aren't any guarantees, and it may take more than a minute."

"I know, I know. Just get here soon. I'm up on the mezzanine level. *Waiting.*"

I hung up on him.

He was an impatient bastard, but I tried to keep in mind that he worked with very strict deadlines for a living. He'd moved here from up north—from a Midwestern NBC affiliate to our local Tennessee one. There were rumors that naughty conduct had prompted him to seek professional asylum in Chattanooga, but it was hard to prove and I didn't really care, so I hadn't asked.

I first met Nick a year ago, when Old Green Eyes had wandered off from his post at the Chickamauga battlefield. Nick was both a help and a hindrance down there in Georgia, but in the end he worked out to be more useful than useless, so I chatted with him when I saw him around town.

This wasn't to say we were friends or anything.

I'd agreed to meet him that afternoon because he wanted some unofficial assistance with a story. Mostly I was curious, partly I was bored, and partly I wanted to be distracted from my upcoming family meeting.

Besides, it was the Lady in White. Granted, that's not the most original name for a ghost, but this one was almost as famous as Old Green Eyes, the quiet, elusive battlefield ghoul.

To tell the truth, I'd very much doubted that she existed at all—at least until recently. Stories about the mysterious lady sounded entirely too made-up. According to local lore, she wandered the second and third floors of the historic hotel, crying piteously and vanishing spookily. There were thousands like her, woven into the history of old buildings across the globe. Often she's a spurned bride, a widow, or a scorned lover. Usually she's upset about a man.

I'd long suspected it was a tourist thing, something contrived to lure in curious travelers.

But then I saw it happening, the same thing that always happens when a nervous rumor becomes a real fear: people began leaving. First the housekeeping staff refused to clean a certain room. Then they avoided an entire wing, then an entire floor.

Soon the repair people began refusing to fix the strange damage in that first tainted room. A light fixture here, a curtain rod there. A busted marble-top vanity. A hole in the wall. It didn't matter if they got fixed, anyway: other acts of vandalism would soon undo the careful repairs.

Before long, the people who were paying to rent the room began leaving, too—in the middle of the night, without pausing to seek a refund. Sometimes without collecting their belongings, or without being fully dressed. They left without looking back.

Though it would seem that at least one traveler had made a phone call to the front desk after taking his leave. He wasn't a superstitious man, or so he told the concierge. He wasn't an overly imaginative man either, but there was something awful in that room and he thought they should speak with a priest.

Instead, the hotel management simply quit allowing visitors to stay in room 236.

But the awfulness spread—from the room, to the hall, to the floor.

To the whole building. And then to the media.

To Nick.

I parked down at the end of the block, across the street from the Read House hotel. It's a ten-story brick affair, built in the 1920s to replace an earlier structure that burned. Part of this one burned too, years ago, but it's been rebuilt and joined by a parking garage. But I didn't have any cash on me except for a handful of change, so I fed the meter rather than keep my car close.

Inside, the hotel is made of mirrors and brass, with shiny marble floors for my heels to click against. The ceilings are high and the carpets are patterned with a baroque kind of lushness that wouldn't look right anyplace at all except in the corridors of a fancy old hotel.

In short, a ghost was all it needed to become a perfect cliché of vintage southern hospitality.

I'd made Nick promise not to bring a camera crew, and I was pleased to see he'd behaved himself. This wasn't an exposé. It was just an investigation—an attempt to see if I could give him anything to work with. Nick wanted a name, or a motive, or an excuse. He wanted a historical figure to hang this ghost story on, so he'd have something to take to the network in a tidy, three-minute package.

I met him up on the mezzanine, where he was lounging on one of the big pseudo-Victorian couches. A bright chandelier loomed above him, bathing the area in sparkling brightness.

He grinned at me and rose, opening his arms in a gesture that encompassed the entire floor. "What do you think? Spooky, or what?"

I smiled back at him, because I didn't really have a choice. His

TV face is contagious when he turns it on and lights it up. "*Or what*, at the moment. It's tough to get a good chill going before suppertime."

"That's no way to get into the spirit of things," he cheerily fussed. With one hand he lifted a satchel off the couch and slung it over his shoulder. I was happy to see that he wasn't in "about to go live" mode. His hair wasn't sprayed into immobility, he hadn't bothered with a suit, and, to my astonishment, the man was wearing jeans. I would've sworn he didn't own any.

"I have to say, I think this is a good look for you. Less…" I looked for a word, and found it. "Smarmy."

"You think? Damn. I should've worn a suit. I didn't mean to put you at ease or anything."

"Then consider your day a failure and brief me already. What's the story? Or, should I say, what's the scoop?"

"There's no scoop, yet—not past what you already know. Weird shit keeps happening, and the hotel's new owners are freaking out. The long and short of it is that room 236 would prefer to remain unoccupied." He pulled a digital voice recorder out of his pocket and held it out to me. "We need one of these, right? Isn't this what you used when you worked with Dana Marshall?"

I shrugged. "Can't hurt. Might help. Probably won't be necessary. And what do you mean 'new owners'? I thought this place was family-owned or something."

He cocked an elbow towards a bit of repair scaffolding at the end of the hall. A major chain logo was emblazoned on the side. "It's been bought out. Back in November. That's why all this renovating is underway—they're going to revamp the place and set up a storefront down on the first floor. They've already gotten the Starbucks open and ready for business."

"I know, it's revolting. And right down the street from Greyfriar's, too."

"Hey, I *like* Starbucks."

"Philistine." I glanced around and noticed, for the first time, that there were corners marked off with construction signs, and an elevator door with an "Out of Service" notice across it. "I don't know. Maybe the old place needs a facelift. Maybe the previous owners couldn't afford it."

"Maybe. But I bet you a five-dollar espresso beverage that that's not the reason they sold the place."

"You're thinking they couldn't handle the ghost."

"Precisely. Half their night staff has walked out and the other half demanded hearty raises for hazard pay. According to the day manager, the big chains had been circling like sharks for a while anyway, making offers, courting the family—hoping to pick the place up. It's on the historic registry now, and with a little spit and polish, the big boys could turn this into a five-star affair."

I guessed the rest. "And when the owners changed their minds about keeping it in the family, it didn't take any time at all to find a corporate sucker with deep pockets to take it off their hands. Have you talked to the old owners?"

"I tried. They weren't feeling very forthcoming."

"That figures." We stood there for a minute, looking and listening around. Seeing and hearing nothing. "This is just a fact-finding mission, right?" I asked, noting the room number nearest me and assuming we must be close to the troublesome quarters.

"Sure," he agreed, tapping his fingers at the recorder I was still holding. "But wouldn't it be nice if we found some spooky facts and got them on tape? Wouldn't that make for a marvelous addition to the story?"

"You don't really think they'd let you run it, do you? They'd get letters, I'm sure. We can't have our local affiliates promoting the occult, inviting the presence of Satan and all that jazz."

"You can't be serious."

I smiled while I fiddled with the recorder. "Oh yeah, that's right. You're not from around here, are you?"

"No, thank God. But Chattanooga residential temperament is neither here nor there. If this turns out well enough, I can always take a stab at going to the network. I'll just label it a human interest piece and see who bites."

"Or 'post-human interest,' as the case may be." The recorder he'd handed me was an expensive model with plastic wrap still clinging to it. I picked off the leftover packaging and flipped it on. "Just so you know, this might not get you anywhere. It might not turn up anything at all. Even if the room *is* haunted, ghosts don't always feel very talkative."

"Why else would they act up, though, if they didn't want to communicate?"

"Any number of reasons. From what you've given me so far, I think maybe this one wants to be left alone. Maybe the remodeling is making her crazy. The dead are like cats, in my experience. They don't like change. You start messing with their familiar surroundings and they get antsy."

"But this one started acting up before the buyout and the construction."

"Maybe I'm wrong then. I don't know."

He pointed down one of the wide corridors and jutted his chin towards a door. "That's it. Room 236. Go take a stab at finding out. Uh—is there anything I need to do? Should I come with you? Stay out here?"

"Stay out here. I probably won't be long. If there's something in there and it wants to talk, great. If not, you're out of luck."

"Try to get me a name, or something I can check out on the Internet, or through genealogy records. Maybe we'll turn up a grisly murder."

"Yeah, wouldn't that be great?" I said, but he didn't seem to get that I was joking.

"Hell yes it would. If she bleeds, she leads. Even if she bled out a hundred years ago. People eat this stuff up."

"Your selfless pursuit of justice does you credit."

"They're going to give me a Nobel any day now, I can feel it. But I'd settle for a Pulitzer."

"I bet you would." I checked that the digital recorder was on, and then I took the card key.

"Feel free to chat into the mic yourself. Share your impressions of the room, the things you see. The stuff you hear. By all means sound a little panicky if you want. People dig panic."

I slipped the card key into the slot lock and a green light appeared, letting me know that it was open. "Sure. And while I'm at it, I'll slip into something flimsy and investigate a strange sound in the basement. Would that work for you?"

"Like a *charm*."

"Stay put," I told him. "I'll be back out in a few minutes. Keep quiet, and don't knock or anything."

"What if you need help?"

"I don't see that happening. Shut up and wait."

I slipped inside and let the door slide close behind me with a hydraulic click. Within the room it was fairly dark, but afternoon sun oozed around the edges of the thick tapestry curtains.

I went to the window and found the long white rod and

pulled it to the right, drawing the curtains and their thick shade liner aside.

Thick puffs of dust accompanied the swishing of the curtains, and when the daylight poured in I saw that yes, it had been a while since the place was cleaned. With two fingers I swiped a shiny trail in the finish of the nightstand.

The bed was covered with a floral print spread, laid out in shades of green, maroon, and cream. A sturdy, cherry-stained headboard was fastened to the wall, and a large armoire held a television. I didn't see a remote control. There was a coffeemaker, though, and an empty ice bucket beside the vanity sink.

"Hello?" I asked the room. "Anybody here?"

I don't go in for too much formality, because in my experience it doesn't help much. More often than not, the trigger is something simpler—something obscure and important that you'd never think about in a million years, anyway. You may as well wing it.

I tried a mental rundown of all the things a maid might disturb.

I pictured a big cart, laden with towels and shampoo samples. I imagined a vacuum. Dust rags. When would it begin? What would rouse the Lady in White?

"Anybody?" The red light on the recorder shined an electric thumbs-up that said all was well and ready. "Can anyone hear me? Would anyone like to come out and talk? Or is the staff here completely bananas?"

I muttered that last part.

A tiny electric shock zapped my hand, and I dropped the recorder. I shook my hand to chase the prickling sensation away, and bent over to retrieve Nick's little toy.

Then the television sparked too, over on my left. It gave a halfhearted spit of electricity, sending a bright line across the center of the screen. Then the screen went dark again, except for the square reflection of the big open window.

I saw a pattern there, on the screen. It was illuminated by the slanting sun.

I left the recorder where I'd dropped it and approached the TV. I knelt before it and angled my head to best see the dusty residue in full relief.

"Now we're talking," I breathed. "You are here, aren't you? You can come out if you want. I'm not afraid of you. I'll listen if you've got something you'd like to say. I'm good at passing messages around."

Pressed into the dust on the screen was a flattened imprint. "Is this you?" I asked, sneaking my fingertip up along the gray glass. "Is this your face? Did you put this here?"

Very clearly I saw it, and the closer I looked the more details became apparent. A cheek was pushed into the set, with an open mouth, and a closed eye. Along the edges of the eye I spied faint feathering, where lashes had brushed themselves against the dirty monitor.

The face was hard to read, since I could see only the half impression. It might have been angry, or sad. Or frightened.

A quick tickle of movement caught my eye. Something flickered through the window's reflection, but it moved too fast to watch, to register what it was. It might have been an arm, or a sleeve. Something that waves, or directs, or hits.

But when I looked away from the screen there was nothing there in the gold patch of light beside the bed.

No matter how hard I squinted I couldn't make anything out of it, not any proper shape or message. Only… if I used my imagination, I might have said that there was a place in the beam where the dust didn't swirl or float. There may have been a blank spot, where the air was clear. If I thought about it. If I was looking for something to see.

"You're going to have to do better than that," I told the mostly unseen presence. "You'll have to be more direct. I want you to know, I'm not here to cast you out or anything. I'm not here on God's behalf, or for anyone who'd try and make you leave. You can stay, go, or wreak havoc. I don't care. I just want to know *why*. Maybe I can help you."

Over on my right, I thought I saw it again—that half-seen blip of motion, relegated to the farthest corner of my eye.

It was a mistake.

I stood up straight, having been crouched beside the TV up until that moment. "What was a mistake? Hey, I heard that. Come on, come out. Let's talk."

She didn't answer right away, and didn't come forward.

"I'm Eden," I told her. "Who are you? Is there something you want? Something I can help you with? I'm here to listen, if you want to talk."

It was a mistake.

"What was a mistake? What happened?"

A loud popping noise startled me. It took me a moment to figure out where it was coming from—the curtains. Up at the top of the rod, one of the circular wooden rings broke and the end of the curtain sagged. Then another did the same. And one more, right next to it. The curtain began to fall.

"Do you want the curtains open? I can open them for you. Do you want more light? Is that it?"

Let it burn.

"Let what burn?"

The Klan will burn it. All of it.

The curtain was nearly on the floor, now hanging from just two small rings. These also broke and dropped, and the window was exposed. "All of what?"

All of us.

"Did—did you burn? I know there were fires here." There were at least two—one when the first hotel burned down a hundred years ago, and another when the new building nearly went up in smoke sometime more recently. "Did you die in a fire here?"

It would almost be too easy.

No.

"Okay. Then please, tell me your name. Tell me who you are."

She started to form, as if the question required more of her presence. She was pacing from one corner of the room to the other, holding up and dragging the curtains, tugging at the faucet handles. Bit by bit they began to turn.

Caroline.

"Caroline? Okay. Caroline." Nick would be delighted. "Caroline who?"

She wasn't really in white, I didn't think—but she had that light, faded look that spirits get when they're only half holding on anymore. By her clothes I thought she might have been from the 1930s; she was wearing a short-sleeved dress that stopped just past her knees, chunky-heeled shoes, and a small hat with a decorative bit of mesh. Her hair was ragged and she was wearing one gray glove, but missing the other.

She scratched at her wrist—the one without a glove covering it—and I wished I could see it better. I wondered what habit she'd had in life that made her keep up the gesture even after death.

But she wasn't solid enough to show me any details.

"Caroline," I tried again. "Do you know where you are? Do you know what's happened?"

Read, she said, in an offhand sort of way that implied she was barely answering me, or not paying attention. I wasn't sure how well the Q&A was going to go, if she was this distracted and confused.

I tried to encourage her, to keep her talking. "That's right, you're in the Read House. The hotel is being remodeled. Did you know that?"

The hotel. Again she spoke with her voice and her eyes in different places.

Since the events with Old Green Eyes, I'd spent a great deal of time on the phone and on the Internet with Dana Marshall, who chased ghosts professionally for a big cable TV station. She'd taught me a lot. I was learning to categorize the dead people I encountered, which was useful because it gave me a better idea of what to expect from them.

Before Dana and her methodical approach to the supernatural, I'd always walked into these situations freeform. I approached every strange event with an attitude of, "Hey, I'm here and ghosts talk to me. Let's get this party started." But it didn't always work very well, and I never knew why.

Come to find out, it's because there are different kinds of hauntings—with ghosts that show varying degrees of sentience. Dana had it all worked out, with charts and everything; but I still preferred to take a more casual approach when I could get away with it.

I assumed, based on the general unresponsive nature of Caroline, that she fell into the popular "barely there" category.

More often than not, these are the legendary dead who routinely follow some habitual path. They walk the afterlife in a loop of practice, no longer remembering much about what they're doing or why they're doing it. In time, most of them fade away to wherever it is they go, having completely forgotten why they stayed in the first place. Sometimes they need help, but more often they refuse it. Occasionally they're too far gone to accept it.

The vast majority of the hauntings Dana and her crew investigate for her TV shows fall into this camp, and I was afraid that Caroline did too. Maybe she'd only been seen more regularly because there were more people around.

It could be as simple as that.

Nick wouldn't like it, though. It wouldn't make much of a story. Oh well. Everything unexplained can't be a fascinating narrative. At best, most of it is charmingly mundane. Only at worst is it sinister, and therefore interesting.

But I tried again anyway. "Caroline, is there something you want? Something you're looking for here in the world of the living?"

She hovered there, not really looking at me. Scratching at her wrist.

"Do you even know you're dead?"

Burned. All of them. Burned them up. Blamed the flu.

Dana had told me about keywords, and how it was sometimes the only way to get them to speak. You had to find the keywords—the things they remembered enough to recollect. She told me to try repeating the ghosts' own phrases back to them, and to build on them gradually; so I gave that a shot.

"Burned? Who burned, Caroline?"

In the church.

44

"The church—not the hotel here? Then you're not talking about the Read House?"

In the church, she nodded. *The mistake.*

Outside the room I heard Nick pacing back and forth, gently kicking his foot against the bottom of the door. "How's it going in there?" he asked, impatient like a man waiting for his turn in the bathroom.

I ignored him. He might have another key, but I didn't think he'd try to follow me inside.

I hear them. Coming.

"No one's coming. That's just Nick. He won't come in, I asked him to stay out."

She was flustered, though. Restless—like she'd been reminded of something unpleasant, and now she couldn't forget it. I knew, though I didn't know why, that she wasn't talking about Nick. She didn't care about him; she probably didn't know about him.

Caroline looked directly at me, and she saw me this time instead of looking through me. Something about the nasty gleam in her eyes told me I'd have been better off otherwise.

You brought them here.

"Me? No. I didn't bring anyone here."

They're coming. You brought them.

"Who? Caroline, who? Work with me here." She came towards me, not slow, but not as fast as she could have. I backed away out of instinct or reflex. "Caroline, I didn't bring anyone. Just Nick, and, and, I didn't bring him. He brought me."

The TV armoire stopped me. I leaned against it.

She came up close, and she was angry. *It wasn't me, it was you!* It was an accusation, now. Not a suspicious guess.

Out, she breathed. She pushed the word against me, wanting to push herself, too. But ghosts so rarely have anything more than breath, if that. I wondered what she thought she'd do to back up the order.

"I only want to help."

Out!

She darted, flashed, and was gone. And the television beside me shattered.

My heart jumped; I moved too late. Gray glass sprayed across the room, grazing my cheek and scattering across the floor and the bed. The vanity mirror broke too—violently and with messy abandon, but into larger pieces than the TV screen. In the bathroom the shower curtain came toppling into the tub's interior, and the toilet lid beat itself up and down.

I couldn't see her, but she was everywhere. She tore the room with a whirlwind that shocked me; I'd never felt anything like it from the dead. At most, some of them would lift small things and leave small messages.

"Caroline!" I yelled, because the wind in the room was loud in my ears and it was only getting louder.

On the other side of the door I heard Nick again. He was knocking, beating. Wanting to know what was going on. Demanding that I let him in. Swearing. And if I heard right, there was someone else with him. I tugged at the door's latch-like knob but it wouldn't budge.

"Caroline, stop it!"

They are coming for me. They are coming for all of us.

"They who? Who's coming for you?"

Into the wind she sucked up the big shards of mirrored glass, and the missing television remote scooted along the carpet. Pillows peeled themselves forward and twisted in the sheets on the bed. The chandelier lamp rocked back and forth, back and forth, and dropped. It bounced when it hit the bed, but rolled and fell and tinkled into pieces when it hit the floor.

I didn't like the look of those shiny, long pieces of glass. I didn't like the way they started to swirl, picking up momentum as if they were being wound up like a pitch, to be thrown.

It was a mistake! I heard her shriek, though I still couldn't see her. It took away too much of her energy to manifest, and she had other uses for it. She would rather use it to terrorize me, and it was working.

When the first finger-wide slivers of mirror were flung, I ducked and they blasted themselves to dust on the wall behind me, and into the thick wood of the armoire.

"Caroline, this isn't funny. Let me out. I'm not here to—"

Another round of missiles went sweeping my way. One stuck in my hair, and another cut a slice in my sweater. "All right, you want me out. I'm leaving. I'm leaving right now, but you've got to let me go—"

Next she chose the remote. It hit me in the head.

I dug the card key out of my back pocket. "Okay lady, you're pissing me off. Knock it off, and I'll get out of your hair!"

But Caroline didn't care if I stayed or left, so long as she could hurt me.

A large painted picture was bolted to the wall above the bed, but it started to rock and I heard the brittle tearing sound of screws working their way free from plaster. The picture must have weighed fifty pounds, but what Caroline wanted, Caroline got. She rocked it free and when it crashed onto the bed it bounced immediately to the floor, and then to the window—which crunched under the weight of the frame.

"Don't—don't do that. Caroline, don't. Look. I'm leaving. I'm leaving."

I had the card key in my hand and I was retreating what few inches I could. Nick's recorder was still on the floor; I reached towards it with the toe of my boot and dragged it to my hand. As I bent to pick it up, something too heavy to be the TV remote clocked me on the head.

Stars like static blurred my vision, but I had the recorder in one hand and the card key was still in the other. I stumbled backwards, into the miniature hall in front of the door—beside the coat closet with the mirrored door.

But Caroline liked the mirrors.

As my eyesight fought to return, I saw the bottom half of a lamp beside me and I knew what she must have thrown. It rose again and I tripped over myself to move away from it.

"Nick!" I called out, not knowing how much he could hear, but wishing to God that he'd open the door. "*Nick!*"

He replied, but whatever he said, I couldn't make it out.

I only wanted her to stay. But it was my mistake.

"Who? Jesus H. Christ, Caroline—stop being so goddamned vague!"

Damned, she echoed. *All of us, burned up—just like him. Just like her.*

She lifted the lamp base again and, God, it was made of terracotta or painted plaster—something heavy and hurtful. She cast it forward into me. I was too close for it to bruise, but it knocked the wind out of me and it pushed me into that mirrored closet door.

I went through it, not cleanly. I pitched and fell, and the glass tinkled around me, dusting me with shining powder and pretty slivers that I'd pick out of my clothes for days.

I felt my skin tear with a dozen little carvings, on my arms and on my neck. Through a soft spot on my belly something pierced, and I shrieked. It didn't hurt as much as it looked like it should, but it hurt plenty bad. It went in clean, with a burning puncture like a big needle. When I pulled it out it was as long as my hand, and my hand was bleeding too. It was so horrifying I couldn't feel it properly; I couldn't think about it rationally. I could only drop the shard and stupidly shake my hand as if it were on fire.

I reached up to pull myself out of the closet and nearly grabbed more glass at the edge of the closet frame, or what remained of it. I pushed myself out instead, one hand against the back wall.

The door was right there, but the card key was slippery in my hand and Caroline was excited by the blood. She threw more glass and other objects—a soap dish, a complimentary bottle of lotion, and a roll of toilet paper—which weren't bad at all by comparison.

Back on the floor, on hands and knees that were collecting splinters, I pushed the card key underneath the door. Within a couple of seconds, I heard the whooshing click of the electronic lock. The door opened into the room and caught me on the shoulder, but at least it was open.

And the moment it opened, the wild microcosm of paranormal misery calmed. Completely ceased, even as arms reached inside and dragged me out into the corridor.

Another man and a woman were there with Nick. Both of them were wearing uniforms that implied they worked at the hotel, and both of them gazed down at me as if they couldn't decide whether to help me out or smack me.

I didn't care. I was thrilled silly to see them, and I told them so.

Nick didn't squeal like a little girl, but he looked like he wanted to. I was a mess, and I knew it.

"That room is off limits for a reason," the man in uniform griped.

Nick ignored him and started barking orders. "Shut the fuck up and call a doctor, or a nurse, or somebody—you've got to have somebody on staff here, right? Get somebody, she's a mess!"

I sat against the wall and tried to wave him quiet. "This isn't a school, Nick. And don't—please, whoever you are. Don't. I'm all right. It looks worse than it is."

"Eden, you're bleeding all over the place."

"Not so much, exactly." I didn't even have to check. I knew, because I could feel it. I knew the scrapes were mending, and the cuts both large and small were knitting themselves into smooth skin. But I hugged my sweater close across my stomach and chest. I didn't want him to see the one really bad wound, the one that was probably still leaking.

Warm wetness was seeping through my shirt and getting sticky. The sweater was black, though. Blood might not show too badly. I crossed my arms across my breasts and put my face down into my hands.

"Get a doctor," Nick repeated, but I shook my head and protested.

"No. No doctors. I'm all right, it's just a scratch. Some scratches. Gimme a pack of Band-Aids and some peroxide. I'll be fine."

"This is all my fault."

I couldn't argue with him there. "It sure is. I'm okay though. Rattled, but okay."

"Was it bad in there? You look terrible."

"It was bad, yeah. But it's not a big deal. It's not something to get all excited over. It was just…"

"What?" He asked it eagerly, but not too eagerly. He was trying to hold back until he was sure I was all right, but his curiosity was eating him alive. "What was it? Did you see her? Did she say anything? I heard you talking, but I didn't catch anything else. And then stuff started breaking. We heard *that*."

"Can you give me a minute?" I asked, bracing myself against the wall and pushing myself to a standing position. Nick tried to help, but I didn't let him. I didn't want him to touch me. I didn't want anyone to touch me, including the nervous-looking maid or her boss—if that's who he was.

"Give the lady some room," Nick ordered, even though the other two spectators had already done so.

"Is there a restroom I could use? Could you let me just—let me wash my hands and see the damage for myself."

"Down the hall on the left," the maid indicated.

"Thanks," I nodded, and with one hand holding on to the vintage papered walls, I drew myself towards the ladies' room. "Give me a minute. I'll only be a minute."

4

AFTER AVERY

"And how about a first-aid kit?" Nick demanded, but it wasn't aimed at me. He projected the suggestion the other way down the hall, and I suppose someone would either see about getting one or say they didn't have one.

I stumbled into the bathroom and it was empty, thank heaven. With a twist of my wrist I summoned steaming hot water from the tap and let it run while I pumped pearly white soap into my palm and lathered it up.

The mirror told me that Nick had been understating when he used the words "mess" and "terrible" to describe my appearance. I looked like hell.

I held my head over the basin and shook it, sending pixie-dust flakes of broken glass down the drain. They fell off my collar, and out of my hair. They sprang from my shirt when I pulled it away from my skin and flicked the fabric with my fingers. Fine lines of drying crimson crisscrossed my forehead and my left cheek. My hands stung when I held them under the faucet because they too were lacerated. But even as I ran the floral-smelling suds over my knuckles, even though it hurt in a sharp, medicinal way to feel the soap, the small cuts healed themselves.

It's been this way ever since the swamp—ever since I killed Avery. He was my grandfather, plus a couple of greats, and he was more wicked and old than any living human ought to be.

But that's the thing, I think. He wasn't human anymore. And whatever he was, he passed it on to me. He called it a curse.

For a long time, I didn't believe him. I almost forgot about it.

Then, after a while, I noticed that I'd stopped getting sick. Ever. And the little nicks, bumps, and bruises that came with being alive began to vanish as soon as I'd acquired them. Some curse, I thought. My health insurance premiums would plummet.

But there was more to it than that, of course. There always is.

I've always had a tendency to "see things," as it was euphemistically described when I was a kid. You write it off to imagination when you're young. You let people call it something else because you don't want to stand out too much. But it is what it is, and it does not care what you want.

After Avery it was different. After Avery, I saw the dead in all their states—I saw the ones who hung on hard and kept their forms, and the weaker ones too. I saw the ghosts that sensitive people perceive as chilly spots in stairways. I felt their chill and I spied them, too—huddled in their corners, looking at me with accusatory stares and sometimes holding out their hands.

When they know you can see them, they want your attention.

I shuddered. I hate mirrors. I picked more pieces of them out of my hair, and with my fingernail I dug a shard out of my thumb.

"How's it going in there?" Nick knocked on the bathroom door. He pushed it open an inch to call inside. "Everything all right? I've got a first-aid kit. They had one in the manager's office downstairs."

"I'm fine, Nick."

"A few Band-Aids never hurt anybody. That I know of," he added, still not closing the door, but not sidling around it either.

"I'll get them in a minute. Hang on, will you?"

"Do you need any help?"

"No."

"Do you have the recorder?"

"Yes. Thanks for caring."

"I just meant—"

I left the sink running but walked over to the door and kicked it closed.

I went back to the sink and ran my hands under the faucet stream some more. What the hell had happened in there, anyway? The first thing I always tell people who are nervous about a haunting is, "There's nothing they can do to hurt you." Truth was, I'd never heard of an ordinary ghost harming anyone, or even trying.

Poltergeists were something different, but no one knew what. And I was confident that Caroline was not one, though she certainly behaved as badly.

I pulled my sweater open and it stung. Drying blood wanted to hold everything closed. It wanted to keep me covered and sealed. But I lifted my long-sleeved black shirt and winced. The injury was writhing, the ends of the neatly sliced puncture wound reaching out for one another. It almost made me ill to watch.

"What is *wrong* with me?" I asked no one in particular.

I took a handful of paper towels and ran them under the steaming water. The heat didn't bother me; I liked the way it made my fingers tingle. It distracted me from the tickle at my belly.

I wrung them out and flipped them open to wipe, and wipe, and wipe. I threw them away. They sat at the top of the pile of trash in the aluminum bin, pink and red on brown paper. I took another few sheets and used them to cram the others down, out of sight and out of mind.

Under my shirt, the transformation was wrapping up. It still hurt like hell, but it wasn't so open-feeling and raw. When I flapped my shirt to breeze the damp skin, I didn't feel the air whistling into the wound.

I did feel light-headed, though. No wonder, with all the blood. Other people's doesn't make me squeamish, but seeing so much of my own displaced fluid made me want to close my eyes, so I did.

Nick knocked the door open again, this time ignoring propriety and strolling inside the bathroom.

I dropped my shirt back down and turned to snarl at him. "Out."

"No. Not until—"

"This isn't up for negotiation. *Out*."

"Let me see."

"Not on your life." I closed my arms around my chest, even though my sweater was sticky and wet. But I'd rinsed the worst of it out, and a sideways glance into the mirror told me that I looked all right, so far as all right went.

He held his ground and made a grab for my shoulders, but I stepped back out of his way. "Shit, woman. They opened the room back up a minute ago and it looks like the shower scene from *Psycho* in there. I know you're hurt, just let me take a look."

"It's not that bad, and some of it isn't mine," I lied. What did he know about paranormal phenomena, anyway?

"Bullshit. Let me see."

"Touch me, and lose an arm."

He threw his hands in the air and said, "Fine. Have it your way then. But I'm only trying to help."

I heard another knocking on the door, from someone identifying himself as a manager.

"I'm fine," I assured him. "Please go away."

"Now, that guy," Nick pointed a thumb at the door. "He's worried because he doesn't want you to sue the hotel for getting hurt here. But me? My motives are pure."

"I have no doubt. But that doesn't mean I want you in here while I clean up."

"I brought a first-aid kit. It's got… stuff in it. Some, uh…" he opened the metal case and fiddled through it. "Some Band Aids and gauze and stuff. Hey, look, antibacterial goop. Use some of this. And take some of these." He handed me big patchy bandages that would have covered half my face.

"Thank you," I mumbled, figuring it might be easier to let his concern run its course and then see him off, since fighting with him wasn't getting me anywhere.

"Ooh, look—spray stuff." He popped the green cap and accidentally hit the nozzle, sending alcohol-smelling mist over his shoulder. The cap rolled around on the floor, but he picked it up and put it back in place. "Use this, too."

"Hey." I reached down and scooted the metal kit towards myself across the counter. "I've got it under control. Look—do I look okay? Mostly? Not gushing bodily fluids or anything."

"You look pale. I mean, pale for *you*. Blanched, I think that's the word."

"Like I've seen a ghost? Ha-ha."

"No, like you've donated blood and you could use a cookie and a glass of orange juice."

Actually, that didn't sound too far off. The simmering stings of my injuries had worried their way down to an idle throb, but I needed to refuel. I wasn't sure what I wanted, but I wanted something. And I was thirsty.

"How about this, Nick. Let's do this: give me five more minutes in here, then I'll come out and you can take me out to supper. I'll fill you in, and if you pick someplace quiet, we can play with the recording a little."

"Yes." He nodded, hard. "Yes, we can do that. I'll just see myself out. For five minutes—any longer than that, and I'm coming back in."

"Is that a threat or a promise?"

"Yes," he said, retreating backwards to the door. "Five minutes."

"While you're out there, would you do me a favor and tell the manager that no one's going to sue him? Just tell him to go away. Everything's fine."

"Lie to him, sure. Got it."

"*Nick*," I said, but he was already gone.

The faucet was still running—it had been running all this time, because I couldn't stand the thought of the quiet if I turned it off. So I washed my hands again, and my face, too. I pulled off my sweater and slung it over the hand-dryer, and pressed the big round button to start the warm air. A full cycle didn't dry the thing completely, but it warmed it up enough that I didn't mind putting it back on.

My five minutes was mostly up, and I didn't doubt for a moment that Nick would come barging back in.

Later, there would be time to sit and recollect... to sort things out and think my way through them.

I shut the faucet off and let the silence fill my ears. Other things joined it, of course. A toilet that wouldn't stop running. The bickering talk of people outside the door—the manager probably, and Nick. And the maid or someone else. Maybe another woman wanting to use the facilities. There was no telling.

It sounded like Nick was shooing the other two people away, and I was glad for it. Between the light-headed fuzziness and the tingling along my stomach, I wasn't in the mood to deal with even the best-intentioned people—much less curious folks who feared I might bring legal action against them.

When I finally emerged from the bathroom, Nick swept one arm protectively around my shoulders. I would have shrugged him off, but he was herding me away from the hotel employees so I let him leave it.

Back down the shiny marble stairs we went, and down the brightly lit halls with the sky-high ceilings. "Talk to me," Nick said. "What went on in there? What happened?"

"A bunch of things," I breathed. "Just get me some food. I'll tell you anything you want to know if you just feed me."

Parked on the street not far from my own car, a white SUV emblazoned with TV station stickers awaited. Nick unlocked it and hustled me inside, then climbed into the driver's seat. "What are you hungry for?"

"Sleep," I said, then shook my head. "I don't know. I don't care. Something fast and easy. Whatever's close and cheap."

He nodded like he understood, but took a turn up Fourth Street towards the Bluff View art district. There's an Italian restaurant on the bluff, and it's close but it isn't cheap. "What do you care?" Nick shrugged when I mentioned this. "I'm buying, remember?"

"Yes, but I had something with paper cups in mind." Going to the bluff felt too much like a date, except I looked like hell and Nick only wanted me for my information gathering.

"I guess you'll have to settle for real food and a tablecloth on someone else's dime. Sucks to be you." He led me inside and I didn't argue because I didn't have the energy. All of my supernatural run-ins recently had done this to me—left me feeling drained and stupid.

It used to be only the really intense encounters had such an exhausting effect, but these days every shadow and whisper takes it out of me. This was the number one reason I'd declined Dana Marshall's repeated offers to join her crew and investigate the weirdness of the world for a cable channel on TV.

We were seated off in a corner, away from the few other patrons. The place wasn't crowded; it was the wrong time of day for mealtime rush—too late for lunch, and too early yet for supper. I liked it that way. So did Nick, who flapped open his napkin like he was straightening a bedsheet.

"Look, I want you to know—if I'd had any idea this was going to be so demanding and, um, bloody, I never would've asked you to look into it. I was just taking a shortcut, asking you to come in."

"I know," I assured him, scanning the menu. "And don't worry about it. It's usually not such a *thing*. And I don't mind telling you—that's the first time a spirit has ever tried to hurt me. Usually they're harmless, even when they're angry. Caroline's a real piece of work, though. She knocked the wind out of me."

"She did worse than that. I saw the floor in there. And that closet? What did you do—go straight through the door? There was blood *everywhere*. If I've learned anything from watching *Law & Order* reruns, it's that dead people don't spurt blood."

"It always looks worse than it is. It's the very *nature* of bleeding. One little cut looks like a massacre."

"Where? Where was this 'one little cut' of which you speak? When we first opened that door and you were there on the ground, it looked like someone had thrown a basketful of razor blades at you. Then you come out of the bathroom looking damp but unharmed. You want to explain that to me?"

"I *did* explain it. It wasn't as bad as it looked. I cleaned up, and there were only a few small nicks. No big deal."

"Show me."

"No." Even though he couldn't see through my shirt and sweater, I closed my arms around my stomach again. It still hurt, some—but not too bad, and only when I thought about it. "And knock it off, already. If I was hurt, I'd tell you and show you just to get you off my back. But I'm not. Can we let it go?"

"Fine." He picked up his menu and studied it to make a point of ignoring me.

Our waiter returned to take our orders and left us again to our sulking. He knew I was lying, and I knew there was no way to tell him the truth. We turned our attention to the digital recorder, since it was safer territory.

"I don't know how much useful chat you'll find on here. She didn't say anything much except that her name was Caroline and someone had made a mistake," I said as I slipped it across the table to him. "I'd be shocked if there's anything on there I didn't hear."

He toyed with the buttons and turned the device over in his hands. "Caroline, huh? That's all she gave you to work with?"

"Sorry." I wanted to add that she was only halfway in our

world anymore, but that seemed incongruous with the fact that she'd slapped me around so successfully. Another possibility occurred to me, so I put it out there for him to chew on. "I think maybe she was mentally ill. She's violent and angry, and she wants something—but she's no good at communicating it."

"You think she's a crazy ghost?"

"It happens more often than you'd think. People who die in despair, or frustration, they tend to stick around. But she's not all faded out like so many of them are. She's pretty powerful, so I have to assume her weirdness is a relic of her living personality."

The waiter showed up with our drinks, and we paused our conversation while he set them down and retreated. I sipped at mine for a few seconds, then removed the straw and gulped most of the soda down. I was so thirsty I could hardly stand it.

"Excuse me?" I called the waiter back and he returned with another drink a few seconds later.

While I worked on the next soda, Nick played with the recorder. He turned the volume down and rewound a bit, letting it run a few seconds at a time. "I can hear you, but nothing responding."

"On that? I can't either. But maybe with the sound up all the way, you'll be able to pick her up. Her voice is funny. It's faraway one second, and screaming in your face the next. She's disoriented, which isn't so strange. But I have a feeling she's been dead a long time."

"How do you figure that?"

"The way she was dressed, for one thing. And for another... well, it's just a feeling. The more I think about it, the more I think something woke her up. Maybe the remodeling, that's my best guess."

He zipped the recording forward and stopped it. My voice jumped out of it. "They who? Who's coming for you?" I'd said.

"Did she answer?"

I shook my head. "No. She just went on about some mistake. She mentioned the Klan, but that may or may not mean anything."

"Do you think it's the remodeling guys?"

"Who knows? I don't think *she* knows anymore. She hears strange people moving around, tearing up the place she occupies. I can see how she'd think it meant someone was coming for her. If that doesn't explain her, then I sure as hell don't know what does."

"Caroline," he mused. "It's a common name, but not that common. Not anymore. And you said something about her clothes. Tell me everything—every stupid little thing. You never know what'll turn out to be important."

I went ahead and filled him in on most of the details, which is to say, I left out the parts that involved me bleeding all over the place. By the time our food arrived I'd given him enough to make a loose police description of her. Perhaps it would be enough for him to find some historical notation, but I didn't think he'd have much luck.

She could have been anyone: an employee, a visitor—someone passing through who passed on instead. I suspected that Nick's big news scoop was going to be a bust, but if he was honestly interested and deeply bored, he might turn up a likely ghost candidate. If he did, he was welcome to tell me about it, but I didn't have any intention whatsoever of going back into that room.

He said he didn't blame me.

5

REVITALIZED

They were still wrapping up the last of the construction, but the North Shore Apartments would be ready by spring—in time for me to get moved in before school started, or so I hoped. I was already planning my living space and collecting household goods. I was already chatting up friends with pickup trucks.

But they weren't finished yet. Down by the river, workers were laying down turf and rocks to cover the banks they'd stripped; and along the waterfront, cement was being poured. Rumors were being stifled.

One of the workers wrote an anonymous letter to the newspaper, but they wouldn't print it. So he sent it on to the local free rag that sits in racks outside of coffee shops.

They printed it. And I read it.

Everybody did.

We all believed it too, to some degree or another. Nothing surprises us around here when it comes to government corruption. Ever since the big Tennessee Waltz bust—when a whole slew of state and local officials were brought up on federal corruption charges—we've all figured that the ones who remain in power are just better at being crooked than the ones who got caught. No one thinks for a minute that the city is being planned and operated by honest men and women.

This really begs the question of why they keep getting voted into office. I haven't got a good answer for it, except for the obvious one: money. The winners all seem to have a lot of it.

But down by the river where the new apartments were going up on the north banks, bad things were happening. The letter sent into the local rag summed it up while missing the point.

I'm just a guy trying to earn a living. That's why I took the job at the north shore, same as the rest of them down there working. But what I'm seeing is enough to drive you crazy.

Money flows in all the wrong directions, but that's usual. Do you even know who's paying for these things? Do you even know who owns the property? Did you know it was Jane Reynolds? It's her company, anyway. You've got to give her credit for thinking ahead. When she was Mayor, the way she fought for the north side development—you didn't think she was doing that for the north shore economy, did you? No way. She just saw another opportunity to make a killing, that's all, and that's why she pushed for the rezoning over there.

And she's the reason people are getting fired and quitting left and right, too. She doesn't want people to know what they're turning up down by the river. Everybody knows the whole city's sitting on history, but there are laws about what happens when you turn it up. You're not supposed to bury it again and pour concrete over it. You're not supposed to pretend you never saw it.

But that's the policy here when you're working for Jane. You keep your mouth shut or you get thrown out on your ass. You close your eyes if you see something you shouldn't.

Those apartments and that little strip mall center they're trying to put up next to them—none of that should've been built. It should've been roped off and checked out. There's weird stuff down there.

And I know at least two guys who left this job, even though it pays well enough to keep most of us quiet. Two of them found something bad down there, and neither one of them would talk about it. One of them went home and went crazy. He wouldn't come back to the site, anyway. His wife won't let anyone talk to him.

So it's up to you people, then, since it doesn't work when we try it—you've got to go to her and demand to know what's under the concrete they poured yesterday afternoon. Go and ask her, even though she'll lie to you. I want to know, too. I want to see what's under there, but I need the money too bad to get myself fired for being curious. But none of this is right. It's screwed up bad, and even though the housing is on track, I've got a bad feeling that it'll never be finished.

We should've called the authorities before any of it ever got started. We should've left that spot alone.

I reread his letter a couple of times while sitting in Greyfriar's, sipping on a cup of coffee and waiting for Harry to call. I had a question for him. It was going to surprise the hell out of him, but I didn't know who else to direct it to.

The letter in the paper distracted me, though, even if it didn't really surprise or bother me. It was easy to infer the obvious—that the crew had turned up artifacts, maybe even human remains of some kind, and then built over them. I was curious about it, but not too excited or worried. It's something you get accustomed to, living in a city like this one. Every place, every spot, every home and every business is sitting on top of somebody's dead ancestors.

It's easy to understand why the reconstructed South is so rife with superstition. If you're uncomfortable living on top of a graveyard, you'll just have to find another part of the country to squat in. Entire neighborhoods here are built on Civil War battlefields. You can't go to a McDonald's without seeing a historical marker recounting all the people who died there a century or two ago.

But it's funny how many people know about the undocumented stuff, too. The secrets live on in urban legends and in small pockets of family lore. The city remembers, even when it would prefer to forget.

Someone always knows.

I thought of Caroline, and I wondered what *she* knows.

But I didn't wonder for long, because my cell phone rang and it was Harry. First, he wanted to know if I was absolutely sure about the upcoming visit and if I had any reservations at all, because I'd have to speak now or forever hold my peace. Malachi was bouncing off the walls, and if I was one hundred percent positive that this was what I wanted, they'd be there on Friday.

Yes, I was sure. Well, I wasn't really—but I told him otherwise. I'd made up my mind, and that would have to be good enough.

"Listen, I need to talk to you," I said, not sure of how I meant to phrase what I meant to ask. "I'm having some trouble… with my abilities."

"What kind of trouble? And with what abilities, specifically?"

I tried to clarify. "It's draining me, Harry. It's eating me up a bit, every time something happens. It's wearing me out."

He paused. "Let's start with the first thing—it's draining you, you say. What precisely? Are you seeing things, getting headaches? That sort of thing?"

"Yes. Sort of. All of that, yes. Except when you ask if I've been seeing things, it sounds like I'm crazy."

"Aren't you, though?" He said it with a smile; I could hear it over the line.

"Sure. But not like this. Not sick. Lately, it's making me sick. It's getting me hurt, only the hurt is fixing itself too fast. Jesus." I rubbed at my eyes for a second, then pulled the phone back up to my mouth. I lowered my volume. "I can't keep hiding this forever. I thought maybe I could, before. But one of these days, someone's going to find me out."

"Find out what?" I glanced around the room, but he spoke again before I could answer. "It's hard to articulate, isn't it? It's hard to say what it is, and what it's like. I'm not sure there's any precedent for it, or if there is—"

"That's what I wanted to ask you about. The only one I can think of to ask is Eliza. I was wondering if you could put me in touch with her. Is she still at that house in Macon?"

"Eden—"

"Harry, she's the only one who ever drank that stuff of Avery's. Except for him, I mean, and..." I looked around again. "And I happen to know for a pretty good fact that he's dead. There's nobody else. I need to know if this is normal, what's going on with me. Or at least if it's to be expected."

He didn't answer for a few seconds, and he sounded very

tired when he did. "She'll lie to you."

"Probably," I agreed. "But it's better than nothing."

"Maybe, maybe not. She'll see it as a victory—you'll be giving her control over something, and she'll devour you alive for it. Look, instead… instead, why don't you come down here for a while? Before school starts for you, I mean? Even a week or two would be something. We could run some experiments. Do you remember Marcus? He'd love to sit you down and pick your brain. We could—"

"No. I don't think so. No."

"It'd be safe here," he argued.

"It's safe *here*," I returned. "And 'safe' is relative, everywhere." He thought on this for a few seconds before changing tactics on me. "There's something you should know, though. Your cantankerous old aunt is 103 now—and not in the greatest health since her 'herbal remedy' supply was cut off. In addition to her usual cryptic, malicious runaround, you might also have dementia to contend with. I honestly don't think there's anything she can tell you, or give you."

"You might be wrong. She might know something, or she might be willing to talk. We've got something more than blood in common now. It might mean something to her."

"You give her more credit than she deserves."

"Oh, for God's sake, Harry. Is she at the old Macon house or not? Did she wind up in a home or do I already have her address?"

I could almost hear him rubbing at his temples and running one hand through his graying hair. He was probably mouthing something inappropriate, too. I don't know exactly what all he did before joining the clergy, but whatever it was, it taught him some colorful language. I remembered the downright astonishing garland of words he'd strung together when I called him to tell him I'd found Malachi roaming Moccasin Bend last year.

But he wouldn't aim it at me. He'd swear to the stars or the ceiling, same as he prayed. "She's still at the Macon house. Two in-home care workers basically live there, keeping an eye on her."

"Bless their hearts." I wondered how much she was paying them. Whatever it was, it couldn't possibly be enough.

"You said it. I don't know them, and I don't know how protective of her they are—but I'm betting you could negotiate with them. They'd probably be thrilled silly to have a few minutes away from the old battle-ax. Give it a shot, if you're so determined to do so."

"Thanks, I will."

"It's your free time, and it's your sanity. Put whatever you want on the line. God knows you won't listen to me."

"Damn straight."

I thought the conversation was winding down to a close, but he cut me off before I could hang up. "Just one thing—will you think about it? Between now and when I see you? Just think about coming down here for a little while. It wouldn't be so bad. Nice weather. Sun. Sand. Surf."

"Nosey priests," I added. But when it sounded like he was going to keep pushing, I gave him what he wanted. "Okay. I'll think about it, and we'll talk about it when you get here. Would that make you happy?"

"Yes. That's all I'm asking for. Then, when I get up there, I can badger you further."

"Great. I'll look forward to it."

"Liar," he said, but I could hear him smiling.

6

THE LANDING

Christ went down to the water's edge, or this is how they tell it. He went alone, though he would've preferred to bring someone with him—Christ and Eden's mutual friend Benny, perhaps, but Benny was in North Carolina chasing ghosts with Dana Marshall for the big cable TV show.

No one else would do it. No one else had the balls or was crazy enough, so he went by himself after dark. In his hand he fumbled with a worn-down skateboard wheel that had belonged to a guy named Pat before Pat went missing, or got Taken.

Christ worried at the wheel like it was a talisman that would carry him past the landing unscathed.

It wasn't dark yet, anyway. People still came and went, here and there. One man folded up a dented metal tackle box and began counting small fish in a bucket. Another threw a rope down off the pier to a little boat. The muffled notes of a local radio station filtered up from within it, along with intermittent static from a CB receiver.

On the other side of the river a few white lights speckled the bank where the new apartments were almost ready to be lived in. Christ glared at the sharp, glimmering lamps. In another week—or two, or three—they would be innocuous streetlamps beside cement walkways. Across the rippling expanse of the Tennessee River, they were waiting.

They were calling him.

When in doubt, Christ usually resorted to violence. It was easy to lash out and hard to find the right words, sometimes. Words failed him more often than not. They were inadequate, and they went unbelieved.

He knew all about the boy who cried wolf, of course.

He knew good and well why no one believed him, and he didn't mind. He wouldn't have respected them if they had. Normally he wouldn't have cared if they lived there or not.

But Lisa, Naomi, and Eden—all three had reserved apartments in the new space beside the river, and it bothered him. Eden, at least, should have believed him. She should have given him a chance to tell her what he knew... but even as he nursed a sharp, itching grudge over the way she'd rebuffed him, he was aware that he should know better.

Of the three women he'd approached to warn, Eden was the only one who knew anything about the other side; and she thought that the story he offered was more madness than anything.

But it wasn't a lie.

Just this once he wished he could convince her, but he knew it wouldn't happen. He couldn't sell her on the danger, because the harder he pushed, the more stubbornly she'd dig in. He didn't know her as well as he thought he did, but he understood her kind.

All right then. He'd *make* her see things his way.

Before the darkness sprawled out too thick across the water and spilled up over the banks. Before all the people retreated to their homes and locked their doors and pulled down their shades. He'd take a stand.

In his oversized pants pockets, besides the skateboard wheel, there was an eight-ounce can of lighter fluid and a Zippo.

He picked up his board from underneath his haunches, dropped it to the ground and stepped on it with one sure foot. With the other, he pushed himself off and forward, away from the landing and back towards the cascading fountain, back towards the remaining few people and the gleam of civilization.

On the board he sailed smoothly past the last of the aquarium workers and one sleepy cop who only shrugged with one eyebrow when Christ flipped him the bird.

He navigated the sidewalks and alternately kicked and glided his way up the bank, past the fountains, and up to street and bridge level. The big blue Walnut Street pedestrian bridge was well lit even though it was still dusk. It used to send two lanes of cars back and forth, but due to advanced age and municipal revitalization, it now served mostly hand-holding couples, joggers, and people with baby strollers.

A black iron sign prohibited dogs, skateboards, and a host of other things that were making their leisurely way over the water regardless. Christ joined their trickling flow. His skateboard clacked and echoed over the wooden planks as he went.

No one bothered him. He considered it a good sign. A blessing, even—and like the Blues Brothers before him, he was on a mission from God.

The trip across the river was more than half a mile, but it took barely five minutes on Christ's rattling board. He skidded onto the sidewalk on the other side, and zipped past a couple of Frasier Avenue shopkeepers locking up. The restaurants were still open. It was late for supper, though, and there were hardly any customers. The wine bar across the street looked warm, but empty.

No cars came rumbling over the Market Street bridge, so Christ didn't wait for the signal. He picked up his board to walk the rest of the distance to the construction site. Otherwise, the tell-tale clatter of his wheels would give him away. It was a sound every cop knew, and none of them welcomed.

In the near-dark the river was bright, its waves rippling reflections from the cityscape and casting back the glow in ribbons.

The apartments were shells, empty and beautiful with nothing inside and without their finishing touches. Christ stopped at the edge of the complex. He propped his board up in a doorway where it wasn't likely to be spotted or disturbed.

His sneakers were held together with duct tape, and they were quiet against the crisp white sidewalks. He tied his hair back with a dirty bandana and stood stock-still, listening. Over the bank, the river lapped gently against the rocks. The hearty hum of southern insects buzzed here and there, rising in volume as the sun set farther and the sky went darker.

He put a hand down into his pocket and shook the tin bottle of lighter fluid. It was maybe two-thirds full... enough to start something, but not enough to keep it fed for very long. He'd have to find something willing to catch and burn.

A trash bin full of newspapers and rags looked promising. He thought about rolling the bin down to the building closest to the water, but changed his mind. It'd be better to find an open one first.

One by one he tried the doors, and was disappointed. The windows were easy, but breaking them was a fast way to get unwanted attention. He kept them in mind as a last resort, and scanned the grounds for an easier target. Quickly, though. Darker and darker it grew, and the streetlamps were too few and far between to be of much assistance.

At some point, the night would have to level off, wouldn't it? There must be some plateau with dawn on the other side. But dawn was a long ways off and he planned to be long gone by then.

Something splashed nearby, and he jumped.

Hurry. Do it and go.

At the end of the row closest to the river, one strip of homes was not yet finished. The front door was locked, but that was irrelevant since one wall was comprised of exposed beams and plastic wrap.

In the trash bin with the papers, Christ found a Coke bottle. He struck it against the sidewalk until it broke, then used one of the sharp edges to draw a jagged slit in the plastic, big enough for him to pass through. Inside it was dark like everything else, filled with drywall dust and piles of junk he couldn't make out clearly. Some of it was bound to be flammable.

He pulled the lighter fluid out of his pocket, and with its tiny nozzle he squirted the contents on the walls, on the drywall, on the plastic wrapping that'd been piled up in the corners. Then he went back to the trash bin and grabbed an armload. He had to squeeze through the slit sideways. On the second trip he tore it a little more, and on the third he stretched it wide enough that he could step through it with ease.

There wasn't much point in a fifth trip. Everything that would light had been retrieved, and there wouldn't be enough fluid to treat more than that, anyway.

Sparingly, Christ sprinkled the newspapers, sandwich wrappers, and other trash until there was nothing left in the can, then threw the can in on top of the pile. He pulled out his lighter. He couldn't remember who he'd stolen it from, so it wasn't likely to be traced back to him.

He struck the wheel with his thumb and the tall, steady flame nearly blinded him. He looked away and let his eyes adjust, retreating to the improvised doorway he'd made with the soda bottle.

He stepped outside, glanced around to make sure he wasn't being watched, checked that his skateboard was still where he'd stashed it… and threw the lighter inside, onto the nearest pile of trash.

The trash caught quickly. A crackling whoosh, a flare of light, and a burst of heat announced that the arson was underway.

Christ ran.

With one swift swoop he grabbed the skateboard and swung it around to the nearest window on the fly. The back wheels cracked through, and the sound of tinkling glass joined the hisses and pops of the fire. Christ skipped the next window along his escape route, but hit two more with that same fast swing, knocking brand-new panes clear of their frames.

"That's for Pat," he grumbled, changing course and doubling back to a second row of buildings. He might as well hit as many windows as possible on the way out. He swung the board again and brought it through a big kitchen window. "That one's for Catfood Dude."

Next building down. His skateboard went through a bay window that faced the river. It wouldn't be enough, not to stop them. He'd need an army of kids to do enough damage for that.

Even two or three people could have started more trouble than a few broken windows.

It was too bad. A few minors would have been helpful. Reckless, and only minimally prosecutable—they would have made glorious mayhem, delightful anarchy. They would have torn the place up like hell.

But when you're thirty and still wearing duct tape on your shoes, you have to get a little careful. The courts are more forgiving of young hooligans than old ones.

Old hooligans have used up all of their second chances.

And maybe the courts were right, thought Christ as he swung the board again, as hard as he could, at a patio door. But the patio was sturdier than the kitchen glass, or maybe he was getting tired. The door didn't break.

Behind him, the fire was gaining a good foothold and the sound and smell of crackling ashes climbed up out of the half-built apartment block. If it hadn't been noticed yet, someone would spot it soon.

Forget it. Forget the patio door.

His hands were starting to shake, and he didn't know why. Just the force of it all, he guessed—the skateboard against the glass, his arms laden down with debris, his feet numb from running over concrete blocks and vinyl siding.

He shook his head, maybe to clear it. He felt disoriented, and turned around. He knew where he was, and how to leave the compound. Back to the main drag, or over to Manufacturers Row, where the darkness wasn't so loaded.

The sidewalks ended, the pavement was broken, and there was nowhere to ride—so Christ had to run. Somewhere off to his right, he heard the sound of sirens. They weren't cop cars. He knew the wail of a cop car, and this siren was longer and louder in its caterwauling—either a fire engine or an ambulance.

Run, then.

His footsteps staggered into something like a jog, and then faster, into a sprint towards the edge of the brand-new complex and into the warehouse district. It wasn't far. It wouldn't take him long.

That siren was definitely getting louder.

He hoped it was an ambulance—something headed for the hospital just over the river. Not a fire engine, not yet. Let it burn. Let it get going good, and let it spread. It wouldn't take the whole place down, but it might do enough damage to set back the opening.

It might give him time. He needed time to gather proof, or to wear Eden down. The other two wouldn't have the nerve to come with him, and they wouldn't know what to do with proof if it bit them on the ass. But Eden would know. If he could show her, she'd understand.

At least he hoped so.

7

UNWILLING FAMILY

Even though it was a pain in the ass, I decided to do Macon as a daytrip. The local news was predicting nasty weather over the weekend, and Malachi and Harry would be here then anyway.

Great. We'd be stormed in together.

Lu and Dave would be *delighted*.

If I didn't seek out Eliza soon, it might be weeks before I could make it down again—and when the object of my road trip was a bitchy old crone over a hundred years old, it didn't make sense to wait any longer than absolutely necessary. I didn't warn her I was coming either, lest she spontaneously die from pure spite.

Instead, I woke up at the crack of dawn and left a note for my aunt and uncle that said, "Short road trip to Georgia. Back tonight. Call cell if overwhelmed with fretfulness." I hoped they'd assume I'd gone down to Atlanta or Athens for a concert or some other event. Like Mr. Spock used to say, "Never lie when you can misdirect."

Tatie Eliza is family—exactly the sort of family that you only approach as a last resort, and even then, she probably wouldn't spit on you if you were on fire. She's my great-great-aunt, or something like that. The family relationships are a little convoluted that far down the tree, and Eliza likes to pretend that no one on my branch ever existed.

She's the daughter of a carpetbagger who moved to Macon after the war, and she's half-sister to my grandfather Avery, give or take a "great" or three. Avery's the same grandfather who tried to kill me once, tried to kill us all: me and Lu and every blood relative who came before us, after him. He's the one who gave me this gift of his, and challenged me to live with it. At the time I thought nothing of it, but now I'm not so sure.

And now, if I correctly read between the lines of Harry's hesitant help, it sounded like the scheming old matriarch must be dying at last. It was hard to believe. I never loved her and I won't miss her, but she seemed eternal. Nothing that hates so damn hard can pass away easily. It takes a certain brand of tenacity to harbor and nurture such a whole-body grudge.

I once joked to her that Lu and I were the niggers in her family woodpile, and if it hadn't been perfectly true, she might have laughed. But skin color is no laughing matter to an old white woman like her, especially one who's the daughter of a scalawag. Fitting in must have been hard enough on her before she knew about us.

I wondered, sometimes, if that's why Avery had stayed in touch with her all those years—if that's why he'd kept her medicated with his elixir. He didn't have to. He must have done it because he wanted to.

Maybe he wanted her to stop hating him.

Or maybe he was just lonely, or bored, or he liked having a

feeling of power over her. Family is so complicated, even under the most mundane of circumstances. I don't think I'll ever sort out the intricacies of my own.

But that doesn't stop me from trying, sometimes—like when I invite my half-brother to come up and visit, even though it means my aunt and uncle may well drop dead of simultaneous coronaries. Jesus, I hope they understand.

But I bet they won't.

The drive to Macon took three hours, but finding Eliza's house again took me another thirty minutes because I'd forgotten how far out in the boonies it was.

I pulled into the big, semicircular driveway in front of the Georgian brick house, then stood on the stoop for a few seconds gathering the nerve to ring the bell. The paint on the doorframe was peeling and the little windows on the door were cloudy. Eliza might have nurse aids on staff, but I doubted she'd found a replacement for Harry, whose service was terminated when he tied her up in the dining room and helped me ransack the house.

I finally jammed my thumb into the button. It stuck as if the corrosion had crusted it into place, but then slipped and sank. Deep within the house I heard a low gonging noise.

Through the clouded door pane, I saw a swiftly moving figure, coming my way in a light-colored outfit with a dark sweater.

The heavy old door swung inward, and I found myself looking down at a small woman wearing a brown bun and a glum, irritable expression. Her casual scrubs had rainbows and teddy bears on them.

"Can I help you?" she asked, in a voice that implied she didn't have any real intention of helping me whatsoever, because she had her hands full already, thank you very much.

"I know I'm unannounced, but I'm here hoping to have a chat with Eliza Dufresne. I understand she's in ill health—"

The nurse ducked her head away and mumbled something that might have been, "Not ill enough." She shrugged at me and said so I could hear her plainly, "Come inside, then." She stood aside and held the door open.

I followed after her and she slapped the door shut behind us. "Are you—are you one of her caretakers?"

"Yes."

"How's she doing these days? We haven't spoken in a while, but—"

"She's fine."

"Fine?"

The nurse, who still had not identified herself by any name, said, "Fine for 103."

I threw her a bone. "You can just tell me she's a pain in the ass, if you want. I know that much already."

"She's a paying client." She didn't relax, but she slumped a little. "She's… a real piece of work, as my mother would have said. The other girl took the day off. I'm here alone with Miss D today."

"Oh shit, I'm sorry."

"That makes two of us. Right this way, please."

"Doesn't someone… I mean, as old as she is—doesn't someone live here with her?" I asked, feeling a great swell of pity for anyone with such a post.

"Used to. They keep quitting. Right now we're working in shifts. There's a third girl, comes in on weekends and sometimes at night."

Through the halls we went, and up the stairs, and down the corridors where all the furnishings were threadbare but expensive. The wood paneling threw back every footstep, creak, and breath.

Each step and syllable happened twice, or three times where the rug was thin and there was nothing to cushion the noise.

"Look, I don't mean to sound harsh," the nurse said, as she stopped and turned to face me. "But if you were close family or friends, I'd have seen you before now, so I'll just tell you how it is. She's very old, and we don't expect her to be with us much longer. She was hale and hardy up until these last few years, or that's how I understand it. But when they reach this age, sometimes they go downhill suddenly. She's as bad as you said and more. I don't know how she'll receive you, and I can't even promise you she'll be lucid. She isn't, not always."

"That's okay. She can't stand the sight of me, so I'm not expecting any charm or manners here. There's no need to warn me."

"Good—because if you don't know what she's like already, there's not much bracing you for her. But remember, would you? Remember she's a dying old lady. Keep it in mind, before you're too hard on her when she's hard on you."

"I can take it, and I won't bite her head off. I know what I'm getting myself into."

"All right, then." She shook her head, and took another few steps down the hall.

I knew where we were; I remembered the place. I remembered every nook and cranny from when Harry and I had stripped the house bare, looking for a book that was six hundred miles away. When we finally found it there, we let it burn with everything else in that swamp house. We let it burn with Avery, and with his bubbling stove and glass bottles and smelly mixtures.

If we hadn't, Eliza would still be up and around, going strong for another twenty years or more like Avery had. So if she hated me, and if she wanted me dead, and if she had no intention at all of speaking to me in anything kinder than a spit and a shout… I couldn't blame her.

Maybe it would be easier, with her mind half gone. Maybe I'd find what I needed more easily in the wreckage of her head.

I stepped around the corner into Eliza's bedroom.

"I'll be downstairs if you need anything. Just holler. I'll hear you."

"Thanks," I told the nurse.

She left me there in the doorway. I stared down at the tiny shell on the bed and tried to superimpose another image over it— the image of the fierce little woman I'd met before. But I couldn't. It didn't work.

She'd been petite to start with and had lost twenty pounds since then, at least. Her thin white hair was all but gone; her scalp crawled with veins and was dotted with liver spots. The hollows of her eyes and cheeks were cavernous and tinged with blue. The nurses had dressed her in a mint green nightgown. It looked like it had been laid down over a scattered pile of forks.

She didn't hear me come in, so I said her name. "Eliza?" I said it softly, like I didn't really want her to answer.

Her neck craned up against a pillow.

"Hey there, Eliza," I said. It was easy to sound gentle. All the nurse had said aside, this was only a shadow of the woman I knew and loathed.

"Who?"

"Eliza, it's me. Do you remember me?" I crossed the stale-smelling room and stepped past a pile of crumpled tissues. There was a seat beside her with a magazine on it, face down. I moved the magazine and took the seat.

Eliza turned to see me, sort of. She twisted her neck with a series of pops that sounded like potato chips being squeezed in a bag. Her eyes were wet and big, with tiny pupils that made her look sharp even as she reclined, an invalid.

I couldn't tell if she recognized me or not. She didn't say anything. Her expression of general sourness didn't change.

"Eliza, I want to talk to you. I came all the way down from Chattanooga to see you. How, uh, how are you doing these days, huh?" I found myself softening the edges of the words, like I was talking to a sick child.

"Louise," she barked.

I jumped. Her voice was stronger than she looked. "No, I'm not—I'm not Louise," I told her. If she heard me, she didn't believe me.

"That girl, I think she killed him," she said. "Otherwise, he'd come home." There was sadness there, and betrayal, and something else I couldn't put a finger on.

I thought about arguing with her, and telling her the truth—that her nephew was alive and well and safe in north Florida. I thought about telling her that he hadn't come back because she was the one who betrayed him. But it wouldn't have meant anything, and she wouldn't have believed me about that, either.

It hurt her to think that he was dead, but I suspected it would hurt her more if she knew he wasn't, that he stayed away because he chose to. But that one was Malachi's to fix, if he felt like it. It wasn't up to me.

"I'm sorry to hear that," I told her, playing along. "My sympathies on that nephew of yours." I could have said more, but I had a feeling that Lu would've stopped there, so I stopped too.

Eliza nodded as if she accepted the sympathies, even though

she was aware they weren't heartfelt. Sometimes, appearances really *are* everything.

"Tatie, something's wrong with Eden. I don't know what, and I don't know who to ask. You were the only one I could think of."

She made a little "harrumph" noise to say she didn't give two little shits what was wrong with me, but her sense of schadenfreude had been alerted and she wanted to know more. "What is it?"

I leaned forward to put my elbows on my knees, then thought better of it. If she got a good look at me, she might figure out I wasn't Louise and then I'd be a mile back from square one, if I was lucky.

"She's having trouble with… with visions. And when she sees the dead, it takes a lot out of her—even though she always recovers quickly. Too quickly, really," I mumbled. "Every encounter costs her more."

Eliza nodded, this time with a smile. "It's the draught. Dumb girl drank it."

"But what did it *do*?"

"Nothing bad to me, because I never saw the dead. But if a crazy little thing like you were to take it…"

It came out of her in a rush. It came out quick, and clear, and she looked dead at me and I could tell that she knew me. She knew I wasn't Louise. She looks down on Louise, but she doesn't hate her like she hates me, so it was easy to see it in her eyes and hear it in her voice.

Then it was gone as fast as it had happened. She settled back down onto her pillow and shut her eyes again.

"A witch has to be more careful." It was another full sentence, but not as snappy as before. "Didn't know what she was doing. Dumb girl."

"So what did it do to her? Your medicine, I mean? Did it hurt her?"

"Who knows?" She attempted a little shrug there on the bed, but it only barely showed. "Avery might've known. He's dead now."

"Is there anyone else who'd know? I know you don't *want* to help her, but I thought maybe we could make some kind of deal."

"A deal?" She laughed until she coughed, and it sounded like she was spitting up dust. "You can't make a deal with me. I don't even want more *time*. Not anymore."

"Jesus, Eliza. What's wrong with *her*? Just tell me, for God's sake. It don't cost you nothing, and heaven's watching."

"There's no fixing her. Two-way street," she said.

"I don't get it."

"She goes closer to them, they come closer to her." Her eyes were still closed. She twisted her thin little hands in the nightgown, balling up the fabric in her fists. "That's how it works."

I shook my head, even though she couldn't see me. "That doesn't help much."

Eliza snorted, a tiny bit. It breezed through her nose like a baby's sneeze. "If she's close enough to touch them, they're close enough to touch *her*."

She started coughing again, weakly and with some halfhearted thrashing. When she settled down, she picked up the thread of thought. "It's no gift. No power. Touch and be touched, that's all."

Touch and be touched? I could see the logic there, but I didn't like it. It didn't mean power. It meant vulnerability.

I rose and pushed the chair back with my leg.

Eliza's hand shot out and nabbed my wrist.

Her grip was strong and angry, and when she rolled her head

to look at me, that old recognition was back. "Girl, you give me back my boy."

"Eliza," I protested, and I picked at her fingers. I tried not to hurt her, which was more than she'd ever done for me. "Eliza, let me go."

"Bring him back to me. Bring him back and bury him here with me. That's the only deal I've got for you. That's what I want, and that's the only thing."

I worked my thumb beneath her pinky and twisted myself free from the rest. "I can't."

She settled back onto the pillow; again she looked sallow and fragile. She looked beaten, but wary. "Get out. Out of my house."

"I'm way ahead of you."

"Out!" she shouted again, and again—and by the third time the nurse came running. "What did you do to her?" the nurse asked, but I had a feeling it was only professional curiosity.

"Nothing. I showed up, and it was a bad idea." I turned sideways and we passed each other in the doorway. "I'm sorry. I'll see myself out."

I nearly ran downstairs, back to the corridor, and to the front door. It was ridiculous, and I knew it. Eliza wasn't going to leap up and come after me, and there was no one else in the house who would chase me.

I tried to feel sorry for her—I worked on it for a few minutes while I wrestled with my keys and slammed myself safely into the cab of my car. She's old, and she's dying, and she's alone.

That's sad, right?

But she'd done it all to herself. And she'd done it to Malachi, too. It was one thing to be alone in life, I suppose, and another to lie alone after it's finished. But that's not an excuse, and it's barely a reason.

I was absurdly glad that Malachi was still alive, for it was the one thing I could still deny Eliza. The malice I felt was resounding, and pure, and I liked it. I didn't even bother to kick it back down or force it aside.

I just let it stew.

Driving home, through the long, flat stretches of Georgia where nobody lives once Atlanta's past, I wasn't even bothered by the way the feeling stayed. I didn't care if it lingered. She hated me to the bitter end, and I could hate her too, if it came to that.

That mad little troll of a woman didn't want to be forgiven, and who was I to go against her wishes? She could stay there and rot for all I cared. She could lie there alone, and when she died, I'd never talk to her—even if I still could. Even if she wanted me to.

I dug my foot down into the gas pedal and wished myself home.

8

VANDALS ARE WE ALL

I slept in the next day and missed my aunt and uncle, but they were thinking of me—or at least Lu was. On the dining room table was our morning copy of the newspaper. A big red circle highlighted one of the front page stories. ARSON AT RIVERSIDE DEVELOPMENT.

I snatched the paper and started reading. A fire had destroyed one of the newer, unfinished units. Windows had been broken in several other apartments. Opening date had been delayed. Police had no suspects.

I dropped the newspaper and picked up the phone. "Nick," I said when he picked up, "what the hell is going on?"

"Crazy psychics," he mumbled.

"Were you asleep?"

"No. Yes. I'm at work."

"Sleeping at work?"

"You should try it sometime. Hey, I was just going to call you."

"When you woke up?"

"When I woke up," he confirmed. "But you've beat me to the punch."

"We crazy psychics are good for that," I said. "So tell me, what happened down at Riverside last night?"

"Huh? Oh. Someone set fire to something."

"I know that much; I can read the paper. I want to know what else happened. What's going on?"

"What do you care?"

"Because I'm supposed to move into one of those apartments soon, and I'll be real pissed off if it doesn't work out."

He yawned, and behind the yawn I heard the rustling of papers, clicking of pens, and the ringing of phones. "What makes you think I can tell you anything about it? I can give you the same blurb I spit out for the morning news, but it won't tell you more than the paper, I don't think. Someone torched one of the half-finished buildings. Dragged in a bunch of trash, doused it with an accelerant and tossed in a lighter. Dumb kids. Same old bullshit tricks. They'll get it cleaned up soon, and you'll have a spanky new place to live. Don't worry about it."

"I'm not worried, exactly. Never mind. What were you going to call me about, anyway?"

"Huh? Oh. The Read House thing. I think I know who Caroline was. You want to do lunch and talk about it? We'll get pizza, and I'll see if I can scare up any skinny on the arsonist."

"Yeah, okay. That sounds fine. Say noonish?"

"I can live with noonish. Come on down to the station, would you?"

"All right. Noonish."

I hung up on him and stood there in the kitchen, staring down at the newspaper. I had an idea about the vandalism, and I didn't like it at all. The arsonist *might* have been a dumb kid. But I doubted it.

I killed a little time around the house and took a shower before dressing to go see Nick at Channel 3. I didn't go too crazy with it—just jeans and a T-shirt. The weather couldn't seem to decide what it wanted to do, so I carried a sweater with me in case it cooled off beyond my comfort level. January in Tennessee is funny sometimes—it might be single-digit temperatures, might be in the seventies.

A glance outside reminded me to bring an umbrella, too. It wasn't raining yet, but there was a whiff of ozone in the air and the clouds hung low and bleak.

By the time I'd made it down the mountain and over to the TV station, the first droplets of a shower were beginning to slap against my windshield. It wasn't enough to warrant the umbrella yet, so I left it in the back seat and made a quick dash inside.

The receptionist called Nick's desk and invited me to wait in a cheesy little lounge with '80s furnishings. I sat down on an oversized beige couch that faced a big television tuned to Channel 3. Since the remote control was missing, I stared vacantly at the mid-afternoon news broadcast while a woman talked about using garden vegetables in homemade bread.

The door to the main set of offices and cubicles popped open. Nick emerged with a couple of bags and a suit wrapped in dry-cleaner's plastic.

"There you are," he said, shifting sideways to pull himself and all his baggage out into the lobby. "Let me stash this shit in the news Bronco. And I know I said lunch, but I need to make a stop first. I think you might be interested."

I rose and held out a hand, offering to help carry something.

He pushed the suit towards me and I grabbed it. "All right. Where to?"

"Riverside." He flashed one of the big bags, and I saw that it held a video camera. "I was going to take a few minutes of tragic-looking arson footage to layer with a voiceover for the 5:30 show," he added.

"Didn't you do the morning show today, too?"

"I did, and it sucked ass. A couple of people are out sick and one guy's on vacation. But I'm flexible. I'm *versatile*."

As we made our way outside and out of the secretary's earshot, I clarified for him. "You're sucking up."

"Not exactly. I've been on shaky footing here ever since—well, pretty much ever since I met *you*. Besides, I think they're looking for an excuse to dump me and pick up someone blonder, perkier, and breastier."

"Yipe."

He shrugged. "It's the nature of the business. I'm just trying to stay relevant."

"Gotcha. Didn't you used to have a cameraman for this sort of thing?"

"Still do. But I'm learning to do some of my own staging. One-man-bands are more useful than one-trick-ponies. Besides, Steve's out too. Kid's sick. It's all right. I can handle it—oh *Jesus* no. Is it raining?"

"It's sprinkling. Nothing to get too excited about."

"We'll have to make this quick."

After laying his suit across the back seat, I climbed into the SUV and tried not to feel ridiculous. I'd never ridden in anything with so many logos on it before.

"Are you going to be investigating the arson?" I asked as I

fastened my seatbelt, while noting that he didn't bother to do likewise.

"Reporting, not investigating. I'm beat, Eden. I need some fucking *sleep*. Being at work at 4:00 a.m. is going to be the death of me. I don't know how the regular morning guys do it, but if I don't get my evening shift back soon, I'm going to pass out or say something completely stupid on air. People lose jobs that way all the time. I'd prefer not to be one of them."

"Four o'clock in the morning?"

"Tomorrow, too. And today, before suppertime, I've got to put together a three-minute piece on the Riverside arson. Since you were asking about it on the phone, I didn't figure you'd cry too hard about the detour." His tone changed suddenly, lowering and going all conspiratorial on me. "You wouldn't know anything about it, would you? Anything psychically helpful?"

"Don't be ridiculous," I told him. My suspicions had nothing to do with being psychic and everything to do with knowing Christ. "If I knew anything, I wouldn't have called you to ask for the information hook-up."

"Good point. And I don't know anything, by the way. The paper got most of the details as I heard them—broken windows, obvious arson with the rags and a lighter, stuff like that. It looks like a drive-by party to me."

"But why?"

"Why do punks do anything?" he said. "Anyway, as I mentioned earlier, I think I know who Caroline is."

"Really?" I asked, not sure how interested I was in her identity. I was still rattled from the incident in the hotel, and I didn't know how much I actually cared who she was or what she was doing there.

"Caroline Read," he said, grinning. "She told us. At the beginning, when you asked her if she knew who she was and where she was, she answered 'Read.' When I listened to the recording I assumed the same thing you did, that she was saying that she knew where she was. But now I don't think so. I think she was telling you her name."

"*Was* there a Caroline Read at the Read House?"

"Indeed there *was*. And get this—she went crazy and killed herself there at the hotel back in 1933."

I nodded. "I'd say that makes her a pretty likely candidate for our ghost, then."

"You *did* say you thought her behavior was off the deep end, even for a dead woman. I think it's definitely her. I wish I knew what her problem was, though."

"Crazy life, crazy afterlife. She kept saying that someone was coming for her—she accused me of bringing them to her, and saying that 'It was all a mistake.' The building renovation is as likely as any reason. New noises, new people coming and going. It's enough to drive anyone to distraction."

He held back, not asking for what he really wanted. I didn't prompt him. Regardless of whether we knew who she was or not, I didn't want to go back to that room, and Nick knew better than to beg.

We rode the short distance to the Riverside site in silence.

Nick parked the SUV a block or two inside the development, just outside the police tape that warned against trespassing. Either he had permission to ignore the tape or he didn't give a damn; he lifted it up and held it for me. He gazed sleepily at the soot-covered carnage while I scanned the area for some hint or sign of a skateboard's passage.

A row of broken windows tracked the vandal's progress. I pointed at them and asked, "What do you think they took out the windows with?"

"Baseball bat? Tire iron?"

A few years before, a fight had broken out downtown near the coffee shop. I'd been there, and I'd watched as a blue-haired kid had taken his skateboard and smashed out a car window with it. People don't think of those boards as weapons, but I knew better.

I didn't say it to Nick, though. I wanted to have a chat with Christ before I sent the cops or the reporters after him. Besides, I didn't have any proof—just a gut-filling hunch.

"Give me a minute, here," Nick said, scoping for a good spot to set up shop. He settled on a driveway and unfolded his tripod there, motioning for me to bring the rest of his stuff.

I dutifully lugged the bag over and set it down beside him, waiting while he checked batteries and assembled bits and pieces of equipment.

"So you bought into this place, did you?"

"Yeah," I said.

"Having second thoughts?"

"Why would I?"

"I don't know." He shrugged the camera up onto his shoulder. "You're acting funny."

"Funny?"

"Quieter, but with more questions. If I didn't like having my balls right where they are, I might pry."

The big gray sky was swirling low, though the sprinkling had stopped for the moment. I shaded my eyes with the back of my hand and watched the clouds boil. "It's a good thing you're so smart," I said. "Hey, you'd better get a move on. We're about to get soaked out here."

"I'm working on it. Shut up unless you want to go on tape."

He zoomed and panned, grabbing footage of the burned-out block and some of the broken windows. Then he stepped up over the curb and got a closer look at the worst of it. True to his word, it didn't take long.

"That ought to be enough. If it's not, I'll shuffle it up and loop it," he said, unshouldering the camera and folding the tripod he hadn't even used. "And because I'm feeling bold—or maybe stupid from sleep deprivation—I'll go ahead and say this: I get the impression that something's going on down here. And not just from you, either. Did you see that letter in the *Enigma*? The one from that construction worker?"

"I saw it, yeah."

"It didn't bother you?"

"Not particularly."

"Then what *did*?"

A loaded drop of rain landed on my forehead. "Let's go. I bet this equipment doesn't like getting wet. If you really must know, my aunt has been bugging me about moving down here too. I can handle a little arson. I can even handle a little haunting, if there's been some kind of archeological cover-up down here. But when Lu throws a fit about something, she's usually got a good reason for it. This time, she won't give me one."

"How so?"

"She says I ought to move farther from the river in case of flooding, and that's ridiculous. It'd be like me telling you I didn't want to live here because I heard some punk had torched an empty building here twenty years ago. It's a bullshit reason; it doesn't stick. But she doesn't seem interested in clueing me in to her real motives, so. Well. Whatever," I finished lamely.

"I see."

"No you don't."

"All right. I don't. But I'll quit asking, if that's good enough."

"That's good enough." I zipped up one of his bags while he finished stuffing the other one, and within minutes we were back in the gaudy SUV.

Though Nick had promised pizza, he recommended a Mexican place for lunch. I didn't care, so I said it was fine. Over burritos, he dragged the conversation back to the Read House, and to Caroline.

"There was a flu epidemic," he said, a trace of guacamole dangling from a crease in his lip. "Around 1919. Killed a whole bunch of people. Any cemetery will show you that much. It's depressing; you wander around and see all these itty-bitty headstones—for kids, you know—and they'll all have these expiration dates in the same year."

"Expiration date. Real sensitive way to put it."

"You know what I meant. I only mention it because that's about the time our girl Caroline started going batty. According to the records I've found, they had her briefly institutionalized in 1919, but it didn't work out and they moved her back home the next year."

"Didn't work out?"

"She was starving herself there, and Daddy brought her home. A few years later, they brought her into the hotel, and there she stayed until she killed herself in '33. At first I thought maybe they'd sent her away because of the flu, like they wanted to get her safely out of town. But it doesn't sound right, and the rest of the facts don't line up with it."

I chewed on my chips and tried not to get interested in the story. If I got too interested, I'd get weak to the idea of going back inside. I don't know if Nick knew me well enough to understand that or not, but he kept feeding me bits and pieces of it until I started asking questions. "Why didn't they put her in the hotel right away? It seems like an easy halfway house, if she was too crazy to live at home and if they weren't worried about the flu epidemic."

"They were busy rebuilding it. It burned down a couple of times and was eventually rebuilt as the big brick monster we know and love, but it wasn't finished until 1927."

"So she wasn't there very long."

"It doesn't sound like it. And for what it's worth, I'm totally *not* going to ask you to go back inside and have another sit-down with her. I wouldn't dream of it."

"You know better."

"I *do* know better. Which is why I wouldn't ask. Not in a million years. But—"

"Here it comes," I grumbled.

"But, if you ever *do* decide you'd like to give it another shot, I hope you wouldn't do it alone. I'd like to think you'd give me a call, for back-up purposes."

"You're a sneaky bastard."

"That's what they tell me."

Behind him there was a window, and as he wrapped up his non-proposal, the sky opened up in earnest. A flash of lightning and its follow-up thunderclap warned that the worst was yet to come.

Nick peeked over his shoulder and noticed it too. "We timed that well. Thanks for coming with me. I appreciated the company."

It came out awkwardly and he knew it; he busied himself with his own burrito.

I didn't know how to respond, so I just said, "No problem," and kept on eating.

"If I hear anything," he said quickly, "about the fire and everything, I'll let you know."

"Thanks. That'd be great."

I would have reciprocated the offer, but I needed to talk to Christ first.

9

ACCUSATIONS

For a second there, I thought Nick was going to bring up coffee or dessert, so I preemptively begged out by telling him I had to meet a friend. It was true, more or less; except I probably couldn't call Christ a friend without deliberately deceiving myself.

I rode with Nick back to the station and reclaimed my car.

The rain was gaining real momentum, but that wouldn't necessarily deter Christ and his friends from skating. However, since I didn't feel like going down to Ross's Landing and looking for them in the unsheltered out-of-doors, I decided to check my second guess: the library.

As any good delinquent will tell you, the beauty of public property is that you can't be kicked out of it easily. If the boys felt like taking a breather from the rain, they'd probably hole up beneath the library's overhang and noodle around on the cement stairs there—if no one was watching.

I parked on the street and sat in my car for a minute, listening to rain hammer down on the windshield and wishing it would quit long enough for me to dash to the library's overhang.

A harder hammering startled me. There were hands knocking against the passenger's side window, and a glimpse of crayon-bright hair through the streaming downpour told me that Christ wanted me to let him inside.

I popped the locks. He flung the Death Nugget's door open and a great spray of precipitation came into the cabin with him. He shook himself like a dog, sending the water all over my vehicle.

"What the—knock it off, would you? Some of us are smart enough to come in from the rain. I'm trying to stay dry over here."

"Give up. It's pissing like hell, and it's only going to get worse. Good thing I can walk on water, right?"

"Whatever. Hey, I've been looking for you." I tried to lend the words some threat, not that I thought it would bother him. I was right, he didn't care. "Good. I was wondering what it would take to bring you around. We need to talk, me and you."

"Yeah we need to talk, but I'm not sure you're going to like it much. How about we start this with you telling me what happened over at the North Shore Apartments last night?"

"North Shore. Yeah. So you heard about that, good."

"What do you mean, 'good'? It's vandalism, and it's all over the news."

He kicked my dashboard with his torn-up shoes and swore loudly. "Goddammit, woman—people are dying, and you're worried about a few broken windows?"

"First of all, I don't know of anybody who's actually dead yet, and second, those are windows in the place where I intend to live in a few weeks. So at the risk of sounding callous, yes, I'm more worried about the broken windows. I know you had something to do with it, too."

He dropped the adolescent whine, and, just for a sentence or two, he sounded his age. "If I did—and that's if—then it would have been an attempt to alert you to the underlying problems of that location."

"You're an idiot. And get your feet off my dashboard."

"A prophet is never loved in his own land, I know, but this is important! Look outside, and what do you see?"

"Rain. Lots and lots of rain."

"Exactly. It's the water. At first I thought it was just the river, but now I think there's more to it than that. It's *all* the water—the rain, the river, the creeks and the runoff. It feeds a greater system. It sustains the chaos. It..." He fumbled for words.

I interrupted while I had the chance. "What are you talking about? And I mean it—I'm asking like a serious human being here, and I'd appreciate it if you'd do me the courtesy of answering like one. Drop the bullshit, and drop the slam-poetry speak. You've got exactly one minute to explain to me why I shouldn't make an anonymous tip to the cops about the North Shore vandalism."

"Tip all you like. They'll never find me."

"And again I say, you're an idiot. It took *me* about thirty seconds to find you."

"But *you* knew where to look. I wanted you to find me. I orchestrated this. I made myself available."

I rolled my eyes and pushed the back of my head against my seat. "You're down to forty-five seconds, asshole. Behave like a grown-up, or get the hell out of my car. You're making the place smell like wet dog."

He pulled his feet down off the dashboard and turned to face me, drawing one leg up underneath himself. "All right. Something nasty is buried down there, by the river. Some*things*, I guess I should say. At first I thought it was just one—whatever they are—but now I know better. There's a handful of them, at least. And they are *pissed*."

"Why?"

"I have no idea. But they're coming up more often. Eden, I swear to you—" He held out his hands, palms forward. "I swear. No bullshit. No bullshit this time. They're killers. And they don't just come out whenever, it's got something to do with the river. It has to be a certain level, maybe. That's all I can figure out for now. That's all that makes sense to me."

I thought again of Lu, and her one stupid argument for keeping me away from the North Shore Apartments. "The water rises," I said slowly. "The banks flood. And… and what? Something's buried in the banks? What, do monsters reconstitute themselves like sea monkeys? I still don't get it."

"I don't either," he admitted, again with his thirty-year-old man voice. "But the more weird shit happens, the more I'm sure of it. And I think—I don't know, but I think—they're working their way farther up into the city each time. They're looking for something."

"Now you're just grasping at straws."

"I'm brainstorming. At first, the only people who went missing were right down by the water's edge. But now they're disappearing from farther and farther uptown. It's only a matter of time, especially with the rain like this. They're tied to the river somehow, and when the river rises, it—I don't know. It might expand their reach. And with all this rain, the river's *bound* to rise."

"That's what the TVA is for."

Yeah, and the TVA has *never* fucked up."

103

"I didn't say that." His minute was up and we both knew it, but I didn't kick him out of the car yet. "This is crazy," I told him instead. "There aren't any monsters down by the river."

"Then where's Pat? Where's Catfood Dude? And where's Ann Alice? Has anyone seen her lately? Because I found her jacket down under the Walnut Street Bridge. And I can't find any other sign of her."

"Wait—what? For a guy who's afraid of the river so much, what were you doing down under the bridge?"

"Looking for Ann Alice!" He almost shouted it at me, and in the added volume I heard a hint of real despair. "She used to meet a dealer down there—she sold off her ADD prescription for lunch money. But he went missing last week, and I tried to tell her not to go down there looking for him. Now they're both gone. And I found her jacket."

He mumbled the last part, as if he wasn't sure how to finish and he was becoming aware of how silly it sounded.

"Okay," I said, trying to tie it all together in my head.

He hunkered down in the bucket seat and crossed his arms over his chest. "At first I thought that you could go talk to them like you talk to ghosts, and then it would all clear up. But now I don't know. Now it seems weirder than that. It seems worse than that."

"So why are you in my car, then? What happens now, if I can't help?"

"I don't know." The way he said it, I thought for a second that he was going to start crying. I was glad he didn't. I wouldn't have known what to do with it. "And you can tell the cops if you want to, if that's what you're going to do. But I was only trying to buy some time."

"For what? For things to get worse?"

"Sure. And it *is* going to get worse. Eventually, you'll be able to see it too. You won't be able to pretend it isn't there, and then maybe you'll get involved."

I shrugged and rolled my head back and forth on the headrest. "And then what?"

"Who knows? But they sure as hell won't believe *me*." He tried to peer through the rain sloughing down the window, but the shapes out on the library steps were only half-formed blotches of color. "They won't believe *us*." He waved a hand at the other skaters on the steps.

"And why do you think that is?" I asked, half serious and half accusing.

"I know why people think what they think. But I can't change it now, not in time to fix this."

Under different circumstances, I wouldn't have put up with his cryptic weirdness for nearly so long; but I had a niggling thought that wouldn't go away, and he was stroking it—whether he meant to or not.

"I need to talk to Lu," I said out loud.

"Your aunt?"

"Yeah. I need to talk to her."

"About this?"

"Not exactly, but maybe."

"What does that mean?" he asked.

"I need to find out why she really doesn't want me moving down by the river. It's like you said—when the river rises, maybe it brings something with it." I shook my head and gripped the steering wheel, just so I had a place to put my hands. "Lu and her sisters, they grew up over there—on the other side of the river.

In North Chatt. I wonder if she knows something she isn't telling me. I wonder, if I tell her what you've told me, if she'll change her story at all."

"Can't hurt to ask."

"That's how I see it." Another long pause hung between us. I broke it first. "Get out of my car."

"What?"

"Get out. Go back to your playmates. I'm going to go back up the mountain now. I'm going to corner Lu before Dave gets home. Divide and conquer, in case it matters. Dave might not know. He doesn't care if I take the apartment. *She's* the one giving me a hassle about it."

"Are you going to call the cops? Not like you've got any proof or anything, but if you send them my way, just do me the courtesy of warning me first, would you?"

"I'm not going to call the cops."

"Or your buddy down at Channel Three?"

"Not him either. Get out, and shut the door fast behind you." He finally did as I ordered, leaving me sitting alone in front of the library. I wouldn't have given his conspiracy theory a minute's thought if it weren't for Lu. I had no good reason to think there was anything linking her reluctance and Christ's warnings, but there were enough tiny similarities to make me wonder.

The drive home took me longer than it sometimes does, because rain makes people drive stupid—on the mountains more than in the valley, I think. People never take those hairpin turns faster or meaner than when it's wet outside, so I had to be careful.

Lu was there when I got home, as I thought she probably would be. I found her on the back porch, sipping something icy that smelled like sweet rum and watching the rain.

"Welcome back. How's it going?" she asked, doing a little toast in my direction. "You saw the newspaper this morning." It wasn't a question. She knew I'd seen it; I'd taken it with me when I left the house.

"I saw it. Thanks for leaving it out. I went down there, actually."

"Did you?"

"I did."

"Not by yourself, I hope."

"Not by myself, no."

She let loose a half-smile and took another drink. "Went down there with that Nick guy, didn't you?"

I had no reason to deny it, so I pulled up one of the wooden deck chairs and made myself comfortable. "Yeah, I did. I thought maybe he'd heard a few extra details, so I called him up. He wasn't helpful, but I went down there with him while he shot some film for the 5:30 show. We took a look around."

"Find anything helpful?"

"How do you mean?"

She crossed her legs and leaned back. "Useful, I mean. Clues, or whatever."

"Why do you do this?"

"Do what?"

"You get weird every time the subject of me moving out comes up. You bugged me to get my own place for ages, then when I picked one—well, anyway. You get weird when it comes to the North Shore Apartments."

"I do?"

"You know you do, and I want to know why. Is it because you used to live down there, back when you were a kid?"

She didn't wince, or flinch. But her posture changed. She

hardened. "Who told you we used to live down there?"

I couldn't remember. "You told me," I said, because it was likely to be true. "Or I overheard it somewhere. You lived over near Frasier, back in North Chatt, up in the hills—right?"

Lu flashed me a face like she'd just bit into a lemon. "Up in the hills. Sure. Up there. Back on Tremont. In that area, anyway."

"Where?"

"Don't bother looking for it. That house burned down fifteen years ago. It burned down not long after my mother left it."

"Where was it?"

"Oh, hell," she said. "Over there—not far from where the gas station is. Up Tremont a little ways, but not far. In that strip where now they've got little businesses in those old houses. You know. Florists and the like."

"Not far from the river."

"Not far from the river." She was still subtly rigid. She was trying not to look tense, and it wasn't working. "But that was a long time ago."

"Did it ever flood back then? I know the river used to flood sometimes, even after the TVA got a foothold here. I was just wondering, since you were so close to the river."

"Sometimes, it flooded."

"Sometimes?"

She dipped her glass and her head. "Once or twice."

"What was it like?"

Lu set her glass down on the small patio table beside her.

"Are you fishing for something, sweetheart?"

"Yeah, but I don't know what." In the backyard, the rain came splattering down—surrounding us with curtains of water. It felt isolated and quiet, despite the drumming white noise.

She stalled, fretting with the arm of the chair and tapping her fingers against her glass. "What do you want to hear? What are you trying to ask?"

"Why don't you want me moving down by the river? What's the real reason, and why do you keep tap-dancing around it? I'm plenty old enough to get my own place, and you've been hinting ever since I dropped out of college that I ought to find one. So I picked this one, and it looks like a good pick. Why won't you let me take it without giving me all this grief? What is it that you don't like about the place?"

"I told you the truth," she insisted. "It's down in the flood zone, down there by the river. One bad storm…" She gestured out at the puddle-pocked yard. "One flub-up at TVA, and you're living underwater."

"That's true of half the city, though—even the university, I bet. Where do you want me to go?"

"Maybe the dormitories? At least they're farther away from the water. And what about the old buildings they converted downtown, and on MLK? There are lots of perfectly good places that would get you up on dry land and keep you near the university."

"The dormitories suck, and MLK is still pretty ghetto. These apartments are nicer. What's wrong with them that you're not telling me?"

She reclaimed her drink and took another swallow, and she stared out through the sheets of water that boxed us in. "Look at all this," she said softly. "Look at all this rain. The river will rise with it, locks or no locks."

"Funny you should say that. Not an hour ago I was talking to someone else about the river rising. He's trying to tell me that the river's edge is an unhealthy place to be; and he's been saying that when the water's high, bad things happen to people who frequent the banks down there."

She didn't say anything, so I kept talking.

"Of course, he's talking about the south banks—there at Ross's Landing. He's not talking about the north riverbanks."

"Like it matters," she grumbled. "Same river."

"And if I told you that this friend of mine says that people are disappearing from down by the river, might you believe him?"

"That depends on the friend. You know some real... pieces of work." How funny, that she used the same phrase as Eliza's nurse.

"Fair enough." I didn't think she'd ever met Christ, but I couldn't say for sure. "Let's say he's someone reliable, and he was ready to commit crimes to keep people away from—"

"You know who set the fire down there?"

"I didn't say that. Let me finish. But say I did know—and he swore to me in front of God and everybody that he had a good reason and that everyone needed to steer clear of that place. Would you say he's a fool, or that he's got a good head on him?"

"Jesus," she whispered.

"Practically."

"What?"

"Never mind. Just talk to me. Just *tell* me. What are you really worried about?"

"I can't tell you, because I can't say. I never saw anything."

She sounded like she was ready to stonewall, but she was starting to talk and that was better than nothing. "Your mother, though. She saw something there—or she thought she did. She used to dream she did."

"But you didn't see anything."

"I heard something. It was…" She was still sorting out how much to share, and I let her. Some was better than none. "It was a long time ago. Back down on Frasier. Do you remember there used to be an armory there?"

"Sure." I nodded. I was too young for the big rave parties that used to happen there before they tore it down, but I knew about them. "Where Coolidge Park is now. Where they put the carousel."

"That's right. One night, I was down there with Leslie, 'cause she wanted to see inside it. It's a long story. The short version is, we got inside and we couldn't get out. The river rose up behind us and flooded the place, and we were stuck in the attic all night. I don't think I've ever been so scared in my life."

"Of what?"

"Girl, we were just kids. It was dark, and we were trapped away from home."

"And?"

"And." She let the word drop like she wasn't going to pick it up again, but then she did. "And we weren't alone. The river… something came up with it. I don't know what. But I heard it. Them."

"Them?"

The drumming hum of the steady rain backed me up and filled in the silence while she worked her way up to what she meant.

"Them. Yeah. Jesus. I don't know." She took another swig and swallow, and stared out past me into the yard where the water was accumulating into ponds instead of puddles. "I swear, there were people. Dead people. I heard them all night long, beating their fists up against the floor and trying to reach us—it's hard to explain. I counted maybe a dozen of them, using my ears, tracking the sounds around the floor."

"The floor?" I asked. "I don't understand."

"We were up in the attic, I told you. The floor underneath us was the ceiling of the main storage area. And down there, everything had filled up with water. I guess they were floating in it, trying to get up. And whatever they were, they must have been bad, because Leslie twitched and mumbled about it all night even while she dozed off and on. Sometime the next morning, after the water went down a little, we were rescued by the police."

"Was there any sign of—of whatever you heard?"

"No, of course not. No one saw a thing except for us, and who were we? Two kids who were too dumb to come in out of the rain. Even if we'd talked, no one would have believed us. Except for Momma, maybe. But we weren't *about* to tell her." She laughed a little, and it came out hoarse, and forced. "Your mother, though. She had these nightmares for a long time—where she would kick and fuss in bed, like a dog dreaming about chasing a car. But she could see, better than I can."

I knew what she meant, and I didn't ask her to elaborate. She continued on her own, though.

"It always *was* like that. She'd tell me about things she saw, and it wasn't like I didn't believe her, because I *did*. But I was jealous, a little. I wished I could see things too, like she did. Like you do." She nodded at me for emphasis.

"Don't say that," I told her. "It's not like you think. It makes me nuts."

"That's what Leslie used to say, too. I believe you—like I believed her. But you know how kids are, especially when there's a set of three. Each of us wanted to stand out in some way. That's all. But we didn't tell Momma. We didn't tell her anything, ever, if we could help it. She had a way of using things against you. She had a way of taking things you were proud of and making you self-conscious. I don't know if she meant to. She was just one of those people."

I mumbled some sound like I was agreeing with her, or listening, or paying attention, at least. If I'd ever met my grandmother, I didn't remember it.

"Well, you know how it is. Anyway. After the thing at the armory, your mother would dream and fuss about burned-up people. She used to cry that they were coming for her, or something. And when she was really out of it, in the middle of the night, she'd try to talk to them—I guess she was trying to talk to them, anyway. She'd repeat over and over again, 'It was a mistake.' Like she was apologizing."

"Wait," I stopped her. "What did you say? Burned-up people?"

"Yeah. She said they looked like someone had set them on fire. And there was a little girl there too, she had something important to do with it. I never understood it any better than Leslie did, and that wasn't much."

All burned up, just like them, Caroline had said. Her words echoed in my head alongside Lu's, folding the two stories together and shuffling them like cards. *It was a mistake*.

"Lu, what if—" I started, but didn't know how to finish. How strange, if they were connected.

"What?"

"There's a ghost down at the Read House," I said. "Her name's Caroline. And she said something like that, like what you just told me. It's not much to go on, but they could be related."

"A thirty-year-old incident and the White Lady?"

"You know about her?"

"Doesn't everybody? Darling, I've lived here all my life. The White Lady's name is Caroline, huh?"

"That's what she said."

She looked interested then, and set the drink down. "You went and talked to her?"

"With Nick, yes. That's what we've been doing hanging around together for the last few days—in case you were wondering. She's been making trouble for the new hotel owners, and Nick wanted to see if he could get a human interest story out of it. He wanted to see if she'd talk to me, so we could flesh out the mystery a little."

"Did it work?"

"Sort of. She's mad as a hatter—same as when she was alive. Back in the twenties, her family had her institutionalized, but then they checked her out and she lived in the hotel until she killed herself a few years later."

"Delightful. But she talked to you? She tried to communicate?"

"Mostly *I* was the one trying to communicate, and she was the one trying to be left alone."

"That's certainly a coincidence, but maybe nothing more. There's thirty years and several miles between our night in the armory and whatever Caroline was going on about."

There was more to it than that—there was a problem down by the river again, at practically the same place where the armory used to be—but I wasn't sure if I was ready to speculate just yet. They were three distant stepping stones, Caroline's ghost, the armory, and the North Shore Apartments. But I couldn't shake the idea that they were connected. It was simultaneously too unlikely and too obvious.

I was seized with the urge to call Nick, but I wasn't sure what I'd tell him if I reached him, so I sat there with Lu and we watched the rain for a few more minutes. My mind kept wandering back to something else Caroline had said, and it too made me wonder.

They are coming for me. They are coming for all of us.

Who? But the answer was obvious. It was written all over Christ's face when he sat in my car and tried to tell me about the things stalking the riverfront.

The more I thought about it, the more I concluded that it was no answer at all; it only raised more questions. Who were they—and what did they want?

And why did Caroline think it was all about her?

10

DEAD ON MARKET STREET

I ended up calling Nick anyway, because who else was I going to tell? Christ didn't know the whole skinny on Caroline's haunting and I didn't feel like catching him up. So, really it was a matter of mere convenience.

He said he wanted to meet up and compare notes again, if that was all right, so we planned to meet at the Starbucks downstairs at the Read House. It was centrally located, and Nick had scheduled an interview with the head of the cleaning staff later that afternoon anyway. After all, what would Caroline do? Come downstairs and kick my ass over a latte? I doubted it. I would have been astonished to find her out of her room, much less downstairs in the café.

Nick blew it, though. He called after I'd been waiting on him for fifteen minutes and had to postpone; there was an apartment fire somewhere in southside and he'd been the closest man with a camera. We agreed to reschedule and I threw away my empty coffee cup.

I let myself out of the café and stood under the overhang at the Starbucks. It was raining again. With the water came a chill I didn't like, but there was nothing to be done about it except tighten my sweater and stamp my feet. It wasn't worth complaining about.

Then I saw her out of the corner of my right eye, standing at the intersection of Broad and MLK.

She looked familiar, but she wasn't a friend, so it took me a second to figure out who she was. I might not have looked at her twice except that the sight of her set my senses tingling. She was looking in my direction, *at* me, I thought, but she might have only been waiting for the light to change.

Her hair finally clued me in. It was soaked, drowned-rat style, and so were her clothes. It was raining, but it wasn't raining *that* hard. She must have been standing there a long time to get so wet... unless she wasn't standing there at all.

"Ann Alice?" I said, and even though the girl across the street couldn't have heard me, she nodded.

I knew her from around town in the same way I knew a lot of people, by sight alone. If I'd ever exchanged two words with her, I couldn't have told you what they were. But there she was, wet and staring.

And hers was the last name Christ had added to his litany of the missing.

And there she was, dead on Market Street.

Once she knew she had my attention, she turned away and dropped her skateboard from its position at her knees. She stepped onto it and kicked, scooting across the street against the light. There weren't any cars. There wasn't anyone else to see her anyway.

The Death Nugget was parked a block away, and with it I'd left the umbrella I'd made a point of putting in the back seat. The rain wasn't so bad, though, and Ann Alice wanted me to follow her.

"All right," I told her. "I'm coming. Wait."

She didn't wait.

I ducked out from under the awning and went after her because I didn't know what else to do. "Ann Alice?"

The back of her apple-red dyed head was retreating fast, and I stumbled trying to keep up. I hopped up onto the next curb and was on the sidewalk then, closer to her without being near at all.

I watched her duck and weave between the few people she met, and no one reacted at all—but no one ever did, even when she was alive. You keep your head down when the kids skate through, trying to get a rise out of you or bum money. It wasn't strange at all that no one looked up. It wasn't strange at all that no one moved to get out of her way.

Except this time they really couldn't see her.

So I followed, but it's hard to follow on foot when your quarry has wheels. "Slow down," I told her, tripping over my own feet and the uneven walkway.

Down along Market she went, scooting in the general direction of the Choo-Choo, and I figured that was where we were going, maybe. But I lost her before we got there, at a corner where an old bank building squatted empty. She zipped around its side and vanished.

I ran up to the building and pressed myself against it. A small overhang let me hide from the worst of the water, so I stayed there and panted. "Ann Alice?" I called, but nothing and no one answered. "Ann Alice?"

Across the street, a homeless guy with a shopping cart looked up at me and shouted back, "Ann Alice!" in a hoarse voice. He went on his slow, rattling way, still shouting it every few seconds, still calling it out in an idiot's echo.

I waited until his progress took him out of earshot, and I was mostly alone. A car or two pulled up to the stoplight and idled, but no one was watching me between their squeaking, slapping windshield wipers. It was safe enough to follow.

Around the corner I slipped back into the rain and let it hit me, since there was no avoiding it.

The building was being remodeled, or maybe only stripped for salvage before it was torn down. You never know, there on southside. Maybe someone had bought it to turn it into condo space, or maybe it was going to be leveled for another stupid stadium. Anyway, it was empty and boarded up with sheets of plywood and "no trespassing" signs flashing orange and black warnings.

But Ann Alice knew what she was doing. One board had been kicked in or pulled down, and there was a gap large enough to fit through. I saw no further sign of her, so I assumed I'd found what she wanted me to find.

I crouched and squeezed, pulling my shoulders through with a little bit of nervousness. The edges of the boards picked at my sweater and pulled my hair. I scraped my back on the wall's edge and winced, but kept going inside, into the dark and dusty closeness of a shut-up place.

"All right, you've got me here. What is it?"

I stood up straight and took in the sights. All the windows had been covered from the bottom up, though some of them were left exposed near the ceiling and there was light enough dribbling in from the gray afternoon. The air was thick and tasted like sawdust mixed with chalk. A few crates and pieces of debris littered the floors and corners.

On the floor, my boot grazed a flyer for a big moving sale.

That was right, I remembered. It used to be a furniture store after it was a bank. I had no idea where it'd relocated to. Didn't matter, though.

Ann Alice was lying low. I squinted into the corners and examined every watery beam of light, but there was no hint of her. Then, upstairs, I thought I heard something like a footstep, or a soft scuffling. It was an impatient little sound.

Immediately in front of where I'd entered was a big empty expanse that must have been a showroom. Back deeper into the corner there was more to see and explore. There were partitions and divisions, remnants of the place's first incarnation as a bank, maybe. Since there weren't any stairs to be seen in the showroom, I headed back, watching for nails and trying to remember when I'd had my last tetanus shot.

A narrow door that looked like it might have covered a closet proved instead to hide a skinny set of stairs. I saw a suggestion of more light where they ended; but between me and the top, there was only blackness.

I pressed a hand against the wall, feeling for a rail but not finding one.

I started to climb anyway. I tested each wooden stair before I put all my weight on it. Every one of them creaked a complaint, but held.

"What have we got up here?" I asked under my breath, not expecting an answer and not receiving one.

The door at the top was hanging open and half off its hinges. I nudged it aside with my foot and stepped into a finished attic with a high triangular ceiling. My nose wrinkled. I detected death, but it was something small. The gnawed papers and pulped clothing suggested rats.

"Ann Alice, you're not up here, are you?"

A human would stink worse than this, I thought. She wanted to show me something else.

Hey.

I jumped. It was an idle greeting, the kind I passed back and forth with people every day. When I turned around, she wasn't there—but I was left with the thought that she *had* been.

"Jesus, kid. What are you doing?" She kept her silence, but I tried to track the syllable to a location. Maybe I'd heard it from the other side of the room, or maybe it came from the big window that overlooked Market Street.

I went with my second guess. I climbed clear of the staircase and went creaking across the floor. Every step kicked up more dust.

Look.

It came out in a whisper, but it was close. Over my shoulder. It was a whisper that pointed.

"At what?" I asked, on the verge of exasperation. "If you've got something to share, I'm listening—but I'm not in the mood to play tag."

Even as I spoke, my eyes were drawn to a cracked patch of crumbling plaster, there on the wall by the window. But I thought I saw something else under the plaster. Color. A line or two that didn't fit.

I hunkered down and examined the patch, which was smaller than a fist. There was something underneath it. I took the edge of my thumbnail and gave it a needling pick. A flat bit flicked away and exposed more color—brown, black, and white.

"Okay," I breathed. "What have we got here?"

The plaster was old and brittle. It didn't take much to pry

121

it free. I whacked the wall with the back of my hand and more chunks fell.

A hoof.

"Huh." The hoof wasn't life-sized or anything, but it meant a much bigger drawing or painting was still hidden. I glanced around the room for something larger and more solid than my hand, and I saw a rusty shovel lying beside the stairwell door.

I picked it up, got a good grip, then swung it.

After the first impact or two, I had to hold my breath against the airborne grime and close my eyes against the dust. But it gave me more of the horse, and part of a rider. I swung the shovel higher. More wall dissolved. More plaster came down.

After a few minutes of effort, I'd revealed a magnificently amateur painting of a white-hooded man on a galloping steed. "Huh." I said, and then I said it again because I couldn't think of anything new to add.

The mural was somewhat smaller than the window next to it, and composed in a style that could best be described as earnest but unpolished. It displayed thick lines, flat color work, and a shabby grip on the basics of proportion. It was obviously meant to be inspiring, or possibly intimidating, but it was damn-near comical.

I stood back and made another scan of the room, paying closer attention to the walls. Here and there more similar pieces—probably by the same artist—peeked through the plaster. I gave one of the more perplexing spots a slap with the shovel and turned up a burning cross that looked almost jolly.

I also found two more partial horses and riders, but I couldn't see the point in exposing them. Whatever was lurking beneath the plaster was no lost Picasso, after all. I'd gotten the message, or at least the general idea of it.

The bank building was old, probably from the middle of the nineteenth century. An upstairs room in a professional establishment—a secret Klan meeting place? Sure. It wasn't surprising. Hell, it was only marginally interesting.

"What am I supposed to do with this?" I asked Ann Alice, but she didn't feel like being helpful anymore.

My phone rang, cluttering up the quiet with a jingling tune. It was Nick.

"All done here. You still want coffee?"

"Sure," I said, eyes still firmly planted on the first horseman. "But let's go somewhere else. I'll meet you at Greyfriar's in about twenty minutes."

When I met him twenty minutes later, Nick was his usual charmingly direct self, and greeted me with a grimace.

"What the hell happened to you? You look like you've been—"

"Climbing around in a dirty old attic?"

"Yeah, but worse. What's the deal?" He used his foot to kick a chair out for me, but I shook my head at him.

"Give me a minute to go clean up a tad." I left him for the bathroom, where I learned that his reaction had once again been understated. I was covered in streaked drywall dust and century-old plaster, which had transformed to a pale, muddy state in every crevice of my clothing.

I washed up, tied my hair back into a fat bun, and joined him again.

"Better," he appraised.

I sat down. "You're not going to believe what I just found."

"In Grandma's attic?"

"In the attic of the old Clark's furniture building, over on Market Street."

He lifted an eyebrow, then lifted his mug. "What were you doing *there*?"

"Long story. Not important. The important part is what I found up there. Under the plaster in the second-story storage space, somebody painted a bunch of old Klan murals."

"Seriously?"

"Seriously. They were plastered over ages ago, but the plaster's falling down and you can see them if you poke at it."

"That accounts for the peculiar new 'product' you've got going on in your hair."

"Oh, shut up. But yes, yes it does."

"And what does this mean?" he asked.

"I don't know if it means anything at all," I fibbed. It must have meant something to Ann Alice, or else why would she have gone to the trouble of showing it to me? Why not lead me to her body—wouldn't that make more sense?

"I know the building you're talking about. It used to be a bank, didn't it?"

"Eons ago, yeah. It was a furniture store most recently, though. Now someone's bought it out and they're gutting it, by the looks of things. Maybe they'll put up condos or something. How hard do you think it would be to find out about the place?"

"What, like if it was used by the Klan?"

"Yeah," I said. "That's what I mean. There must be records of that kind of thing."

"Maybe, maybe not. I don't know. The Klan, I mean—let's be honest. Even these days they aren't the most organized bastards around. Have you seen their white power flyers? Have they no spellcheck—or is that an oppressive tool of the Jews and the blacks too?"

"I found one of those flyers on my car the other day, so I'm thinking they need to research their target demographic a little better. I wonder what they'd do if I showed up for a meeting?"

"Do you still have it?"

"The flyer? No." I frowned at him, and he hastily explained himself.

"Might be an interesting sort of investigative piece, that's all. It's been a while since anybody's bothered with the Klan in the news. And hey, I'm a white guy. I could probably get past the bouncer to take a peek at a meeting."

"Ew."

"For research purposes!" he protested.

"For whatever purposes—*ew*. But if you wanted to take a camera into the old Clark's building, it might make an interesting quickie piece. Tell the boss you got an anonymous tip and found the place open."

"Is it open?"

"Technically. You can get inside if you're willing to get dirty. If you can make a few phone calls, you might not even need to. Some sweet talk might get you past the front door in a more legal fashion."

If there was one thing I'd learned from hanging around Nick, it was that journalism credentials opened doors and got people talking—so if he wanted to check into the paintings, I'd be happy to let him. He'd almost certainly find out more about them than I could.

In my experience, if a ghost isn't trying to lead you to a body, she's trying to lead you to a killer. I didn't know what an old Klan meetinghouse had to do with Ann Alice's demise, but it must have been important one way or another. Ann Alice was Caucasian and non-confrontational, so far as skater kids go. I had a hard time believing any neo-Nazis had gotten her.

"I'll make a note of it," Nick said, and I knew he'd remember. If nothing else, he'd get bored and short of ideas some afternoon and go poking around. "But that's not what you wanted to talk about. You wanted to talk about Caroline, right?"

"Right."

"Good. So did I. I found her grave. She's buried in that big spread over at the foot of Lookout. You want to go check it out?"

"Why?" I asked. What was the point of seeing where her body was? It was the rest of her that was making trouble.

"Why not?"

"It's raining, for one thing. And who cares, for another?"

"Do you think *she* cares? You've talked before about ghosts who don't know they're dead. If she knew where her body was, might this solve the problem?"

I shook my head and stood up, having suddenly realized that I had no coffee. "Whatever's wrong with her isn't going to be fixed with a little show and tell." I fished a couple dollars out of my jeans pocket and took them to the counter, where I exchanged them for a to-go cup.

When I returned, I'd had some time to think. But I still didn't believe her grave was going to do us any good. "Here's what I think would work better," I began. "We know she was institutionalized somewhere, right? Do we know where?"

"I've got it written down someplace."

"Good. So wherever she was, they'd have records, wouldn't they? Treatment records, maybe. Maybe we'd get dumb and lucky enough to stumble across a journal or something, but I wouldn't hold my breath. There's always the chance we might scare up a few doctor's notes."

"Good point. Patient/client privilege doesn't hold up when patient and client have both been dead for years. It's worth looking into."

A flash of Technicolor hair at the window caught my attention. I looked out and saw Christ there, chewing on the filter end of a cigarette. "Excuse me for a minute," I said to Nick.

"Again?"

"Again. Just for a minute."

I pushed open the heavy glass door and Christ flinched, as if he couldn't decide whether or not to run. "Christ, I want to talk to you."

He was glaring over my shoulder at Nick. Nick didn't know what was going on, but he knew malice when he saw it. He made a tense, defensive shrug that asked through the glass, "What the fuck's your problem?"

I turned my back on him and took Christ by the shoulder, gently pushing him away from the storefront and back to a spot where we were less easily observed. "I saw Ann Alice today," I told him, and to his infinite credit he knew *exactly* what I meant.

"I told you!" he almost shouted, but I held him down with one hand and made a shushing gesture with the other.

"I know you told me, and hey—now I believe you."

"What'd she say? Where is she? What happened?" The questions came flapping out of his mouth one after the other, but I had to sit him down and quiet him with the truth.

"I don't know—she didn't say anything. She just led me to something, and I don't know what it means. She wasn't very helpful."

"Maybe you just didn't *understand*."

"Oh, there's no 'maybe' about it. She took me to that old bank building on Market Street, the one on the corner that used to be a furniture store."

"Did you find her body?"

"No. Good Lord, no. I would've had to call the cops over that, and I wouldn't be sitting here talking to you if that had happened. I didn't find any trace of her. But I *did* find something weird. I think it's what she wanted to show me, but I don't get it."

"Well?"

"Well, it was a series of paintings on the wall, underneath the plaster."

"Wait. What?" Christ deflated with confusion. "Murals? *Under* the plaster? How did you—"

"They were old KKK murals, pictures of hooded bozos on horses with burning crosses. But they'd been there a while, probably a hundred years or more. Someone had plastered over them ages ago, and the plaster's coming down; that's why I could see them. That's what Ann Alice was trying to show me. As soon as I twigged on, she disappeared. I'd ask if you know what she meant by it, but I can tell by looking at you that you're as stumped as I am."

"I'm not stumped," he argued. "I'm never stumped. I'm just temporarily unaware."

"You're nuts, is what you are."

"But Ann Alice wasn't."

"Is that why she was selling her behavioral modification meds down by the river?"

He stood up. "Yeah, because she didn't need them. That's the point. She wasn't crazy and she wasn't stupid. If she showed you the furniture building, then she must have had a reason."

"But what would that reason be? That's what I'm asking *you*."

I hadn't known Ann Alice very well. She'd always struck me as a pretty little burn-out tomboy. It seems to take ghosts a lot of trouble and effort to manifest, though, so when they do, there's almost always method to their madness. Of course, sometimes madness *is* the method, and that's where it gets tricky.

"I… I have no idea. But maybe I should go check the place out—get a look around. You didn't find anything, but *I* might."

"Knock yourself out. Keep your eyes open, though. It's private property and there could be cops hanging around. There's a hole in the plywood covering one of the side doors. Go in that way and take a look. But be warned, you might end up running into Nick there too. He may do a local interest piece about it."

"Is that what you're doing here? Talking with him about this, I mean?"

"Yes. Why? What did you think I was doing?"

"You *said* you wouldn't rat me out to the media, but for all I know—"

"I meant what I said, dumbass. But I did tell him about the paintings, because he's got access to research options I don't."

He laughed, a half-dismal little cough of mirth. "I get it. You're not above using him to do your legwork."

"What's *that* supposed to mean?"

"Take it however you like it. I don't give a shit. Thanks for the heads-up, though. I'll go check the place out before Ned Nickerson over there gets his paws on it."

With that, he dropped his board to the ground and took off down the sidewalk. I should've known more than to expect any gratitude, but it still annoyed me.

I went back inside and Nick was waiting with a refill. "What was that about?"

"Nothing important. I had a message for him, that's all."

"He looks… charming."

"You are… lying," I said, imitating his joking tone. "He's a right bastard, but I owe him a favor. Sort of."

"Long story?"

"Long story. Wouldn't fit into a three-minute piece, I assure you. But hey, stupid question," I warned. "Do you know who Ned Nickerson is?"

He scrunched his forehead, then brightened. "Nancy Drew's boyfriend, I think. Not that I ever read them; I was a Hardy Boys man all the way. But my sister couldn't get enough of them. Why do you ask?"

"No reason. It's just a name that came up in passing. I thought it sounded familiar but couldn't place it. You know."

"Sure," he said, but it didn't sound like he believed me.

11

SEEING AND KNOWING

It rained again the next day and the river was up, which is how it goes. With bad weather comes a higher river, fewer people downtown, nastier roads, and construction breaks, so the North Shore Apartments would have to wait for repairs and completion.

Rainy days always make me restless anyway; I turn into a little kid again, wanting to go outside and feeling thwarted.

My mood wasn't helped by the fact that I was on borrowed time at Lu and Dave's. They knew I was leaving. I knew I was leaving. I was all packed and *prepared* to leave. We'd made our peace with it, but for one reason after another I couldn't actually get the hell out.

It really *was* time, I knew. A lot of my friends still lived at home, but even with guardians as laid-back as my aunt and uncle, past twenty-five a girl tends to want her own space. And once everything had been arranged but delayed, my impatience was killing me.

I was itching for an excuse to leave the house when Harry

called and gave me an even better reason to want to flee.

"You ready?" he asked, as if I could possibly tell him "Yes."

"Ready as I'll ever be. What's your ETA?"

"Tomorrow afternoon. Does that work for you?" In the background I could hear Malachi jabbering happily.

"Tomorrow afternoon. In time for supper?"

"In time for supper," he confirmed. "How do you want to do this?"

"Preferably? In body armor. But failing Kevlar, how about you two show up here at the house around six. I'll sit down with the 'rents and warn them. I've been putting this off long enough. I think it's time to have that little chat, whether I like it or not."

"I don't envy you. Be gentle with them."

"I won't have a choice. Hey, do you know how to get here?"

I gave him directions and we hung up. Tomorrow afternoon.

Supper with the family, plus Harry and Malachi. It was enough to make me break out in hives, but it would only be worse if it was a surprise.

Lu and Dave were lounging on the back porch together, watching the rain like Lu and I had the day before. We lived in a quiet patch of Signal Mountain. Our nearest neighbors were two lots away on either side, so we had plenty of trees in our backyard and no one to bother us.

It was easy to feel isolated; but then again, it was easy to feel secure.

I made myself a stiff drink—then I thought further ahead and made three. I used up the last of Lu's sweet rum and a two-liter bottle of soda, but it would be worth the replacement costs to have an alcoholic buffer. I finished the drinks off with ice and straws, then stuck them on a TV dinner tray and took a deep breath.

I pushed the patio door open with my foot.

"Frosty beverages?" I offered, trying to sound jolly.

"Absolutely!" Dave agreed first, reaching forward and taking a blue plastic tumbler off the tray. Lu took the orange one and I was saddled with the pink. "Now what do you want?" he asked.

"Want?"

"Or need?" Lu clarified. "You look positively ill. What's wrong?"

"Nothing's wrong, exactly. Nothing's *wrong*. Can't I bring my two favorite people a drink without getting the third degree?"

Lu sipped hard through the straw and smirked. "Maybe you should pick two other people—possibly people who don't know you very well."

"Oh, that wouldn't be any fun. I just wanted to run something past you before tomorrow afternoon." I settled in, taking the patio chaise longue and pushing it a foot or so back, up against the wall. I did my best to look relaxed, and almost certainly failed.

"You in some kind of trouble?" Lu asked, taking the safe route because she was unsure whether to be concerned or amused.

"Do you need money? What have you done now?"

"I haven't *done* anything. But I'm about to do something you might take objection to, and I want to warn you rather than spring it on you."

"Whoa, boy." Dave made a show of taking a deep drink. "It must be serious. These are pretty strong."

"Well, serious is sort of relative, isn't it?"

"Sweet Jesus." Lu followed Dave's example.

"No—no, really. Okay. Before you get worked up, let me make some disclaimers. First of all, I'm not in any kind of trouble. Second, no one's gotten hurt, and no one needs money. I'm not moving to Europe and I'm not plotting anything illegal." The minute I said the last part, I wondered how true it was. In the interest of full disclosure I backpedaled carefully. "Actually, we might be in a gray area, there. Like, I don't know if it could be called 'harboring a fugitive' if the police stopped looking for him because they think he's dead."

It was as big of a preparatory hint as I could deliver. Lu and Dave both froze and stared, each of them trying to parse out what I was so reluctant to divulge. Neither one knew what to ask, so neither one asked anything. They waited me out. So when the moment had reached its critical mass of awkwardness, I kept going.

"It's like this. You know a couple of years ago—when I went to Florida." It wasn't a question. We all knew what I was talking about. I had a quick flashback to the swamp, and to Avery with his dank little cabin. I remembered the smoke and the ashes, and the way Malachi—even hog-tied—had repented enough to lend a hand.

"Go on," Dave said. He was trying to sound tough and warning, but I heard eagerness there too.

"You guys remember Harry, right?"

"Sure," Lu said. "Older guy. Tall and tough-looking. The Jack Palance of clergy."

"Used to work for Eliza," Dave added.

"That's him. He went back to the monastery in St. Augustine after all the craziness happened. And it's hard for me to overstate how seriously crazy all that was. But I need you to take my word for it."

Lu definitely didn't like this. The toughness Dave feigned was iron-clad in her voice. "Word taken."

"So what if I told you that maybe I wasn't entirely complete in my description of what happened there, that I might have left out the part of the story that I didn't think you'd like very much? Say, hypothetically, well… you remember Malachi?"

It was the stupidest possible way I could have brought him up, but they were making me manic with their tense, stoic audience. Of course they remembered him. He'd tried to kill me. Twice.

Neither of them answered.

"Okay. So. Malachi. As I think we can all agree, he had some issues. But those issues sprung from a series of misconceptions he had—"

"Oh God," Lu breathed. She'd already caught on, but I kept talking.

"And it is very, *very* safe to say that—in the swamp, at that batty old guy's shack—those misconceptions were cleared up. Malachi even tried to help me. I won't say he saved my life or anything, but he definitely helped. And once he realized how wrong he'd been, I… um… I might have pulled him out of the burning shack."

"Oh God." It was Dave's turn.

"Well, sure, God. With Malachi, y'know, it was always 'God this' and 'God that.' He was hurt pretty badly and I had a moment where I couldn't help helping him. And then I gave him over to Harry."

"Harry." They said it in stereo, and I knew they were both thinking back to the regularity with which Harry continued to call me.

"Sure. Harry. And Harry is… not exactly *rehabilitating* him, or anything, but Harry's been keeping an eye on him for the last couple of years. And, *yes*, before you even ask, *yes* Malachi and I have been in semi-regular contact. And please don't freak out or anything, but—"

"But?"

"But Harry's bringing him over here tomorrow night because we're all going to have supper together and it's going to be *lovely*."

I've heard about situations where people have heart attacks or strokes and death strikes them so swiftly that they remain upright for a time, and other people don't know they've died because their eyes are still open. For about thirty seconds, I was afraid that this weird mishap had spontaneously struck both my aunt and uncle, that I had killed them both with the news of Malachi's imminent arrival.

"Somebody say something," I whispered.

They gave me another thirty seconds or so before Lu finally asked, in a cracking voice, "What time?"

"Six-ish."

"Now, wait," Dave said, but he said it slowly like he was still catching up—not like he intended to put his foot down. "Wait. This is. Wait."

"Weird. Believe me, I know how weird it is. I've been thinking about how weird it is for years now. All kinds of weird. But at the end of the day, he's had an enlightenment and a change of heart, and he *is* my half-brother."

"Well, yes. *Technically*." Lu said it like a disavowal.

"Technically, and literally. Like it or not." Then it was my turn to disavow. "It's not like we're suddenly best friends or anything. It's not like that at all. But he's really fucking *eager*, you know? He wants to make it up to me; he's got something to prove. He wants to be friends and… and, he's alone, except for Harry. He's got nobody but me, and while I realize that this is *deeply* screwed up, that's the way it is. He's coming tomorrow. And…"

Dave downed the last of the drink in a long swallow. "And?"

"And I'd appreciate it if you didn't try to kill him. He's harmless. I swear to God."

"He tried to *kill* you."

"Yes, but he was never any *good* at it."

"What about that girl at the poetry slam? He killed *her*, Eden." Lu had hardly touched the drink since I'd started talking, which was possibly a bad sign.

"It was an accident! Look, do you really think I don't know how bad this is? Why do you think I've kept quiet all this time? Why do you think I haven't said anything, that I just let Dave think I had a creepy long-distance thing going on with Harry?"

"I *did* kind of think that," he confessed.

"I know you did. But hey, look on the bright side, right? I'm not having an *affaire de coeur* with a man old enough to be my grandfather."

"Some bright side," Lu grumbled.

"It's *a* bright side. I didn't say it was the brightest of all possible sides."

Lu shook her head like she was still thinking and all this talking was distracting her. "Have you—have you seen him since then? Since Florida?"

"Yes. Once. He came up here last year, but I kept him out of sight and sent him back to Florida." I thought I might as well build up some trust by offering a partial confession.

"Oh God."

"Lu, stop saying that."

"Well, what do you want me to say? Seriously? Should we go out and buy some streamers? Should we throw him a party? Would that make you happy?" She was creeping up to shrillness, and I knew that the calm before the storm was just about over.

Dave put a hand on her arm and withdrew it, like her skin was burning hot.

"No, but I want you to be civil. I want you to let a little water flow under the bridge and give him a chance to say his piece. He's pathetic, all right? I feel sorry for him, and I let myself get talked into this when I probably shouldn't have, but it's too late to do anything about it now."

"The hell it is." Lu put her glass down and stood. She put her face in her hands, then ran her hands back through her hair and faced me. "This is *unbelievable*."

"I know. Just—I'm asking you, just be cool. Harry will be with him, and he'll be fine. We'll be fine. We'll be fucked up and fine. It's just supper, and he'll be back on his way to Florida the next morning."

"Water under the bridge," she repeated. She turned away from me and Dave both and glared into the backyard.

"If I can forgive and forget, I'd hope you can too."

"It's different."

"How?"

"It's different because he tried to *kill* you. He tried to take you away from me. I don't know how much forgiveness I've got left, and I sure as all get-out don't know if there's enough left in me to cover *that*."

"Then don't forgive him. I'm not asking you to like him, I'm asking you to tolerate him for an hour. Don't do it for him, or because he deserves it. Do it for me, because I'm asking you to."

"This is the stupidest thing you've ever done."

Dave raised a finger like he might have wanted to argue, but his desire to interrupt was overruled by his reluctance to get between Lu and me.

"So? Something has to take that title. Let it be this—at least it's something harmless."

"Harmless." She used the word again, throwing it back at me. "Harmless. And I guess that's your call, isn't it? You wouldn't bring him here if you thought for a second he'd do anything to either of us, I know."

"See? That's more like it."

"But you've been fooled before. And I don't like it. I don't like the idea of it, of him being here in this house. I don't like it that you think this is okay. None of this is okay. None of it."

I stood up then, too, because I wanted to be on eye level with her. I didn't want her to stand there, looking down at me while she talked. "Jesus, Lu. If you'd just *meet* him, you wouldn't be half so worried. He's innocent and stupid. If you do this and you meet him, you'll never worry again. You'll never wonder."

"I don't want to wonder," Dave finally joined in. "I'd rather see him and *know*—and if I don't know the second I set eyes on him, I don't want to go through with it. But I'd be willing to set eyes on him. I'd be willing to find out. Lu? I think we should. I think we should at least take a look at him."

"So it's both of you then, lining up against me?"

"No one's against you," I told her, and I meant it. "No one's for or against anybody. That's the thing—there's no reason to struggle anymore. There's no reason to feel that way anymore, and I want you to *see* it. I want you to *know* it, and to stop being afraid."

Out of pure frustration, I went ahead and left it at that— taking my leave while the leaving was good. I picked up my still-mostly-full drink and went back into the house, and I tried not to listen as they continued the conversation without me. It was tough to resist the urge to go back out there and argue some more, but there was nothing else I could tell them. Malachi was coming one way or another, and they were going to have to get used to it.

Maybe Dave would calm Lu down, and maybe she'd rile him up.

They'd have to work it out without me.

12

THE RIVER WALK

Christ's voice whispered hard over the connection, and into my voicemail box.

"I found Ann Alice's body. Not in the old furniture place, but up in the undersides. I wouldn't have recognized her except for the old Smurfette tattoo on her wrist. You can barely see it anymore. She's... I don't know. I don't know what could've done this to her. But nobody cares."

He'd hung up then. The callback number was one I didn't recognize, probably a payphone. He must have called overnight, when I had the phone turned off. He must be in trouble, or he wouldn't bother.

I knew what he meant by "undersides." Lots of us downtown people knew about the undersides—the place where the city's water runoff drains down into the Tennessee River. You have to know where it is to find it, but if you know how to find it, it's plenty big enough to climb up inside. Some people talk about it like it's the Underground, down in Atlanta. But it isn't.

It's just some water runoff tunnels and a few hollow places underneath the city where there used to be roads.

But the rain.

I looked out the window and it was still coming down as determined as ever.

It made me think of Christ in his ratty clothes and taped-together shoes, sloshing knee-deep up into the undersides and standing there, in the low, cement-domed rooms with Ann Alice's mortal remains floating and stinking.

I knew better than to wonder if Christ had called the police. Of course he hadn't. I readied my thumb to dial 911, and thought better of it. What would I say? And would anyone believe me?

If it was flooded down there like I imagined it must be, would they even send anyone looking for her—even if they believed me?

Another possibility made me close the phone and slip it back into my pocket. It was entirely possible that Christ had moved her himself. I wondered what he'd do with her if he did. I wondered where he would put her.

Although fully twelve hours had passed since I dropped the Malachi bomb, Lu and Dave were eating breakfast on the back porch, still discussing the finer points of my idiocy and working out their future reactions to Malachi. I didn't want to bother them. I left them a note on the fridge saying I was going downtown and to call my cell if they needed me.

Once I got into the car I called my old friend Jamie, who hadn't seen Christ in several days and didn't know what he was doing.

"What's going on?" he asked, and I tried to give him the fifty-cent version.

"You've heard him fussing about missing friends, right?"

142

"Monsters down by the river? I've heard about it. But he went running off after the last poetry slam and no one's seen him since. I just assumed he was being a drama queen."

I was concentrating on getting down the mountain without killing myself in the storm or I might have rolled my eyes. "You'd know it when you saw it, wouldn't you, darling?"

"But of course. We know our kind. Look, he does this once in a while. You know him. I wouldn't worry about it too much. Frankly, I'm not sure why you're bothering to call around about it. Since when does Christ have any cred with you?"

"Since I think he might be telling the truth."

"Really?"

"Just this once," I said. "Try to contain your astonishment."

"My heart is doing poundy things in my chest. Could this be the seventh seal? Is Armageddon upon us?"

"You never know. Listen, where are you right now?"

"Now? I'm at home with Becca. Why?"

"I'm on my way downtown. I think Christ is in some kind of trouble—or, if he isn't yet, he's gonna be. So I'm headed down to Greyfriar's. It's always a good spot to start looking for people. I'll be down there soon."

"No you won't," he said with his own special kind of nonchalance.

"Yes I will. I'm sliding down the mountain right now. Would you believe this rain?"

"Sure I'd believe it—but you're not going to get far. You'll never make it over the river. They've started shutting the bridges down. The river's rising, cutie. TVA sucks ass, in case you didn't know."

"What?"

143

"Look out of your windshield. It's raining, not just diddling around anymore. It's been going on for days, and there's some problem up at the dam. They're trying to keep people off the bridges."

"Then Christ is definitely in trouble. I think he's down at the undersides." I lost traction then and had to drop the phone into the passenger's seat while I regained control of the Death Nugget. "Hang on a second," I said, and I hoped he heard me.

With the squeal and squeak of four angry tires, I pulled the car back into its correct lane.

I picked the phone back up. Jamie was mid-way through saying something, but since I'd missed the first part I cut him off. "Wait. Call the cops. Christ won't like it, but if the river's really coming up, I think he might be in real trouble."

"If he's down at the undersides then, well, *yeah*. What's he doing there? And how do *you* know he's there?"

"He left me a voicemail. He went there looking for one of his missing friends, and he said—" I stopped myself. "He said he was down there, but the signal was all shitty and I could hardly understand him."

"Shit." Somewhere behind him, his girlfriend asked what was going on. He shooed her away with a promise to fill her in later. "He'll kick my ass if I call the cops on him."

"Then call the cops *for* him. At least see if someone will go down there and look for him, you know?"

"What are the odds?"

"Probably not good. But try it, please? I'm going to try to get downtown now, and if I do, I'm going to start at Greyfriar's. If he made it out of the tunnels, he might go dry off there. Or the library. I don't know."

The white noise of the rain around my car made it hard to hear, but I think Jamie was getting up and moving around. "Eden, stay on the mountain. Just stay up there and I'll look into it. I'm not doing anything right now anyway; I got sent home from work. The restaurant closed up when they started talking about shutting the bridges. That goofy little car of yours isn't made for wading."

"Don't insult the wheels, man."

"The Nugget isn't exactly an SUV. Half of Red Bank is already underwater," he said, but that didn't tell me anything. Every time it rains too bad, big chunks of the main drag lose their sidewalks and storefronts.

"You're going to get stuck down there. Don't do it. Stay put, and I'll see if I can get a lead on Christ."

"Oh, I *will* get across the river. You just watch me. And be at the 'Friar in half an hour. But first—call the cops."

"And tell them what, exactly?"

"Tell them—tell them you heard someone calling out for help down at the undersides entrance, the one beside the amphitheater under the pedestrian bridge. Tell them you think someone's trapped down there, by the river. Tell them anything, except don't tell them it's Christ. And I mean it: thirty minutes. Be there."

I hung up on him and threw the phone back onto the seat. I was almost down off the mountain, and 27 was beginning to straighten out. But it unnerved me, the way the unrelenting rain gave everything such a weird sense of urgency—between the pounding noise and the zero visibility, it was enough to make you crazy.

The very thought that they'd shut down the bridges was ridiculous. They never shut down the bridges except for road work. The bridges were plenty high off the ground, and plenty high away from the river.

But Jamie was right. The road began backing up and the loud blue and red lights of cop cars beamed wetly through the storm. Flashing lights with arrows indicated detours and recommended shelters.

"I need to watch more TV," I said to myself, pulling up next to a raincoat-bedecked officer waving a flashlight.

I rolled down the window. "Excuse me? What's the situation? I'm trying to get downtown."

"Emergency," he told me, blinking through the droplets that ran down his nose and dripped off his mustache. "Trouble with the locks at the dam. We're trying to keep everyone up away from the river until the situation is resolved."

"But—"

"I realize it's an inconvenience, ma'am. If you're trying to get to work—"

"I'm not trying to get to work. I'm trying to get home," I lied.

"Sorry, ma'am. Give us a few hours to sort things out. Right now, we've got a couple of businesses that look like they're headed underwater, and we're shutting down the Veterans Bridge."

"No way! Has this ever happened before?"

"Not so far as I know. Ma'am, please move along."

"What about the hospitals? What about the interstates?" I shouted over the rain.

"Ma'am, I'm going to have to ask you—"

"To move along. Yeah, I got it."

My phone rang, and I rolled up my window. I wiped rain off my face and checked the phone's display; the call was coming from home. Lu and Dave watched more TV than I did, and probably were calling to warn me about the closings.

I ignored the phone. Now I had a *challenge*.

I was probably a couple of miles from the river, but I knew a whole lot of back roads, and I'd told Jamie I'd meet him in half an hour.

My first thought was to try the long way around, via the Chickamauga Dam—but if the dam was having issues, I could safely bet they'd shut down driving over that spot, too. The cop said they'd closed the Veterans Bridge. That left the Olgiati and Market Street bridges, but since those were within a mile of the closed one, they'd be jam-packed or shut down as well.

I felt stupid, but beyond those three arteries I had no earthly idea how to get across the water. I'd never needed another route before. How far around the city would I have to drive? Chattanooga doesn't have a ferry or anything, so it wasn't like I could chase down a boat.

Well, there was always the chance I could chase down a private craft; but I'd have to get next to the water for *that*.

I tried to imagine all the boats I could think of, and they all docked in approximately the same place on the north bank—down by the pedestrian bridge. But if I could make it down to the pedestrian bridge, then I could walk across the river myself. It's less than a mile.

The more I pondered the plan, the better I liked it. The cops would be busy chasing cars, and the bike cops would have better sense than to patrol the bridge in that weather. Who on earth would be trying to walk it, anyway? Only a damn fool.

But I happened to know that at the end of that bridge, on the other side, there was a set of cement runoff tunnels down at the river's edge. And down there, under the city and up beneath the banks, there might be proof of something horrible. And there might be a dumb punk drowning.

147

I didn't know how high he could crawl in those tunnels, but I knew there were several "up" vents here and there with rusty metal ladders heading up to the street. But those street entrances were often locked or covered with manholes too heavy to budge without equipment.

I didn't want to think about it. I just had to get there. But the prospect was daunting: traffic had become a Gordian knot, and every stray off-road was getting clogged with people who had the same bright idea I did. There are a lot of back ways to reach a destination around here, but the trouble is, everybody knows all those back roads too.

Finally—and well past my thirty-minute meeting command—I worked my slow, aggravating way through a north Chattanooga neighborhood and came out near Frasier Avenue, the old warehousing district-turned-tourist strip.

I'd never seen so many cars there.

I'd been out for the big Riverbend music festival and thought *that* was bad, but this was insane. Cars were stopped in every available street, corner, and curb—jammed into parking lots, halfway onto sidewalks, and parked on people's yards wherever private houses met the shopping district. Everyone was trying to turn around, which was almost perfectly impossible.

"Oh God." I said it out loud, for no one to hear. I'd really done it this time. There was no leaving, and no going forward. I'd stopped at the top of a hill, and I still had a tiny bit of wiggle room between the curious and desperate cars, but my window was closing fast as people crushed themselves as close to the water's edge as they could get.

I thought about my almost-apartment a few blocks away and wondered how it was faring. I thought of Christ down in the runoff. And I thought of Greyfriar's, and the stores, and the boats, and the bridges.

I could run for it. I could find a place to leave the car and make a dash for it. The path to the river was straight downhill and only a matter of blocks.

It was hard to see what was going on down there. The chaos had reached some kind of critical mass, and police were chasing or arresting everyone within arm's reach, or that's what it looked like. Down closer to the water, people were starting to turn back—abandoning cars and retreating to the tree-filled neighborhoods up the hills.

My windshield wipers slapped a nerve-wracking rhythm as they barely managed to swipe the glass clear for a split second at a time.

"This is going to suck," I said to no one in particular, though it was followed by an apology. "Okay, little Death Nugget. I'm going to have to find a place to leave you for a while. It won't be so bad," I assured it. "Up here on the hill, it's not like you're going to get flooded. Worst case scenario? You get towed and I'll have to pay a big fat fine to get you back."

But really, what were the chances that a tow truck was going to make it into north Chattanooga any time in the next few days?

I peered through the sheets of rain sliding over my windows and figured, "Not any time soon." Cars were crushed together, fender to fender, on every street that was not obscured by trees or buildings. People were standing outside their vehicles swearing and shouting, making threats, and starting fights—which only rarely drew the attention of the overwhelmed police presence.

Behind me, cars were clogging the roadways. If I didn't pull over and switch off now, I'd be stuck in the lane where I idled.

A truck in front of me gave up and pulled up the curb onto what looked like the yard of an old apartment building, but the neighborhoods up there are so jumbled it was hard to tell.

Since he'd set the precedent, I did likewise, compelling my small black compact to hike the curb and take to the grass.

From the minimally higher vantage point of somebody's grass, I spied a parking lot catty-cornered from the block. It was full, but people were still turning into it as if they could make a complicated U-turn and find their way back home by nightfall.

It wasn't going to happen.

Too many abandoned cars and too many angry, confused people.

I added my own car to the pile, zipping over the soggy grass, down one curb, over a sidewalk, and up a second curb. This put me in the back part of the lot, where, behind a pair of monster SUVs, there was a small open space where a little black car fit perfectly.

I hadn't even gotten the keys out of the ignition before someone whipped in behind me and blocked me there, but it didn't really matter. This was a vehicular suicide mission and we all knew it. No one was leaving by car today.

A nasty gust of wind roared its way past, rocking the Death Nugget back and forth.

I knew I had that umbrella in the back seat somewhere, so I fumbled around until I found it and yanked it forward. Another gust of wind sideswiped the car, and I had a feeling that the umbrella wouldn't really help. The rain was sweeping down sideways.

I tried to be calm and thoughtful.

Sure, Mother Nature was raising hell; and I was now

effectively trapped miles from home; and, yes, the city was in an uproar; and, of course, Christ was down by the river possibly drowning even as I sat there; and obviously I'd told Jamie I'd meet him in half an hour, a deadline which had passed twenty minutes ago. Never mind the fact that Harry and Malachi had chosen this particular weekend to try and visit, and they were down there somewhere now—not in town yet, I hoped. I could only pray they were running late. It was the only thing that would save them.

I was increasingly afraid that I was going to have to stand them all up, but I was determined to do my best. If I made it to the pedestrian bridge, I'd be closer to Christ than to Greyfriar's. I'd have to check the undersides first.

I wished to God that I wasn't alone.

At least when I'd gone tearing through the battlefield, I'd had Benny and Dana with me. At least then, if I stumbled, there was someone to know what had happened and someone to keep pushing me forward. Not here. Not now.

So, all right, it was me against the world. What should I bring?

My cell phone was lying forlorn upon the passenger's seat. I picked it up and shoved it into its protective holster—but the holster wasn't going to keep it from getting wet. Thanking heaven that I didn't clean out my car too regularly, I reached down to the floor and found an empty potato chip bag. I shook out the leftover crumbs of salt and snack, then dumped the cell phone into it, holster and all. I rolled this up and stuffed it into my purse, zipping it into a side pocket.

The purse itself was a large bag with a strap long enough to sling across my chest for hands-free carrying. It was black leather and slightly worn, but it had been treated with a protective spray and would keep out most of the wet so long as I didn't go swimming.

Again I looked outside, through the waterfall window.

Swimming might be in my future whether I liked it or not. But the cell phone couldn't stay in the car.

I picked through my purse and pulled out a small notebook, a checkbook, some makeup, and my wallet. I stuffed the notebook and checkbook into my glove compartment, and put the wallet back inside. Most of the contents were plastic anyway, and unlikely to be damaged in case of baptism by immersion.

In the glove box I found my tiny, trusty flashlight. It was made to be durable and maybe even waterproof, but I'd have to take my chances on it regardless. I chucked it into the bag. I also found a knife—one of my old favorites, the one with the leather sheath that snapped shut around it.

I'd started leaving it at home or in the car because the blade was too long to be legal, but thinking of the chaos at the bottom of the hill, I decided that it was worth the risk to carry it. I undid my belt and slipped it through the loops, then fastened myself up.

Better than nothing.

I had to use my leg to help pry open the car door, which was resisting because of the wind. I knew in an instant that the umbrella wouldn't do me a bit of good, so I left it. I climbed out of the car, crawled through my purse strap, and locked the doors behind me.

Standing there, overlooking the river and the city from the top of that hill, I wondered what I was doing and how I planned to do it.

But I couldn't just stand there, so I braced myself against the slashing, driving rain, and started to run.

13

THE GAUNTLET

Crowds were forming, milling, and moving in an agitated fashion up and down the hills of north Chattanooga. People were coming together, chattering angrily, swelling into big groups, breaking into smaller ones. Cars were abandoned at every juncture as the obvious hopelessness of the situation became clear.

I was only a kid when the Berlin Wall came down, but I've seen old movies about people who were trapped on either side when the barrier rose. Those movies were what I was thinking of.

People were angry and frightened, and here were the police and the emergency services folks—here were the officials in charge of protecting us. Here they were, not letting us go home, or go to work, or simply *go*.

I used to joke that you never know how many people live here until Riverbend, that ridiculous festival that consumes the downtown area for a week each spring. In that week, it seems that the Tennessee Valley residents number in the millions, and every goddamn one of them wants to loiter inappropriately. And this was even worse than Riverbend: so many people and so many vehicles—and so much noise.

They were furious at being stopped and they were blaming the people in uniforms because it was easier than blaming the river.

But any fool could see that it was the river rising between us; any fool could stand still and stare for a minute and see what was happening. Any fool could tell that trouble was coming. I could smell it in the fear, in the confusion and desperation that made the throngs crowd forward towards the river—even as the river stretched itself up and out to meet them.

There were men and women at the river's edge with their backs to the water. They were trying with megaphones and skyaimed gunshots to spread a little sense. It was such a simple message—get away from the water; here it comes.

It took my breath away.

And I joined them, these stupid, swearing people who pushed themselves against the water. I saw people with small kids on their shoulders, sopping wet and getting wetter; I saw people carrying dogs. I saw cats, some with collars and some without, charging up the hills, dashing between legs and climbing trees. I worried for the dogs, but the cats—I figured the cats would be all right, left to their own devices.

And I saw the rats. They live down by the river, a pestilence on tiny clawed feet. By the hundreds they were fleeing the river. Rats, for God's sake. Even the rats had better sense than the people did.

Than *I* did.

But I was in too deep now. I'd missed my date with Jamie, but I was as stuck as everybody else and I wasn't leaving Christ to drown beneath the city. And I wasn't answering my phone either, though I could feel it throbbing on vibrate against my ribcage, through the sides of the leather purse.

I wasn't going back. I'd gotten this far.

But Frasier Avenue fought me. It was mobbed and packed, and there was no moving. Glass was breaking everywhere and at first I didn't know why or what was causing it; and then I saw people throwing things into the store windows—and people being pushed and crowded into the stores, through the windows, through the doors.

From street level I couldn't see the river, and it was a blessing. I didn't want to see it. From the top of the hill with the church, I'd looked down and seen it creeping up and out, saturating Coolidge Park and working its way up to enfold the carousel. The river was only yards away and rising fast, and people were still fighting to get to the bridges.

I wasn't the only one with the idea of hitting the pedestrian bridge, either. Police had blocked it off with their cars, but people were climbing around them, on them, and over them. Someone had a Taser out, and I imagined that it was probably a bad idea to fire one off in the middle of a flood, so I did my best to stay clear.

Up came the water.

Behind me, I heard a dog barking and I saw the poor thing, chained to a parking meter and apparently abandoned. I shoved my way back to him, and I clung to the meter like it could anchor me in the sea of people.

He wasn't a big fellow, twenty pounds of a little boxer mutt-mix. He was shaking, and cold, and I didn't know what to do for him except let him off his chain. I reached down and unclasped it, my hands slipping all over it because I was shaking too.

The dog strained against my hand and against his collar and

against the meter pole. Between the pair of us, he got loose. He head-butted me like a cat and barked frantically, and I didn't know what to do, or what to tell him.

"Go on!" I said.

With a yap and a kick, he took a dive into the forest of legs and weaved through them with a speed I envied.

That done, I tried to go back across the street. Somebody was still sitting in a car and trying to honk his way through. He was pinned by people on all sides, and on the verge of gassing it anyway. Before he could do this, I climbed up on his hood, slipping and sliding, but getting high enough to see—for a few seconds before I fell—how close we all were to real trouble.

The Walnut Street Bridge is a metal frame stacked on old stone pillars that have risen out of the water for over a century. I'd never seen those pillars look so *short*.

Over the park grounds where thirty years ago there'd been an armory, the water slipped up and swallowed the fountains with their lions and elephant statues that squirted water at tourists. The water was gray and rougher than I'd ever seen it, even as it pooled up in that insidious way.

It was eating at the bridge's ground supports, too. The water bases were stone, but over land the bridge was supported by huge blue metal supports with rivets the size of soda cans.

Already people were in the water, swimming in one direction or another—hanging on to whatever unmoving things they could grasp. I didn't know if they'd been caught midstream in the rising current or they'd been dumb enough to jump for it.

The man driving the car I was standing on hit the brakes and the gas at nearly the same time. I fell, but not hard. I caught myself on someone else, who pushed me away, causing me to fall again, into another person who treated me similarly.

But in that glance from the car, seeing folks grasp at the underpinnings of the bridge had given me an idea. It wasn't a great idea, but it was the only one I had.

I slam-danced my way through to the far curb, closest to the river. Police were starting to back up on the bridges, forced that way by the crowd and the water. As people pressed forward and the river gushed higher, there was no other way to get up and out.

I almost didn't notice when the water first reached my ankles, I was so wet anyway. Everything was wet and horrible and I could hardly see for my hair hanging in my face. I wiped it back and wiped my eyes and looked down; and what gathered to hold my legs was not rainwater. Rain doesn't usually bring driftwood and dead rats. It doesn't often bring the floating carcasses of fish.

By then it was less crowded, but only by a bit. As the water climbed and crawled its slow, unstoppable way up from the riverbed, people were getting the hint—for all the good it did them. Retreat was almost as hard as a forward march. The panic each caused was a different kind, but no less urgent and no less difficult to navigate.

Here it comes.

I tried to hold my ground and failed. Forward, backward, or in circles—yes. But there was no holding still.

Someone hit me in the eye with a sharp body part—an elbow, maybe. It hurt, and I yelped, but no one heard me. Everything was getting hit anyway, so I couldn't stay still. The water was coming up hard and I was wondering about all these people behind me and around me.

The hills that line the river, they're technically part of the river valley gorge, I think. They're high hills and they would surely offer safety, even in the rain, and even from the water. It could only rise so high, so fast.

But these people around me, the ones trying to retreat—would they make it? This was no tsunami, but the basin was filling and the good citizens of Chattanooga were too disorganized and terrified to make practical preparations—they weren't even heading for higher ground in any significant numbers.

It was getting hard to run. The water on the street was up to my knees and it was thick and filled with detritus. The rain would not relent and everything was slippery. Everything was hard to grab and hold, so it was with great difficulty that I hauled myself up onto a street lamp stand and tried to find something else to reach for, something to climb for and crawl for.

I wasn't more than a few yards from the police cars on the end of the Walnut Street Bridge, and those police cars were wheel-deep in the river. How could the water come so high? It wasn't possible.

In the back of my mind, a merry little riverboat was tootling down Market Street in an antique photograph. So it was possible, yes. I knew it had happened before. But that's what the TVA was for. That's what the dams were for.

Where were they now?

If the rain had let up for five seconds I would've praised God. But it didn't, and my hair was hopeless in a way that isn't vanity but pragmatism. I couldn't see through it and I couldn't get it out of my face even by tying it back. Nothing short of a razor would have kept it off me by that point. Everything was impossible. It would be easier, I thought, if I went into the water. It would be easier to swim or wade for the nearest pillar and climb up onto the high, arching bridge on the other side of the police barricade.

I reached for the sharp brick edge of a corner building and caught it, fumbling. I held it and pulled myself around it, pressed to it by the current. I had no choice. I hadn't thought of the current. Even in its slow, pooling rise, the Tennessee had a lot of pull. There was no way I could swim against it.

Off to my left in the street, people were starting to scream with a different timbre, and I turned to look even as I tried to brace my feet and half crawl, half swim backwards up the side of the building. It was the cars—that's what they were screaming about. The cars were filling up and being tugged, pulled, or pushed. The water was in the street, flooding Frasier up to a thigh's height, or to the waist of a smaller person.

Now they fled in earnest, trying their best to push their way up the hills, but the hills were blocked and crowded by those who were still crushing forward because they didn't know or understand what was going on down below.

It became easier to approach the river as the other people fled. The river was approaching me, after all. I did it a foot or two at a time. I did it by reaching and pulling myself, and by using my height to stretch myself out in the water—until I was in up to my chest and bracing against anything I could find.

When my hands finally groped the blue-painted rail of the bridge's edge, I tightened my fingers around it and locked them fast. Like climbing the monkey bars on a school playground, I heaved myself along until I was high enough to sling my legs up over the edge and stand on drier stuff.

I hung there for a moment and caught my breath. The boards of the bridge's deck were slippery and my legs were shaking, so I had a hard time standing at first. But once I did, the bridge curved high enough that there wasn't any water up around my feet. The police cars were door-deep then, and I didn't see the officers who had once driven them, not at first. Then I spied them down on the street, herding those who could be herded—skimming them from the water as best they could and pulling them out, pushing them up stairs and up onto roofs where the water height allowed it.

Of course, I wasn't alone on the bridge. Maybe a hundred others had made it up there too. It was busy but not crowded. I didn't have to fight my way through anybody to pass; I just wandered between them. The pedestrians were clinging, clustering together in groups or running for the middle, where the peak was highest. The river was far enough below that we were sure it couldn't get *that* high, because if it did then we'd need a fucking *ark* and there was no hope for any of us.

It's about two-thirds of a mile across the Walnut Street Bridge, so it takes some time to traverse. It's a nice jaunt if you're on a bike or on roller skates, or if you've got a skateboard. But when the water is coming at you from above and below, the thunder won't stop, and people are crying from every direction, it isn't pleasant.

I made my way as fast as I could.

It got slower towards the end, towards the south side of the bridge. The water was coming up there too, same as on the north side. It wasn't quite as bad, but it was bad enough. Up to my left there was the Hunter Museum of Art, perched above the river on a cliff and probably safer than the aquarium, which was down to my right. The banks are sharper on the south side than the north side, but they're both pretty high. Still, I couldn't help feeling a brief, paralyzing sort of fear for the animals inside. It was stupid of me. There were people too, maybe *lots* of people drowning and dying, but I still breathed a little prayer for all the swimming things in their glass cages.

When I got to the end of the bridge, I was pretty sure that prayers weren't going to do Christ any good. No one could have made it in or out of the undersides without a scuba tank. If he was still down there, there was nothing anyone could do for him.

The water had eaten the riverfront boardwalk and absolutely filled the little amphitheater beneath my feet. Crowding on the south side—the downtown side—of the river wasn't as bad as the north side—which was mostly residential—had been. People inside the city had other places to go—they had farther to retreat, and so they spread out farther than the folks who were backed up to the mountains. But it was still bad. Cops and other officials in yellow-lettered blue jackets made valiant efforts to direct traffic and people, but nothing much was changing. Just getting off the bridge was an adventure in its own right; the police wanted me to stay where I was, but I had no intention of listening.

It eventually registered that these crowds were also drier, not waterlogged like the people on the other end of the bridges. Like me.

There were also more sirens there downtown; more ambulances and fire trucks and police, too. I heard a helicopter overhead and looked up to see it swoop past me, towards the hospital. That meant that the hospital wasn't perfectly cut off, which was something, at least.

On this side of the river, too, there were the news vans. There are always the news vans, aren't there? I wondered how they'd gotten there; I knew Channel 3 had its headquarters on the north side, but maybe they had roving reporters.

I was seized with a sudden urge to find Nick, but there were too many other urges pulling me in too many other directions. Harry and Malachi were out there somewhere, and Jamie, though

I knew he must've written me off by then.

So where should I go first? I had to find some shelter, even if it was temporary. I needed to dig out my phone and see if I could reach anyone, now that I'd more or less arrived at the place where I'd meant to go. My best prospect seemed to be Greyfriar's, my standby coffeehouse and the meeting place of everyone in my approximate age and social group. If not there, where? And it was only a couple of blocks away, all of that downhill.

Downhill. The thought worried me. I could recover from the disappointment of the sinking of the North Shore Apartments—I wanted to live there, but they weren't mine yet. And although I enjoyed shopping on Frasier, I never rode the carousel and I wouldn't miss the park.

But what if Greyfriar's went under?

I backtracked, because I had to, going out of my way to avoid the worst thronging and the tightest knots of people. Only a couple of blocks. I could do that in a mad dash.

I did, though I was panting and on the verge of tears by the time I reached Broad Street. I was also wading again. The water was sloshing up high over my boot laces, but I hardly felt it. The rest of me was soaked to the bone already. I only noted the added damp because of the sound of my feet slapping and snagging in the muck.

When I reached the intersection at Fourth Street, I saw the horses. They were being led up out of their stables from the place where they usually waited to draw tourist buggies. They stamped and snorted in the water while one of the bigger Clydesdales held steady and still, letting himself be hitched up to the rigging.

I wondered for a moment why they were binding the horse into his harness and cranking up the buggy's roof. Then I saw the ambulance mired in the road, one wheel dropped into an open manhole that was gushing brown froth. There was a patient in the back of the ambulance, a paramedic covering him with a tarp so they could move him.

Any port in a storm. The water was knee-high in some spots, and if it kept on rising like this, a horse and a sturdy wagon would get farther than a low-built van, emergency lights or no.

I went to the right, squeezing between the tight bumpers of cars that were either abandoned or on the verge of being abandoned. I kept on going, because if I didn't get to Greyfriar's, I didn't know where else I'd go.

When I got there, people were working to sandbag the doors, just like some of the other shops on the street. That end of Broad, the one that runs up against the aquarium at the water's edge, is up on an embankment that helps protect it a little, but not much. The sandbags weren't going to do any good and I think everyone knew it. But if you didn't fill the bags and push them into place, what else could you do?

There isn't any overhanging shade at the coffee shop, so when I beat my hands against the glass I was standing outside being rained on, as if I even felt it anymore.

Inside there was a crowd. I saw a few people I knew, and a lot of people I didn't.

I saw Jamie's girlfriend Becca, with sticky wet strands of dark blond hair plastered down over her shoulders. She saw me too, and waved. She gestured, and when she reached back through the crowd, her arm pulled Jamie forward.

"Let me in!" I demanded.

The people stacking sandbags yelled something back, but

we were all yelling and no one was understanding much. I think they were saying something about trying not to open and close the door. Whatever it was, I disregarded them and pushed my shoulder against the entrance.

The door shoved two or three people back and there were complaints all around, but people eventually made room and I came in.

It was miserably hot in there, and crowded like I couldn't believe. Back down by the roasting room I heard the manager trying to make himself heard, but it wasn't working for him. He was saying something about wanting to clear out the store and lock it up, which meant he didn't have a very good idea of what was going on outside.

He wasn't going to get these people out, not without a shotgun—and maybe not then.

Jamie took one of my hands and dragged me towards him, around a pair of quivering college girls. "Hey, glad you could make it."

"I always do, don't I?"

"Just a little late."

"I ran into some difficulties." I nodded at Becca, who nodded back. Together we crowded into a front corner beside a fake plant and watched the madness around us.

"Say, you haven't seen—" I started to ask about Harry and Malachi, but it wasn't a good idea and they wouldn't have known who I meant, anyway.

"Who?"

"Never mind." I unzipped my bag with a series of faltering jerks. The zipper was clogged with grass and mud, and the bag was dripping a nasty-looking puddle there where I stood. But inside the zippered compartment, wrapped in the discarded chip bag, my cell phone was dry enough to dial.

I flipped it open and started hitting buttons.

Harry's number came up and I pressed Send. When the call connected, the signal was bad and I was surrounded on all sides by people shouting into cell phones.

"Where are you?" he answered without a friendly preamble. He was shouting too.

"Greyfriar's—downtown. Where are you?"

"With your brother, at a Waffle House on the south side of town. What the hell is going on?"

"I don't know," I said, but I offered him what I could. "Something about a dam, or some locks. Something's gone wrong and *bad*. They've shut down the bridges over the river. And I've got to tell you, it can only get worse."

"No kidding," he agreed. "But you made it downtown? How? What did you do?"

"Long story. Not important. You two are going to have to get out of here—I think that's the main thing. Get out. Go back to where you came from and we'll reschedule this little date with no hard feelings."

Malachi whined something in the background, but I didn't catch it. "Easier said than done, sweetheart. Traffic is blocked in both directions, from the ridges to the 24/59 split. There's no way out, north or south. We're stuck here, and I don't know what the hell I'm going to do with Mal. The police are everywhere."

"But they've got other things to think about right now. I wouldn't worry about that. I guess you should just… hole up someplace safe. And we'll have to wait this out." At least they were all right. That's what I kept telling myself; at least they were all right. "Listen, I'm going to go. Lu and Dave have called…" I checked the display, "eight times in the last hour. They're going to kill me if I don't get back to them ASAP. Just stay where you are, or find a safer spot if you need to."

"Thanks," he said, but I think I heard a pretty distinct eyeball rolling. "I'll do my best to follow that advice. Do you have any recommendations? We can't hang out here forever."

"Recommendations?" I thought about it, but didn't know what to suggest. I had a good idea of which Waffle House he meant, but I didn't know the area well. "Maybe back across the interstate and up. You're there by East Ridge, aren't you? Near the interstate?"

"Yeah."

"That's low country there, you know. If you find yourself ass-deep in alligators and you need to move, the ridge is right behind you and there are lots of roads to take you up."

"That's… almost completely unhelpful, given the situation. But I'll take it under consideration."

"I'm only trying to help," I said.

"I know. I know, and I'm sorry. But I'm only trying to keep myself and your brother from drowning—and do keep in mind, there's a lot of other trouble he's capable of getting into."

"Okay, well, good luck. Look, I've got to call Lu and Dave. Keep me posted, would you?"

"I'll try."

We hung up, and I was looking to dial Lu back when a policeman pushed his way inside and hollered for everyone's attention. He then began to give evacuation orders, and people started arguing with him before he got the first sentence all the way out of his mouth. The chaos grew so dense I almost dropped the phone. I only held on to it by virtue of a death grip and total stubbornness.

"We can't stay here," Becca condensed and repeated the cop's message. "They're going to make us leave."

"To go *where*?" Jamie asked before I could.

"No one gets out, no one gets in; what do they think is going to happen here? Where are we supposed to go?" I took another push to the hip and went face-first against the window, which clanked but held. "But no, we can't stay here."

"What's happening?" Jamie asked, not really expecting an answer, but sensing a new bleakness and urgency to the officer's mood. "He's talking about evacuating to higher ground, and talking about roofs. That's crazy; it won't get that high, will it? Could it?"

"I don't know," I said, but he didn't hear me and it didn't matter. I wasn't looking at him anymore. I was looking back through the window, where my face had left a greasy imprint on the glass. On the other side of the cheek-shaped smudge, out on the street in the rain, I saw someone and knew that nobody else did.

The neighborhood kids called him Catfood Dude because there was a rumor that he'd eat cat food if you gave it to him. He was half homeless, or maybe more than half; and I had always gotten the distinct impression that he was in need of brain-chemical-modifying meds. He chattered to himself and didn't ever bathe, and he'd do anything stupid on a dare for a dollar. His hair was tangled up in dreads, but not the cool kind that trustafarians cultivate.

For the first time since I'd been aware of his existence, he was looking me square in the eyes. He wasn't twitching and he wasn't fretting in that worrisome way that made people on the sidewalks move away from him.

The cop was trying to urge people outside. Without saying a word to Jamie or Becca, I let him herd me around the frame and out the door. As he held it, water came spilling in over the sandbags, but the sandbags were less than useless and we all could see it.

My friends called out to me, but over the din I could pretend I hadn't heard them. Catfood Dude had something to say and I wasn't doing anything useful there in the 'Friar anyway. "All right," I told him as I pushed my way outside. "All right, what have you got for me?"

It won't be long now, he said.

"What? What won't be long now?" Another couple of people trickled and tripped out of the clogged coffeeshop behind me. It was almost better, out there in the rain. You could see the sky at least, you weren't packed against other people like crayons, and the water didn't mean much. Everything was wet anyway. What was a little more?

"Eden!"

It was Jamie, behind me now, leaving Becca back inside and forbidding her to follow. I don't know why she obeyed, but she stayed there, watching from the other side of the glass while he kicked a sandbag over and joined me.

"Go back in there," I told him. I realized I was still holding my cell phone, but the water wasn't as bad, tapering off at least for a while. It was coming up fast from the ground level, but the sky was giving us a break. I twisted the phone in my fingers, wondering what to do next.

"Forget it," he told me. "What's going on? What are you doing?"

"Trying to sort some things out. There's not anything you can do to help. Just go back. Take care of Becca. I don't need any help."

"Where will you go? You're not getting back up to the mountain."

"I know, I know, but… I don't know."

"Now you're just—"

"Drop it. I have some things to take care of." Catfood Dude was watching patiently, waiting for me to finish. I'd never seen him hold still for so long, and I didn't trust it.

The pigs are right. Everyone should go. It isn't safe.

Behind us there was more commotion, more shouting, and Becca squeezed around the door to join us. "Let's go home," she urged, taking Jamie's arm in a way that wasn't whiny so much as insistent. "My place. I live up on top of the hill." She pointed up Fourth Street and I nodded. It would probably be the driest spot in town short of Cameron Hill. "The blue building. Buzz number eighteen and we'll let you up if you need a place to crash."

"Thanks," I said.

"I guess that means we're walking," Jamie said.

"Unless you think your car will start and move in this. They're blocking the roads anyway. Walk or drown, I think. I've got some things to take care of, but I might take you up on your offer later on, tonight maybe. I've got—"

"Yeah, we got it," he interrupted. "Things to do. I get it."

"Go," I urged. "Go while the rain is light."

I left them there. We turned our backs and went our different directions. Jamie went with Becca sloshing up the hill and I went after Catfood Dude, who was walking towards downtown—towards the horses and the Tivoli Theater, and the big bank buildings and the old empty storefronts. I followed as fast as I could.

The ghost led me forward, and as I went deeper into the valley, the water became less troublesome. A couple of blocks made a huge difference—the difference between knee-deep and puddle-deep. I even started seeing cars moving again, though not fast and not very far. But it was drivable, except for the way the streetlights were failing more often than they were working.

The buses weren't working, not the gas ones or the electric shuttles, but the horses were. Tourist guides with hansom cabs were piling as many people onboard as the beasts could drag—mostly triaged to the elderly, the handicapped, and kids, or that's how it looked to me. They took the carts up onto the sidewalks and along the alleys where cars don't go because they can't or shouldn't.

So people were leaving—they were getting out, maybe to the ridge tunnels or to the mountains. Not many people, but some people. The most vulnerable people, I hoped. It wasn't the world's fastest evacuation because there weren't *that* many horses and the going was slow; but it was happening. It was underway. It was better than nothing.

Foot power or hoof power—fastest and best. I ran after Catfood Dude and he led me to a square, squat building with boarded windows and an ornate front that was sad under the plywood.

Inside, he said.

I stood there and caught my breath, hands on my knees. "What's inside?"

Nothing, yet.

He vanished, and I was alone except for the dimmer chaos of the confused city's heart, where the water was still a threat and not a reality. The roads were jammed and cars were being abandoned even as I watched. Why not? Everyone could see the horses, and with the sweating, steaming, determined animals in our midst the writing was on the wall. Get out however you can. But *get out*.

No one was watching me, and the police I saw weren't watching for the kind of looting I was likely to do.

I think it might have been a bank like the old furniture building had been, once upon a time. The lettering was faded above the door and on the side plaque, and I didn't take the time to squint for it. The place had been empty as long as I could remember. I only remembered it at all because it was odd, a place in such a good location sitting so vacant and old, and no one had torn it down or built anything new to replace it.

But the ghost had said "inside," so I took him at his word. I pulled my knife out of my belt holster and used it to pry at the sodden wood and rusty nails covering one of the lower windows. It didn't take any time at all to pull it free. The window it covered was broken and ragged.

When I got the sheet of wood free, I held it on the ground and stepped on it until I broke it, and then I took the biggest piece and used it to swipe the glass away from the termite-eaten frame. I climbed inside and blinked.

The interior was as dark as night. Time to find out how waterproof that tiny flashlight was.

I wrested it free of my bag and flipped it on. It surprised me by sparking to life.

There wasn't much to see—just the usual crates and trash, though not much indication that people had been squatting there. Usually abandoned buildings in that area have clear signs of teenagers or the homeless, but not this one. Instead I found a stray cable or two—like for audio equipment—which was weird. I stepped forward and heard a change in my footsteps' echo;

when I looked down I saw that the original flooring surface had transitioned to something new.

I retreated for fear of falling through into heaven knew what. But when I found the edge I tapped at it and shined the light down low.

It was metal, a grate. On top of it, someone had thrown a couple of shipping pallets. It took some real effort, but I pushed them aside and saw the rusted square of grating that covered... what? I thought of the street elevators built into the sidewalks—the ones that allow city workers access to the sewers. This looked something like that, only I didn't think it had been used in years.

And it wasn't locked. The grate was only laid down atop the hole.

I beamed the light down and saw nothing of interest. It could have been a basement or an unfinished cellar.

Or a tunnel.

I looked down as hard as I could and saw no sign of the cement work that identifies the undersides—not even any walls, or support structures. No floor. No, this was more like a tunnel than a water runoff system.

"The underground?" I said aloud.

I felt ridiculous the moment it was out of my mouth, whether or not there was anyone to hear. Everyone sort of *believed* in the underground, but no one actually took it as a point of fact.

The true facts are slim pickings, but you know how it goes. In old cities where the water level is unpredictable, sometimes things *stack*. Where the old buildings are too damaged to restore, and the sediment level has grown high enough, sometimes builders wind up constructing right on top of them.

Everybody knew about the underground like everyone

knew about Old Green Eyes out at the battlefield; and everyone had a story about winding up in a clammy spot of dirt beneath a building or beside the river. Most of it wasn't true, or it referred to the concrete water runoff system we called "the undersides." But enough of the bullshit tales had legs to make you wonder if it wasn't something else, maybe.

I'd read that during the war, people spoke of tunnels dug all over the place so soldiers could quietly move goods from the river. In the 1860s the city was held by north and south in turn, and tunnels were a known Civil War-era tactic of hiding and transporting soldiers and supplies.

It made more sense to me than a precariously piled mound of underground city fragments, anyway. But people around here believe what they like.

I didn't really believe it. Not before, when the urban legend was passed around by my friends, and not even then, when staring down into an open hole covered by a grate.

But I knew, without believing any of it necessarily, that I was breathing down into something bigger, deeper, and longer than an unfinished basement. I listened, kneeling there beside the edge, because I thought I heard something strange—something that wasn't coming from outside, but coming from underneath.

I leaned my head and pressed my ear down low, and there it was. A scratching, or a scuffling. Something slow-moving, but too big to be a rat. Something distant, but not so far away that I couldn't detect the struggling pattern of feet in mud.

Yes, it was distant still. But there wasn't a doubt in my mind that it was coming closer.

14

HELP ME

"Nick," I started repeating into the phone long before he picked up on the other end. I was shivering and cold and unhappy, and I was trying to tune out the faint sloshing scratchings coming from the hole behind me. But it was dry inside the old building, so I made use of the roof and made a phone call.

"Nick here."

"Nick," I said again. "Something extremely fucked up is going on."

"You're not just whistling Dixie." He sounded tired, but a little bit happy to hear from me. "Where are you, woman? And please please *please* tell me that you're up on the mountain still. Because if you're down here in the city, I'm going to have to freak out."

"Sorry. Commence freaking out—but be warned, I'm way ahead of you. I'm in that old building—I don't know what it's called—the old building down off MLK. The one that's boarded up and looks like it used to be a bank or something. You know what I'm talking about?"

"I don't know. MLK and what street?"

"Martin Luther King and—" I raised my head as if I could see outside to the street sign. I couldn't, so I guessed. "Broad, I think. Maybe Market, or Cherry? It's on the corner. Catty-cornered and down the street from the library and the Read House."

"I don't know it. But I could find it, if I could get there—and I've got to tell you the truth, I don't know if I can get there."

"Where are *you*?"

"I'm—" It sounded like he was doing the same thing I'd just done—taking a look around and not learning much. "I'm at the bridge. City-side, not Signal-side. The 27 bridge, Olgiati. It's—it's chaos. I've never seen anything like this."

"What are you doing there?" I asked.

"Trying to keep from getting trampled. I'm on foot, at the moment; the news SUV was commandeered by a couple of cops for use as an ambulance—but I can't imagine how far they've gotten with it. So what's going on where you are? You sound dry and alone, and if that's the case, then I applaud you—because it couldn't have been easy."

He was hollering into the phone in the middle of a crowd, and it made him hard to understand.

"It wasn't easy. It was creepy, and I'm really worried. I need to get out of here and… and I've got some family that just came into town, and I'm not sure exactly what I expect you to do about this, but I guess I'm glad you're all right and I could really use some company. But if you're all the way down at the bridge, then I don't know. I guess just stay safe, and I'll catch up to you when I can."

For all the trouble I'd gone to in order to get dry and alone, I wasn't liking it much.

"I'm going to try to work my way back down in your direction," he said slowly. "I think I'm going to try to get to the Read House. You must be rubbing off on me or something because I found something this morning—something I shouldn't have found, not in a million years."

"What did you find?"

"The Spanish Flu, a fire, and those juvenile murals you found in the old furniture store—they're all related. I think Caroline knows why. And I think we need to talk to her, because if we don't…"

"If we don't, *what*?"

He was quiet, like he was listening to someone else. Then he said abruptly, "If we don't, this could get a whole lot worse. Something's down there in the river, Eden. Fuck me, something is *down there*. But it's not going to stay down."

Behind me, I heard the *scritch, scritch, scritch* of the faraway something crawling beneath the city. "You're right. But what is it?"

"I don't know. But I'm starting to get a few ideas."

"If you get to the Read House," I started. "I mean, *when* you get to the Read House, give me a call. I'll come and help."

The burned-up man.

The thought flicked through my head and it almost hurt. I squeezed my temples between my thumb and ring finger. And my phone began to beep. "Nick, I've got another call coming. I'll catch you later. Call me when you get here."

"Will do," he said, and hung up.

I hit the button to transfer the next call over. "Harry? Is that you?"

"It's me. We're at the Choo-Choo."

I groaned. "That is *not* where I told you to go."

"No, but it's where we were taken. It's being set up as a shelter and it's a nightmare. But we're here, and we're safe, more or less. You don't think it'll flood up this far inland do you?"

"I've got no idea. Surely not? But you're at the Choo-Choo?"

"Yes. We're here. We're in the main terminal building, the front one, you know. We're back in the area that's a bar. Lots of brass and glass, and red. There's a piano, too. Do you know where I'm talking about?"

"I do, yeah. And I'm coming—I'll be there in a few minutes. Give me maybe twenty. I'm not real far away."

"All right. We'll be here waiting."

I folded my phone and wrapped it carefully in its foil protective pouch before putting it back into my purse. And then, before I left—as if it would do any good—I pushed all those wooden shipping pallets back on top of the grate. I threw on a couple of crates and a whole lot of trash too, just for good measure. My phone rang again while I was doing this, but it was someone calling from home so I didn't answer it. And then I exited the way I'd come in, out through the window.

Back outside the sky was low and sulking, but it wasn't raining—or it was, but only in dribbles. I blinked hard, rubbed my eyes, and tried to orient myself. I was less than a block from the Read House, but it would probably take Nick the better part of an hour to make his way there from the bridge. First came Harry and Malachi.

Harry and Mal were a few blocks south. I was too tired to sprint the distance, and suddenly a little hungry, too. I hadn't eaten since breakfast, and breakfast felt like ancient history.

Onward and upward I walked. Out of the central district and away towards the south side, where there were fewer people than down by the river. But as I got closer to the Choo-Choo,

177

the crowds began to thicken; and by the time I reached it I was surrounded again by crying babies, worried women, old people in wheelchairs, and a handful of men in lettered jackets trying to direct the human flow of traffic. I staggered up to the nearest such official and tried to get his attention.

"Sir?"

"Ma'am, if you could step aside unless there's a medical emergency?"

I let it go, because I think I only wanted to be told that someone knew what was going on—that somebody was in control, even if I knew better. I gathered in five minutes of crowd surfing that at least this was a shelter and that the Red Cross was there. And under the great painted dome in the old train station, hundreds of people crushed together on the gleaming marble floors and waited for word, waited for food, or waited for the water to go down.

I sidestepped as many of them as possible and made it to the piano bar with its wall of mirrors and shelves loaded with brightly colored bottles of liquor. And there, in the back corner, behind the piano and under a gilt-framed mirror the size of a patio door, waited Harry and my brother, who leaped to his feet and started waving as soon as he saw me.

I stumbled towards them, over a few people and around a few others. I pushed my way past the edge of the bar and joined them.

"You made it!" Malachi wheezed, flushed with excitement and sticky with sweat and water.

"Was there ever any doubt?"

Harry stood up too, and I'd forgotten how tall he was until he wrapped an arm around me and I was chin-forward into his shoulder. He looked the same as always, thin in a strong way that's often called wiry, and with a face full of sharp angles that made him look smart. He was wearing a longsleeved gray sweater and jeans, while Malachi's sweater was white.

Malachi the Ageless still looked twenty, though I knew good and well he was in his late thirties. His hair was growing out again, into that straggly blond haystack he wore when I first met him on that playground in the rain. When he had a gun. When he wanted to kill me.

I hugged him—and for perhaps the first time, I meant it. I was genuinely happy to see him. I grabbed Harry again too, because I was happy to see him as well. Their timing was terrible and the circumstances of their arrival could've been better, but they were here and they were alive. And, in the back of my head, I knew they'd gone to an awful lot of trouble to be here. It's hard not to be flattered by that. It's also hard not to feel some sense of obligation to someone who has climbed through hell and high water to see you.

So I sat down there with them in their little corner. We exchanged gossip that didn't amount to much more than, "Holy shit, look at all this water."

My phone rang again while we were playing catch-up, and it was Lu. It was loud and crowded there in the corner of the bar, but I finally felt calm enough to answer her, so I did… and immediately wished I hadn't. I'd expected to find myself on the receiving end of a nasty verbal beating and she didn't disappoint. At some point, Dave picked up the other receiver and they tag-teamed me until my ears rang.

When they were finished, I told them that I was all right and I didn't know what else to say. It had all happened so quickly, after all. When I'd left the mountain the threat of the closed bridges was still just that—a threat. Within two hours, the city was shut off and I was downtown. I'd only meant to go meet some friends; I hadn't anticipated this. I swore all this was true, and I was only lying a little bit. I'd been expecting a mess, but the sheer extent of the mess—how could I have known? How could anyone have known?

They conceded that point. Because really, I was right: how could anyone have known?

Lu and Dave were watching TV at home, safe and dry up on the mountain. I was glad for that much. Two fewer people for me to worry about, that's what it meant. "And you guys are staying up there, right? You're not going to do something crazy like come down off the mountain and try and get me, are you?"

"No, of course not," Lu answered for the pair of them. "I don't think we could get down the mountain if we tried right now. And even if we did, we'd never make it out to the Choo-Choo. They're declaring martial law down there, did you know that?"

"I didn't know we had enough police in this city to enforce martial law."

"We don't. They're calling them in from all over the place. Eden, this is—this is historic. This is fucking *epic*. This is like New Orleans," she said, and I could hear an edge of excitement in her voice. It wasn't happy excitement, exactly—it was more like a keen interest tempered with fear. "Hey," she went on to add. "I saw that reporter friend of yours on the news. If he ever wanted a stab at a Pulitzer, this is his chance."

"I'll be sure to pass that along to him."

"Will you be seeing him at any point soon? I ask because, I mean—look. I'm *glad* you've found… well, I'm not exactly glad you've found Harry and you-know-who, but I'm glad you're not alone. But really—one old guy and your crazy-assed brother? I wish there was someone else with you, too."

I glanced over at Harry, who looked ready to beat the ass of the entire world at a moment's notice; and I thought of Nick, who is only a little taller than me and probably drinks fussy coffee drinks when he feels like butching up. "What exactly are you trying to say, Lu?"

"I'm trying to say that I'd feel better if you were someplace with—with more people. Or better access to technology. Or more civilization, or—"

"Or someplace you could keep better tabs on me?"

"Something like that," Dave finished for her. "You're over at the train station?"

"Yes, I'm here now. But if it makes you feel better, Nick and I are supposed to catch up with each other in a little while. If he happens to have a satellite hidden under his shirt, I'll be sure to use it to phone home."

"You'd damn well better," Lu all but growled. "Next time you fail to answer that phone, I'm going to assume you're dead; or if you're not, I'm going to have to hunt you down and kill you."

"Got it, sure. Love you too."

Dave backed her up, but more gently. "Really. Please leave the thing on, and answer it. Make a couple of old fogies happy?"

"I'll do what I can, but these batteries don't magically last forever. Please keep that in mind."

In the end, they agreed not to call every hour on the hour and I agreed to answer when they did call; but in real life, I knew better. Their idea of nervous moderation was to phone every *other* hour, and my idea of answering judiciously was to pick up every *other* time.

Harry and Malachi were happy to have my undivided attention again, though none of us seemed to know what to do now. We exchanged harrowing stories of sloshing our way through the city, and they shared their bottled water with me. The Red Cross was handing it out along with granola bars and Little Debbies; it wasn't high cuisine, but it would suffice.

Above us, fits and starts of rain echoed loud against the ceiling and the world began to go dark outside. Inside, things weren't much better. We accepted thin but sturdy blankets from one of the volunteers, and we huddled down, waiting for word or morning.

15

MEET ME

Around eleven o'clock that night, Nick called. My phone was stuffed into my purse, which was acting double-duty as a pillow, so the vibrating ring startled me into stupidity. I fumbled the thing open and was amazed to note that I hadn't awakened either Malachi or Harry, both of whom slept awkwardly beneath the piano and behind it.

"Hello?" I said, keeping my voice down but not to a whisper. Even after hours there was a dull roar in the room, the tired complaints of refugees who wanted to go home. Most of them probably still had homes to go to. As far as I knew, the flooding centered on the old business and tourist districts. The residential areas tend to be on higher ground, or on cheaper ground farther inland.

"Where are you?" Nick asked, as usual without a greeting.

"I'm still at the Choo-Choo." I rubbed at my eyes and twisted my shoulders, trying to crack my back.

"I just got to the Read House. Can you get down here?"

AN EDEN MOORE STORY

"I guess," I said, almost wishing I hadn't. I ached all over from the swimming and the climbing and the running. I was bone tired, but now that I was awake I didn't think I could get back to sleep if I tried.

"You'll have to sneak in, but I really want you here. There's something fucked-up going on."

"Haven't we already had this conversation?"

"Yeah. But now I've got a better idea of what it is. Sort of. Kind of. It's all got something to do with the First Congregationalist Church of Chattanooga."

"Never heard of it."

"It burned down in 1919. City officials swore that the church was deliberately closed and burned because of the Spanish Flu epidemic. Communities closed a lot of public buildings then, theaters and churches and the like. They didn't really understand how the flu was spread, so they tried all sorts of things to slow it down. But I've never heard of burning buildings to prevent the spread of disease. That sounds excessive, doesn't it?"

I closed my eyes and leaned my head back against the side of the glossy black piano. "If you're grasping at straws, I guess controlled arson doesn't sound so wacky. But why do we care why the church burned down?"

"Well, contemporary newspapers called the fire 'suspicious' too; wrote about it like they didn't believe the city's official line. Also: it was Caroline's church. And that's when Caroline first went crazy—when her family started sending her to doctors and sanitoriums. Her first stint in the crazy house was in November of 1919. And we don't believe in coincidence, right? So it had to be related. Somebody burned that place down to hide something, Caroline knew about it, and the rest of the city helped bury it."

My head was hurting again, throbbing in time with his words. Again I heard that phrase in my head, clear as day and surprisingly loud: *the burned-up man*. "What do you mean by that? Helped bury what?"

"I don't know. But—Jesus. I don't even know how to say it. I don't have the vocabulary I need. I can't… look. Listen. There's something going on down by the river."

The pit of my stomach dropped, because I thought of Christ. "You said that last time we talked, too. What are you talking about?"

"I'm not even sure. I'm seeing dead people, everywhere. But not all of them stay down. Some of them—they're coming up out of the water, out of the river. I don't know. Nobody knows. The police are trying to force a lockdown and get everyone as far away as they can. But I've had people grabbing me when they recognize me, trying to tell me stories about—shit. About dead people wrapped in chains, walking around."

"What, like… like zombies?"

"No, of course I don't mean *zombies*. I mean dead people up walking around and wreaking havoc. That's totally different, isn't it?" Around the edge of his voice I heard something close to hysterics, barely controlled.

"Did you, personally, see anything?"

"I don't know what I saw, okay? It could've been anything. It could've been anyone. But I tell you this—they're looking for something. I don't know what or who or why. But there's something coming out of the water, and I think it's going to be something nastier than this city has ever seen. I think it's going to be bad. Can you please, please, *please* get over here to the Read House?"

"It'll take some time," I said, but it wasn't prohibitively far. "I heard they've declared martial law. Is that why you said I was going to have to sneak?"

"Yeah. But the more I think about it, the less I think the cops are going to be a problem. The authorities are calling everyone down to the river's edge—which, might I add, is now somewhere around Third Street. And the higher the water gets, the more—the more range these things get. They're being reported deeper and deeper inside the city. Shit, Eden. Shit."

"Third Street," I echoed. "Okay. Third Street. That's still a long way from us, and a long way from the Read House."

"It's only a few blocks!"

"But it's a few *whole* blocks. Don't get all girlie on me, damn it. You're high and dry right now, and I'm high and dry right now, and the cops are down by the water keeping people out of it—right?"

"They're trying. But it's dark, and not everyone knows that there are *things* down there. But I shit thee not, Eden. There *are* things down there."

And then I could almost hear his frantic, shifting gaze, and I could recognize his horror. It was the horror of someone who had long believed but never *known*. This was a man who *knew*, now. And it had rattled something loose inside him. I wondered what he'd seen, and if he'd ever tell me—but if I could pull it out of him, it wouldn't be over the phone.

"Eden?"

"I'm still here."

"Eden, get here. I need to understand this. I think Caroline understands it. I think she might even be able to help."

"You're guessing."

186

"What choice is there? And come on—what *else* are you doing tonight? Sleeping?"

"I *was* sleeping," I informed him with a grumble. "But I can come out. Let me warn my company here, and I'll do my best to be out there within an hour."

"An hour? It's not that far away."

"No, but I've got to go to the bathroom, and it's dark, all right? I'm not even sure if my flashlight still works. Give me an hour and I'll do my best. I'll get there. Just don't freak out on me if it takes more time than you think it should. I'm tired, and slow. I'm really tired," I repeated. It bore repeating.

I closed the phone. I'd lost my potato chip bag but I located a large Little Debbie wrapper and made do. I couldn't tell if it was raining or not, but it was bound to be wet off and on, and my purse had been so thoroughly soaked that it'd never be the same.

I pushed against Harry and woke him up. He looked at me like he didn't know who I was. "What? Um, what? What's going on?"

"Nothing, nothing really. I just wanted to warn you—I'm going to take a little field trip."

"What? Are you kidding?"

"No, I'm not. A friend of mine is stuck over at the Read House and I'm going to try to catch up with him."

"Do you know what 'martial law' means?"

"I do, yes. But I hear the cops are headed down towards the river right now. It ought to be quiet between here and the hotel, and it's only a couple of blocks," I told him, betting he didn't know the exact distance.

"All right. Sure. But why? What time is it?" He patted himself down, feeling for his watch or a cell phone.

"It's about eleven. It's not that late. I won't be gone but a few hours, probably," I said, but even as it came out of my mouth, I knew there was no telling if it was true.

He sighed and leaned back, putting his hand over his eyes for a minute as if he were trying to think. "All right. Do what you're going to. There's nothing happening here, anyway. And don't get me wrong—I'm glad you took the time to try and work with nervous-boy over here, but I'm not one hundred percent crushed that the family meeting fell through. Granted, I couldn't have anticipated how *spectacularly* it would fall through, and I wish that the circumstances could have been different, obviously—"

"Well, obviously, yeah."

"Yes. But. Maybe a rescheduling isn't the worst of all possible ideas."

"I'm relieved to hear you say it."

We both looked down at the sleeping Malachi, as if he were our own weird child. "You want to wake him up and say goodbye?" Harry asked, and I knew that he knew I wasn't coming back any time soon. I don't know why I'd bothered to try to reassure him otherwise.

"No. Better not. He'll only make a stink. I think you two should pack up and make your way out as soon as they let you. Get back to Florida safely. There's nothing y'all can do here except be refugees. If you can get out, get out."

"There ought to be shuttles before long, or buses," he murmured. "Something to take us outside the city, past the ridges."

"One would think," I agreed.

"We can't stay here forever. They'll have to start shipping us out soon. Worst comes to worst, when the rain lets up and we're awake good, we'll make a walk for it. Once we get beyond the tunnels, it shouldn't be too bad."

"I hope not," I said, and I kissed him on the cheek. "Look, I'm going to go. If it looks like I'll be able to come back before morning, I will. If I can't, I can't. I'll call."

I took one last look at my sleeping brother and nodded at Harry, who nodded back. Then, with carefully placed steps, I began to tiptoe my way through the sprawled people and their improvised camping places.

The bathroom was up front near the entrance, past the big dome. Getting there was a trick, because it felt like every square foot was occupied. And even late at night there was a short line; it wasn't a restroom designed to serve hundreds of people at a time.

While I waited for a stall I busied myself at a sink. I washed my face and shook out my hair, then tied it back again in a filthy scarf. What else was I going to do?

I finally scored a stall and spent entirely too long peeling my sticky-damp clothes away. I'd gotten mud and bits of dead grass into crevices I wouldn't have admitted to knowing about. But there weren't any showers except in the hotel rooms, and those were being parceled out to the elderly and to people with small children.

But I would have *really* loved a shower.

People were waiting. I finished up and left the stall to someone else. Outside the big swinging door, the lobby was piled with people, and I picked my way past them to the front door.

Someone at the front desk saw me. She was on the phone and she waved a finger at me, like she wanted me to stop and come talk to her. I ignored her and pushed on the entrance until it gave way. I slipped myself outside.

It wasn't too cold, but with my clothes still clinging to my skin it felt chillier than it should have. I shivered and closed my arms around myself.

"Miss?" It was a young guy in a security uniform that didn't fit him well. "Miss? What's your business out here? We're trying to keep everyone indoors if possible." He beamed a light towards me, but not into my face.

To my right, I saw a couple of guys smoking. Before I could even ask, one of them offered me a cigarette and I took it. I held it up at the security guy and he nodded.

"Thanks," I said to the guy who'd shared.

"No problem. It's too crowded in there, man." He didn't look at me when he spoke; he stared out across the train loading zone, packed with cars and blocked off by a big fire engine.

He looked familiar. I thought I placed him, so I asked, "Don't you work down at Greyfriar's?"

"Yeah. I did."

"Did?"

He turned to face me and he looked as tired as I felt. He was a tall guy with a long, lean torso and a shock of red hair that matched his beard. "It's probably underwater by now."

"Nah," I said, unwilling to even consider the possibility. "No way. TVA will get its act together and—"

"Are you kidding?" He took a deep drag, then gestured as he exhaled. "TVA. It's bullshit. On the radio they were talking about a problem at the dam. The locks are broken or something. Can't let any water in or out. They're working on it, sure, but it won't get fixed in time to undo any of this. We're all fucked. Look around, sister. Or, hell, just ask Brian over there. He knows how fucked we are."

The other smoker rubbed his cigarette butt against the building wall and slipped back inside as if he didn't know we were talking about him—or he didn't care.

"Why? What would he know?"

"You know he moved here from New Orleans, right?"

"This isn't New Orleans. And the water's got to go down someday," I said. "The river's got to run regular eventually."

"You keep telling yourself that," he said, as he stubbed out his own butt and went back inside.

I didn't see where the security boy ran off to, so I took this as my cue to leave while the leaving was good. I walked fast around the cars in the traffic circle, past a fire engine, and out into Market Street, where more cars were parked and abandoned.

Inside some of them I saw people sleeping or sitting up talking. Made sense. There was no point in crushing inside the Choo-Choo with the rest of the masses if you had an enclosed space of your own.

Across the street from the old train station there's a strip of abandoned stores and an old hotel that saw better days fifty years ago. Most of the boards had been pulled off the windows and a lot of them were broken. People were camping inside, burning fires in steel construction drums. The firelight sent weird shadows sprouting from the broken windows, cutting themselves into orange rainbows on the glass.

At least it wasn't raining anymore. But as soon as I began to feel a chilly sort of happiness over that fact, a distant growl of thunder promised more water to come. God. How much more could there be?

I didn't break out my little flashlight because I didn't really need it. Most of the streetlamps were still lit and I didn't need to draw extra attention to myself. No one paid me any mind and I liked it that way. I was just one more person on the sidewalk.

I tucked my hands under my armpits to warm them up and walked with my head down, mentally daring anybody to stop me or bother me, or say one *word* in my general direction.

I knew the area and I walked it fast. Everywhere people were talking, sometimes loud, sometimes crying, sometimes whispering and worried. Everybody was scared, not least of all because rumors were flying quickly from the river to the outlying areas, and to the deeper corners downtown.

And I was going towards the river, not away from it. But just to the Read House. I'd make it in a few minutes, and it wouldn't be so bad. Nick would be waiting for me, and I would be happy to see him, in a complicated sort of way that I didn't want to think about too hard.

I kept my head so low that I almost didn't see Pat. But he stepped in front of me and I could either walk through him or stop, so I stopped. I looked over and out, and there he was—wet and angry looking, like something bad had happened but there was nothing to be done about it now.

He looked just like he had the last time I saw him, big pants and big shirt on a frame that was skinny like a coatrack.

He's right, you know. About the church.

"What?" I said, and I said it softly. People could see me, there on the sidewalk, through the wet and across the train tracks.

The church. It all started there.

I hesitated, unsure of what to ask. "Then, um. Where's the church? Should I go there, if that's where all this started?"

Naw. It's been gone for years, Nick told you. Burned to the ground. Starting at the beginning won't get you shit. It ended at the river. You'll have better luck starting there.

"Why? I don't get it—I don't know what I'm supposed to be looking for, or what I'm supposed to do when I find it!"

They're coming back. Don't worry. You're headed the right way.

"Hey lady, you coming from the Choo-Choo?"

I whirled around and nearly hit the guy who was standing there, even though he wasn't being threatening at all. He was older and a little stooped; he looked tired and wet like everybody else.

"Yeah," I told him.

"It's a shelter, right? They're letting people sleep there?"

"Yeah. The Red Cross is there."

"Okay. There's food?"

"Sure," I said.

He wandered off, back the way I'd come. When I looked back towards the river, Pat was gone.

A street or two away I heard glass breaking, and people throwing instructions back and forth. I clung to the edge of a building and walked in the shadows. They didn't see me; but I watched them while I passed. They were letting themselves into a super-nice restaurant on the corner across from the train tracks.

Tired of Little Debbies, I guess.

I didn't get the impression they were a violent lot, just a nervously looting gang in search of some silverware or maybe a bit of pâté. I made sure not to step on anything loud and kept my head down, because that's what you do. It's what we all were doing. We were all walking with shoulders pointed and heads aimed at the streets in front of us. So unsure. So confused. Just don't touch us. Just don't stop us. We're desperate and hardened, even those of us wearing open-toed sandals.

I could see tiers beginning to form, and it was strange, and clannish. Some people hid and hunkered with children or in dry places where food could be stashed. Some people went walkabout because we had business to attend to, or maybe because we couldn't just sit still and wait to drown or starve.

All around, in patches of gold, small fires lit up the night between the wet spots.

I went past all of them. I did not stop to warm my hands except by holding my own ribs harder. I stuck to the sidewalks and as close to the buildings as I could; I hid against the walls and scraped my shoulder against the bricks, ducking into doorways and sliding into recessed entryways, always trying to keep myself out of the flickering light.

After all, you never knew who was out there.

Nick knew. And Nick thought Caroline knew, too.

Above an intersection clogged with empty cars, the streetlights repeatedly flashed red above me. The dim, crimson light cast an intermittent sheen across the cars and the roads, and the wet patches blinked it back.

All around me, from everywhere and nowhere in particular, voices and crashes cut the quiet into pieces. I learned fast that it was best not to look too hard. It was best not to hang around and wonder. Best to keep moving, to keep hopscotching the blocks to the Read House, where I might find civilization.

The Read House is down the street from the big convention center, so it's surrounded by less deluxe lodgings and a few restaurants, coffeeshops, and banks. Now necessity had forced it to give shelter to a greater capacity than it was ever meant to serve. The halls were strewn with blankets and bodies, arms and legs beneath every step.

I pushed open the big glass doors and past a man in a uniform. "Nick? Nick?" I said it loud but not in a yell. Not while people were trying to settle into something more peaceful than flight, even if it was only for a little while.

I went for my phone again and called him, because I didn't know how else to track him down.

"I see you."

"What?"

"Look up at the mezzanine." I did, and there he was, waving. I flipped the phone shut and stuffed it into my pocket, which was marginally drier than my purse. "There you are," I said, even though he probably couldn't hear me from where he was.

"This way," he said, with a finger pointing at the stairwell door. I nodded. "Hang on."

More careful stepping took me to the stairwell, which was propped open—possibly as a result of some fire code. A couple of people came and went, clomping up and down the cement stairs with unadorned iron rails.

When I emerged on the next floor, he was waiting for me. "I think the most telling thing about any of this is that no one will take Caroline's room."

"What?"

"Look around. People are fighting for a square foot or two of space, any place to set a baby or a broken leg. But you can't put anyone in Caroline's room. They opened it at first, because, you know, they basically had to. But within an hour she'd chased them out. She chases everybody out. She'll probably try to chase us out too."

He was fidgeting and frightened-sounding, and I wasn't used to it. Not from him. I liked him better brazen, but what can you do? He'd learned something new and it changed him.

I never do get used to it, the way it changes people. I've known for so long that it isn't fair for me to be impatient.

"But that's where we're going, isn't it?"

"Where else?" he said and sounded downright happy about it. "She's got answers, Eden. She's got them, and I want them, so we're going to go in there, and we're going to *get* them."

Ah, that was more like it—more like *him*.

"You keep talking about answers, and you mentioned something new and weird down by the water. Are you going to fill me in or leave me guessing? Because I've got to tell you, it's a madhouse out there—a mad city, anyway. I've never seen anything like it."

Overhead and past the windows we heard the hearty flapping of a helicopter's blades cutting low near the buildings. It flew in the company of several others too, or so it sounded. Nick lifted his chin and gestured at the big noise, pointing towards it with his face. "They'd better hurry up."

"Who? What?"

"Evacuating. They're starting with the hospitals. They'll hit the shelters next. They'll get the people who've done what they're told out first. But have you noticed? The National Guard is gathering at the ridges and moving people over them, too. We've got to empty the city. We've got to move everyone before the *things* get any faster, and higher, and farther into downtown. And, you know, I don't think it will be long now. I think it's just a matter of time."

I followed him while he fumed his little tirade. He reached back behind and grabbed my hand; I wasn't following fast enough, climbing my way over the sniffling kids and wide-eyed old people on blankets.

"What's—" I started, but he cut me off.

"The police are figuring it out now, too. We're all coming around. We're all starting to see. The lock failure? You think that was an accident? I don't. It was an event. It was a deliberate *event*."

I yanked on his hand because at least it gave me an ounce of leverage to pry his attention towards me. "You're about to lose me here, hero." I let go of his hand. "Start talking sense already, would you? I don't know what's going on, so you're going to have to tell me. And you're going to have to do it like a civilized, sane human being if you want me to pay attention."

I released him and let my hands drop to my sides. I was so tired. "I'm sorry," I amended it. "It's been a rough day. Just, please. Just spell it out for me. I'm beat, over here."

He stopped and looked me up and down, almost like he was seeing me for the first time—but not really. More like he'd just noticed something that had been there all along, but he didn't have a reason to see it before. "Okay," he said in a half-whisper, the kind that comes out when you exhale while your mouth holds the shape of a word.

"Okay," I echoed.

"Let's do it like this, then. The elevators are working but crowded. I've scored a pass for the service elevator. Let's take that, and I'll tell you what I saw on the way up."

"Okay," I said again, and I let him guide me down a hall and around a corner. He pressed the button on an elevator that didn't look half so shiny as the ones in the lobby, but would be serviceable enough if the doors ever opened.

They did. We stepped inside. He picked a key from his pocket and plugged it into the hole beneath the list of floor buttons. The doors closed and we were lifted up with that stomach-dropping whoosh that comes from an elevator built for speed, not comfort.

"Down by the river, where the green grass grows," he said in a sing-song. "Down by the river, something is coming up, and coming out. I don't know how many of them there are, and I don't know what they want. But they're dead. They're very, very dead. And they are *pissed*."

"I beg you to be a touch more specific."

The elevator pinged and the doors split open to the next floor. We stepped out into another shiny tile hallway and immediately began working our way past more refugees who were scattered around on the floor. All ages, all sizes, all shapes, and all colors were crowded together, trying to stay on the carpeted places but not altogether able to do so.

I hesitated when we reached the hall with Caroline's door. There was a space around it like it was quarantined, or banned, or just plain smelled bad. I didn't want to go back in. Not yet. Not without knowing.

"Keep talking," I told Nick. "Tell me everything you can before I do this. I don't want to talk to her again without knowing what I need to ask." I hated myself because it came out so close to a whine. But I was tired, and she'd hurt me so much the last time. I didn't want to go in there cold, not again.

Nick's eyes shifted back and forth, sweeping the floor and seeing no private place to speak, or even stand. "Hmm. Back into the elevator. Just for a minute."

"What?"

"Not out here, in the hallway. Not here where people can hear."

"Fine," I said, and I even agreed. There'd be no point in scaring people silly who were already frightened and confused.

Back into the elevator we went, though we had to wait for it. Once inside, we let the doors close and Nick plugged his key in again, turning it and pressing a button that would lock us there.

He turned to face me, then leaned back into the corner and sat against the support rails there while he spoke. "It's like this: *I have no idea*. I have to start with *that*. I've got a million and one questions, but I'm running short on answers."

"That's all right. Start with what you've got."

"There are people coming out of the river—dead people. Some of them are wrapped in chains, and some of them are all blackened and wet, like they were burned and then soaked. They look like they dug their way out of hell and into the Tennessee River. So they're wrapped up in these chains, and they're using them as weapons, sometimes. They're swinging them at people, using them like whips—" He made an Indiana Jones flip with his wrist. "And they're pulling people under. They're dragging people down."

"And you saw this? You saw them?"

He nodded vigorously, as if by sheer sincerity he could convince me. "I saw one of them, more up close and personal than I would have liked. He was standing in knee-deep water over near the aquarium. I saw him, and he was huge—he was just insanely tall and black. Not black like a black person," he clarified quickly, but changed his mind. "Or, I don't know, maybe he *was* a black guy. It was hard to tell. He was all burned up, with his skin all cracked around the edges and this gray *tissuey*-looking stuff underneath, showing through in the places where the skin peeled away. And his eyes. Jesus. They were dead. I thought maybe he was just a crazy homeless nutter until I saw his eyes, under the streetlamp."

"Okay," I said, bobbing my head slowly, trying to think and finding the task difficult. "Okay. So the ghost of a burned-up dead guy."

"No!" He said it loud, and quick. It startled me. "No, not a ghost. Caroline in there—" Nick pointed out towards the hall. "Caroline's a ghost. I may not have ever properly seen one, but I've got an idea of what they're supposed to look like, and that thing—that guy down by the river—he was no ghost."

I thought about arguing with him, but I had a feeling it wouldn't be worth my trouble.

"This was no ghost. This was something solid, something with real strength. It was a monster. It was swinging that big rusty chain and I could hear it creaking and wet, splashing around and crashing through windows. Ghosts don't do shit like that. They can't do shit like that, right? That's what *you* always tell people. The dead can't hurt you. The dead are just dead. They're not anything to be afraid of. Well, I hate to tell you this, but those things out there, they're dead. And they are going to kill everyone they can reach."

He seemed to have run out of steam, so I took a deep breath and waited another beat, another second, just to be sure. "They," I said slowly. "You said 'they'—but you only saw one?"

"No, I saw two. But the other one, I didn't realize what she was, not until I was up close to her. Not until I was right on top of her. I tried to help her. I thought she was in trouble."

"So the other one's a woman?"

"I don't think you're getting it." He swore under his breath. "I could hear them, and I could see the shapes squirming up out of the water, wriggling out of the riverbed like turtles or eels or rats. I saw the girl because I tried to help her, because I didn't know any better. She didn't need any help, and she didn't want any."

"What did she want? What did this woman—"

"Not a woman," he interjected. "A girl. A little girl, or not a very big one, anyway. She was maybe ten or twelve, tops. And half of her face was all burned away, and one of her arms, and maybe more of her. It was dark, though, and I didn't see her in time to realize it." He rubbed his hands together, squeezing his fingers tight, trying to think. "And, and, she was wearing a little yellow dress. I think it was yellow. It might have just been old and got yellowed-looking, like old clothes do. It had a pattern on it, once. Flowers, or maybe butterflies."

"All right. Now we're getting somewhere," I said, even though I wasn't sure. "You're a news man. You've got a head for details. Give them to me. Tell me more, about what they were wearing and what they were doing."

"That's all I can think of."

"No it's not. Do your goddamn job, Nick. Report. Report to me. Call it like you saw it. Leave nothing out, because any little thing could help. What was the tall guy wearing? Did their clothes look like they fit any particular historical period? Did they say anything? Did they seem to be looking for something? Someone? What do they want?"

"I don't know!" he nearly shouted, which was almost painful in the close space. "I don't know," he repeated, but I could see that the wheels in his head were turning, even as he denied it.

"Think," I commanded, though the command was frail and needed a nap.

"I'm—I'm thinking the clothes looked old, but, Jesus, I couldn't tell you how old. Maybe a hundred years? I didn't see any women in hoop skirts or bustles, but then again, I didn't see any women—just the girl and the man. Men's clothes—it's harder to tell. He was wearing pants, not jeans. And suspenders. I remember seeing a suspender hanging down, unhooked. The girl was just wearing a smock, you know. A little girl's smock, one piece, with little buttons on the front. Yellow. And…" He closed his eyes. "And she wasn't very dark-skinned, but I'm pretty sure she was black. Her hair was braided up like little girls do, you know. Or maybe it was just the burned-off skin showing through. Fuck, I don't know."

"Keep going, you're doing good. What else?"

"What else? I got the impression they were looking for something. Well, my *first* impression was that they were crazed zombies bent on wreaking havoc, but now I think they were looking for something."

"Something? Or someone?"

"Maybe. It's hard to say. They were swinging chains and groaning."

"Groaning? You didn't mention any groaning. So they weren't talking or anything?"

"No. Not talking, not exactly. Wheezing, maybe. Groaning, yeah. They didn't make much noise. They were mostly breaking things and killing people. Everything else was making all the noise."

I wiped a stray curl or two off my face and leaned back against the elevator wall opposite Nick's spot. I slid down until I was sitting, and he did the same, mirroring my knees-up pose. "If they're dead, they shouldn't have these *bodies* left to manipulate. They shouldn't be walking anywhere, not in flesh. You're right and wrong about Caroline, though. She's a ghost, but she's got something funny about her, too. She's got something in common with these things. She's got physicality on her side, and I don't know how or why."

It was his turn to look confused. "Physicality? Like what?"

"Like she can move things. Interfere, and interact. Throw shit and break things." I wound down. "I've never encountered that before. Before Caroline, all the dead folks I knew were just voices and shadows. They were leftovers, with no bodies left and no power to affect the physical world. But Caroline can. And those things you're talking about, apparently *they* can. And assuming you're right, and they're dead, this is definitely a strange and bad thing."

"You can always assume I'm right," he said, and for a spark's worth of a second, he was his old self.

"I wouldn't go *that* far, but in a pinch, I'd trust your eyesight."

He laughed, more because he was tired than because I was funny. "Hey, I'll take it. Whatever I can get."

"Stick around, and I'll see if I can't make you a better offer later on," I said, and even as the words came out, I wasn't sure if I meant them, or *how* I meant them. I was getting slap-happy from exhaustion, or that's what I told myself.

"Holy shit, woman. Are you flirting with me?"

"I have no idea. Get me out of this box, you bastard. Let's go see if Caroline feels like shedding any light on the situation."

He hopped to his feet with a new kind of energy, and I followed suit. With a twist he removed the key and the doors slipped apart, letting us back into the hall and into the press of people trying to rest, or sleep, or just stay dry.

When we reached the door, Nick pulled out the plastic card that would let us in. He pointed at me with it and said, "This time, I'm coming with you."

203

"Yeah, sure. All right." I didn't have the energy or motivation to argue. I had hit a wall of the fuck-its and I honestly didn't care what he learned or what he saw. "Come on in, but prepare to duck and run. She's got one hell of a throwing arm." I tilted my head to indicate the room, which was still a wreck from my last visit.

The lights were off. Nick knocked the nearest switch with the back of his hand and stood aside to let me in, and to let the door shut behind us with a soft click. I walked past him and found the next light, the one for the big lamps at the corners. Then I went to the bedside lamps and flipped those switches too. Bring it all in, all the light. Every stray ray or beam.

Let her see *us*.

"Hey Caroline," I called, sitting down on the edge of the bed. "Hey, Caroline Read. We know who you are and we want to talk. Show yourself, you crazy old broad. We want to know what's going on, and we think you can tell us."

Nothing. Nick froze, deer-in-the-headlights.

"Come out and talk. You remember me—you beat me up and threw me out a few days ago. Work with me, and I'll see if I can't help you."

And there she was, in the mirror. I hadn't realized I was facing it until I caught the movement above my head, from the corner of my eye. There she was, holding still and steady, eyes narrow and hair wild.

I don't need your help.

Nick didn't see her, but he saw me looking at her, so it must have looked like I was talking to myself in the mirror. She appeared over my right shoulder. Kneeling on the bed behind me. I didn't feel it, though. I didn't detect any pressure on the mattress, or see any crinkling of the covers to indicate a body's pressure on it.

204

"Maybe you do, maybe you don't. But everyone else thought you needed help, didn't they? That's why they sent you away. You wanted help, or you needed help, but you didn't know how to ask for it."

You don't know what you're talking about. She didn't move or lash out, and she was speaking in full sentences—which was an improvement over our last meeting.

"Then explain it to me."

No one to tell. No one to hear.

"You're not making any sense."

They did it to make me quiet. I couldn't tell on them, even when I tried. No one believed. No one listened. And I'm the crazy one? I'm the crazy one? I'm... where's my other glove?

She looked confused for a moment. *It's a riddle,* she told me. *Have you heard it?*

"What are you talking about?"

They have not flesh nor feathers, nor scales nor bone, but they have fingers and thumbs of their own.

"I don't get it."

My gloves. I lost one, and now you can see the cut I made.

"Caroline, did you kill yourself?" I tried to get a better look at her naked wrist, but she wasn't solid enough to see much there.

I know what they said. I know what they told people, and I know why. Because if I'm mad, if I'm mad like a hatter in a storybook, then nothing I say matters. None of the truth means anything because it came from me. So if I'm mad, then no one has to listen.

"Caroline, no more riddles. Say your piece or we're leaving."

Leave then. I don't care.

"You should. We might have news. Better yet, tell us the truth, and we might believe you."

Nick kept his mouth shut but watched where my eyes went, and watched me close. I appreciated his patience. I knew it looked like I was talking to myself, but I also knew that he trusted me and would wait.

I saw what they did, she said. When she said it, her hair—which had been shining and swimming around her head—began to settle, lying down against her scalp and to sit on her shoulders.

"What did they do?"

Killed them. All twenty-nine of them. In the church.

"You're right," I whispered to Nick. "She's said something about the church."

Burned the church down to hide what they did. Blamed it on the flu. She stopped. For a second, I thought she was going to fade away altogether.

"Don't—no, don't. Caroline, come back. Caroline?"

They killed them all, but it was too cold to bury them. Not enough wood to burn them. Weighted them down and threw them in.

"What's going on?" Nick asked, since the moment was slipping.

"Not sure. She came on strong, and now her mind's wandering. Caroline, who killed them? Can you tell me who killed them?"

She sharpened around the edges and her hair began to crackle again, signaling something the way a cat's tail does. *Wrong question*, she said.

"All right. Not the killers, but the killed. Who were they? What happened?"

It was a good church, and they were good people. It was insistent, the way she said it—an apology for something else, too. Or maybe I was reading too far into it.

Outside we heard a hint of commotion, like an argument was brewing. Nick and I turned our attention to the door, but then let it drop when nothing followed the initial outburst. When I turned back to the mirror, she was gone.

"Caroline?"

My fault. They're coming for me. She's coming for me.

I didn't see her, but I heard the words as clear, soft, and sharp as if she'd breathed them into my ear. The room felt lighter, and changed. It felt empty, even though Nick and I sat together at the edge of the bed.

"She's gone."

"I felt it," he said. "It was quick, like the air letting out of an untied balloon. Did she give you anything helpful?"

"Here's a better question—where'd she go? She doesn't ever leave the hotel, does she?"

"No, but she's been seen out in the halls, and on the mezzanine. Maybe she went for a walk."

"Sure. Why not?" I rose then, and the bed squeaked underneath me when I left it. "We could go looking for her, but I don't think it'd do any good. She's finished talking for now. And she might have told me enough. It's hard to extrapolate from crazy dead people, though. Especially—especially right now. God, I'm tired."

"Me too. But what do you want to do? Sleep? We might miss something."

I smiled at the thought of it, knowing he was right. We were acting like little kids who won't take a nap for fear of being left out—and for the horror of it all, and the fascination. I couldn't sleep yet, not anymore. I'd nabbed a couple of hours at the Choo-Choo and that much would have to suffice. I didn't know when

Nick had last slept, but we were in it together now, regardless.

"Do you think the Starbucks downstairs has any coffee left?"

"They did an hour or two ago. How do you think I'm still able to hold myself upright? But the odds are good they're running out now, if they haven't already. I told you, there's a retreat beginning. People are getting the hell out of the river area and working their way back here."

"Well, I'd hope so, if what you've told me is even *close* to right. Let's see if we can scare up a cup of caffeine from them, and then sit down or something. I need to think, but I'm out of energy for thinking. I think I used it all up getting here."

He lifted himself up off the bed with sleepy reluctance. He led the way to the door and opened it, feeling around with his foot and saying, "Pardon me," to whomever he nearly stepped on.

"Sounds like a plan to me," he said. "And I meant to say—if I didn't already—that it was really cool of you to make it here so fast. After we talked on the phone," he turned sideways to let me pass, "I felt sort of bad about it. I kept hearing these stories from the cops and firefighters who were filtering back here. They were talking like it's a war zone out there. I know you were coming from the heart of downtown—not the river—and I thought maybe it'd be better that way, but I hear it's not. I hear there's looting."

"There is, in fact, a lot of looting."

"Yeah. Gunshots? I heard there were gangs running the streets—"

"The most quickly organized gangs in the history of gangs, you mean? I didn't see any *gangs*—just groups of loosely affiliated people breaking shit and stealing things. If you want to call that 'gang activity' in a press report, you can go right ahead. But it's a reach."

He was quiet and I thought maybe I'd annoyed him, though I wasn't sure why or how. "I wasn't thinking about it that way," he said with a touch of complaint. "I wasn't thinking about what a great story it was. I was thinking that I was an asshole for asking you to come hiking through it all to appease my curiosity."

"That's not what I meant, either. We're too tired to talk, I think. We're just going to piss each other off if we keep it up. You think I'm calling you a mercenary jackass, and I was just trying to anticipate... well... that you might be one at a later date. Wait, this isn't coming out right. Let me put it this way," I backpedaled as I stepped carefully over a sleeping pair of little girls, wrapped up together in some large man's jacket. "It was bad out there, but it wasn't as bad as it could be. And it sure as hell wasn't bad enough to stop me, and I don't hold the trip against you."

"Okay," he said, and it was a tired sort of surrender, offered under duress. We backed up against a wall in order to let a pair of harried-looking paramedics carry bags of supplies through a hall and over the people who were already camped there. When they were gone, he turned to me again and asked, as if I knew how to answer it, "Then, now what?"

I closed my eyes and leaned the back of my head hard against the patterned wallpaper. "God, I don't know. We're out of leads here, aren't we? What do we chase next?"

"Caroline was my only idea, and she wasn't too helpful, was she?"

"Yes and no. She's conflicted, and willing to lie to herself or to us—whichever makes her feel better. And she said what you said, that the church was burned and it was blamed on the flu. What church was it? I forget."

"First Congregationalist Church."

"Right. Burned down. Fire. That's what we're going to have to start with. We've got burned bodies and a burned church. What follows logically?"

"The bodies were burned in the church," he prompted. "And don't forget the Klan. I might be a Midwestern lad at heart, but if there's one thing I know about the Klan, it's that they liked to burn things—and the First Congregationalist Church would've been a tempting target."

"Why's that?" I asked.

"It was a racially diverse congregation—one of the first in the country. Black people, white people, coming together to worship. But mostly the church is just a footnote in an occasional history buff's article. I couldn't even find out for sure where it used to be, only that it burned down in 1919 and no one could agree on why."

"And it was Caroline's church?"

"Apparently."

"Weird," I said.

"Why?"

"The Reads have been a rich, prestigious family around here for generations. I have a hard time believing they'd send their kids to a church where there was any mixing. I guess they could have been enlightened before their time, but I wouldn't bet on it."

He shrugged and tiptoed his way out of the corridor, into the stairwell. "Oh ye of little faith," he said.

"I have plenty of faith."

"Just not in other people, huh?"

I wanted to argue with him, because I didn't like the way it sounded when he said it—like an accusation, or an observation that he found distasteful. I could've argued, but he'd said it himself: he was a Midwestern lad. He wouldn't understand.

There were boundaries here, south of the Mason-Dixon; and there still *are*. Time moves slower here. History drags this place along, kicking and screaming, until a city like Chattanooga takes on polish enough to resemble its northern or western brethren. So when people come to it cold from somewhere else, they take a look around and they think, "This is just like some other place I've seen."

But it isn't.

Back downstairs there was nowhere to sit and almost nowhere to stand in the Starbucks. But coffee was still brewing, and it was being passed out for free with help from the Red Cross people.

Nick and I each took a cup, and neither of us diluted it with anything sweet before we drank it.

16

THE ARCHIVES

My phone rang, and even though I was crouched in a corner without room to flex my elbows, I wrangled my arms around enough to answer it. "What's going on? Are you still down there?" Dave asked, seeming to assume that I was awake and alive despite the hour.

I checked the back of the phone, and it told me we were creeping up on 3:00 a.m. "I'm still down here," I confirmed. "Down at the Read House, now."

"What? Why?"

"Because… it's a long story. Nick's here," I told him, as if it explained everything—even though it didn't.

"Lu's asleep finally, but barely. I couldn't join her though, so I thought I'd call. What about—I mean, have you reached or seen Harry? Or you know, Malachi?" It cost him to say that second name. I could hear him trying to keep the syllables from sounding too angry.

"I found them. They're over at the Choo-Choo. They stayed

there; I told them to. They're going to go on home, whenever they can. So you can tell Lu she can rest a little easier, not having to sit down at the same table with them."

"That's not going to help her. Not going to help me, either. We want you to come home."

"You and me both, man. But right now? I can't imagine how it could happen. I'll just hole up for the night, and one of these days they'll *have* to open the bridges again. Won't they?"

"I thought you were going to hole up with Harry and your brother?"

"It didn't work out. But I didn't go far and I made it somewhere safe, so you can stop worrying. Go get some sleep for yourself."

Nick wrangled his way back to me, having briefly left my side to see if he could beg a refill from the Red Cross people. "Who is it?"

I pulled the phone down against my neck to quickly answer, "My uncle," then returned my attention to Dave. "I'm safe. Everything's fine. Go to bed."

He begged to differ. "Everything's pretty far from fine, princess. Chattanooga's on CNN and all the major networks. And there are rumors coming out—there's *footage*, baby." Oh, I could really hear it then—the worry. The fear. The wish that we could reverse time a day or two and have nothing more to fear than an awkward dinner with strange relatives.

"Footage," I echoed weakly.

"Footage, yeah. Things in the river, down there. And there are riots, and gangs, and there's looting, and—"

"And right here at the Read House," I cut him off, "there's Red Cross coffee that actually tastes better than the Starbucks stuff they were handing out earlier. There are people sleeping on the floor wrapped in jackets and blankets, and there isn't enough space to go around. But it's pretty quiet. There are cops, and there are a few firefighters, and we passed some paramedics in the hall a few minutes ago. Dave, I swear to God, it's not that bad here. Not like what you're seeing on the news."

Nick heard that much and his interest was piqued, but he knew better than to interrupt. Instead, he shimmied himself closer to me and listened.

"Stay there, then," Dave begged. "Promise me you'll stay put. They'll be evacuating people for days—but if you've got to stay someplace, better the hotel than anywhere down by the river. No one knows what to call it, but I've seen the footage, from people with little digital cameras and from some of the more ballsy news guys. It looks like hell down there. Please promise you'll stay at the hotel."

"I… I can't promise you that. I don't know what's going to happen an hour from now, or come morning. They might make us move—like you said, they're evacuating people all over the place."

"Then promise me you won't leave unless they make you. Promise you'll stay unless it's safe to leave." He was begging. He didn't ever beg, not like that.

"I promise I'll do my best to stay safe," was all I managed. It was a watered-down promise and we both knew it. But it was the best I could do.

"That's not enough to let us sleep."

"But this is—this is a fluid situation," I told him, borrowing some sound bite I'd overheard on television. "I'll do my best. It's what I always do. And—I'd like to point out—I've survived this long with nothing but my best. You're going to have to trust me to take care of myself."

"I do trust you that far. I do, I swear. But please—don't take any unnecessary chances. Just stay away from those chances. Think of your poor old Lu and Dave up here, and then, if you get a chance to do something crazy—think twice. Will you do that for us?"

"Of course I will. You don't even have to drag the promise out of me. You ought to know better."

"Then why don't I feel any better?"

"I don't know," I said, and I almost felt like crying, except that it wouldn't have done either of us any good. "But I'll be careful. And I'll call. Or you can call me, just as long as this phone lasts."

"Hey," Nick squeezed my arm and pointed out through the glass doors. "Friends of yours."

Outside I saw Jamie half-carrying Christ, dragging him up to the nearest person in uniform—a woman with a jacket that said "EMT" in yellow letters on the back. Jamie's bushy black mane was slicked and soaked down his back, nearly down to the top of his pants. His shirt was torn and he was either muddy or bloody, I couldn't tell which.

"Dave, I've got to go. Jamie just got here with a friend of ours. I think he's hurt."

"The friend, or Jamie?"

"Yeah," I said, even though it didn't answer him very well. "Look, I've got to go. I'll be careful, though. I'll take care of myself. You go get some rest. Love you both," I added, and closed the phone.

"Thanks," I said to Nick as I pushed past him and out to the front, through the glass door and into the night—which had gone cold. Or maybe I was only tired, and drained, and hungry, and the world felt cold even though it wasn't.

"Jamie? Christ?"

215

"What are you doing here?" Jamie lowered Christ into a crumpled sitting position against the building, where the EMT shined a light into his eyes and tried to talk to him.

"Same as everybody else, I guess."

He grabbed me by one arm and gave me a hug that I was preposterously happy to receive. He felt slim and tight under my arms, but comfortingly, comfortably strong.

"Glad to see you made it in one piece," he said into my hair, then pulled back to look at me. "But I thought you were headed for the Choo-Choo?"

"I was, yeah. I made it, too. But then I ended up doubling back. Long story."

Nick emerged behind me, squeezing into the space beneath the overhang.

"Ah," Jamie said, as if it answered everything. He pointed a thumb down at Christ. "Lookit what I found. He was floundering around on Fourth Street; Becca and me nearly tripped over him on the way back up to her place."

"Hey darling," I said, crouching down beside Christ. His orange semi-Mohawk was flattened and brown, and his cheeks looked even more gaunt than usual. Around his eyes a blue-gray cloud smudged itself deep, giving him the look of a corpse, though his chest rose and fell, fast and hard.

"Hey," he mumbled back, the single sound stretching over a wheezing pair of breaths.

"Jesus, Christ. I thought you were still down there, you know that? I half swam across the river and half climbed the damn bridges trying to get you."

Something tight and curved stretched on his mouth, almost a grin. "Dumbass."

"Tell me about it."

"We're all dead, now. Get off of me, lady," he said to the EMT. "I'm fine. Get the fuck off of me."

She backed away, but came back a second or two later with a towel and a bottle of water. "I don't know if you're fine or not, but here—take these."

He took the towel and wrapped it around his shoulders, then opened the water and downed it in a few quick gulps while I watched. "Didn't realize," he gasped. "Didn't realize how thirsty I was. Water, water everywhere—and all the boards did shrink," he bubbled, killing off the last of the bottle and dropping it empty down at his side.

"You're alive, though. Christ, you're alive. And now... now I sort of want to *kill* you."

"Nothing but love for you too, Eden. And I didn't tell you to come out and get me. I didn't ask for help."

"Yeah you did. Like, a dozen times you asked for help."

"Oh. Well. I meant today. Or yesterday. Whichever. I didn't ask for help then. There wasn't any help for Ann Alice, and I could find my own goddamn way out of the undersides. How exactly did you plan to contribute to my survival, anyway?"

"I don't know," I admitted. "But if you'd drowned, I would've felt guilty for years to come."

"Drowning was the least of my problems," he said, putting his hands down on his knees, and putting his head down on his hands.

Guilt, I thought.

I sat down next to Christ and tugged at the leg of Nick's jeans. "Guilt—that's what it is," I told him—realizing I was abruptly shifting subjects, but lacking the vitality to summon up a good transition.

"Guilt? Who, Caroline, you mean?" Nick said.

"Yeah," I nodded, glad that he'd managed to follow my disjointed train of logic. "She's all et up with guilt, as my aunt would say. She said that they blame her for everything. Maybe it wasn't just whiny self-flagellation; maybe the fire really *was* her fault."

"How?" Nick slipped his back down the glass and it squeaked where his shirt was still damp. When he was sitting next to me, Christ, and Jamie, he added, "If the fire was in 1919, she would've been just a kid."

Jamie piped up then, leaning on the glass instead of sitting to join us. "Kids do stupid destructive things all the time without meaning to."

"True," I said. "But how many kids ever do things *that* stupid? I mean, stupid enough to burn down buildings and kill people?"

Nick looked at me like I'd just beamed down from a pyramid-shaped spacecraft. "Do you even *watch* the news at all? Ever? Even sometimes, just because I'm on it? That sort of thing happens all the time."

"I *do* watch the news sometimes, sure. But never just because *you*'re on it," I clarified, even though it was practically a baldfaced lie. "I've got the Internet, too. Fascinating stuff, real life."

"Fascinating and fucked-up," Nick said. "More fucked-up than you'd ever believe, the stuff that happens every day."

"Today? Sure. But eighty years ago, a little girl burned down a church full of people? Or maybe," I thought out loud, "maybe she did something that got the church burned down. She wouldn't need to have struck the match to feel awful about it. Especially not if…"

"What?" Jamie asked. He was still eyeing Christ like a mother hen, but Christ didn't do anything except sit there and pant.

"Nick, you said—you said you saw a girl. Didn't you? A little girl, maybe, what—ten or twelve years old? That's how old Caroline would've been, give or take. What if that little girl was a friend of hers?"

Nick bobbed his head slowly, thinking right along with me. "I see where you're going with this, and I like it. The church burns down and her little friend dies. If she thought it was all her fault—whether it was or not—that could easily be the sort of trauma that would oh, say, make her batshit insane."

"Thus the ensuing institutionalization."

"Who? What? Who's Caroline?" Jamie wanted to know. Nick tried to fill him in the long way. "Well, about eighty years ago, we think—"

"She's the Lady in White," I said, giving him the shorthand that would let him fill in the rest.

"For real? In here? You went looking for her?"

"It was this guy's idea," I said, jacking my thumb over at Nick. "And yes, we went looking for her, and yes, we found her. Furthermore, we think she has something to do with whatever's going on down at the river."

"What's going on down at the river?" Jamie asked.

Christ snorted, but didn't offer any information on the matter. "You mean you don't know?" Everyone seemed to know—even Dave, stuck high on top of Signal Mountain, well out of the reach of any dead, grasping hands.

"Why would I? Becca and me went up the hill back to her place, just like we told you. We found him on the way. I sent her on up, then dragged this asshole from pillar to post, trying to find a shelter that would take him. But they're disassembling the shelters and moving people out, pushing back farther into the city—away from the river. I figured it was because the water's still rising."

"Oh, it's still rising," Christ said without looking up. "But that's not the problem. It's just the catalyst for the problem. That's what I think, anyway."

"Just this once, let's pretend that what you think might be helpful," Jamie said. He was joking more than not, but it still sounded harsh. I guess we all sounded harsh, by then. We were all so worn out.

"All right, let's *do*," Christ obliged. His voice dropped to its usual timbre of skepticism and cattiness, and even though it was defensive, it was *him*—not the tattered little guy who could hardly breathe who had been there a moment ago.

"I know what I saw," he told us. "They're zombies, of a kind. They're dead, and they move, and they kill—but they aren't totally mindless. They want something, and whatever it is, they can't have it. So they kill. They kill everyone they can reach."

"Don't you think that's a little alarmist?" My caution came out like flippancy, but it wasn't.

"Alarmist? Alarmist? Take a look around, for my sake, would you? Look at this place—look at this city. It's as bad as it can possibly get, isn't it? But that's what a tragedy is!"

"What? Settle down, Christ." Jamie put a hand on his shoulder as if it would hold him down.

"It's when you think things have gotten as bad as they can possibly get… but you're only halfway there. That's what a tragedy is. *That's* what this is. So the city's flooded, and that's bad. That's really fucking bad, but before TVA came along it used to happen all the time."

"Not like this." Nick said it with a certainty that implied he'd looked it up. Maybe he'd been doing some research in his free time.

"Not like this, maybe. But only because there have never been so many people living here. I mean, you can't look around and say, 'It isn't that bad' because obviously it is. But this—all of this, the people sleeping on the floor, and the police, and the helicopters flying overhead all the motherfucking time, and the lights flashing, and the windows breaking, all of this bullshit—this isn't even half of it. It's not even half of how bad it's *going* to get when the river gets here."

It was hard not to be struck silent. Christ was a man prone to hyperbole, but even his vast store of exaggeration wasn't sufficient to paint the scene.

"I'm talking about fucking zombies, man! Zombies!"

"And… now we've got to settle down for a little quiet time, don't we, Christ?" I said, pulling at the towel and pulling him closer to me with it. I wrapped one arm around him and put my mouth against his ear.

"Christ, dear, we believe you. We believe you."

"You do?" he asked, and he looked up at me with clouded blue eyes, and I thought there was no way in hell he could be thirty years old. He had to be fifteen under all that bravado. He had to be a boy. "You believe me?" He asked it again, and his eyes were watering.

"Yeah, we believe you. We do. We *do*."

I held on to him and let him rock back and forth against me, between me and Jamie, who lapped his arm over mine so we could hug him together. Nick looked like he felt left out, but he didn't offer to join the pile and we didn't invite him to.

"But," I whispered down into that manky, wet, rat's nest of

vibrantly fake-colored hair, "right now everybody else doesn't know yet. And right now, everybody else is trying very hard *not* to believe, and not to hear. Right now, it's rumor. Right now, it's scary shit being passed along from refugee to refugee."

His autistic rocking lurched itself into a nod.

"No one's saying this ain't a mess, and it ain't bad, because we all know it is. We can look around and see it's bad. And look—there are official-type people here. They're getting out everyone they can, starting with the sick, and the families with kids, and with old people. It's slow but steady. I've been watching it all night, starting at the Choo-Choo. It's not perfect, but it's working."

I lowered my voice even farther, and brought my lips even closer to his ear. "But if you keep yelling like this, you're going to start a panic."

"And they ought to panic!" He started to rise, but Jamie and I forced him to stay down.

"*No.* No panic. Not yet—not while the real danger, as you put it, is still down by the river. Let them get the most vulnerable people up and out of the way. And then, when the panic comes—like we all know it's going to—then we can all make a run for it, and we'll all have better odds. Better to get the slow and weak ones out of the way now."

"Mercenary of you," he growled.

"Let's all be mercenary, if it's like you say—and I believe it is. This time, under these circumstances, in this life-or-death situation, it's good for everyone. If there's going to be a stampede, fine. But the fewer in the herd, the better our chances are."

He was silent, except for the tiny rhythmic squish of his rocking in wet clothes. "All right," he said. "All right. All for all and one for one. I can see that. I can make that work."

"Good," I told him, rubbing at his shoulder.

"As per usual, Eden my darling," Jamie said, patting me around Christ's shoulder, "I can't tell if you're brilliant, or completely deranged."

Nick combined an eye roll and a sniff into a gently derisive facial gesture. "Hey cuddle pile, it's starting to rain again. Let's get inside if we can, eh?"

"Inside, sure, but not here." Christ perked up and looked nervous. "Not while the zombies are coming."

Nick offered him a hand, and despite the fact that both Jamie and I were ready to help him up, he took it. "No panicking the peasantry, remember?"

"I remember. But we can't stay here, it's too close. I mean, the river is just a couple of blocks that way." He pointed to the left, towards the aquarium at the end of Broad Street. From our vantage point we could barely see its outline, a sharp-edged structure made of glass with the emergency lights glowing green and yellow from within.

"Where should we go, then?" I asked him, but I could watch the tweaks and shadows of ambivalence working across his face.

He drew away from us and faced us, looking from one pair of eyes to the next. "What do you think, how far can the water really come up? It's only a river. How far up can it go?"

None of us knew, so nobody answered. He went on talking his way up to a point that I could see coming a mile away.

"I think they're stuck there, in the water. I've never seen them in water less deep than knee-high. They can't leave the river, so they can't go any farther than the river lets them. And if that's right, then once the TVA gets the locks straightened out—once the rain stops—"

Even as he spoke, a crunching growl of thunder rumbled across the valley.

"Once the rain stops," he went on, "down goes the water. And down go the zombies."

"But that'd be a temporary fix at best." I put my hands on my hips and peered out into the darkness, attaching my eyes to that distant marker of the aquarium. I couldn't even tell if I could really see it, or if it was just an illusion of exhaustion and hope.

The road between the hotel and the river was straight and dark except for the flashing, thrusting lights of the emergency vehicles and the police blockades with the yellow-striped saw horses. Cops and feds were trying to keep us unpredictable refugees as close to the hotel shelter as they could. They were rounding up strays on the street and forcing them up to the ambulances, inside the nearest open doors. Anything to get us off the streets.

I watched them and felt an urgency different from the one that had driven us all all day long. They knew something we didn't.

Rather, they knew something *most* of us didn't.

I looked back and forth between this weird little group and wondered what the hell we were going to do. Be quiet, sure. Be wary, of course. Wait for the water to go down.

"How long do you think it would take, anyway?" I asked no one in particular. "How long before it goes down?"

"Days." Nick lifted and dropped an eyebrow and a shoulder. "Weeks, maybe. Longer than we can hold out here, that's for sure. They'll cart us away before that happens."

Jamie folded his arms and squinted into the shadows, same as I was. "That's not going to work. The river's going to get higher before it goes lower. Look around. Listen to the radios—can you

224

hear them? They're trying to talk around it, talk about it low, you know. But if you listen, you can tell."

"And with the water comes something worse. Even once it goes down, they'll still be there, waiting." Christ banged his head up and down against his chest. "It was the construction, what woke them up. It was those apartments, Eden. Your apartments. That money-grubbing ex-mayor didn't want anyone finding out about what the workers found, so she covered them up again. And they aren't going to go away now, whether the water recedes or not."

"Thanks for trying to make this *my* fault. Thanks. Yeah. I appreciate that."

"Not your fault *personally*," he was quick to qualify. "But I'd like to think that you get it now. Not like before, when you were bullshitting me. You get it now, right? Why I did it?"

"Why you did—" Nick started to ask, but before he had the question all the way past his lips, he'd figured it out. "You're the little shit who set the apartment fire the other day."

"*Big* shit, thank you very much. And what are you going to do about it? Put it on the news, motherfucker?"

"I ought to," he said. I didn't hear much conviction behind it, though.

"Call the cops on me?"

"Somebody should." Jamie said it with a smile, though.

"So you've known all along?" Nick demanded, and I'd either forgotten or never realized that he hadn't. So much of my life had overlapped in the last twenty-four hours, I felt like I'd never get it all straight.

"Yeah, I've known. I've been trying to tell her," and here Christ pointed a long, accusing finger at my face, "for days. It's not her fault that there are zombies overrunning the city, but she should've listened to me in the first place, and then maybe things would have been different."

"Why?" I asked. I held my ground even though the rain was coming down good and we were all getting wet again. But I wasn't keeping anyone but Christ out with me, so if the rest of them wanted to soak, that was fine and not my problem. "Why should I have believed you, not just this time, but ever? You've built a lifetime and a reputation on being full of shit, of crying wolf, and generally trying to stir up as much trouble as you possibly can while staying out of jail."

"Broken clock, bitch, broken fucking *clock*!"

Jamie took Christ by both shoulders and backed him down, away from me and away from the road. A cop car was trying to pull up and around, using the curb as a lane and weaving a tight trip up to the hotel. "Out of the road, Christ. Out of the rain, everybody. This isn't doing anyone any good."

I asked over his shoulder, into Christ's face, "What do you mean by that, 'broken clock'?"

Jamie answered for him, or around him. "Twice a day. Even a broken clock is right sometimes. He did a poem on it a couple of slams ago, right?"

"Right," Christ said. He was trying to muster complaint, but was so flattered that someone remembered his poem that he was temporarily disarmed. "That means I've got once more to be right before the day is out, doesn't it?"

"Metaphorically, I suppose." A huge splat of water slid off the canopy above us and hit me in the eye. I wiped it away and stepped sideways, trying to crush my way under the shelter but only meeting limited success. "Literally, there's no way of knowing.

And I wouldn't set down Vegas odds on it any day of the week."

"Fuck you," he told me, and there was only a residue of venom there. We were all too worn out to even swear at each other properly.

"Sure, sure. Fuck me. Whatever. Even with all your prophetic warnings, we still don't know what to do. I think our current plan is, 'Wait for the water to go down while we sit around with our thumbs up our asses.' Isn't that about what we've got so far? Anyone want to correct me? Please?"

Even as I said it, I was still peering down that black and yellow corridor towards the river. And I saw shapes there, indistinct and unmoving. Three of them. Side by side in a little line, just like me, Jamie, Nick, and Christ. Catfood Dude. Pat. Ann Alice. Watching us as I was watching them.

Knowing that I saw them.

You are so close, Ann Alice said, jerking her head at Nick.

Pat shook his head. *No she isn't. Newspaper and TV aren't the same thing.*

"Newspaper?" I said, and everyone suddenly looked at me like I'd lost my mind. "Nothing. Just. Huh. The newspaper." The ghosts were gone, and I could once again see the black, back end of the city against the river.

"What about it?" Nick asked. "The newspaper building's out at the other end of town—back towards the Choo-Choo and a couple of blocks past it. They ought to be high and dry right now. I bet they're having a field day with this."

"Like Channel Three?" I said, to the tune of a pot calling a kettle black.

"And Nine, and Twelve, and everybody else. It's a job, isn't it? We're helping how we can. Why do you think I haven't got a vehicle right now? And what do you think I'm doing here with you, instead of being back up at the Olgiati showing the world what it looks like down there, huh? Why do you think that is?"

"Because you're a goddamn idiot," I growled.

Everyone looked startled except for Nick, who looked like he'd expected it. "Truer words were never spoken. Say them again, if you like."

"No, thanks. I didn't even mean it that way—"

"Point is, I'm here now. You're here now. These two schmucks are here now."

Jamie let go of Christ, who slumped back down against the wall and let himself flop there. "I object to the designation of 'schmuck,' you cheesy-ass microphone masturbator."

"Enough!" I waved my hands. "Enough. Look. We're tired and pissy. Stop it. Both of you. All of us. Stop it. I don't have the energy to do all this by myself and argue with you all, too."

"You started it," Nick said, but he sidled up next to me anyway, striving to get out of the rain and underneath the old-fashioned hotel canopy. It didn't give us much protection from anything; but when the wind came swooping down and the thunder rang out loud again, it gave us all an excuse to fold in closer together, and watch the sky without feeling alone.

"The newspaper," I said again when the thunder strike had petered away. Two ideas were struggling hard to collide in my brain, and when they did I still wasn't sure they made any sense side by side. "That building over there—next block over, and down one—didn't that used to be the newspaper building?"

"Naw." Nick shook his head. "Don't think so. It's been in the old warehouse building, or bottling plant, or whatever back in southside for ages. Like I said, high and dry."

"Naw." Jamie sided with Nick, then corrected him. "She means the old *Free Press* building, from back before the two big papers merged. You know the place—back behind the Pickle Barrel. It looks like the *Daily Planet*, all chrome and shiny stuff. That's the old newspaper building."

"Older than that," I murmured. "I know about the *Daily Planet* building, and that's not what I meant. On one of the old buildings near the Bijou theater, there's a historical marker. I remember it, down by—"

"The river," Nick finished for me.

"Yeah, how did you know?"

"Lucky guess. If it wasn't towards the river, it wouldn't be bad, and you wouldn't be thinking about checking it out. That's just the sort of luck we've got."

I slapped his arm. "*You're* the one who got me this close to the water. I was back over at the Choo-Choo until you called. What's another block or so in a bad direction?"

"Towards zombies and the river," Christ said from his spot down on the sidewalk. Jamie kicked him gently with the back of his boot.

"Ix-nay on the ombie-zays," he said, catching a pointed look from a nearby cop with a clipboard. "Seriously. Knock it off. We believe you already, but don't make a big case about it. You're going to get us hauled off to the loony bin."

"How?" he asked, palms up. "Right now, I'd *take* a ride to the loony bin just to get the hell out of *here*."

He had a point. "Regardless," Jamie fussed. "Just… don't. You hang around shouting about zombies and they might find a way to make you a priority—in a way you most definitely won't like."

"Who cares? This guy's going to rat me out to the news anyway."

Nick acted like he hadn't heard it. "Let me make a phone call or two. The producer down on the other side of the river, he's lived here forever. He might know about the building you're talking about. Though I have to ask—even if he does know where it is, what do you think you're going to do? Break in?"

"Probably won't have to," I said. "Stay under the cops' radar. Look around inside, if I can. See if there's something important there—something that has to do with all this."

"Ghosts talking again?" Christ asked.

"They *were*."

"They never seem to be very helpful, really," he observed.

"I know, and I wish I knew why. Most of the time it's like they've only got a few minutes to say their piece; and sometimes it's like they don't know what's important and what's not. The rest of the time, I think they're just being contrary."

"Why would dead people be contrary?" Jamie wanted to know.

"Why are living people contrary? Same reasons. They aren't so different from those of us with a pulse, especially the ones who have strong enough personalities to stay or linger. I think maybe they like the attention, because being dead makes them feel left out."

Christ had found a cigarette—or part of one—that wasn't completely soaked. He pulled a plastic lighter out of a cargo pocket and managed to light the remainder. "I don't know about you people, but I wouldn't put up with that kind of shit," he said.

"I put up with it because it's different. It beats to hell the scores of sad, frightened dead people who just want one more chance to say the things they should've said every day while they were alive."

Nick had his back turned while he chattered into his cell phone. Jamie asked what I meant. "What, so the rest of it is just static?"

I closed my eyes and tried to nod at him. "It's always the same thing. 'Tell him I'm okay and I love him. Tell her I love her. Tell them I love them.' I'm not saying it's not important, but come *on*. Say it while you've got the breath to do it. And you know what? I think it's one reason people disbelieve psychics so much—the way the message is always the same. Love and roses. Warm fuzzy feelings from dead child, dead husband, dead mother or wife. It's rarely specific or checkable. But that doesn't mean it's any less true."

Jamie thought about it for a second. He reached down and took a drag from the semi-cigarette Christ had found on the street. "I guess that does make it easier for the phonies to work—especially if it's true. Especially if that's all the dead have to say—that they're okay and they love us."

"It's true. Eighty-five percent of the time, that's all it is."

"Bullshit," Christ said, reclaiming his cigarette. "If you're going to come back from the dead, at least have something important to say."

"What could be more important?" Jamie asked him.

"Anything. Lottery numbers. Where the gold is buried. Why zombies are attacking the city."

I nudged him with my shoe. "Think of 9/11. Think of all those phone calls, tying up the cell towers—from the buildings and from that plane that went down in Pennsylvania. People everywhere who knew it was their last phone call—they sent the same messages, 'I love you,' over and over again."

That shut him up, at least temporarily.

Nick flipped his cell phone shut and rejoined the circle. "You're right. There was an old newspaper in one of the buildings down there, near the aquarium. And here's an interesting corollary—just as our First Congregationalist Church was significant for having black and white members, the newspaper was noted for being owned by a black family. You see? All this shit is sort of coming together, isn't it?"

"Maybe," I said.

"What shit?" Christ wanted to know, so I caught him and Jamie up as fast as possible. "Themes emerging. Motives. A church fire and some burned-up bodies, an integrated congregation and a black-owned paper, the KKK—these are things which ought to, if we knew a little bit more, merge to form a more complete picture of whatever the bloody red hell is going on down here."

Nick tapped his phone against his elbow while he thought. "What do you want to bet, since it's not too far away—that the family who owned the paper also went to Caroline's church?"

"I doubt it was Caroline's church," I said again, even though I didn't have any good reason to. "I just can't picture it. A rich, respectable black family might have gone to an integrated church eighty years ago, but a rich, respectable white family probably wouldn't have, that's all."

"Whatever. Allen says the place is something else now, though. No trace of what it used to be except the historical marker you spoke of. He thinks maybe it's owned by Blue Cross or the Electric Power Board now."

"So?"

"So, I can't imagine what good it will do us to check it out."

"What else are we doing right now?" I asked, and they all looked at me like I was deranged.

NOT FLESH NOR FEATHERS

"Well," Christ glared up at me from his spot on the sidewalk, "for one thing, we're not running towards a rising river full of—"

"I'm just trying to brainstorm here, and think of something useful and practical we can do."

Behind us, another ambulance was trying hard to work its way up to the Read House and meeting limited success. Too many cars were in the way, and too many people wanted too many things from it. Folks who were on the sidewalks, standing there clumped together and getting wet, tried to mob the vehicle. Police pushed them back. A foot or two at a time the stubby medical van crawled forward.

Nick sighed and the rest of us did it too—like a yawn that gets passed around a circle. "Right now, maybe the most practical thing we can do is find a corner, close our eyes, and get some sleep. We're running on empty here. We all know it."

"Speak for yourself," Christ ordered, but he was at the end of his rope too, and not fooling anyone.

"How much longer till morning?" I asked.

Nick turned his phone over and squinted at the display. "A few hours, tops. Maybe less. Maybe in the daylight this won't look so bad. Maybe the things down by the river will slow down."

"Why?" Christ complained. "They aren't vampires."

I thwapped him on the head with the back of my hand. "Have you actually seen any of them? During the day, I mean?"

"Not during the day. But until tonight, pretty much everybody who ever saw them died shortly thereafter. The mere fact that we haven't seen them when the sun's out does not mean they can't wander about in search of a tan, if they want."

"He's right," Nick said.

"Sure, okay. He's right, maybe. But whatever they are, I bet they'll be easier to *see* when the sun's up. Harder for them to sneak up on us. Right?"

Jamie agreed, but with an ulterior motive. "So we might as well grab a cat nap. All of us, if we can. What are we going to do now, anyway? We're stuck here and we're more-or-less safe. If the river keeps rising, and they keep on coming, then we might not find ourselves in such a choice position for long. I'm going to make the hike back up to Becca's place and turn in."

"What? No way," I argued, but he put out his hands and waved me into submission.

"It's straight uphill from here, away from the water. It's dark, but it's not too far and there are plenty of living, breathing, non-zombie people between here and there. It's fine. I'll be fine. I'd be a selfish cad if I tried to score a spot here anyway."

He left us shortly thereafter, and I couldn't blame him or stop him. He was in better physical shape than the rest of us, or so I wanted to think. Maybe he'd gotten more sleep, or had consumed more coffee; but he looked good enough to walk the distance to Becca's place, which couldn't have been more than a mile.

The rest of us agreed that there was nothing else to agree on. Christ fell asleep on the spot where he sat, and a paramedic said he'd keep an eye on him. Nick and I were too tired to ask precisely what that meant, so we didn't.

Nick's phone rang, and it turned out to be the producer from the studio again. He wanted to know if the news SUV had ever made it back down to the Read House, and Nick didn't know.

"The hospital people said they'd leave it down at the shelter if they could get it here," he said.

"Fat lot of good it would do us."

He rubbed at his eyes and then turned off his phone altogether. "It's got a pretty roomy interior. More roomy than any patch of carpet we're going to find in the hotel. And I've got the keys. If we can find it, we can sleep in it. If you want to," he added without any embarrassment or reproach.

I looked up at the Read House, or what I could see of it from beneath the canopy. It was a big brick thing, solid and sturdy-looking, with the weight of history and expensive renovations holding it up and holding the masses safe inside. It struck me as infinitely more secure than an SUV filled with video equipment parked haphazardly outside in the rain, where there were—let's be honest—zombies.

But at every hotel window I saw people crushed and tangled, sleeping however they could cram themselves, with lights, televisions, and radios turned on and turned up in every room.

I looked back out into the rain and still saw no sign of a river lapping its way up onto the cement walkways. And though there were crashes, sirens, and far-flung wails of engines and alarms, the darkness on the street looked quieter.

"All right." I hardly had enough energy to squeeze the words out. "If you can find it, I can sleep in it."

He dashed off into the rain and I waited. Twenty minutes later he reappeared to lead me back behind the hotel and up into the parking garage. Up on the second floor, pinned and squished between a Hummer and a minivan, the Channel 3 SUV was less parked than abandoned.

We wrung out our hair and our clothes.

He reached inside and threw all the expensive equipment out of the back area, into the driver's and passenger's seats. He unloaded the rear a piece at a time, and then, when it was as clear as it was going to get, he reclined the back seat until it lay flat and open.

I crawled into it and stretched out beside him, then curled into a ball.

And then I guess we went to sleep.

17

PICTURE SHOW AT THE PAPER PLANT

Nick was snoring beside me, which was a decidedly peculiar way to wake up.

I came to sometime after dawn, to a sky still gray and a city still heavy with rain. The parking garage had become a temporary camp like every other near-dry place downtown. People were sleeping and sitting in cars, around cars, on top of cars, and in some cases, underneath them—laid out flat like children do when they play under the bed.

Inside the news SUV, the windows were foggy and everything smelled like wet carpet. My clothes reeked. My hair had conspired with the mud and rain to give me dreadlocks that would've done Medusa proud.

The intrepid reporter was out cold, with one leg crooked up on the rear wheel well, and the other stretched out straight. He was using a Channel 3 windbreaker for a pillow.

I didn't see any point in getting him up, so I didn't. I opened the back door as quietly as I could. He didn't budge, or break his routine of soft snores.

I closed the door behind me and stretched.

Things were quieter outside, in the shelter of the concrete parking garage. Everyone was crowded together there, sure—but with the open air things didn't seem quite so oppressive. One thing I wasn't imagining, though—I needed a bathroom.

Inside the hotel there were several large restrooms, but getting into them would be a trick. The elevators were permanently jammed and at least one was serving host to a family of six. The stairs were more promising. I took them down to the valet level and then was pointed to a back way inside the old hotel, underneath the car garage.

One of the huge public restrooms was right around the corner, and it was full, of course. But I waited, because what else was there to do? Find a quiet corner and pee on the floor?

I waited, legs crossed and breath held, until a stall opened up and I could grab it.

The toilet had overflowed and there wasn't any toilet paper, but it was better than nothing, so I used it and pretended I knew nothing at all about germs or public sanitation. When I was finished, I gave it a flush that only partly took. Then I waited for a turn at the sinks.

People were trying to change baby diapers on the floor, or on the counters; but only a few had diapers to use. Some people were sharing and some were hoarding, and a few women were starting to fight over it. I let their argument be the background din to my time at the sink; I tried not to listen too much or I'd get too mad.

I felt like hell. So did everybody else.

I washed my face and gargled some hot water. I peeled off my shirt and it itched when the wrinkled folds unstuck themselves from my skin. Every last inch of me was pruny, but the shirt was nasty, so I stood there in my bra and washed the shirt with a palm-full of pink industrial soap. Better to be clean and wet than dirty and kind of dry.

If it hadn't been so crowded, I probably would've pulled off my jeans and washed them as well; but there's a world of difference between hand-washing a T-shirt in a sink and doing half a load of laundry there.

I was hungry, in an idle way. I was thirstier than I was hungry, though. And my head was pounding and my muscles were sore in all kinds of strange places. I felt like I'd slept on a duffle bag full of garden gnomes.

But at least I'd slept.

Out in the hall there was a clock behind the concierge desk that said it was about 8:30 a.m. I'd accrued maybe four or five hours of sleep altogether on top of the one or two I'd stolen in the Choo-Choo with Harry and Malachi.

I reached for my phone, but it was dead. Either the water or the steady battery drain of nervous relatives could have done it, and I was fortunate that it'd held up as long as it had.

I was almost relieved for the honest excuse not to answer it. It was easier to assume that all was well without me—that Harry and Malachi had been transported beyond the ridges, and that Dave and Lu had finally passed out and turned off the television.

In the hotel lobby, surrounded by dozens of interested faces, there were two televisions displaying the local and national news, respectively.

Chattanooga was the word of the day. I watched Channel 3 first. No surprise for the local news to be self-referential, and the station was on the top of a hill on the north side of town. No surprise they were still up and running full coverage, even though the anchors were looking haggard and in need of more heavy-duty hair products.

I came in at the middle of Terry Sexton's warbly-voiced diatribe. "...thousands of people displaced, hundreds injured, dozens missing."

"Dozens?" I said out loud, and I heard the word bouncing around in the crowd. Everybody knew the toll was higher than that. It had to be.

"Police are having trouble keeping the peace, and looting, rioting, and gang activity is increasing as the hours pass and people are kept away from their homes. Also, we have received some strange reports coming out of the downtown area, down by Ross's Landing and the aquarium. Shots have been fired and barricades are being established; police are not issuing a statement at this time, but there is compelling video footage available and we've been running some of it since last night. Here's a clip now, taken yesterday evening down at the aquarium fountains."

The clip that played was grainy, dark, and shaky—it might've come from a camera phone or a digital camera with a film-clip mode. I weaseled my way through the crowd to watch it closer. I had to see. I had to know.

There was a man, like Nick had said. He was tall and black and burned-looking, visible only in partial profile and shadow, illuminated imperfectly by the flashing rotation of a police car's blue and white lights.

He could have been a refugee, like the rest of us. But I knew better. I could tell from the tittering sobs that leaked from the crowd that others in the crowd did as well.

At the corner of the screen I saw a smaller figure too, about half the size of the man in shadow. Nick said there was a girl, too. This could've been a girl. I couldn't tell. She moved fast, though. They both did. They moved in a jerky way—in a stilted series of lunges—like it had been years since they'd needed to move a body.

You could see it at a glance. They were dead.

And when the tall man's shape turned forty-five degrees so that his face was almost outlined, there in the light of an aquarium lamp, I knew that they were not ghosts. Not spirits. Not haunts.

My spine crawled with a prickling dread, and the absolute silence of the room around me assured me that I wasn't alone.

God, at that last second when the face—when you could see the little girl's face—and you could see the anger there, and the rage, and the pure hatred… it took my breath away. It was hideous and exquisite. It was malicious death, and it was walking.

It was coming.

Terry kept talking, and the clip was rewound, repeated, replayed.

I forced myself to stop watching. I forced myself over to the other television, to watch a broadcast with a little bit of distance. Something not quite so close. Something not quite so personal.

But CNN had picked up the footage too, and I wondered suddenly if it was Nick's footage. He'd told me about a man and a girl, and those were the figures I saw on the screen. He had a camera. He was a journalist. The clip might have been his. But if it was, why hadn't he mentioned it?

Perhaps he didn't know about it. He'd handed over the SUV, and with it, perhaps, the camera. I hadn't seen him carrying it.

"Channel Three reporter Nick Alders…" Terry said his name. I wrenched my attention back to the other screen, but I missed whatever she was saying about him.

CNN had aerial footage of people running and swimming. There was looting, sure. Mostly young men, throwing bricks into windows. Then a few families at the Dollar General, where there were diapers and food. Here and there, with helpful graphic arrows and circles to place them, the national news also noted that something strange was coming up out of the water.

You looked at these things—half a dozen or more, at least, caught on tape—and you saw how they moved with that twisting, aggressive gait, and you thought of old movies. You thought of things in black and white, and monsters without a lot of dialogue. But you didn't say the word. You didn't say it, because if you did then other people would start to say it. It would spread faster and worse than wildfire. It would cause more panic than if you just said "Unknown persons" even though you meant "Unknown things."

But everyone in that room knew.

We glanced around, catching each other's eyes and *knowing* in the worst possible way what was out there. It wasn't here yet— not reaching out to us, not crawling up to the doors and beating with burned and rotted hands—but it was coming, and we needed to get out. But how?

CNN said, "Evacuation is being orchestrated by Homeland Security and FEMA, with helicopters and all-terrain vehicles as well as boats. Old train lines are running again and the transport cars are moving people instead of meat, lumber, and steel. At this point, authorities are concentrating on moving the displaced citizens to established evacuation points where they can be…" The reporter tapped at her earpiece and continued, "Yes, they're moving them into position to be shipped out of town and down to Atlanta—about a hundred and twenty miles away. And—and some are also being sent to Nashville, I understand."

"Not Knoxville, though, I bet," I said under my breath. The river goes right past it or through it, too. If we were having trouble, they were probably having troubles of their own. But I bet they didn't have zombies.

"The Tennessee Valley Authority has not issued a formal statement except to say that they are aware of the problems at the Chickamauga Dam and that they are working at one hundred and ten percent to try to fix the issues that caused the locks to seize. The weather will be a determining factor in the repairs, but the National Weather Service is predicting more rain for the next two days, at least, so Mother Nature isn't ready to cut the Tennessee Valley a break."

"Why should she?" someone nearby grumbled.

I retreated from the edge of the crowd and pushed myself back against a wall, against a mirrored panel that fogged up with the warmth of my body and the damp that just wouldn't leave my clothes or my hair. It was cold on my shoulders, but I didn't care.

They're coming!

I heard her plain as day, but I didn't know where she was until I looked up at the mezzanine—and there she stood, hanging over the rail by one hand. She was shouting, not to me specifically, but to anyone who would listen. A little dog began to howl and a couple of babies started to cry; but for the most part she went unnoticed.

They're coming! she said again. *Jesus, can't you hear them? Up from the river, under the city. Coming, coming, coming, on wetburned feet.*

"Caroline?" I called for her attention, and got it. "What do they want? Just tell us what they want!"

Nothing they can have.

243

"Then what's the point?" I asked too loud, because then she was right beside me, closer than I would have liked. Her breath was ashes against my cheek.

Slow them. Stop them, maybe, for long enough. While you can—while they walk below, while they dig their way through the buried city.

"The underground?" I don't know why I gave it a question mark. I knew exactly what she meant.

How long, do you think—before they emerge?

I thought of the battered little building with its open floor... not a block away, if that far. "But I thought they had to stay with the water? Isn't that how this works, Caroline? They can only rise as far as the water?"

She rolled her eyes at me, then reached out hard and fast—slapping the mirror beside my head and breaking it. *They're dead. They're not supposed to be able to do anything. I don't know what binds or stops them. I don't even know what binds or stops me.*

On the floor a few feet away, I saw a small black boy with eyes turned to me as big as quarters. He'd seen the whole thing, bless his little heart. I held a finger up to my lips and winked at him, trying to make it light or funny. It halfway worked. He mustered up a halfway smile, but it didn't go very far on his face.

"What are we going to do?" he whispered up at me.

"I don't know," I told him. "But I'll think of something. I always do."

I caught a glimpse of Nick's reflection in the mirrored wall. I turned to surprise him before he could sneak up on me. "Let me ask you something," I dove right in. "Say, hypothetically, we needed some explosives of some kind."

"Say, hypothetically, that you're out of your fucking mind."

"Man, there are kids here. Knock it off." I gave a parting nod to the kid on the floor and took Nick's arm, leading him back into the hallway, towards the entrance to the parking garage.

"If the worst thing that happens to them today is that they hear a little bad language, they'll be in ridiculously good shape."

"Yeah, but. Look, the things that are coming—they need to come up and out, and I think I know where. They're working their way up the underground, into the old tunnels beneath the city. I heard them coming, I swear to God. There's a boarded-up little place—I was there when we spoke on the phone yesterday—and they're coming up from underneath it."

"Not all of them, they aren't. I saw them down by the water myself. People are *still* seeing them down there. They're tearing through the things at the river's edge—you know, the restaurants and stores, and the spots around the aquarium."

"Okay. Sure. Some of them are coming up the long way. But *some* of them are coming up from underneath. We don't know how many of these guys exist. You said what—half a dozen, documented? That's not much of a horde."

"Half a dozen caught on tape. Maybe twice that many actually spotted. It's hard to tell at night." He let the thought drop and picked it up again. "But now that the sun's up, it's better than the rain at night. Maybe we could go scouting and—"

"Let's not resort to such drastic tactics yet, all right?"

"Drastic? Last night *you* wanted to storm the old newspaper building, if I recall correctly."

"Not storm it, precisely," I argued. "I merely noted it as a place of interest. It's a spot we should check out if we can, because I think there's something there. The ghosts were talking about it like it means something."

He leaned around me and pushed against the glass door, which opened to let us outside. Even though the air was palpably damp, it was better than the closed-up, recycled oxygen within the old hotel. It was better than breathing everyone else's used-up air; and smelling the rain was better than smelling overdue diapers, sick people, and body odor.

I turned my face to the sky and let the drizzle hit me, because at least it was only drizzle.

"But you've said it yourself, the ghosts don't always know what they're talking about. People who are wrong when they're alive are just as likely to be wrong when they're dead."

"True. But there seems to be a pretty good consensus among the early victims—they're the ones I'm seeing, the skater kids and the homeless guys who went missing before anybody gave a shit. Speaking of which, have you seen Christ?"

We were back at approximately the spot we'd left him the night before, but there was no sign of him.

"Nope. Not since we left him here. Where do you think he went?"

"Heaven knows, but it might not care." I turned myself in a circle and made a cursory glance at the street—occupied from curb to curb with parked cars, the sidewalks lined with people smoking, talking, or just taking a chance to smell something fresh.

"So he's the one who set the apartment fire, huh? I guess you knew about that all along, didn't you?" I heard an accusation there, even though it sounded like he was working to keep it in check.

I tried not to bristle. "All along? You mean, did I know he was going to do it and then somehow fail to report back to you about it?"

"No, that isn't what I mean and you know it."

"I knew he did it, but not until after the fact. I'd guessed he might have done it, and then he went ahead and confirmed it for me. He's not much good at keeping secrets, in case you hadn't noticed."

"I noticed. But you didn't feel compelled to report him to the cops or anything—why's that?"

"Okay, you know what? I'm not one of your three-minute feature packages. I'm not obligated to explain myself to you, so if you could drop the roving reporter act right about now, that would be *great*."

"I'm only making conversation."

"You're digging for dirt and I don't like it." I put my hands over my face and breathed through my fingers. "This was all a bad idea. A *cosmically* bad idea. I should've never..." I stopped myself.

He got the gist of it, whether or not I'd finished it. "Nobody made you."

"I know. I know—but you'd think I'd know better, by now. Forget it. The short answer is yes, I knew Christ set the fire. The rest of it—about why I didn't tell anybody—you ought to have figured out for yourself by now. He was on to something. I didn't know what, and I'm still not positive; but I think we can both agree that *maybe* he was right insomuch as there was definitely something weird going on down by the river."

"Agreed. But here's what I was getting at before when you tried to shut me down for asking questions: what was he right about? What did the construction work over there turn up—the bodies? Some relics of what happened to them?"

"My money's on the bodies, since we have to assume that whatever was dug up prompted all of this. The construction disturbed them, and here they come. Maybe it's just coincidence that the construction here at the Read House disturbed Caroline too, and maybe it isn't. We don't believe in coincidences."

A splash just a heartbeat stronger than the drizzle hit my head, and yes, the rain was working itself back up again. We edged ourselves closer together, and into the crowd that was clotting up under the canopy. Nick wiped his hair back across his skull and coughed softly.

"It can't be as simple as that," he said, wrapping one hand around the metal pole that supported the overhang. "You think that these… things—you think they caused the flood and the problem at the locks?"

I had to think about that one before answering it. "No. No, I think it's a combination of bad timing and opportunism. Catfood Dude went missing first, and that was a couple of weeks ago. They had to wait for the water to rise in order to get any traction. And then—then I don't know. Maybe it's just nasty timing. Or maybe they're more talented than we know. And at the end of the day, given how little we know about them, that's entirely possible. Why does it matter?"

"It matters because, if we know why they're here, we've got a chance of figuring out how to make them leave."

He was right in principle, but Caroline was more right than he was. They were dead but defying all the rules of death.

There might not be a way to send them home, or back from whence they came. Maybe they didn't want to go back. Who could blame them, with a grave like the river banks, in the earth beneath a housing development? It wasn't like we could just offer them a Christian burial, sprinkle a little holy water, and call them satisfied.

That line of thinking brought me back around to the one

Caroline had started. "You never did answer me about those explosives. Where might we procure such things, if we were to hypothetically need them?"

"You're barking up the wrong tree, sweetheart. Do I look like a guy who works with dynamite for a living?"

"Right now you look like a guy who forages under bridges, fighting trolls for a living—but that makes two of us, I'm sure. I don't know about you, but I'd throttle a puppy for a chance at a hot shower and a change of clothes right now."

"Maybe not a puppy. But definitely a dog of some sort." He tried to smile and I tried to encourage him by smiling back; but, like everything else in the world right then, it was watered down and cool.

"We can't talk like this here," I said.

"You're right. Let's go somewhere else."

"Where?"

"Where did you want to go? The old newspaper building? What say we run past the Red Cross station and grab a granola bar, then see about taking a walk. Even zombies need their beauty rest, right?"

"I doubt it."

"So do I," he admitted. "But it beats standing here, waiting for the sky to fall or the water to rise, doesn't it?"

He was right, and it did. I hadn't realized how hungry I was until he mentioned it, and even though I'm not a huge fan of anything granola-based, it sounded like a three-course meal.

We waited our turn in line, in silence for the most part. It was weird how quiet everyone was—like we were all so exhausted by the noise, and panic, and running and swimming and frustration that standing in line waiting for snack food from the back of an ambulance looked like a good chance to take a break.

All the while I was thinking, trying to sort through my store of accumulated life-knowledge. Where do explosives come from? Construction companies, maybe. Demolition sites, obviously. Mining digs, more likely than not. None of these were within immediate walking distance.

Nick asked what was on my mind, so I went ahead and told him.

"Maybe you're thinking about this too narrowly. What sorts of things might be used for explosive purposes, in a pinch?" He asked this between bites of the cereal bar, which he chewed hard because, my God, it was like eating the sole of a dried-out sandal.

"I don't know. Large machinery? Bulldozers, or cranes, or the like—they can be used to knock things down. A backhoe might work. We could fill the hole in or kick the building down on top of it. There you go, man. Thinking outside the box. Or better yet—oh man, it's so obvious." I slapped him with the back of my hand. "Seriously. I've got an idea now."

"Oh God."

"No, it's a good idea."

"I don't believe you," he said.

I took a swallow from the water bottle that came with the granola, and motioned for him to join me as I started a quick pace back around the side of the building. We were in the rain again, but it was becoming a mere condition of life and I was learning to ignore it.

"What's today?" I asked him. "Sunday, right? No, Saturday. It's got to be Saturday by now."

"I don't know. Sure, let's say Saturday. What of it?"

"All this started going down, what, Friday morning? Things

went to hell and they never had the usual Lookouts baseball game this weekend. I'm betting the stadium over there is probably set up as another shelter too."

"Yeah, it's a shelter now, but they're clearing people out of it. The old newspaper building wasn't close enough to trouble for you—now you want to go right into the thick of it?"

I stopped, not because of what he was telling me, but because the flaw in my plan had hit me upside the head. "Huh. Here's the trouble. I have no idea where they keep the fireworks. I know they shoot them off from Cameron Hill, but I don't guess they store them there between firings. They must store them down at BellSouth Park. And you're right that the stadium's right by the water, but it's up there on the hill next to the interstate. It's not underwater, I'm sure. But there's no guarantee that's where the fireworks are kept anyway. For all I know it's handled by some outside company. I don't guess there's any chance you could hop on your cell phone and find out, could you?"

"What's wrong with yours?"

"It rests in peace."

"Well *mine* isn't made of pixie dust. I don't know who I'd call to find out something like that."

"Who was that guy you called to find out about the paper building?"

"Allen, the morning show producer. But he used to work for the *Times-Free Press*, so it wasn't totally off the wall that he might know something like that. You're asking me for a shot in the dark."

I tapped my foot and tried not to listen to it splashing. "The Internet. Maybe if we had access to a computer—ooh! We could go to the library!"

"Right. And you think that's the sort of thing you could find out from a search engine? If the library is even open or has power?"

"Maybe not, but…" But I was backing myself into a corner, and running out of ideas.

"Why are we chasing down fireworks, anyway?" asked Nick.

"Because I bet those industrial-size fireworks could take down a rickety old tunnel and probably the building with it, if we could light enough of them down there."

"You want to fight zombies with fireworks." At least he said it with a straight face.

"Why not? You have any better ideas? Because right now I'd love to hear them."

He threw his hands up and made a gesture that implied he'd love to wring my neck. "Redoubling the efforts when you've lost sight of the objective. Great. We call that *fanaticism*."

"No! I haven't lost sight of anything. I'm just becoming better focused, damn you. Look—they're coming up from under the city, and I know where they'll come out. They were buried for who-knows-how-many years, so let's bury them again! I'm chock-full of objective!"

"You won't get them all that way. Some of them are still trolling the riverbanks."

"It'll get some of them—and some of them's better than none of them. Jesus, if we only knew what they wanted." I started walking then, because the sound of the scratching, scratching, scratching from below that old building was ringing in my ears and I had no idea how close they were.

He followed me and fell into step beside me, because I guess he didn't know what else to do. I hadn't asked him to, though.

I didn't make him do anything. He volunteered for the mission, even if it was only to try and talk me out of it.

"The fireworks might not be there."

"But they might be."

"You think we can just walk out with them?"

"I don't see why not."

"You think the stadium will be empty? Last I heard from the station, it'd been set up as a base of operations. There are cops, feds, FEMAs, and every other authority abbreviation you can pronounce up there. It'll be like trying to break into a police station."

"Then I guess I won't knock. BellSouth Park isn't that big, but it's big enough to have a million side entrances and exits—especially if you're willing to climb. And I, for one, am willing to climb."

The baseball park wasn't terribly far away; in Chattanooga's downtown area, nothing is. You're working with maybe three or four square miles between the river and the ridges, so all the downtown buildings are clustered tight. The stadium is down by the river but on top of a hill like Becca's apartment is—simultaneously closer to danger and higher up away from it.

We walked the way mostly in quiet, ducking under overhangs where it was easy and appropriate to do so, and staying out of the rain less than we would have preferred. But we were getting accustomed to it. You had to. You either got accustomed to it, or you went bananas.

So we stayed out of the rain when we could, and we walked through it when we had to.

"Do you smell that?" Nick asked, drawing up short and ducking beneath the overhang of an old retail store.

I slipped into the mosaic-floored entryway beside him. "Smell what?"

"Smoke. I smell smoke."

Once he'd said it, then yes, I smelled it—faint and acrid. I peered out through the sprinkles and tried to tell if some of the felt-gray cloud cover held anything but humidity. "I smell it now. It's not too bad. What do you think's burning?"

"Not people," he said, which was a weird thing for him to blurt out.

"No... not people. It's not fleshy-smelling. Maybe some of those rioting gang-persons have taken torch to something." Even as I said it, I sniffed for some hint—for that dirty-sweet taint of hair or skin. I didn't detect any, but I failed to find its absence reassuring.

"Are you sure you want to do this?" Nick asked, all seriousness and exhaustion. "It's another couple of blocks, all uphill. And look down," he added, flapping a hand at the street. "Here it comes. How high do you think it goes?"

I'd noticed a block back that yes, we were walking towards the risen water. It didn't rise all of a sudden—sidewalks to open river—but it was slipping up on us nonetheless. The puddles were getting wider, the runoff was coming more steadily along the gutters, and at the end of the street before us there were no traffic lines, no curbs, and no sidewalks. It was all an oily black sheet of water.

"We gonna hike through that?"

"I don't—no. No, we'll go up a street, and over. Up the hill."

"Delaying the inevitable."

"We are *really* on the same page today," I told him. "It's starting to creep me out. But yeah, we'll have to deal with it eventually. For now, though, we can hike. We'll figure out the rest when we get there."

I put my hand on the side of the building as if to pull myself around it and back into the street. Nick thrust an arm out and pulled me back. "Wait a second," he ordered. He craned his head around the corner, then ducked back and urged me to do the same.

I did, because he looked like he meant it.

We retreated as far as we could, to the shallow darkness of the alcove. It wasn't much of a hiding space, but we braced our backs against the old door and crouched until we were sitting there, jammed against each other.

I held my breath, but Nick was cooler than that. He narrowed his eyes and kept his fists tight. He must have ears like a parabolic microphone to have heard it so much sooner than I did—but there it was. An irregular scraping noise—something wet and dense, like a waterlogged tree being pulled over speed bumps.

It was breathing, or trying to.

Air was being dragged back and forth, in and out, of something big but broken. My ears tracked it off to our left, from the water's edge. It was moving slowly but steadily, steps sloshing and squishing. Where it ran out of water, it stopped.

Nick stopped breathing then. His shoulder tensed beside mine until it could've burst through his sleeve.

A plopping swish, a leg turning in ankle-deep liquid. There. And stepping free onto denser ground. Very slow. Very uncertain. But very definite—coming free of the river's overflow. And another step after it. Then the thing stalled and did not move, except to shift and squeeze back and forth, the cool, wet air playing over those rotted lungs.

"Stay there," Nick whispered. He wasn't talking to me, so I didn't listen.

I stood up. He reached to pull me back down, but I didn't let him. I shook off his hand and came free, out of the alcove.

There wasn't any sun, but it was bright anyway. Everything was bright when you were as tired as I was, but it wasn't just me. The white-gray sky was reflected everywhere, especially off the water-smoothed streets down the way. I squinted against the sky and against the rain, even though it barely fell and I barely felt it.

At the edge of the space where the city turned to swamp the creature was standing and staring at me, every bit as hard as I was staring at it.

It was tall, and black from head to toe—but by birth or by fire I couldn't say. Everything was on the verge of peeling off: skin, clothes, hair. Pieces of it sloughed away while it stood there.

I looked to its eyes for some clue, but found none. It had nothing to see with, nothing to stare with—just black pits that might have been gouged out with a thumb. But I knew as surely as I knew my own name that it was watching me. And although it hadn't enough face left to show anything but the horror of a toothy grimace, I knew that when it looked at me, it was displeased.

"What do you want?" I demanded, louder than I should have. It hit the street as a raspy shriek. "Tell me, and I'll do what I can— I'm not like the rest of them. Tell me!"

It did not respond, except to laboriously raise one crooked knee and force its foot farther from the water. Towards me. Towards downtown, and the Read House, and the Choo-Choo, and every place else that still was dry.

"You think you're making some kind of point?" I asked, and I knew it was a stupid question. It wasn't making a point. It was making an escape—from the water, from the river. "You want to prove that you can walk free of the water? Then come for me, then. Come and get me if that's what you're going to do."

Nick was out of the alcove then. He wrapped both arms around me and squeezed, and yanked. "What the fuck is wrong with you?"

"Nothing—nothing! Look at it—*look*."

"Yeah, look at it standing there, *out of the goddamn water*. The river won't hold them forever. And you're *taunting* it."

I wrestled with him, trying to writhe out of his grip. I didn't want to hurt him, but he wasn't going to tell me what to do, either, so I drew back to land an elbow in his solar plexus—but instead he caught my elbow with one hand and spun me around. I didn't know he had it in him.

"Look at it!" I shouted at him. "It can't move yet, not well, not far! This is my chance to talk to it!"

"Fine!" he shouted back. "Talk all you like! But while you waste your breath, take a look around! It's not alone."

I tore myself out of his hands and gasped, because he was right.

One outside the lip of the water. One behind him. One back, and to his right. One kneeling on a bench, heaving and coughing. And there, under the clear plastic shelter of a bus stop, something smaller.

Something watching, in a different way—with eyes still left in a little head.

Its face was burned away, up one side as if it had been hit with a road flare.

"Little girl," I wheezed.

"I told you so," Nick said. "Don't look at her. For Christ's sake, *don't look at her*."

257

She already had me, though. I couldn't look away. She wouldn't let me.

The smell of smoke filled me, even though it wasn't there on the street—it wasn't there in the air. But it was inside *her*, and she was talking. I'd asked them to talk, and she was the only one who could answer.

"No," I said, or I thought I said. It didn't mean anything. It was only a general objection to the powerlessness of it all, to the helplessness and fear—and to the smoke. I couldn't breathe. She wouldn't let me.

Nick was saying something that I couldn't understand. I felt his hands around my forearms, shaking me. He was stronger than I thought. Stronger than I gave him credit for.

It was hot. Terribly hot—ashes and charcoal. It stung my eyes and seared my sinuses. The church. They were burning the church. No—I'm still inside. I'm still inside. We aren't all dead. Didn't kill the rest of us.

How much do you think you can survive? she asked. *If you live through the bullets, and they burn down the rest, how long will your heart keep beating?*

"I don't understand," I moaned.

She didn't either. It was part of her rage.

Nick was still screaming at me, but I couldn't hear him. He was right there, in front of me, clasping my face in his hands, and I couldn't see him.

I was lying down, hiding under a pew by the pastor's podium. Everyone else was dead. Everyone else was lying between the aisles or on the platform, and two of them were thrown into the empty baptismal font. Their dead eyes opened and saw nothing. I was crying and biting my lips to keep them closed so I would say nothing.

I could see the horses outside the window. There were three of them, and three men arguing among themselves—and there were more I couldn't see, but I could hear them talking. "Not the end of the world." *The end of the world.* And through the windows came fire, even as the rain came down outside, slapping great drops against the stained-glass picture of Jesus on the cross.

Behind Jesus, another cross burned and broke and fell down into ashes; I could see it between the flames and where the windows were breaking, broken, coming down and coming apart.

Everything was coming apart.

And I was burning, and breathing.

Still breathing when the sky opened up above and the fire burned itself down to a sizzling bad smell around me. Across me and on top of me. Above me.

Then a shift, though the sky above me looked the same—all heavy and thick, and swirling low. Nick was there, though. His voice worked its way through the haze in my ears and behind my eyes, but he wasn't making any sense to me. I couldn't assemble words from the sounds, but I listened anyway, and after a few minutes the letters arranged themselves more clearly.

"I'd tie you up, but you might get the wrong idea."

"The chains," I mumbled.

"What?"

We were someplace else—not on the street by the water, and not in the alcove. Slick grass was smashed against my face, and the air was clearer. Winching one elbow underneath myself and trying to prop myself up with it; I only succeeded in turning over.

He was sitting beside me, on the grass, on a hill. We were beside the interstate, before the serpentine S-curves that herald the way to the Olgiati bridge. I had mud in my shoes. I could feel it before I could feel the grass, but then the grass started to itch and that was all I felt.

I sat up, but not easily and not very well. There were drag marks leading up to my position, which explained the overflowing footwear.

He'd hauled me clear past the hotel and up, up as far from the water as we could get without an airlift. It was good of him. I lay back down and let the spitting rain go to work on my skin.

"What did you say? What was that?"

"Chains," I said.

"If I had some, I'd cheerfully oblige you."

"Not me. Them. The fire didn't destroy all the evidence, so the Klan took the bodies and threw them into the river. Weighed them down with chains so they'd sink. I'm so tired," I finished.

"I know."

"Thirsty."

"Can't help you there. But if you'll pull yourself together long enough to follow through on your crazy-ass plan…" He pointed down the hill, over to our left just a few hundred yards. "Voilá. Now who's your daddy?"

"If you can help me get upright and point me at that-there stadium, then *you* are."

"That's what I'm talking about."

It wouldn't be as easy as that, I knew. BellSouth Park was almost an island. A loud, crazy flapping overhead signaled the passing of a helicopter, which flew directly over us and then swooped down to land in the middle of the outfield.

"Do you still want to do this?"

I leaned forward, not feeling sturdy enough to stand but sturdy enough to flop my head down over my knees. "I don't know. I don't know if it matters. They're coming anyway, on land or under it. They're working up their strength. She's making them."

"The little girl? You think this is her doing?"

I nodded shakily. "Yup. She lived the longest, and hates the most."

"I don't get it."

"You don't have to. It doesn't matter. She doesn't know what she wants; she only wants to feed, or to destroy. It's the anger of a child. There's no directing it and no appeasing it. She's not going to stop until something makes her."

I held my head up and it was okay—that is, it didn't seem to be in danger of flopping back onto the ground at any moment, so I took a risk and tried to arrange my feet underneath myself to stand. With some help from Nick, it worked. But I was pretty sure I was going to throw up, so I pushed him aside and lost what little I had in my stomach all over the grass.

"What's wrong? Jesus, what now? Are you all right?"

He was kneeling and trying to help, even though I didn't really want any help and I sure as hell don't like people watching me throw up. I was barely strong enough to stand, much less strong enough to hurl, but I did it anyway, repeatedly, until my chest cramped and I had to stop or implode. Most of the time there was nothing but some liquid and the near-recognizable chunks of granola bar.

"No, I'm not okay, exactly." I wiped my mouth on my sleeve, which was so dirty it didn't visibly fix my mouth or soil the shirt. "But I will be. I will be all right. I just need to refuel. I need some *protein*," I added, as the image of a huge, dripping cheeseburger flashed inside my brain like a neon light.

"Was it this bad last time, too? When you were in the bathroom and didn't want to come out?"

"What?"

"At the Read House. A few days ago, when you were—when there was Caroline, for the first time. And you wouldn't come out of the bathroom. Was it this bad then, too?"

I wiped my teeth with my tongue and was disgusted by the taste of bile. I spit a big loogie onto the grass beside the damp pile of vomit. "No. Bad, but not like this. Different. Or not really different, but not as bad. Shit, Nick. I don't know what's wrong with me. Nobody does."

He got all solemn on me, working his way around to face me, and to take my arms again. I noticed how much he was touching me today and I wasn't sure what to make of it, except that I didn't mind it and I was too worn down to object even if I did.

I took a step and slipped on the grass, landing ass-down but not hard enough to do anything but jolt me into tears.

It was one of those crying fits where you swear you aren't crying, but you're sniffling and your eyes are streaming anyway so you're not fooling anybody. I covered my face and gulped for air.

Nick, like just about any guy faced with a crying woman, had no earthly idea what to do. But bless his heart, he did the best thing he could've done: he sat down next to me and waited it out.

"I never told you half of it," I coughed, wishing I had something to blow my nose on, but since there was nothing handy and certainly nothing dry, I took a deep snort and swallowed back as much as I could. This gave me hiccups, which only made me sound more ridiculous.

"Half of what? Of what happened at the hotel?"

"That too. But (hiccup) that's not where it started. That's not where it (hiccup) got weird. It got weird in Florida, a few years ago. It's been (hiccup) getting weirder ever since. And now I can't tell if I'm dying or if I'm invincible, but (hiccup) it's all very confusing."

Nick took it in stride. He reached down to the ground beside his hip and pulled a dandelion, then began picking it apart. "You can tell me about it if you want."

I snorted again and choked on a phlegm-filled hiccup, before blurting out, "Off the record?"

"I think this is about as far off the record as we're ever likely to get."

"I can't trust you."

He didn't answer, and I couldn't see him through my hurricane hairdo and all the crying. God, the crying just wouldn't stop. Now that it had started I couldn't kick it down or force it back—it just came pouring out and it wasn't like a leak in the roof where you throw pans on the floor to catch it. There was nothing to catch it, and nothing to catch me.

"I wish you'd try to trust me," he finally said. "What do you think I'm going to do? Go running to the studio and start editing a package together?"

"I don't know. You would've done it to Christ."

"You're not Christ. And if you'd asked me not to, I wouldn't have done it to him, either. It was a good story, but not one with a lot of proof. The station usually won't run shit like that anyway; they're too afraid of getting sued."

"Good point," I burbled.

"And by this good point, I swear. Are we friends, or what? Because you seem to know a whole lot of people, but you don't really seem to be very good friends with any of them."

I don't know why I answered like I did, why the words just

came falling out of my mouth—faster than I could stop them, even though they didn't appear relevant to his accusation. "I killed somebody. Back in Florida, back in the swamp. That crazy cultist you've heard about, I killed him. I cut off his head and threw it into the swamp. If I hadn't, he was going to kill me and the other person there. Fuck it, it was Malachi. It was my crazy-ass brother."

"Wait—the cultist was your brother?"

"No." I shook my head and resolved not to do it again. I saw black and white static when I did that. No more. "No, the crazy cult guy was going to kill us both. So I killed him first. Malachi helped."

"Wow."

"Uh-huh. But when I killed him… something happened."

"When you killed Malachi?"

"No. Didn't kill him. He's fine. He's… shit, well. He's on his way back to Florida by now. It's a long story."

"I bet."

"But when I killed the other guy, something… happened. I don't know what." I'd lost the hiccups, and was grateful for that small mercy. The crying hadn't turned itself off yet, though, so I still sounded like a blubbering lunatic and I couldn't help it. I couldn't even slow it down.

"It was like… like he cursed me. Sort of. And now whenever I get hurt, it doesn't last. It heals right up. It closes up and it's completely freaky. So I sort of feel invincible (hiccup), right?" No, the hiccups were only delayed, not gone completely. "But then all this psychic shit—it's gotten so much *harder*. It's like it's killing me, every time. Every time it's bad, and it's a real interaction—like with Caroline, or down there—it just takes so much out of me. I'm better at it, but it's killing me."

"Killing you, yeah. You said that part. Stop saying it. I don't like hearing it."

"Well it *is*. And I don't know what to do. No one else knows either, and I've tried *everybody*." I realized that he didn't know Eliza, and therefore couldn't have possibly understood what I meant when I emphasized "everybody," but he got the general idea: everybody within reach, regardless of how unlikely or unpleasant.

"What about…" I think he was going to suggest Dana, maybe, but since he'd heard the "everybody" part, he restrained himself. "Everybody, huh?"

"Everybody." The word came out covered with spit.

I was sitting there, with the water on the grass seeping through my jeans and crying like an inconsolable baby, feeling like a complete idiot, and not having any idea of how to fix it. "And now there's this—there's all of this." I waved, sweeping an arm out to catch the waterlogged city and the stadium on the hill like a lighthouse or an island. "And I'm so tired, and I don't know if I can do this. I only wanted to get some fireworks."

It trailed off in a mumble. Nick patted me on the back.

"Do you still think that's a good idea? You said they're coming up under the city, but I think you believe me now when I say, 'Not all of them.' You'll get some of them, but you won't stop the rest. And now you're telling me that you don't think they can be stopped."

"I didn't say that." I sniffled, then remembered that I *had* said that. "I didn't mean it, if I did."

"So what do we do?"

"We can either (hiccup), we can either sit around and let them all get in, or we can stop some of them. We can (hiccup), we can let the feds and cops handle the topside things, and we can take care of the ones coming up from undersides (hiccup)."

"We could try reporting it first. Down there, at the ball park."

I tried to snort derisively, but I only succeeded in blowing snot around. "They've got their hands full already, don't you think? And what would we tell them? Zombies coming up from underground? We've got zombies running around on the streets where everybody can see them. Let's deal with those first, that's probably what they'll say."

I wiped my whole face on my sleeve again and then propped myself on my arms. Nick leaned back and did likewise. Under different circumstances, we might have looked like a picnic, there overlooking the city beside the interstate.

"How do you think they're handling it?" Nick asked. "What are they doing? I'm going to go out on a limb here and guess that shambling undead aren't exactly in the FEMA handbook."

I turned my head to lay it sideways on my forearm. "Shooting at them, I guess. We've heard gunshots a lot lately, here and there. I mean, if I had a gun and I saw one of those things, I'd probably shoot at it. I'd totally aim for the head, too."

"Do you think it's working?"

"Probably not. I'm forced to assume it's not. They're still out wandering around—but it could be worse. It's not exactly a horde. And I have a feeling—just a feeling (hiccup) that they're not going to spread anything. I think there's a finite number at work. And god*damn* I thought I was done with those hiccups."

"You're getting done with the crying part, at least."

"Yeah," I said, as if I'd noticed before he pointed it out—though I hadn't. But the faucet was creaking itself shut and the sobbing was subsiding. I was almost intelligible. The stupid feeling wouldn't go away so quickly.

"So. Finite number. Shambling undead. Working their way up from the water. Coming by land and by under land. If you really want to go down to the stadium and steal some fireworks, I guess you can count me in."

"Really?"

"Hell yeah. But I don't think we should break in. I think we should walk up and knock. You're doing the hysterical female thing really well right now—or you were a minute ago. I think we can use that."

"You are so mercenary."

"That's why you like me so much."

"What makes you think I like you at all?"

"Reporter's instinct. It's like woman's intuition. Ironclad and perfect, at all times."

He was trying to make me laugh. I let him have a small cackle, because one of us deserved a small victory right about then and it probably wasn't going to be me.

"There you go," he said, nudging me with his shoulder. "But knock that shit off, would you? By the time we get down there, I want you whimpering, cowering, and begging for help. You pull that off, and I'll get us in just fine."

He stood then, bracing himself on the wet grass and offering me his hands. I reached up and took them, and let him hoist me to my feet. He slung an arm over my shoulder as if to keep me close or help me up. Under different circumstances I might have considered it too much, but I kicked my intimacy issues aside and let myself be happy that there was someone else warm there beside me.

Half sliding and half stumbling, we made it together down the hill and came splashing toes-first into the water. There wasn't any way around it.

To our ankles, and to our knees, but not much higher—no swimming—we waded our way past floating trash, swimming rats, dead birds, and shiny slick spots that might have been oil, toxic waste, or anything else.

"Hold it right there," we were ordered.

We held it, shivering even though it wasn't that cold, even in the water. I hoped I looked as pathetic as I felt. Nick stood up straighter and moved his arm to my waist.

"Hey." He waved with the other arm. "I'm Nick Alders—from Channel Three. I let you guys take my SUV yesterday. I was working my way back to the shelter and I found *her*," he said, meaning me. "I think she needs medical attention, and this was closer than the Read House. She can hardly walk, and I can barely carry her."

I slumped against him, as his narrative seemed to require. But I tried not to be too obvious about it.

It worked. At least it worked insomuch as the cop with the very large gun quit aiming it at us and pointed the muzzle down at the water. "Bring her on in. You can't be walking around out here, though. Jesus, what are you thinking?"

"I'm thinking that the son of a bitch who runs the newsroom reamed me out because I was supposed to get a signature from somebody about that fucking SUV. So when I finished screaming his eardrums out, I was too pissed off to stay put."

"Where'd you find her?" He was a blond guy—a Bubba, I suspected, one of those younger, corn-fed local boys who gets way too excited about a little authority. It's a type—thrilled to be in charge, but without enough experience to nail down the proper cop voice for more than a sentence at a time. But he was walking us back through knee-deep sludge to safety, so I couldn't muster too much ill to say about him.

Half a block back we met more water and more cops, who were canvassing the area like crazy and looking jumpy as a long-tailed cat in a room full of rocking chairs. They chattered back and forth through radio receivers strapped onto their chests like bulky black *Star Trek* communicators.

Hard to blame them. I knew what they were patrolling for.

"Get them inside," somebody said, but I couldn't tell who. I was glad for the permission though. Nick was right, it was a whole lot easier than breaking in.

I didn't say anything, just kept my head down. I let Nick lurch me along without either giving him too much help or causing him undue effort, or so I liked to think. He was grunting and sweating by the time we made it to the edge of the stadium, though.

When I did look up there were more police and a bunch of men in wading boots, plus a scattered woman or two. Everyone had a radio or a cell phone stapled against an ear. Everyone was giving orders, pointing, and arguing or demanding more information.

Nick and I were probably the only people there who could've actually told them anything more than they already knew, but nobody asked us and we didn't offer our expertise. Nothing we knew would have made them hold their guns any steadier.

"Shoot them in the head—what kind of advice is that? That's video game advice, numbnuts," one guy was asking, somewhere by the main gate.

"Well it can't hurt. Slows them down, I think. Haven't you ever seen a movie? Always start with a head shot, if you can get one."

"Head shots aren't bringing them down, sir."

"Head shots aren't speeding them up, either."

269

Above us all the back wall of the bleachers rose up high and sharp against the sky, against clouds that were still loaded with enough rain to keep us all mighty uncomfortable. I'd never been to a game there. Never cared much about baseball. Never thought we needed another stupid stadium. But it was definitely big and solid-looking.

There were worse forts you could pick to hide in.

The ticket offices were lined up and empty, closed up and unattended. Vendors' carts had been kicked out of the interior, I guess, and were stacked or pushed out of the way into the parking lot, piled up like barricades.

I saw a few other refugees too—other people who were closer to this shelter than to any of the others farther down, away from the water. We were all being herded back to the interior, so we went. Up into the skyboxes they wanted us to go, but my legs weren't working very well and I had a hard time with the stairs.

"Elevators?" I asked. Someone said they weren't working, or they weren't being used except for emergency personnel or disabled people, so I closed my eyes and locked my knees.

I don't know how many flights I climbed to get up into the skybox, but once I was there it wasn't too bad. Inside, there was climate control—and there were towels, and fans, and even some hot food and fountain sodas. I dropped myself into one of the plush, oversized chairs in a corner and tried not to fall asleep where I flopped.

Nick brought me a Coke and a hot dog, just like it was an ordinary day at the ball park.

I wolfed both down, and wiggled my fingers towards the table for more. He dutifully provided some. I took down the next hot dog in under a minute, but spent more time with the soda. Hard to believe, surrounded by water, but I was getting dehydrated. We all were. That's why the nice Red Cross people were urging us away from the sugary sodas and towards Gatorade and water. Most of us ignored them. We'd had a shitty couple of days and we wanted our junk food, thank you very much.

When I felt a tiny bit more human, I hauled myself out of the chair and went to look out the window. It was a big window, stretching from corner to corner of the skybox; and from it, I had a good view of everything below. An ambulance was parked in right field, or in the puddle that now comprised right field. Above, and very nearby, the air-chopping thunder of a helicopter droned low, then landed beside the pitcher's mound.

White-uniformed people spilled out of it. They were followed by some people in black uniforms and chunky vests, with guns.

When the helicopter was empty, I lost interest.

It was quieter there, in the skybox, than it had been at the Read House. Not so many people, I guessed. Everyone else had been passed up farther along the shelter chain. We were the stragglers. No kids, thank God. No one who was visibly incapacitated or disabled. Just a handful of people who were tired beyond endurance.

I gathered very quickly that the trick was to lie low and stay out of the way. The trick was to hide there in the rich folks' skybox and eat the trashy park food while the authorities sorted out the hard parts. No one wanted to be sent to the Read House or to the Choo-Choo—even though no one but me and Nick knew what those shelters were like. Everyone could guess. Nobody said anything, but we all were thinking about what happened in New Orleans when the hurricane hit. We were thinking about the stadium there, and what it looked like packed with people.

So everyone played it low key.

I did too. I didn't have the strength to do anything else, so I went back to my overstuffed chair and closed my eyes.

I could hear Nick talking, here and there, around the room—doing his Nick thing, asking questions and harvesting information. He was quiet and calm, his voice down in a firm but gentle whisper as he went from group to group. Roving reporter.

I cracked my eyes to track him with idle curiosity.

But I must have dozed off and on, because he'd cleaned up since we arrived. I thought about taking a trip to the loo myself, but couldn't muster the energy, so I didn't bother. I watched him, instead.

He'd combed his hair down and it was drying into waves that sat against his head like they belonged that way. His clothes were drying out too, and lying funny on him, sticking to his chest and legs. Rationally I knew he was about ten years older than me, but it didn't show.

"What are you grinning about, princess?" He caught me looking.

"Not a damn thing," I said.

"Good," he said, and he was smiling back. He dropped whatever mini-conversation he'd started, and came back to squat beside me, putting his hands on the arm of my chair. "Have a nice nap?"

"I don't remember. If I did, it wasn't long enough. What time is it?"

"Too late for lunch, too early for supper. How you feeling?"

"I've been better. But I could use another hot dog."

He shook his head and jerked a thumb at the table. "No more hot stuff. Got chips and the like, though. Popcorn. Beer."

"Ew. No beer."

"Fine. More for the rest of us."

"I'll take a bag of chips, though." I began to unpeel myself from the chair and he objected, but I waved him down. "I've got to get up sometime. Now's as good a time as any."

When I rose I had creases and crinkles in all sorts of strange places from the way the vinyl chair had worked itself into my exposed skin. Nick pointed and laughed, and I kicked at him with the toe of my boot, but I didn't mean anything by it.

I squeezed a bag of Doritos and they opened with a poof of cheese. One at a time I snacked on them, both afraid to eat too quickly and afraid it'd be a while before I ate anything else. These days, I never knew when or what that next meal was going to be.

My bedroom up on Signal Mountain might as well have been a thousand miles away. In the back of my mind, though, I thought I'd walk it for a chance at Lu's kitchen. But you can't walk on water without a degree in theology, so I tried to rally my brain cells together in a different direction. Fireworks. That was the brilliant plan that had gotten me this far. Leave the wading zombies to the men with guns. I'd take care of the tunneling ones.

I took my chips back to my chair, back to Nick. I leaned back in his direction, offering one. He pushed his fist into the aluminum bag and helped himself.

"This is what we need to do," I began, as if beginning to say it would help me to construct it. "We need to find out where they keep the fireworks, but we need to do it without calling too much attention to it. I mean, we can't just corner a cop and say, 'Hey man, how about them fireworks?' So instead—"

"Instead, we could just ask around about where they store the supplies, because one of the Red Cross people is asking if there are more napkins, towels, and the like. I mean, you could try that if you wanted to, but it might look weird because I've already been doing it."

"Seriously?"

"Seriously. Well, I *am* a genius you know."

"I did not know that."

"Well, now you do. But here's what I've gathered, in case you're interested: there's a basement level or two beneath this place, which shouldn't surprise you at all. That's where they keep everything from jockstraps to ketchup packets."

"To fireworks? And if they're in the basement, would they still be dry?"

"Hang on," he said insistently. "The basement in this place is still well above the river; we're on top of a hill, remember? And after asking about fifteen people, most of whom told me the same things all over again, I got one nice guy to warn me about the locked, sealed storage down beneath the food service areas. That's where they keep the dangerous crap, like, I don't know, fireworks and shit by the sounds of things."

I was so stunned I didn't know what to say.

He was grinning ear to stubbly ear, and only when I saw him up close like that did I realize it must've been several days since he'd shaved last. And up close, and after a week like the one we'd had, I had to admit that up close—yes, I could see the extra ten years on him.

In that same split second, my logic centers deactivated due to fatigue, I grabbed him by his shirt collar and kissed him.

18

HOW SHOULD I PUT THIS?

He kissed me back, and one of the other refugees made a halfhearted cat call. It embarrassed me but not enough to let go of him right away. When I did, I pushed him back as quickly as I'd pulled him forward, and then I said, "That is the most competent, reasonable, useful thing and best damn lie anyone's done for me in ages."

Nick looked surprised, but from which part of the last thirty seconds I couldn't tell. "Is that all it takes to get your attention?" he asked. "A minimal display of competency?"

"It's harder to come by than you might expect. And that wasn't just competent, it was thoughtful. A veritable double play, my dear fellow. Help me up and we'll call it a triple."

He did, lifting me out of the chair again by my wrists.

I felt better, if not good. I felt ready to walk again, and maybe even take a few stairs if I was feeling bold. I was gradually shedding that shaky, low-sugar fragility that made me all weepy and needy, or so I liked to think.

One of the guys standing by the window tried to chide us. "I don't think we're supposed to leave the skybox areas," he whined.

"Bathroom," I told him.

"There's one up here."

"I don't like that one." And once we got outside, I pulled away from Nick and said, "I really do need a bathroom. Let me take a quick spit bath. Hang on. Plumbing."

"What?"

"I'll tell you later."

Downstairs and down the hall there was a stadium-sized unit with a long row of stall doors, all of them empty. The sinks were big and battered for such a new stadium, but they were more or less clean, so I more or less stripped and rinsed out my clothes again, except for my jeans. My jeans were almost dry and there was no way in hell I was going to douse them again until I really had to.

At the risk of achieving a nuclear 'fro, I held my head under the faucet and rubbed pink bathroom soap into my scalp, because it smelled better than I did.

I wrung out what I could and wrapped my head in nasty brown paper towels to squeeze out some of the rest. I wadded them up and threw them away under the counter.

I slapped the round metal knob of the hand dryer, flipped the nozzle up, and draped my wet shirt across it. And while the heat took the edge off the dampness, I washed my face a couple of times.

Nick kicked the door. "Hurry up in there. Are we going to kill some zombies today, or are you going to take a spa break?"

"Shut up. I'm coming."

On the floor beside the trash can there was a hair elastic that could've belonged to anybody on earth before it wound up on the bathroom tiles. I didn't give a damn. I picked it up and twisted it around my fingers, then pulled my hair up into a high, raggedy ponytail. The scarf I'd been using was too disgusting to wear anymore. Somebody else's discarded hair twisty was actually a step up.

I yanked my shirt back over my head. It felt clean and hot instead of cool and dirty. I pushed the door open with my foot and said to Nick, "Let's go do this thing."

"You sound positively human again."

"I'm feeling positively human again. Not superhuman, but human. I think I can walk unassisted. Where are we going?"

"Down," he said, taking the lead. "I've been told we'll need a manager's key to get down to the storage levels from the elevators, but there's a service stairway back behind the food places on the first floor that'll get us in without one."

Every sound echoed against the cement floors and the superhigh ceilings that stopped several stories above us. The place was busy but not crowded with emergency workers and cops; but then, the place was just too *big* to be crowded. Several times we were stopped and asked what we were doing outside of the skybox area, but Nick just repeated his story about hunting supplies for the Red Cross and they let him go. A little bit of celebrity in this city goes a long way. I suppose they thought that if it turned out he was lying, at least they'd know where to find him later on.

We tried not to sneak because sneaking called attention to our presence. But we made a general effort to avoid the busier places, because why take extra chances? It was tricky, and it took us a few minutes more than I would've liked, but it worked out. We found ourselves alone together, staring at a scratched metal door that said, "Employees only."

"Is this it?"

"It'd better be," he said, and he pushed the lever latch to move the door aside.

The stairwell was packed with moldy shadows and it smelled like old meat. We took the stairs quickly because it was nasty in there and we didn't like it. The floor was shiny with something gross, and the handrails were covered with old paint that flecked off under our palms.

Our feet tapped way too loud in the narrow space, but there was a door at the bottom so we opened it. I caught it before it closed, just in case, and kicked a little wooden wedge in its way so it couldn't shut and keep us there.

"Where's the goddamn light switch?" Nick demanded. "I'm not going to do a Yosemite Sam down here and strike a match. There's got to be one somewhere."

I spotted it first—a thin, dangling chain, like the kind that dog tags hang from. I gave it a yank and the old-fashioned yellow bulb popped to life, drenching the basement storage with a sick-looking ochre light that was only somewhat better than none at all.

Inside we found stacks and stacks of junk, boxes, and dusty things that smelled a tad tart.

Nick wrinkled his nose. "Gunpowder. You smell it?"

"I guess that's what it is." I gazed around and saw mostly things that looked like ordinary storage.

"We're in the right spot. Jesus, look at this stuff. This has to be it—look at all these warnings."

"So maybe you should be careful about how you pick them up and shuffle them around," I suggested.

"I *am* being careful. Don't be such a worrywart—and holy

shit, these are heavy. We're going to need... huh. How many do you think we'll need? You've seen the hole, I haven't. What are we talking here? Major demolition? Minor cave-in?"

"A minor cave-in ought to do it." I tried to remember all the junk over the hole, and I had to believe that it wouldn't take much to bring it all down and bring the earth down with it. "What do you think those old tunnels are, anyway? Mining tunnels? A lot of the kids out here think they're part of an underground city, but that seems highly unlikely."

He wiped the side of a box, and gray dust coated his sleeve. "I couldn't say. I've heard about it; it's a popular little urban legend here. Maybe tunnels or earthworks left over from the war? I don't think there's any way to know, not anymore. No one has any records of making them, and all the folks without any imagination say that they don't exist anyhow."

"Oh, they *exist*."

"I believe you. But for all you know, it could be a big unfinished basement."

"No way. I heard them down there—"

"You heard *something* down there. I want you to keep in mind that there's an excellent chance we're going to bury a whole bunch of rats and no shambling undead."

"I know what I heard. And they're coming up from the river, so the tunnels have to go at least that far. Anyway, I'm not worried about it. This is a good idea, and it'll work. As long as we can smuggle these things out and back downtown."

"All right then. But we're not going to be able to do it by hand. We're going to need bags, or backpacks, or something. Stay put and start picking out your poison. I'll run upstairs and see about raiding the souvenir shop."

I did as he suggested and stayed behind in the smelly, dark room, while he went upstairs to see what he could steal. I ran my hands along the box seams and popped a few open, taking a peek inside and reading labels.

"Not intended for indoor use—well, no *kidding*. 'Five hundred foot minimum fallout area required.' Five hundred feet?" The canister was cylindrical and heavy, like an oatmeal tin filled with pennies. "Salute," I read aloud from the label—apparently the name of the shell. I thought about trying to pry the shells open, but then remembered that my knife might well make a spark or two, and then we'd have our Yosemite Sam moment after all.

Nick returned with two duffel bags made of sturdy nylon. He'd thrown in a few towels, too, plus a smallish can of paint thinner and a roll of plastic wrap.

"Why the paint thinner? And plastic wrap?"

"We might need something flammable later on. Makeshift running fuse, or some such. As for the wrap, it's raining again. And the towels, you know, to keep all this stuff separate. We're basically going to be playing terrorist here—running around downtown carrying little bombs. I hope that this soothing mental image causes you to rethink this thing, but I bet it won't."

"That'd be a safe bet. We're here now, we've got the fireworks, and I say we load up and get the hell out of Dodge."

"How long are we going to have to carry this crap, anyway? It's fucking heavy."

"Not far," I said, but I had to think about it. "A few blocks. It's back towards the Read House—practically across the street from it, come to think of it. Catty-cornered, anyway. We can't let zombies arise from the earth right near a shelter, where there are old people, sick people, and kids."

He put down the shell he was holding, and looked at me with a fresh glare of disbelief. "But it's okay to set off industrial grade pyrotechnics there?"

"It's *across the street*. Not exactly across the street, but down it. Probably a thousand feet, anyway."

"You have no earthly idea how far a thousand feet is, do you? And that's an awfully specific number; you wouldn't have pulled it out of your ass because you've been reading these labels, would you? Because some of these labels say two thousand feet, not one thousand, and not five hundred."

"No. That's not why," I lied. "Look, Nick, it won't take very much. A couple of these—the ones that say five hundred feet." I carefully hoisted one of the smaller shells, and damn, it was heavy. "We'll start with these, and if it doesn't work, or the place doesn't come crashing down, then we'll give up and call the SWAT team. Grab some directions, though. I haven't the foggiest clue how to light one of these bad boys."

"Sure. Yeah. I'll just grab this 'How to Set Off Giant Fireworks' pamphlet over here… wait, I see no such thing." He was getting frustrated with me, but that made two of us.

"Just… whatever paperwork you see. Take that. Stuff it in, and we'll read it later, or on the way, or something." I started reading from the first sheet I found. "'1.3G fireworks, not intended for use by amateur consumers. Licensed pyrotechnic…' yeah, whatever."

In the end we just took one each, because if it was going to take more than that we were probably screwed anyhow. We wrapped them in the towels and put them in separate duffel bags, each of us toting one of the bags.

There was a hearty moment of awkwardness as we stood there facing one another, stolen goods slung over a shoulder and no real plan. Also, well, I had kissed him, and it was kind of weird, but I sort of wanted to do it again. But I didn't know if the feeling was mutual, and, besides: zombies. We had better things to do with our time than get busy in a ball park basement—but I'd be lying if I said I hadn't thought about it.

"All right. Back to the hotel?"

"Back to the hotel." It felt Freudian to say it, but I didn't stop myself—so there the words hung, and we each waited for the other to take the lead.

He did.

I followed him out and we kept to the shadows, trying not to skulk and trying not to draw too much attention, either. For the most part, everyone was busy running around, talking into radios, reading maps, and toting an ungodly amount of munitions from place to place. If anyone noticed us, it was usually to tell us to get back up to the skybox.

We agreed to do so every time we were told, then immediately returned to our escape.

None of us were prisoners there, so it wasn't very hard. It hadn't occurred to anyone that anybody would be fool enough to dash back out into the undead-populated water outside the park, so all the gates were open and no one was watching them. We hopped the turnstile at the side entrance where the fewest people could see us.

As soon as we were free of the concrete and the parking lot, we were clear—or, rather, we were back in the water.

"It won't go down, will it?" Nick did a prancy girl-step when his foot hit the mush of grass and dirt.

"Apparently not." I tried to be less prissy about it, but, God. I felt like I'd just gotten dry; I wasn't in any huge rush to get dank again. "This is unreal. The river, I mean. How could this happen? I thought TVA was working on it."

"Hard to believe the government hasn't got a handle on it, I know. Just ask New Orleans. I'm sure Uncle Sam is just about to come up with a solution."

We decided to head up, then over. It was a course of action that took us out of our way but kept us drier than simply cutting through downtown. And, since we weren't yet sure how to handle the small horde of splashing undead, it was probably best to stay out of their known domain.

Between us we'd had fewer hours of sleep in the last few days than we usually got in one night, but our store of common sense hadn't left us completely.

It was so strange, though—walking up by the interstate, on the gravel shoulder between all the parked cars. Most of them were abandoned, but here and there a few people had set up camp where they'd stalled or run out of gas. If you had a few candy bars in the glove box, you were just about as well off as the people down the hill in the shelters.

The whole thing was creepy. It felt like one of those post-apocalyptic movies you catch sometimes, where all the trappings of civilization are left in place but there are hardly any people.

From our vantage point up by the interstate, we could look down and see how the water was, yes, still rising, and yes, still eating downtown a block at a time. And if we looked up to Cameron Hill, which overlooks the interstate from an even higher vantage point, we could see what had happened to more than a few of the car-abandoners.

Cameron Hill used to be a big apartment complex, but it was bought by Blue Cross and scheduled for demolition—making way for new office buildings, I imagine. For now, though, the complex stood vacant and high—really, at the highest point in the city that one could still call "downtown."

People had climbed the hill and were camping there, too. Even from down at the road level, we could see how windows had been broken out and the empty apartments had been entered. I didn't know if they still had running water or anything, but it probably beat sleeping all cramped in the car. A big plume of smoke was coming up from the hill, but it looked like a contained sort of smoke, like a bonfire or something. Later I'd learn that the squatters had filled the empty swimming pool with construction debris and lit it like a beacon.

I guess, when it all comes down to it—or it's all stripped away—we just wander back to that primal assurance. "If I have fire, I'm okay."

I thought again of the heavy shell I was toting around. The nylon bag seemed to be sloughing off water well enough to keep everything dry. I checked Nick's bag in front of me, and it appeared to be likewise stable. But seeing it bounce back and forth against his thigh made me nervous.

"We should carry these more carefully, don't you think?"

He stopped and turned around. "Sure. What do you recommend?"

"I don't know. Just. Well. We're banging these things around here and they're full of gunpowder. Seems like a bad idea."

He gave me a look like he wanted to argue or fuss, but gave up on it before he started. Instead, he tightened the shoulder strap so the bag stayed in the crook of his waist, under his arm. I did likewise, and tried to hold it steady as we walked—but it wasn't easy. The road was made for driving, and the shoulder wasn't made for anything but motor emergencies. This was an emergency if I'd ever seen one, but when you're on foot instead of wheels the shoulder is rough walking—a minefield of stripped tires, uneven paving, and broken glass.

Sometimes we'd look down below and see things walking in the water. At such a distance it was hard to tell what was what, or who. After a while, we quit looking and kept our eyes on the road in front of us.

When we reached the Martin Luther King Street exit, we used it to walk down from the main road; and the Read House was right there, on the left. It was still busy in a tired, worn-out, desperate sort of way. From every window inside faces stared out at the street, waiting for a way out or waiting for the water to come to them.

I stared back at the eyes that settled on me, as if I knew what I was doing.

While we were gone, tow trucks and at least one bulldozer had come through moving the cars. It had to happen eventually; and now there was a lane and a half cleared from the front of the hotel to the onramp at the interstate—heading out of town, not towards the bridges. That way was pretty much clear, at least as far as I could see. The trick was still actually getting the ambulances and buses to the hotel, but it was happening. Slowly, but surely.

"Where are we going now?" Nick asked.

I pulled my attention away from the face-filled windows and looked through and past a mound of overturned cars at the intersection of Broad and MLK. "Over there, at the end of the next block up. It's right on the corner."

I dodged a cop with a bulletproof vest bulging under his jacket. "We're asking everyone to get inside," he told me out of the corner of his mouth, without slowing down.

He was too frantic for my taste. A glance at Nick told me that similar thoughts were brewing in his head, too.

Another pair of police officers as well as someone in a uniform I didn't recognize—SWAT? FBI?—came tearing around a corner, waving and chattering into their radios.

Nick took my arm and pulled me back off the sidewalk against the building in order to let them pass. "They're trying to get everyone inside," he said, as if I hadn't heard the first guy. "We're going to have to get while the getting's good."

"Something's about to hit the fan. Can't you feel it?"

"Yes, and I'm no psychic. Come on."

I pulled ahead of him then. I slipped past him and out around the corner where the hotel parking garage was. "Let's go through— underneath. Fewer prying eyes on the back of the block."

He nodded and chased me into the dark first level of the garage, then out into the bright whiteness on the other side. Our shoes made scuff marks on the wet cement of the sidewalk, and I'd been right—there weren't nearly as many people back there. Everyone was concentrating on the front, where people came up begging for food, water, and a corner to sleep in.

We took flight without trouble and without interruption. It was easy to run on the straighter ground, even with the duffel bags and their heavy, illicit contents.

I thought I heard my name.

I looked over my shoulder, mid-step, and didn't see anybody but Nick. "What?"

"What? I didn't say anything."

"Oh. Sorry." So I kept running.

I could've sworn I'd heard it again, but we were almost there.

The next intersection was even worse than Broad and MLK; there had been several wrecks as vehicles tried to ram their way out and failed. You can ram past a couple of cars, maybe, but half the city's fleet of SUVs proved unmoved by the two sedans that had made a charge for it.

I turned sideways and shimmied my way past crumpled hoods and blown tires. Nick did likewise, and between us, we made our way to the boarded and forlorn little building on the corner.

"I don't think I've ever noticed this place before," he said.

"It's been closed up as long as I can remember."

"What did it used to be?"

I shrugged. "Couldn't tell you. But I got inside around the other way. Come on."

"Sure. Let's just add breaking and entering to the list of charges. Swiping these shells has to be some sort of felony, and—"

"And as for the rest, you're only *entering*. I did the breaking before you got here. Stop being such a worrywart."

"I'm mostly worried about what's waiting in there," he confessed.

I found my loose sheet of plywood and gave it a good yank, reopening the window I'd used earlier.

"After you," he said.

"As you like." I crawled through and onto the garbage inside. The scratching, scraping, dragging, shuffling was louder—much louder than when last I'd visited.

Nick came through behind me.

"Watch your step," I told him. "I covered the hole in the floor with a bunch of crap, but the floor isn't very stable, I don't think. Be careful."

We set our bags aside and tried to find a sturdy corner to hold them while we moved the pallets and crates around. "I hear them," he said. "Holy shit, I hear them. You weren't kidding, were you?"

"*No*, I wasn't kidding."

"They're right underneath us!"

"I know that, yes. Thank you. What wonderful timing we have. Here—get that end. Help me with this one, it's heavy."

He wrenched one arm under a pallet with some chains and equipment weighing it down. "Are you sure? I mean, we're sort of opening this up for them, aren't we? Maybe we should pile more shit on, then burn the place down on top of them."

"I don't think that would work," I countered.

"Why not?"

"Because once everything's burned down, they'll just shove the ashes out of the way and come out anyhow. We've got to bury the fuckers. It's the only thing that's ever kept them down and out of trouble."

"You've got a point there. So how are we going to do this? I mean, what are we going to do, treat these things like Molotov cocktails and do a chuck and run? And don't these canisters say five hundred feet of clearance?"

"Technically yes, but I figure that the five hundred feet thing doesn't really apply if you set them off underground."

"You figure that, do you?" He heaved a set of two-by-fours aside and we were almost there, almost done. We almost had the thing open. "Hey, give me that flashlight of yours. You've still got it?"

"In my purse, yeah." I unzipped it and shoved my hand inside. Everything I touched was waterlogged and disgusting; the makeup would be a lost cause, but I didn't really care. The flashlight was a hardy little bastard, and it was working just fine. I tossed it to him, and he caught it, then flipped it on.

He aimed it down the hole exposed by the missing planks.

"What do you see?"

"Nothing," he answered. "Not a damn thing. Either they're not there, or they're still hiding. But shit, you can hear them, can't you? That's amazing—but it might be a trick of the acoustics. If it's a tunnel, then they might still be a ways off."

"Wave it around. Go on. Lean down in there, or give it to me and let me do it."

"I'm *looking*," he swore, swiveling the beam and apparently not meeting any resistance with it. "There's nothing there yet, nothing *right there*, anyway."

I didn't know if that was good or bad. On the one hand, we'd arrived ahead of them; but on the other hand, we might need to get closer to them to really stop them with improvised explosives like ours.

"I'm going down there," I told him, even as he was already stepping around the pit to stop me.

"No you're not."

"Watch me."

"Don't be an idiot."

"I have my reasons."

"I bet you do. If one of them is trying to get me to make a spectacle of myself on your behalf, you're almost there, darling. But you are not going down in there. We'll set these off up here, or light them and drop them, I don't care. But there's no good reason whatsoever to risk going down there."

"I want to try to talk to them. I want to see what they want."

"You already tried that, and it left you a blubbering, weepy mess. I'd prefer not to see that again, if it's all right with you. It worried me."

"But that was different," I argued.

"Different how?" he demanded.

"Those were *different dead people*. I've got a theory and I want to see if it holds up. The more we know, the better chance we have of stopping them for good—not just covering them with dirt and hoping for the best."

"Eden, this is—"

"Hear me out, okay? Whatever they're capable of, it's got nothing to do with omnipresence. They can't be in two places at once. The ones up there holding the attention of the police and the firefighters—they might be some kind of distraction, and these guys are up to the real trouble."

I kicked at the nearest set of boards and they collapsed into the pit under their own weight. They clattered down like giant pixie sticks, and the noise of their fall was shockingly loud. The noise of the approaching others did not dim or slow. They may as well not have heard it, or if they did hear it, they surely did not care.

Reassured by the loudness of the falling debris, which sounded close relative to the wheezing, stomping approach of the things under the city, I took the light back from Nick and beamed it down myself.

"It's not very deep," I said.

"Probably deeper than it looks. How do you plan to get back up once you're down there? And do you think you can do it fast enough to clear that five hundred feet?"

"I told you, I don't think five hundred feet is a strict requirement under these circumstances. And it looks like I can probably hoist myself on up, if there's someone up here to help me out."

"Mother*fuck*," he spit. "Hang on, then. The bags."

"Yeah, the bags."

He grabbed them both and put one over each arm. I didn't realize what he was doing until it was too late to stop him. "If it's going to be one or the other of us, it might as well be me."

"What are you doing?"

But he had already hit the wet, sucking ground down below. He sank a few inches; I could hear the slurp of the mud taking his feet. He staggered, went one hand down into the mud, and recovered himself.

"What the hell are you doing?" I screamed at him, because we'd already established that the zombie things didn't care if we were there. Whatever they were coming after, we weren't it— which wouldn't necessarily stop them from tearing us limb from limb when they caught us.

"This, you crazy woman. And I say that with nothing but pure affection," he added. "But for one thing, I'm taller than you and I'll have an easier time climbing out; and for another, I'm trying to be the hero here and keep you out of trouble. Let me, already. And throw me the flashlight, I'm going to need it."

"Taller than me? By like—an *inch*, maybe. And when did this become about—"

Before I could finish it, I knew something was wrong—really wrong. I felt a crack underneath myself. I felt the tiny, awful give of something that ought to be holding me up. I felt it decide that I was too heavy, and that this wasn't going to work out.

But I didn't have time to jump. I tried, and the jumping only made it worse.

When my feet pushed off the wood flooring objected all the more, and broke all the faster. I fell fast and hard, and no matter what I grabbed for, all of it fell with me—down almost on top of Nick, who was swearing loudly and colorfully.

I landed shoulder down. Nothing broke my descent except for the mud, because, hero or no, Nick didn't have time to get under me to help cushion the fall. The consistency of the stuff beneath us couldn't fairly be called "floor," but might, with a measure of semantic slipperiness, be described as "ground." It was more mud than anything else, at any rate.

Even in my ungraceful entry, I hadn't let go of the flashlight. It was blacked out with earth, though, so I wiped it on my jeans and realized that my hand was bleeding from some wound I didn't remember getting. I might have scraped it while falling, or rather, while reaching for something to stop me.

The wound stretched across my fingers. It was ragged and nasty, like it'd been caught on a nail.

"Beautiful. Just fucking beautiful. I swear to God, woman—if we get out of this alive, I might have to kill you."

"Check it out," I told him, ignoring what he'd said. "Look, let me show you, what I told you about. Look at this."

I held my hand out, palm forward, to show him the bloody scratch. I could feel it tingling, already. It was closing, and I closed my eyes, like that would speed up the process or at least distract me from how weird it was. I didn't want to look at it myself, but I held the wounded hand out while I pointed the flashlight at it with the unmarred set of fingers.

"Is now really the time for… holy shit. You weren't kidding." He slogged through the earth and took my hand in his, aiming it up so he could see it better. He wiped it on his shirt, across his stomach, then held it up again—this time with the light. I let him take it from me to get a better view.

All around us the echo of that awful, struggling approach banged off the walls in a terrible way. And from there, down by the source, the smell was overpowering—a constant head full of decaying things crawling with rot and insects.

I pulled my hand away from him, but I let him keep the light.

"What are we going to do?" I asked.

"Eden?"

That voice again, from up above. This time, I was definitely not imagining it. Nick pointed the light up and there, holding one hand up to his eyes, was Malachi.

"Mal? What? What the hell are you doing here, what…? And, get away—get away from the edge! That's how I got down here. Back up!"

"Harry said you'd be coming back down to the Read House, and I wanted to see you before we left. I saw you just now, down there. I tried to get your attention, but you ran off so fast. Hey, who's that?"

"That's Nick. Nick, that's Malachi."

"That's—wait a minute. *That* Malachi?"

"That's the one, yeah. Hey, Malachi, I'm actually real happy to see you. We could use a hand here. Is there a rope or anything? Anything at all like that up there that you could use to help us out?"

He looked around, that shaggy blond head bobbing left to right, and not meeting with any resistance in the form of potentially helpful objects. "No. I don't see anything like that. What's that sound? And what's that smell?"

"It's—shit, Malachi. Not now. Later, okay? Now we need out. Or we need a way to get out quick. Where's Harry?"

He looked a little hurt, but I was feeling too worried by the nearness of the sucking, sloshing feet to get worked up about it. "I lost him back at the Choo-Choo. Well, no. Probably around the Read House. He knew where I was going."

"Is there any chance you could—"

"Eden." Nick said my name with a note of panic kept loosely in check.

"Get Harry. You should try to get Harry—or any of the feds or cops you see running around out there. Go get them, and bring them here. We're about to need some *very* serious assistance."

"Eden." He said it again. He was waving the flashlight back towards the dark end of the tunnel. The walls were propped here and there with big square beams—the kind you see in old mines— but they looked like they'd fall apart if you touched them with your fingertips. They were so waterlogged and old they couldn't possibly be offering much support.

And there, in the back—at the very, very edge of the light, maybe thirty or forty feet away from us, there was motion. Movement, in jerks and short reflections of the light on slime.

"Malachi, *hurry*!"

He scrambled above us and I heard more creaking, cracking; and I was afraid for a few seconds that he'd surely drop down to join us at any second. But whatever he was walking on held, and he crashed through the hole in the wall, almost certainly widening it with his body to get out so fast.

"Come on, superhero. Do something," Nick said, taking a mud-anchored step back against me.

"For example?"

"Talk to them. They're dead. They're *different* dead people, remember?"

I tried. I tried for all I was worth—concentrating, as Dana had tried to tell me last year. She'd worked with me some, trying to give me focus for it, and I wanted to think I'd improved.

But I couldn't make any kind of contact with them at all. I didn't even sense them as present; they weren't *there*, except that they were crawling towards us and gasping, wheezing, grimacing along the tunnel.

"I can't," I breathed, trying to lift one foot out of the muck and put it behind the other one—trying to retreat as far as I could, even though there wasn't any room, really. "I can't. There's nothing there to talk to."

"They're right *there*!" he shouted, gesturing with the flashlight as if I didn't know good and well where they were.

"In body, sure. In spirit? Not so much. They're empty, Nick."

"Then how come you gathered all that information above, in the water? All that shit about the church and the fire, and the little girl—"

"That's it," I said. "What you just said. The little girl. She's the one doing this. She's sending these ahead, moving them like pieces on a game board."

"But you said she didn't want anything."

"No, I said she couldn't be satisfied or stopped. Whatever she wants, she can't have it. Whatever she's looking for, it's been gone for years. It's only going to make her angrier, and more destructive. And you said it yourself, they're right there—and I'm as open to them as I can possibly make myself, but I'm not getting a damn thing."

"Then what do we do?" He was backing up too, and there was nothing to back against. Either the tunnel ended there beneath the old building, or it had caved in beyond it. There was nowhere to go except into the earth, which was packed and wet where there should have been walls.

The stink was unbearable, and unbelievable.

"Wait for Malachi?" I said, and I didn't mean for it to sound like a question, but it did.

"Fuck that noise. Help me with these things—get them up, come on."

Nick was yanking at the beams that had fallen down with us. They had half buried themselves with the weight of their collapse, but he dug them out and wrenched them forward, setting them upright and then changing his mind.

"What are you doing?"

"I was thinking barricades, but there aren't enough of these. There might be enough to stack and climb though, so help me out here. They're slow, but they're *coming*."

"I *know* that, thank you!" So I did what he said, and I grabbed two or three, whatever I could hold. And they were all slippery, but I held on tight and scored a few splinters, didn't let go of them. I swung them around and gave them to Nick, who was arranging a stack like a baby's blocks.

Everything sank, though. No matter what we put down there, it slid, slipped, and squished down into the mud. So we stacked it higher. We piled it for all we were worth, and when we had everything we could stand on, it still wasn't enough.

And they were *coming*.

I held the flashlight in my mouth. It tasted like earth and dead things, but I was afraid to drop it, too afraid to wedge it into the wall or put it down. Even without looking, I could see them writhing at the edge of the flashlight's beam, at the fringe of the light's circle, where the ribs of the tunnel were weak and crumbling as they clutched them, reaching forward, pushing past, slogging through.

"Malachi!" I screamed up at him, but the word was warped around the barrel of the flashlight.

"Hurry up!" Nick added. We couldn't hear anything up there to suggest he'd come back, but we weren't above hollering for help at that point, so we did. We blew our lungs out with the effort of it; we yelled until we were hoarse, and until the foul-smelling crew was too close to ignore.

"Up." Nick braced himself. "Up—maybe I can lift you from here. Then you can help pull me up. Come on."

"No, I'll lift you."

"This is no time for feminism, babe. I weigh more than you do. Pure mercenary. Come on." He locked his hands together and held them low.

Christ, they were close. I could see their eyes, scooped-out empty sockets that saw nothing. I could hear the gushing gasps leaking from their chests like they were squeezed out of old bellows. All that blackened, barbecued skin peeling in pieces, and all those broken fingers clawing forward—they moved so slow, but it was a horrifying kind of slow, a slow that will never stop. It was a slowness that you could run from your entire life, and you *would* run your entire life, because you'd have to.

I nodded at Nick, because he was right—and because it would only be a matter of minutes before they were on us. Maybe a matter of seconds.

I wiggled my feet free of the mess on the ground and pulled myself onto a pair of two-by-fours that offered something like stability. And from there, I jumped—putting one foot into Nick's locked fingers and letting him lift me.

I caught the rotted edge of the floor above and it came apart in my hands. I flipped backwards from the inertia of my flight, and I landed on my back—half on the boards and half in the mud. The mud half hurt less.

"You all right?"

"No, but I will be." I accepted his hand when he offered it, and I let him help pull me up, back onto our little island of detritus. "Try again. It was close." I shook my shoulders, trying to loosen the pain that knotted there, coiled between the bones in my neck and my arm.

He held his hands back down and I took a deep breath.

He threw, I grasped. I caught the edge again and it held, or part of it held. Part of it fell away. I scrambled, digging in with fingernails, with fingertips, with slapping palms and kicking feet, pumping knees.

Beneath me, Nick's hands were fighting to help—to give me something to push against. But it wasn't working. I could feel myself sliding; too much weight remained over the edge and there wasn't enough to cling to. And the floor above wasn't stable enough. It wouldn't hold me. I knew it wasn't going to hold me.

Then, bursting through the window where we'd all made our entry, came Malachi.

"Get low!" I told him. "Lie down—spread your weight out! It won't hold us otherwise!"

He did as he was told, and he did it fast—lying as flat as he could and holding out his hands just in time to give me one last thing to grab before toppling back into the pit. His fingers wormed their way around my wrists, and he'd anchored his feet somewhere beyond where I could see. He wiggled me back away from the edge. The floor objected like mad. The boards cracked and threatened collapse with every elbow jab and every knee knock.

But it held, and he had me out.

"Where's Harry?"

"Couldn't find him!"

"That's all right—that's fine. We'll do without him. Help me—help me get Nick, he's still down there."

"Okay—what do I do?"

Frantic but determined, I stalked the perimeter of the pit. "Throw me the flashlight," Nick said. It seemed like the least I could do, so I dropped it down and he caught it. "What are you doing?"

"Get out of here."

"What are you doing?"

"*Get out of here!* " He was rummaging with the duffel; he was pulling the shells out of the towels that wrapped them. He set the shell on a board.

"Tie them together! Tie them together, we'll use them as a rope. Throw them up and we'll pull you out, goddamn you!"

"Not long enough," he said. "The floor won't hold us, anyway."

"It'll hold," Malachi insisted, creeping around the opposite side of the lip. "Man, tie the towels together!"

Below us, Nick flexed an arm and there was a ripping sound where he'd pulled off the hem of the towel. He held the strip of fabric in his teeth and pointed the flashlight down at one of the sheets of paper we'd swiped from beneath the ball park.

He read quickly, then dropped the paper and examined the shell, all of this so fast, like he didn't know what he was doing but he figured he'd better learn in a hurry. "We're not going to get more than one chance at this. Keep looking around up there. Look for something—a ladder or a rope, something real that might be useful. I haven't got but another minute or two and I'm going to make it *count*."

Now well beyond frantic, I stood up and stared around at the storage—at all the trash, all the warped crates, and the disused leftovers of long-forgotten cleaning instruments and construction tools.

Nothing looked promising, but Malachi was rifling through the stash on the other side of the room with the pure tenacity of a terrier on a rat.

"Wait a minute," he said, stopping and turning to dash right back outside.

"What are you doing? Get back here!" I shouted, but he was already gone so I kept thrashing around, looking for something—anything.

Seconds later my brother returned with a long red cable wound up around his arm. "Like this?"

"Like that!" I reached out and took them from him. "Jumper cables?"

Big, long jumper cables—good ones. "I saw them inside a car on my way here. I broke the window, but I figured this was an emergency."

"Indeed. Good job," I mumbled, unwinding them and looking for a solid spot to brace myself. "I'm going to need your help here," I told him. "We're going to do this the long way, the stretchy way. I don't think the floor will put up with anything else."

"Just tell me what to do."

"Back to the hole. Back to solid ground—lie down and grab my feet."

I put myself belly-down on the dusty, muddy, messy floor and twisted one end of the cables around my wrist, then for further leverage, I clamped the alligator jaws to my leather belt.

Then I used the other end like a lasso and threw them over the edge. "Get my feet, Malachi—get my feet!"

He took them and held them hard.

"Nick?" I called, almost glad I couldn't see what he was up to. "Nick, do you see the—"

"I see them. Just a second."

"Have you got a second?"

"Yes, shut up. Hang on." He tugged at the cable end, and he was quiet for a moment before hollering more. "When I say 'now,' do your damnedest—but if it doesn't hold, or if I let go, you've got to run."

"No way!"

"*Way*, or I'm not taking the cable. Because when I say 'now' I'm going to light this wacky improvised wick and we're going to see what happens—and it's going to be loud, and it's going to be messy, and you don't want to be on top of it."

"Okay, okay—just do it. Just, come on!"

I pulled myself forward on my elbows to peek over the edge, and I wished I hadn't. The halo of light permitted by the edges of the pit was populated. They were coming. So slow, but so steady. Winning the race.

And in the center, at the end of our makeshift rescue rope, there was Nick with the paint thinner and the scrap of towel. He'd stacked the shells one on top of each other. Probably only needed to blow one to set the other. Good plan. Smart man.

"Nick?"

He looked up at me and I saw his face white against the mud

at his feet. "You can do this. I can do this." Then he pulled the lighter out of his pocket—a nice Zippo. Did everybody have one of those things but me?

"Ready?"

Nick wrapped his wrist up in the cable, and I scooted back away from the edge to give him room. I looked over my shoulder at Malachi, who nodded that he was ready, so I told Nick that I was ready too.

"Three, two…" I heard the wheel snap and spark below.

A new, warmer glow came rising up out of the pit, and a puff of warmth came with it.

"Now!"

Malachi heard it too and locked himself around my feet, and together we pulled, yanked, and heaved.

"*Hurryhurryhurrryhurryfaster!*"

Beneath me, I could feel the floor objecting. I ignored it, because I had to, except to try, even as I hauled for all I was worth, to distribute my weight more broadly. It didn't work, or maybe it did—but Malachi was having trouble behind us, and I could see that glow rising, climbing up before I could see Nick's hands on the other end of the line.

When I did see them, blackened, muddied, and white around the knuckles, I pulled one arm back and sent the other one forward, grabbing him and giving him a wrist to hold. "Take it," I commanded, and he did. "Take it, I can hold you. Come on."

He climbed my arms like he climbed the cable and in a few seconds we had him out, and he had Malachi to help steady him too, and we needed to leave. Needed to stand on something firmer, needed to put our feet on something that wouldn't fall.

But Nick looked back, down into the pit.

302

"Shit," he said, and the urgency had drained from him. "Shit, it went out. Fuck, it went out!"

"What?" Malachi came closer then, even though I tried to hold him back with my forearm.

"Don't," I told him. "Don't—it won't hold."

The floor answered me, believing me. Something too old and too eaten by termites and damp made a crunching sound.

"What's down there? Oh God," he said, and I only then realized he hadn't seen them yet. But he looked over the edge, as near to it as he could come, and there they were—all charred, reaching arms and raspy, struggling throats, shambling into the halo of light where the pit let in the leftovers of sun that could make it through the window.

"Malachi, move away from the edge. Come on. It didn't work, but okay. It didn't work. But we can't stay here—and we had such a hard time getting up, surely it'll take them some time. Forget it, this was—shit, Nick. You were right, it was a stupid idea."

"I never said it was a stupid idea."

"You didn't? You definitely implied it. Let's just go get the cops; we'll find some of the nice SWAT boys with all the Kevlar."

"What *are* they? We can't just—they're going to come up through that, aren't they? You were going to—oh God. Oh *God*."

The floor was warning us and I didn't want to wait for another collapse. "Come on, out now."

Nick was way ahead of us, already at the hole in the window with the pried-apart plywood. "People!" he said like he couldn't believe this was taking so long. "Let's move it, shall we?"

But by then I was as transfixed as Malachi was. We could see them, just over the edge. They weren't looking up at us. They weren't paying attention to us. But they were coming for us, and they were assembling together, kneeling and bracing. They were making their own ladder, out of their own bodies.

"Something is making them do this," I breathed, hardly believing what I was seeing. "They can't do it themselves. They haven't got it in them, there's not enough left. Someone is telling them—moving them—to do this."

It was fascinating, so fascinating that even though they were climbing up close, I couldn't look away. I tried to reach them again, tried my hardest to concentrate and project and all those other hippy-trippy terms Dana liked to use, but they just weren't there anymore; their minds were completely gone, rotted out their ears or burned out their noses. Nothing.

But their emptiness didn't make them any less dangerous, or disgusting. And when one reached the lip of the hole I didn't step back fast enough to keep it from grabbing my leg.

It gave my ankle a yank hard and fast enough to bring me down, but Malachi caught me under the arms and tried to draw me back. I kicked with the other leg, using the heel of my boot as a chisel, but not meeting a whole lot of success.

Nick came back in and tried to help Malachi, but I tried to scream them both away—the floor, it wasn't going to hold. "Can't you hear it?"

With the added weight of Nick, the guys pulled hard enough to loosen the thing's grip; its bony black fingers slipping down to close around my toes. It might have been the least of our problems. Two more of the things were reaching the edge, using their arms, elbows, and creaking old shoulders to creep onto the jagged rim.

Malachi stiffened, and I thought it was fear because I didn't understand. I didn't get it because I couldn't have imagined or predicted it, or else I would never have let him do it.

I didn't understand until after he slung one arm lower, under my ribcage—and hefted me back with such force that part of the thing's fingers got caught in my laces, and the crumbling flesh came away with me too. I didn't understand because I didn't know he was that strong.

He moved so fast, too. He backed up and into Nick, who stumbled backwards but caught my hand as he went. Together we tumbled away from the edge while Malachi went towards it.

With a running jump he took the top two creatures headlong and toppled with them down into the hole.

I yelled his name, and would have jumped forward if Nick hadn't gripped me like a vise and held me in place, back by the wall, back by the hole where we could get out if only we would push the plywood aside.

Down below in the hole with the writhing, teeming creatures, all arms and legs and mindless limbs, Malachi struggled. And spark, spark, spark—I could hear the wheel turning on the little lighter Nick had left down with the bags. It was sitting on top where it would have been easy to see and find. My brother might not have always been the sharpest crayon in the box, but he was a decisive son of a bitch—that much I knew. That much I'd always known, from the first moment I saw him on a rain-wet playground on Signal Mountain.

It seemed like a thousand years ago.

It felt like somebody else's lifetime, lived, died, and forgotten. I could hear him down there—even above the scattering din of the wrestling, restless dead, slopping their limbs together in the mud and trying to reorganize, and rebuild.

And above it all, or under it—a pocket of sound where I could hear the spinning clicks with every twist of his thumb—I heard

Malachi striking the lighter, over and over again, and then he stopped.

"Eden?"

"Malachi?"

"I'm sorry about everything. For ever. Since the beginning."

"Malachi?"

"Run."

There was more in the word than when Nick had said it.

Nick was frantic, making it into an order too frightening not to be obeyed. Malachi was offering it up as a calm, certain warning. It wasn't a threat, or even a promise. It was a fact.

Nick was thinking more clearly than I was, but I think I can be forgiven for it. He was dragging me to the exit. I wasn't fighting him exactly, but I couldn't make my legs cooperate enough to pull my balance together and help him help me.

We didn't make it through, all the way.

The first percussion hit—a shockwave, a pulse of sound and pressure that lifted the floor and shook us all. I sucked in a breath just in time to hold it for the second, greater blast—accompanied by a tremendous whistle and wail, and then I couldn't hear anything, really. It was all gone, just a shaking, warbling set of waves that ate the floor and rocked the walls.

Nick was saying something into my ear—he was screaming it against the side of my face, and I couldn't hear him. When I looked up, the roof was swaying, or maybe it was my vision, I couldn't tell. I couldn't sort anything out—there was only the sound, a living, breathing thing that swelled and shouted.

Then there was another pop. Though it must have been as loud as the first one, it seemed a junior version of the real thing. And following it, there was a second big blow—the second shell igniting.

Below me the world was falling away.

Nick had me, and he held on to me, and he lifted me out. I scraped my back on the window frame and was pulled into the gray-white day outside. It was cool there, and raining again, like it had been for days.

19

DROP BY DROP

We staggered into the street and dropped ourselves down behind the nearest vehicle—a blue and tan Ford Explorer, circa 1994. It's funny, the details you remember afterwards. It's funny the way the small things that you might have overlooked—that you should've overlooked—stick in your head, like your brain is looking for something else to think about.

Anything else.

I looked down at our ankles and there was more water, coming up still, and coming up slowly. Unstoppable. Like the things underground. Looking up, above our heads—it was more water, in drips and drabs, not firmly resolved to rain but too heavy to stay aloft. And I was wrong about the sky, about my first impression of it. It was yellowed then, more than a gray-white.

It looked sick, the color of an almost-healed bruise.

Looking across, there against the vehicle—I saw water running down in rivulets, creeping its way down to splash on the road. There was a scratch, too, made with a key or heaven knows what. It was shaped like a bird, sort of—like a kid's version of a bird, a flappy M shape as it flies away into a background made with crayons or watercolors. The cheap kind, in rainbow colors on a plastic palette.

Around us the water pattered down but we didn't hear it. We saw it bubble and bead and drop. All we could hear was the pounding, firing, pulsing of the contained blast—and after it, the crumbling fall of the building above it; and after that, the settling of the earth in sliding clumps into the tunnels. Filling them up. Covering them up. Like I'd planned.

Like I'd planned, but not like I'd expected.

"This wasn't what I meant," I said, leaning my head against the Explorer.

Nick slid down beside me to sit there, even though the water was there and it was filthy. He sat beside me and put an arm around me and I was mostly just stunned and listening, waiting.

But after the last of the settling, and the last of the cracking boards folding in upon themselves, there was no sound at all except for the hissing of water filtering down to where the fireworks sparked, here and there, under the leftovers. There wouldn't be any cries for help. I knew that already. I knew he was dead. I felt him leave, and now I wanted to feel him come back. But there was nothing.

Also, though, there was no crawling, shoving, climbing of dead things. None of that either.

"It worked," Nick said, as if that made everything okay.

"Who cares?"

"You do. It worked," he said again, trying to pull me up.

I didn't exactly fight him over it, but I made him work for it.

When I was on my feet, toes pruning in the disgusting water,

I answered him. "It worked. But it shouldn't have… it shouldn't have cost that much."

He braced himself like he thought I was going to start bawling again, but I didn't. I was calm, because there was nothing else left inside me. I'd burned the rest of it out, or burned it off, and used it up.

"Look, I'm really sorry about… *him*, and everything, but we've got to get moving. We should go to the Read House. We need to—"

"What?" I interrupted him.

"Clean up. Regroup."

"There's more you mean to say, isn't there?"

He ran one hand across his forehead, moving the dirt-dreaded hair back above his eyebrows. "They're still coming—the ones up above here. You know he didn't bury but some of them. They're going to need help getting people out, moving people away. They know it at the ball park now, too. If we hadn't left when we did, they would've flown us out shortly."

"How do you know that?"

He cocked his head towards the park. "I don't know it, but I suspect it. Bits of things overheard, you know. They were trying to empty the place. And now they're going to try to empty the Read House. It's a tiered approach to evacuation, they were calling it. Getting the population out in stages."

At the risk of changing the subject, I said, "Harry. We've got to go find Harry. I have to tell him so he can leave—so he can get out of here before it gets any worse. Harry won't leave without him."

The last of it came out in a babble, but Nick was patient with it and nodded as he started to lead me back up the street to the hotel. "Good idea. Good plan."

"Not a plan, really."

"Good start of a plan. It'll get us moving, anyway, and we'll figure out the rest when we get there. We'll figure it out. Come on. We'll figure out something."

"Stop that."

"Stop what?"

"Talking to me like I'm four years old."

"Sorry."

I shouldn't have snapped at him. He was only trying to help.

But I couldn't muster an apology for it, and he didn't act like he needed one, so I just walked beside him and tried not to notice that we were moving through water. It was higher even than earlier that morning—it was at the very doorstep of the shelter when we arrived.

Nick was right, they were moving people out.

Emergency personnel directed human traffic, and the bulldozers and tow trucks had cleared another lane of traffic to the interstate leaving town. It moved in a steady flow if not a heavy one—ambulances, fire trucks, police cars, and the occasional bus somebody scared up from a schoolyard or Greyhound.

They made up a caravan that moved in lurches. Park, load. Creep forward to the onramp. Follow the arms of the policemen and -women in their wet blue uniforms. Slow but steady. Running the race, if not winning it.

"Harry?" I called over the low-buzzing din. "Harry? Are you here?"

I thought of my cell phone and remembered it was dead and wouldn't be of any help to me. I turned to Nick and said, "He's a tall guy with white hair, wearing—I don't remember. I can't remember what he's wearing—but he's in his sixties, maybe. Real good shape though—thin, but on the tough-looking side. I think he used to be a boxer or something. He told me once but I don't remember."

"All right, I'll keep my eyes open."

Before I could holler too much more, Harry found me first. He got a good handful of my arm through the crowd and tugged, commanding my attention and Nick's too—since Nick was still moving in "protective alpha male" mode.

"There you are!" he said, and Nick figured out that this was the guy we were looking for.

"You're Harry?"

"I'm Harry. You two looking for me?"

"Yes," I said. "Trying to find you."

"Well *I'm* trying to find your brother. Have you seen him? Crazy little bastard took off looking for you here. I tried to keep tabs on him, but you know what he's like once he's got some stupid idea in his head."

I don't know what my face told him, but it gave him an inkling that all wasn't well with the world. This would probably have been a good time to burst into tears again, but it didn't happen.

"What's going on? You've seen him."

I nodded and tried to answer, but nothing came out. Nick took over. "We've seen him. He helped us out of trouble, and it cost him."

Harry went still as a statue, then changed his mind and opened up that impressive, long-armed wingspan of his—herding us both off to a corner where we were out of traffic's flow and could construct the illusion of privacy. "Where is he now?"

Nick answered again, and it was just as well. "Somewhere underneath Broad Street. He's gone, man."

Harry exhaled through lips pursed in the shape of an O. "Oh. Okay. Oh. Are—are you sure?"

My turn to talk and nod. "Pretty damn sure. We were stuck down there, under the city—there was a tunnel, the old underground, you know?" I was babbling again, but it wouldn't slow down so I let it flow. "We were down there because there were things down there—we saw them, and we were going to stop them from coming up underneath the city, out of that old building down there on the corner, which you can't see from here but that's okay because it's not there anymore anyway. And Malachi helped us get out after the floor collapsed, but then he went back in because, I don't know why because, but he was trying to help, or trying to make up for it all, that's what he said. And he lit the fuse on the shells and—"

"Wait, *artillery* shells? Where did you get your hands on—"

"No, fireworks shells. Big ones, though. We stole them from the ball park, and we were going to set them off down there and close the tunnel because you have to bury them—you have to bury them again, it's the only thing that's ever kept them down and quiet. You have to bury them," I said again, because hearing myself pronounce the refrain made the story something I could process.

"It was my fault," I tacked on at the end. "Harry, don't be mad at him, it was all my fault."

"Not mad at him, not mad at you," he told me, trying to smooth it over or soothe it down. "Not mad at anybody. Calm down, okay? Calm down."

"Okay, I'm calm. I'm *perfectly* calm; there isn't anything left for me to be. But it's time for you to get out of here. You were here for him, and for me. But you should go now. They're still coming and we've all got to leave—we've all got to move."

"To where? Where are you going to go, Eden? What are you going to do?"

"I don't know. Out, I guess. Home, eventually—someplace the river can't catch me. Isn't that what's important right now? Just get away from it. Do you see where it is? It's coming for us, and it won't stop, and we've all got to get out of its way."

"It'll go down eventually, darling. TVA will fix the locks and the rain will end, and everything will go back down to normal."

"No. I'm leaving. I want away from it. I want to be done with it, and with those things that won't stop coming. And, Harry, when people see them—when people here at this shelter see them? And it won't be long, you can believe me when I tell you that. When people see them it's going to be fucking *panic*, do you hear me? There won't be any more of this organized retreat, tidy like this. It's going to be pandemonium. Chaos. It's going to be screaming and running and dying. That's what it's going to be. They want out, and they want up, and *they are coming*."

"What are you talking about? You've completely lost me."

"You'll catch up, whether you want to or not. You'll find out. You'll see."

"All right, I'll see, then. You—damn. You look like hell. Let's get you inside and cleaned up, straightened up. Maybe get you a cookie or something, some orange juice."

I shook my arm out of his grasp and scowled. "I didn't just donate blood, Harry. I don't need any of that. I just need away from her. I mean, here. I need away from here."

I didn't know why I'd said that, until I'd had time for my few firing synapses to catch up with my Freudian back-brain.

"What? Who is 'her'? What are you talking about?" Harry asked, and I think Nick already knew.

"The little girl," he said. "She's the one running this show, you said it yourself. So, what then? We find her, we deal with her, we wrap it up and write a four-minute piece about it."

I rolled my eyes. "Sure. And it'll be just that easy, too."

"What little girl?"

"All right, let's go sit down somewhere and have a talk. It'll take a few minutes to catch you up." Nick was already scanning the crowd for an island of solitude to which we could retreat, but even before the screaming started, I knew it wasn't going to happen.

And then, it did—the screaming began in earnest, I mean—and I didn't have to look down the street to know why. I only had to look down at my feet, where the edges of my boots were up to their soles in manky black river water.

"Too late," I whispered. "Too late. Harry, go. Nick, go. We've got to get out of here. It's about to get very, very nasty."

The first wave of the stampede cuffed us then, buffeted us back into the building as people who didn't even know why they were running turned themselves towards the road and ran. The human tide parted around the cars and sometimes went over them; but people were really getting frightened. Part of it was that some of them had seen the wobbling, shaking bodies burned black and awful as they lumbered up out of the water. The rest of it was that so many of them hadn't seen anything yet. All they knew was that there was running and screaming, and that to stay in place meant to be trampled—or caught by the unseen things oncoming.

"How do we get out of here?" I yelled, but was cut off by someone's elbow in my face. I ducked aside and pulled Nick and Harry both with me. "And how, precisely, do we 'deal' with a girl who's been dead for eighty years? And who's powerful enough to raise the dead?" I braced one foot on a jutting edge on the

315

building's brick face, and jumped up to give myself a second or two above the crowd. I saw them, coming up the road, and I had to amend my statement. "So to speak."

"So to speak?" Harry asked, tiptoeing to see—and since he's so much taller than me, he had an easier time of it. "Holy shit...."

"I wouldn't call them 'raised' exactly, that's all. They're up and moving, but they're not traveling with all their factory original parts, if you get what I'm saying. They're blind and mindless. They're being moved by the only one who can see—the little girl. She's been using the biggest of them, a really big man, as her front man because he's huge and intimidating-looking. Do you see— Harry, look over that way again, tall man—do you see one that's smaller than the rest of them?"

"No," he said, shaking his head. "What the hell are they?"

"Zombies," Nick said. "She's right, let's just get the hell out of here."

"Where?" Harry asked. "Back to the Choo-Choo?"

"You *could* do that, yeah. Or maybe just get out of town the more direct way—up the ramp there. These things can't get very far out of the water; or even if they can, they can't move very quickly on dry land. Get up there onto the asphalt. I think we'll be pretty safe." The interstate was elevated behind the Read House anyway. It was the same road Nick and I had climbed from the ball park, and it ought to be well out of the water except right at the river.

Though many of the refugees wouldn't be able to get terribly far on foot, they could get far enough. And quite a lot of them could probably make the mad, sprinting run to where 27 meets 24, a mile or two away—and there, the entire road is up on columns, elevated well above the earth.

"We need to spread that around," Nick said, and he was right. I gave Harry a nudge, Nick a nod, and we three split up to burrow through the crowd. It was easier said than done.

People were panicking, and we were going against the flow of human traffic no matter which direction we picked. The Read House parking garage, the places on the sidewalks out front, and the lobby area were all a boiling stew of humanity and there was no way around it.

I peeled my eyes for people in uniform and I located them, here and there. One cop with a radio in one hand and a megaphone in the other had hooked his arm around a lamppost and was standing on its moorings, leaning above the crowd.

I worked my way towards him and when I reached him, I grabbed him by the leg. "Hey," I said, and he looked like he wanted to ignore me. He tried to shake me off, but he didn't have enough leverage to do so.

I had to yell over the din, and I was tired of yelling, but I wasn't giving up yet. "Listen to me—and don't ask any questions. Those things can't get out of the water. They can't leave it, not very far and not very well."

"What?" He looked down at me like I might be mad, but there was hunger in his lean, saggy face—like at least I was telling him something concrete, and this was a first for the day.

"Get everyone away from the water—away, it doesn't matter where. Those things over there, the things you see coming—they can't leave the water hardly at all. When they're out of it, they move slow. Get everybody up onto the interstate—up that onramp and out."

He nodded like he understood but he wasn't sure if there was any good reason to believe me. But right about then, gunshots popped around our ears like fireworks, like baby versions of the Salute shells for all their volume. People started screaming and the press of bodies only got worse, more frightened and desperate.

Glass was breaking and I didn't know where it was coming from. I didn't know what it belonged to.

I think—at least, it looked like it, anyway—most of the gunfire was coming from the authorities and was aimed down the street where the water came creeping high, bringing the dead things with it.

"Headshots," I told the officer, whose calf I still clung to. "Won't stop them, but it'll slow them down."

"Is that how we kill them?" he asked, and I thought he probably hadn't heard me very well.

"No, can't kill them. Already dead. Just distract them, slow them. Get everyone else out of the way."

He nodded again, but that didn't mean anything. He lifted the megaphone to his mouth; it was one of those electronic ones that you push buttons to speak through, not an old-fashioned cheerleader's model. When his voice came through the device the words were murky but much, much louder.

"Everyone go towards Martin Luther King. Go towards 27!"

This was more or less the only direction anyone was running anyway, but they were all running like marbles dumped from a sack, bounding back and forth and around, ricocheting off of cars and off the sides of buildings—a great experiment in chaos flow. Gradually, the place was starting to empty.

The Read House had only held a finite number of fugitives from the water. There were only so many of those who knew they should flee, and only so many who were capable of running farther under their own power. The smaller ones, the older ones, the weaker ones were getting left behind, but that's the way it always goes. That's the way it always works when no one's in charge and there's no way to stop the water, or the monsters, and the only thing you can do is get out of the way.

It's not like the government is there to help you.

So as the first wave poured, drained, and howled away from the building—even though some of them didn't know what they were running from—most of the ones who were left were looking for safe places.

"Up," I told the first one I found, an older woman with two small, shrieking kids who were probably grandchildren. "Up, go up. Get as high as you can. The parking garage—get to the elevators."

"I don't know where—"

"Come with me."

It was the best I could do, even though it trapped them up on the roof. Up on the roof, the helicopters swirled and swooped—the helicopters might see them and get them. And besides, that high up they were so far beyond the water they ought to be safe.

Safer. It was the best I could do.

I grabbed a couple more on my way to the elevators beneath the building. One was a heavily pregnant woman and one was an elderly man in a gray bathrobe; then we picked up a girl with crutches, and were lucky that a hotel employee (in his valet uniform) could lift her into his arms and carry her along with us.

I stuffed the lot of them into the elevator and called others over to do the same. "Go to the top level," I told them. "Get on the roof and flag for the helicopters."

The police officer who'd been hanging on the lamppost caught up to us and saw what we were doing. At first I thought he was going to stop us and start making some official, by-the-book kind of suggestions that would royally piss me off, and then I'd have to kick him in the balls… but he surprised me.

"I'll radio it in. The roof of the parking garage."

He left us, clutching the radio to his mouth and squeezing the buttons on the megaphone, which hung limp from his other hand. On his way back outside, into the stark white afternoon with the ash-gray sky, he waved others in our direction.

They hadn't all been abandoned; someone always stays. A mother, a son, a father, a grandfather here and there, and more grandmothers with little ones in tow. There weren't enough healthy helpers to go around, but even then—even understanding that terrible, awful things were creeping forward—the brave ones understood that there was time. The loyal ones kept one eye on the road and the river trash, calculating the time until there was no time left to run.

Outside and overhead there was at least one helicopter even before the elevator had time to return to us. We watched the digital numbers drop and cursed the seconds while the cars loaded and unloaded.

We cursed the moments as the refugees straggled past and the screaming all around us didn't stop, only muffled itself to crying and shouting, which was no better but at least made it easier to hear—and easier to pass orders back and forth.

Harry found me again, down by the elevators.

He was panting, but still energized and ready to move bodies. "I heard there was some crazy woman stuffing people into elevators and sending them skyward. I figured it had to be you."

"Thanks," I said, handing a little fellow maybe three or four years old to a man I assumed was his father—but the man shook his head.

"Not mine," he said.

"Whose? Who does this one belong to?" He was a redhaired imp with dirty freckles and a nose serving as a snotfaucet. He howled in my face as I held him up. "Who does this one belong to?"

Nobody answered, and everybody shrugged impatiently, because the elevator wasn't rising and everyone wanted to get up, out above the water. The man I'd tried to pass the kid off on changed his mind and said, "Forget it, I'll take him. I'll keep him upstairs if I need to. Come here, little dude."

The little dude screamed, but I foisted him off anyway. Next. Next. Whoever's next. Get on board. Room for one more, no, not the wheelchair—not that much room. You're first on next round, though, I swear to God.

"Ma'am?" Harry addressed the petulant-looking, ancient woman in the chair. "How about you and I take the long way around. It'll be fast, and you'll have to hang on, but I can push you up the ramps."

"Up the ramps," she repeated, and something about her eyes, and her reaction time, implied that maybe she wasn't all there anymore. An Alzheimer's patient? "But I just had a baby!"

"Not in the last sixty years she hasn't," somebody mumbled, but if the woman heard him, she didn't argue with him.

"I'll be careful," Harry promised, then checked her all over to make sure she was all inside and not on the verge of toppling out at high foot-speed. Satisfied that she wouldn't spill out at the first bump, he took hold of the rubber handles and began a hurried retreat towards the coiling car ramp.

I thought I heard her complaining, but then as he rounded the first turn her echoing, weedy voice dribbled down to the elevators. "*Wheeee!*"

Ping.

Elevator number two was open again. People began loading. Nick appeared, with another parentless small child. "Someone said the parking garage, and oh, of course—it's you."

"You have any better ideas?"

"Not at the moment, no. Not any more good ideas, anyway.

Hey, does this little girl belong to anyone here? She's asking for Mommy and I can't find anyone matching that description."

"Bless her heart!" One of the grandmothers with three charges already put out her hands and took her. "Not one of mine, but if no one else claims her, she can ride with us."

"Excellent," he said as he handed her off.

"What did you mean by not any *more* good ideas?" I asked, holding the doors open with my leg and my butt. "You said that like you'd already cashed one in."

"I did. Got on a cop's cell phone to the TV station. The traffic reporter has his own chopper, and he's on his way out here. The hospital only has the one, the cops don't have any, and the feds haven't yet figured out that they need more of them, that they need to start moving people instead of personnel."

"You kick ass, man."

"Tell me about it. He'll be plucking people from the roof in ten or twenty minutes, tops. Probably less, if I know him."

"Doesn't he need some kind of FFA permissions?"

"Probably. That won't stop him, though."

A fresh pattering stomp of running feet and hollered orders went charging past the open area where the parking garage dumped onto Broad Street, and we all knew we were running out of time. On the upshot, we were running out of people, too.

On the downshot, the creatures were so close that I could hear them breathing again. I could hear them walking in that splashing shuffle, which slowed as it reached the edges of the water, but by this point the edges of the water were all around us and all over our feet, even there inside the garage.

And there was a crack of lightning followed almost immediately by an answering thunderclap.

"More fucking *water*," Nick swore, and nobody chastised him for saying it in front of old ladies and little kids.

And we were out of time, just like that.

The elevator numbers were sinking, and freezing, stopping and starting, but there were too many floors and we had maybe a dozen people left, huddled there. Together, we huddled, all of us and all of them—there was nothing else to do. The rest of them were hearing it too, the gagging, gasping, forced crush of air in the crumbled chests.

Not all of them knew what it was, though. Thank God.

Nick knew, and I knew. Nick had the good idea first. "This way," he said quietly. We'd all gone quiet. We were all listening, trying to place the spot where the noise was coming from. "This way—back over here. Come on. One level up, we can walk it."

"Is that where we're going?" a small girl asked way, way too loud.

"Yes," he whispered down at her. "Yes, that's where we're going, and we're going there right now." He looked up at me. "Out of sight might be the best we can do for now."

"Yeah." I hated to admit it but there wasn't much choice. "Okay, yeah. You take them up there."

"Oh, I don't like the sound of that…"

"Because I'm going that way." I pointed out at the square of gray light where the parking garage hit Broad. "They're slow. I'm fast. You do the math. Take these guys up and out, go farther than the vans if you think you can. It's only what—eight or nine floors? Okay, get them up, at least one floor."

"Eden," he warned, and I ignored it.

I had to ignore it. There they were. Two of them. Knees first, into view, then off-balanced torsos, and with them came the dragging scrape of chains.

"Go!" I hissed at him, and the little girl with the big questions started to cry.

I took off. I dashed the thirty yards out into the light, into the open street right in front of the moving, wandering things. Only then did I realize that I was splashing too, and that the river was higher than I'd thought. In the garage it was harder to see, maybe; or maybe it was farther above street level than I thought.

But I was splashing, boots slapping one after the other through maybe three or four inches of navy-black water with a sheen on top like motor oil and a current of leaves, paper coffee cups, and a dead pigeon or two.

One of the things raised a hand at me, but there wasn't much motive behind it. It was the equivalent of "I see you" and "Here I come" rolled into one. So slow. So stupid. So perfectly empty and knowing nothing at all, but there they were—walking. Moving. Breathing in jagged coughs. Seeing me, and recognizing that I was something to be chased. The teethrattling scrape of a rusted chain whipped through the low water with a heavy splatter, and its tail cracked against the bottom of a glass door, shattering it.

"Run, people," I said out the side of my mouth.

"Eden!" It was Nick.

I didn't listen to him, and I knew he was too preoccupied to chase me. "Get them upstairs. I'll join you as soon as I can."

The things were already shifting their forward paths, trying to turn to follow me instead of continuing on whatever course they'd been programmed for.

And there was the sound of those chains again. They were caught on wrists and cinched around waists. Dead hands gripped and swung the brownish links, which slid through the air and ripped messily through the water. Everything they struck broke and feel. A potted plant beside the main entrance, the brass concierge desk, the polished marble panels along the walls, all met the terrible snaking chains and were destroyed.

My back was to the elevators, and to the people there. "You promise?" Nick asked.

"I promise. Go. They won't catch me."

One of them groaned as if in protest, so I went ahead and challenged it. I took three long steps out into the light in front of them—directly in their path. Their wobbly, charred-wet heads swiveled jerkily to follow my movement.

"Come and get me then, if that's what you want. Come on. Over here." The water had reached mid-calf on me. They were not so slow here, in the street where the curbs held a few inches of water in the road.

They made a decision, if it could really be called that. I ought to say instead that they were distracted by the more immediate stimulus of my body's motion, and they pursued me—mindless, quick, like a cat jumps after a bird flying past, even though a closed window separates it from the back yard.

Forward came the things, and faster—now that they'd been given a goal more interesting than "forward" alone. The biggest one hoisted his elbow and flipped his wrist, coiling a length of chain up and reaching back, as if he were preparing to strike.

"That's right," I said, backing up, and backing away from the parking garage. "Follow the bouncing brunette. Come to me. Come and get me."

I had to turn around then, because they were coming approximately as fast as I could walk backwards. They were easy to track, though—tearing through the clotted water behind me they were about as quiet as a flock of angry ducks. I dashed and splashed forward and they came on my heels. They were smelly and loud, but not close enough, not yet.

I'd concocted a half-formed idea that all I really had to do was get them up out of the water. If they'd struggle their way up and out into the road, or onto the grass on the other side of Martin Luther King… if I could get them out onto land where they were weaker and slower, I might be able to—I didn't know, really. Kick them out far enough to strand them, or assault them, or hack them up. With what, I didn't know yet.

But it was a thought, and the germ of a plan. Put them where they're weakest—lure them there. Then beat them down. Into how many pieces must they be broken before they'd stop coming?

I didn't know, but I aimed to find out.

Alas, it's never quite that easy. I heard them slowing behind me; I thought maybe it was just the way the water was getting lower, but then I looked over my shoulder and saw that I was mistaken—or partly mistaken.

Those sons of bitches were getting *sidetracked*.

I'd gotten them as far as the front door, no more than a few yards—which was aggravating, even as I considered it a mini-success. They weren't looking into the parking garage anymore, and from the space beneath the concrete layers of the garage I could hear the scuffling echoes of people moving quietly, quickly, but not easily, across the cement.

The things behind me weren't looking that way, or listening that way. They were stopping in front of the open double doors beneath the main overhang. They were looking inside, with those faces that didn't have any eyes left.

No one within looked back at them; I glanced up at the upper floor windows, wondering how many people might still be left in there. A crowd was assembling on the interstate, less than a quarter mile away. People were hanging off the edge and the guard rails, pointing and chattering, talking, screaming.

I looked up again. Up in the windows I saw a few faces, yes. But only a few.

"Shut the doors!" I shouted up to them. "Wherever you are, shut your doors and hide, for God's sake!"

Most of the few faces disappeared immediately. I'd stayed in the Read House before. I knew good and well you could hear street noise from the rooms. I knew good and well they'd heard me. To the ones who remained, I shouted again, "Shut your doors! Go shut them! Lock them and hide!"

One or two remained transfixed at the panes, but I figured that Darwin would have to sort them out, if that's what it was going to come to… because like it or not, those things were going *in*.

They pushed past the doors—which were still propped open—fell inside, recovered, and staggered on.

On the other side of the building, glass was breaking again

and there was some shrieking. Were they taking the back entrance too?

"What the hell?" I yelled, demanded. "What do you want? What are you doing?"

The rest of them were there too, even though the water was all but nonexistent. It made them slower, as I already knew; but maybe they'd been practicing while we weren't looking, because it didn't stop them. On creaking knees and with reaching hands they dragged themselves up away from the water pooling in the streets and on the sidewalk.

I counted six, no, eight. And there were more on their way. I saw them on the street, still coming and coming faster than those who'd climbed out of the river, because down the street they still moved in their element.

All of them were homing in on the Read House like it was calling them. I had no idea why; but I had an idea who to ask.

I turned on my heels and ran back to the front entrance, where the big green canopy was sagging with the weight of the rain and the glass doors were smeared with greasy black soot and skin. One of the things came close, within arm's reach. I ducked out of its way but it was quicker than it looked and it snared my sweater.

I kicked at it—threw my foot against its torso and hips because that was all I could reach. It hung on for dear death, and when I shoved my heel against it I heard the cracking of old bones.

One more kick, and by sheer force of inertia I fell free from it, taking a finger or two with me. I picked them off my sweater and threw them down onto the carpet, where they wiggled a redundant, round pattern like a rolling egg.

Two more, up from the other corridor. There they were. And another three through the front door. Jesus, how many of them were there? This was the most I'd ever seen at one time.

For a hysterical second or two I wondered what the proper word for a group of zombies would be—a cluster? A shamble?

Then I remembered they were quickly cornering me—not by speed but by numbers. Access to and from the Read House was limited to a few doors, and these were all being filled with jerking, smelly bodies.

Two sides blocked: coming and going. Still free: the main staircase, and one hallway, which led towards the place where the parking garage opened into the first floor. There were elevators there. I dashed forward and slapped at the up-arrow button. It lit up immediately, but there was no corresponding reassuring ping that indicated a car was waiting.

And just like that, I'd lost my third free corridor. Two more things—I thought maybe they liked to move in pairs—were coming in from the parking garage. If the elevator didn't open by the count of five, I'd have to double back and try to take the stairs.

One.

Over my shoulder, still no sign of the shuffling, struggling undead. I could hear them all around me now.

Two.

But they hadn't come into view, which meant the way to the stairs was still free. Not much longer, though.

Three.

The pair at the garage entrance thrashed forward.

Four.

Hands, one missing a couple of fingers, gripped the corner and used it to pull itself forward, bringing a badly burned and barely functioning body along with it. No point in waiting for the stroke of my fifth count.

Now or never. Elevator or stairs.

Judgment call time—elevator was an unknown quantity. Doors might open in a fraction of a second or in another three minutes. Three minutes was not an option. No elevator. I whirled the other way and doubled back, sliding on the slick marble floors still wet with the footprints of refugees.

Inches ahead of the zombie things, I skidded on squeaky-damp boots almost into the mirrored wall, but I caught myself and dropped palms-down onto the stairs.

The stairs were marble too, or some other shiny, polished stone. They were hard to climb on with wet feet, but if it was tough for me, it'd only be tougher for the things coming my way. Were they chasing me again, or had I simply tossed myself into their path?

Up, to Caroline—that's where I was headed. Were they, too? Was that where all of us were going?

I made double, maybe triple the time of my pursuers. If I hadn't been so tired, I could've really put some honest distance between us; but as it was, I was glad to stay even a few steps ahead of them.

I hit the mezzanine floor with a running start and charged towards Caroline's room. The hotel was deserted now, or it looked and sounded deserted except for the crawling things coming up, always coming up. And then there was me—panting like a horse who's run too long but is too afraid to stop.

"Caroline?" I called. "Caroline? Where are you, Caroline?"

She didn't answer, and I had a full hallway between me and the things now, which wrapped around the corner of the mezzanine, overlooking the main common area with its pretty plush couches and lovely brass fixtures that cast warm reflections on a room littered with the trash of hundreds of refugees.

There were more things coming inside, too—one had broken a window and was making its way into the common area to join its fellows.

That made—at my best count—maybe twelve to fourteen.

And more coming. I don't know how I knew it, but I knew it. Not many more—you don't need too many to create a horde. That must be the word for a group of zombies—a horde. How many would you need for that? Two's only a pair, so three or more, right? It might not be Romero-worthy, but I was willing to call a baker's dozen a horde. Again the hysterics were setting in, and I wanted to laugh, but I didn't, because it sounded too much like crying.

"Caroline?" I shouted again, coming to the corridor that housed her room—there on the end, on the right. It was locked.

I kicked at the door.

"Caroline? I know you're in there. Open up, goddammit!" And then the lock clicked, and the door swung open, just like I'd asked. I didn't believe for a moment she'd done it because I told her to, but I was in a bit of a jam at the moment, so I took the invitation and pushed the heavy door against its hydraulic hinge.

I leaned it shut behind me.

"Caroline, what's going on? Why are they coming here, and what do they want? You know, don't you? Where are you?"

She wasn't manifesting yet, but I was in a hurry. Things were coming up the stairs, lurching and tottering down the lovely halls of the old hotel, leaving stinking trails of black oil and sloughed skin.

"They're coming for you, aren't they? I can't think of any other good reason—and they aren't chasing me or the people.

They were coming here all along, weren't they? You tried to tell us, and we didn't know what to make of it. But they were coming for *you*."

Me.

"There you are, you crazy bitch. There you are—now talk, and make it good, because people are dying all over the place." But she probably didn't care about that. Better to turn it into something else; what did she need? What did she care about?

"The hotel," I told her. "They're going to take this hotel. They're going to destroy it and everything in it. When they're through with it, even if there's anything left, the people who own it will just tear it down. Is that what you want?"

No. No, they can't have it.

"The zombies? That's who you were talking about before, right? The ones who were coming for you, the ones you thought I brought. Well *I* didn't bring them. They knew you were here; they knew all along. I tried to keep them away but it didn't work— it isn't working." I talked fast because I could hear them again, through the thick door, though they weren't at the end of the hall yet, or I so I thought and hoped.

She knows.

There was an emphasis on that first word, and I knew exactly who she meant. There wasn't anyone else to move them. *She* was doing all of this. *She* was running the show.

"Why? Why is she coming for you—the little girl, the one who didn't die in the fire? What does she want from you?"

Same as you want. Why.

"Jesus, I do not understand this."

Caroline came into something like a solid image then, looking out the window through the gossamer layer of white curtains beneath the darker lining. She wasn't gazing at anything in particular that I could see, not peering down to the streets below where the dead things crept towards us, only avoidable and not at all stoppable.

It was a mistake. It was a lie.

"I don't understand," I said again.

My sister didn't really go to marry the newspaper man's son. I said it to be mean. I didn't know anyone would go there, to the church. I didn't know Julene was there.

"Julene?" Ah, a name for the small zombie queen. "She wasn't your sister, was she?"

No. Her mother worked in the laundry. Not "seemly." Should play with little white girls, but there weren't too many then, not here.

She sounded positively lucid, and it unnerved me more than when she behaved like a madwoman. "Let me get this straight— your sister, was she older than you?"

Caroline nodded, not turning away from the window. The way the light came in, watery and sick though it was, almost made her more rounded, more solid, when it hit her face. More real.

"And you were jealous, or angry, so you told someone that your sister was going to marry the newspaper man's son—at the church there? At the First Congregationalist...?" I let the title die in my mouth. I didn't need to say it, she knew it already. And the only thing we knew about the old newspaper was that it was owned by a black family.

Outside the door the dragging footsteps neared.

"You were lying, but someone took you seriously. And it was someone with connections to the Klan."

Everyone had connections to them back then. I shouldn't have said it. It was a mistake. Sister wasn't even there. She was on the riverboat with a boyfriend she kept secret. And all that time, I'd wished he was mine.

And I heard it, in a flash—I saw it, with a flicker. Caroline, flesh and blood and maybe twelve years old, all knobbed knees and folded arms. "She keeps it secret because she doesn't want Daddy to know. It would make him crazy to know. You know who it is? That newspaper man's boy. That's why she keeps it quiet. She's going to marry him in that church, you know the one."

Behind the girls, a door closed quiet, like someone was shutting it and not wanting to be seen—not wanting the people in the room to know that they'd been heard.

It was a mistake.

We were both repeating ourselves then. Both of us running out of things to say, but the dead things were still coming and our talk wasn't going to slow them down. So why was I bothering? From that flawed logic, I think—the kind that says, "If I understand how this works, I can fix it."

But the more I listened, the less confident I grew.

"What does she want, then, Caroline? Revenge? She can't very well kill you, if that's what she wants."

I thought, though, of that moment of contact Julene had made with me down by the ball park. It was so blind, her anger—her hatred. Driven like an infuriated child, and I imagined that when she reached this room, nothing she'd find would satisfy her. Just as a child will scream for a toy so long that when she receives it she doesn't want it anymore—that's what this would be like.

And I heard a scratching at the door.

Caroline backed away from the window to sit on the bed. The door would hold a minute more, I thought. I sat down beside her. "I guess you could apologize." It was a pitiful excuse for a suggestion, but she didn't mind it.

That won't work, will it?

"It's worth a try, don't you think? You don't want her to burn this place down around you, do you?" Or around any of the handful of people still here, either, I thought. She probably didn't give a damn who else joined her, but she probably wanted the hotel left standing.

Where would I go?

"I don't know," I shook my head. "I don't know what happens. The only dead people I ever see are the ones like you, who stuck around for some reason. Those who leave don't ever come back to talk about it; not that I know of, anyway."

I'm not ready.

The scratching had turned to banging, which turned to beating, and to the disgruntled squeals of hinges being strained to their breaking point. I looked at the window and thought of the ledge; I wondered if it'd be worth my trouble to try it.

I kept my voice steady by pure force of will. "Caroline, they're here."

I know.

The door burst open in a bent, awkward break where the wood gave out before the hinges and the deadbolt.

Julene came first.

She ducked her head beneath the battered door and entered the room deliberately, carefully, with one foot firm in front of the next. There was a thickly rusted chain on her right wrist, looped there but pried apart and left to hang. Her eyes were still that awful boiled yellow.

I rose from the bed and moved myself as close to the far wall as I could. I positioned myself beside the window and wondered what it would feel like to fall those stories to the ground. It was only a few. People survived worse all the time.

The other blank, wheezing dead things poured into the room after Julene, but they held back in accordance with her wishes. She was the only one who was still angry, and the only one who remembered.

Caroline? I knew it must be an echo of her real voice, but it sounded pure and weirdly sweet. Friendly, even. *Caroline, there you are. Still here, after all this time. I thought they sent you away.*

The ghost, still seated on the bed, did not answer. I responded on her behalf, since it wasn't like they didn't know I was there.

"She came back. She lived and died here. Now she stays here."

How did you die here, Caroline? It wasn't another fire, was it?

She shook her head, no.

How did you die here, Caroline? It wasn't a bloody murder, was it?

She shook her head again, no.

How did you die here, Caroline? Was it sickness or an accident?

You know it wasn't. I did it myself. She turned her arms wrist up, and I saw the long slashes that scarred her remembered skin. *It was a mistake, Julene.*

You should've followed me. You knew where we were. You knew where they put us. And you didn't even tell our families where to get us, so they could bury us right. Instead, some of us washed up on the other side and lay there in the mud.

It was a mistake.

"What do you want her to do?" I asked the small, furious girl with the chain clinking from her wrist. "What should she say to make up for it? She's dead, Julene. You can't kill her. You can't take anything away from her. Look what you've done—look at all these people you've hurt to get here."

It was a mistake, Caroline repeated. *I'm so sorry. I never did get to tell you that.*

"And after Caroline, then what? Then what will you do—where will you go? Will it end here, or will you walk out into the sun and let the police blow you to smithereens with a grenade launcher?"

I might as well not have been there. Neither of them looked at me or responded to me, and the horde at the back of the room was sagging as the girl's attention to them waned. It was possible that through those things was the easiest way out. So long as she ignored me. So long as they all ignored me.

But I couldn't leave yet—I needed to see. I needed to know.

Even again, after they found us where we washed up on the other side of the river, no one cared. They buried us again. They hid us again, and left us.

Caroline did not stand, but she turned on the bed so that she faced her childhood friend; while seated, she was at eye level with the girl. *I was selfish. I didn't want things to change. But they always do. Everything changes but us. How long will you be angry with me? What should I do?*

Julene looked confused, as I'd expected. There was no magic formula. Nothing for her to take, or give.

"You could go together," I blurted out. "You could leave together, to wherever it is that neither of you went back to. Your quarrel can't be resolved here, or now. You'll have to take it somewhere else. You have no ground to meet on here. You can only stare back and forth and toss your accusations and apologies around. For God's sake, you two. *Leave*. Leave together. And let them go, too." I gestured at the things waiting patiently by the door and beside the bed.

They're already gone, Julene told me. *I'm all that's left, and I move them. They are my dolls.*

"Then put them down. Put them down and go."

Now I had their undivided attention, and I didn't know what to do with it.

Where?

And I had no good answer for that, for them. But someone else did.

There was someone else in the room, someone new and not good at this yet—this manifesting thing, this trick by which the dead make themselves solid enough to see. But piece by piece he pulled himself together until he stood in front of the mirror, at the foot of the bed, facing us all.

He looked calm—calmer than I'd ever seen him or known him to be. He looked… smart. Wise, might be a better word. Collected, and determined—but he was always determined. That much carried over. That much, at least, went with him.

I've got them. Don't worry, little sister.

Strange. He'd never called me that before. Always by name, like he was afraid that acknowledging the relation would offend or embarrass me.

Come with me, he said to them both; and since neither of them knew what to make of it, or of him, they didn't move or answer.

A flicker of irritation crossed his face, and it looked familiar. It looked like something I do when I'm annoyed, but not ready to be too vocal about it yet. Jesus, what other ways were we alike?

"Malachi?" I don't know why I turned it into a question,

because of course it was him, and it wasn't until I said his name that I realized I was crying.

No worries—I'm not sticking around to bother you.

"That's not what I meant. You can stay. You can stick around and bother me, I don't mind." And even my disclaimer didn't come out like I meant it.

He grinned.

Pardon me, he said to the girls. *But I'm leaving and I think you should probably come with me. I'll take you where you need to go. Bye, Eden*, he added.

Then there was a light behind him so bright that the reflection in the mirror made my head hurt, and it blinded me to everything else in the room. Everything was eaten up by that sharp, brilliant beam of white—and there was silver around the edges, I thought. Silver and something else, something shining on the other side of the room-eating glow.

There was a noise, too—a buzzing, white noise so loud that it erased everything else and all that remained was quiet. And I was there, blinded and deafened by the light and the sound.

I put my hands over my eyes as if it mattered, and I slipped down the wall to sit with my head in my arms, my arms on my knees, and my feet sideways on the ground.

Nothing held me up anymore.

I closed my eyes and buried my face against my thighs; I drew my legs up close and squeezed them.

There was something like falling—a vibration like heavy things dropping, nearby. And pounding things like footsteps. But I didn't hear them, I only felt them beneath me, coming up from underneath.

Coming up from under the floor like everything else.

20

IN THE END

The Read House was quarantined; and though I tried to tell everyone it wasn't necessary, authorities are trying to round up and isolate everyone who was inside when the place was breached by the creeping dead.

I understand the concern. I've seen plenty of movies, too. But all this precaution isn't called for. None of us are tainted from being there; or if we are, it's only the upper-respiratory crud you might expect from people who've spent too many days being soaked to the bone.

When they found me in Caroline's room, I was unresponsive—but it wasn't because I was sick or injured. I fell asleep, right there. Eyes closed. Ears ringing and muffled from the unearthly noise. I was exhausted. And regardless of whatever the rest of the world thought, I knew I was safe.

If I'd had the good sense or strength to make it all the way to the bed, I don't think the paramedics would have been so worried. If I hadn't argued with them so hard, they might not have crammed me into the back of the ambulance on a board with the straps holding my head and neck straight.

If my phone hadn't been so thoroughly dead, I could have called Lu and Dave. Harry called them for me.

They made it to the hospital before I did. I'd been flown to Erlanger's branch over at the foot of Signal Mountain, mostly by coincidence, and partly because that's where they were triaging everybody brought in from the hotel.

I ended up on a gurney in a hallway crowded with other gurneys, and doctors and nurses and various hospital personnel in scrubs coming and going all around me. I was so tired that I slept there anyway. I slept until Lu and Dave were able to track me down and paw me awake.

It was good to see them.

They took me home and tried to put me to bed, but I smelled like hundred-year-old corpses, body odor, and clothes that had been marinated in the river—which was basically a broth of dead fish, rats, and birds. I wasn't climbing into bed like that, not when I'd scored a whole couple of hours of sleep at the hospital.

That was the best goddamn shower of my life.

I used up all the hot water in the house, and we've got a *huge* heater. I scrubbed like crazy, ruining two washcloths and mangling a perfectly good loofah in the process. Three rounds of shampoo took the worst of the trash and sweat out of my hair.

I wrapped it up in a towel, and wrapped the rest of myself up in a towel. I went back to bed and stayed there for I don't know how long. The damp towel wore a groove on my pillow and it didn't matter at all.

It was dark when I woke up. I hadn't closed my bedroom curtains, so I could see outside into the night on the mountain.

The mountain was dry except where the sky had dumped rain all over it. It could have been storming like a hurricane and I still would have thought of it as dry. No flooding here. Not so high as this.

I lay in bed and listened for rain but there wasn't any, for the first time in days. I heard the television though, tuned low in the living room. Sounded like local news. Was definitely local news—I'd know Nick's voice anywhere.

I couldn't make out what he was saying, but he was back at work, doing his thing. I hoped he'd taken a moment or two to sleep. He needed it as badly as I did.

I thought about kissing him and remembered that it was nice, and I was glad he was all right—but really, I'd never had any doubt. He was Nick, and somewhat invincible. I liked that about him. I liked that I didn't have to worry about him, and that—generally speaking—I could trust him to take care of himself. In a pinch, it turned out, he could take care of me, too.

I wasn't sure what to make of it. I'm not the sort of woman who typically needs a whole lot of rescuing.

I lifted myself up out of the bed and the towel came untied from my head. It stuck to the pillow, which had soaked up enough of the water from my hair to be clammy and cool. With the back of my hand I pushed it off the bed. I shook my head and my hair popped to life, not quite dry, but prepared to commence its regular tactics.

I didn't care. I let it fly.

I checked the alarm clock beside the bed. Blue LED lights told me it was 3:46 a.m., and I believed them, but I wondered what day they meant.

Without turning on the light, I found my bathrobe on the

floor in front of the closet. I shrugged it on for modesty's sake and felt around for the doorknob.

In the hall, the main overhead was switched off, but there was plenty of glow coming from the television and a side table lamp in the living room. Dave and Lu were both asleep there, sharing the couch and a fleece throw like a couple of kids having a sleepover. Out cold, the pair of them. Some other reporter was on the TV then, and I didn't recognize her. But it wasn't Nick so I wasn't interested.

I tiptoed to the kitchen and nearly blinded myself by opening the refrigerator, its illuminated interior like the flashlight of God in the semi-darkness.

I squinted against it and ran my palm around until I found a half gallon of milk, which I drank straight from the jug. Until I downed the milk, I'd thought I was hungry. No, just thirsty; or the milk had enough heft to stifle the hunger. I took the jug with me. I picked up the cordless kitchen phone's receiver and took it with me too, back into my bedroom. I shut the door and crawled into bed, retrieving a dry pillow and shoving it behind my back.

I still hadn't turned on the lamp. The green-glowing keypad was plenty to see by for dialing.

I hesitated, and took the moment to down another swallow of two percent.

I leaned my head back against the headboard and closed my eyes, letting the jug settle onto the covers beside my leg and letting the hand holding the phone drop to my lap.

I didn't quite dream, but I wasn't quite remembering.

It was weird, being pulled from the room where I'd last seen Malachi. It was strange, being wrestled onto the neck brace and seeing myself in the mirror at the foot of the bed. And on the floor, where the medics had covered her with a blanket or a sheet—something white—the gruesome body of Julene had finally settled too, down to the carpet in the rich old hotel. I knew it was her, like I knew the other stack—the pile of things also covered with hotel linens, blocking the doors except where they'd been pushed aside. I knew those remains too.

Wrong place, wrong time—like all the best victims. Unrelated to any conflict or quarrel, simply present at a place where the conflicts and quarrels came together. It may have been an evening service or a choir practice that brought them there on the night Caroline made her impulsive claim. It may have been a study group, or even someone else's wedding—no one knew or remembered now, and I didn't think anyone was left to tell me about it, even if I knew where to ask.

Most of them left when they died; they only came back because she made them—and even then, it was only their bodies she forced to walk. Whoever they were, they had found their peace years before she found hers.

But she did find hers, and it was partly thanks to Malachi, who had saved the day twice. My chest tightened thinking about it, and about him, and I wondered how much was left of him. Would it be enough to bury? Or, when the streets were eventually opened and excavated, would they find only a crushed pile of wet ash and bone?

I never gave him the credit he deserved. I should've answered the phone more. I should've invited him to supper sooner. I should've gone down to visit.

I should've.

I could play that game all night, but there was little point.

I set the milk jug on my nightstand, where condensation from its chill left a foggy little puddle beside my alarm clock. I lifted the phone again and started to dial Nick's number... then stopped.

My thumb pressed the button to disconnect before the call went through.

Again I started to dial, not Nick but Harry. But I stopped. I could tell him where he could find Malachi later. I could ask him later, if he'd make some kind of arrangements for him. Maybe Eliza should get her way after all. I had no idea what my brother's last wishes might have been, but at least one person wanted him to come home, and it was a wish I could conceivably honor.

And where else could I take him? What else could I do but send him home?

What the hell. Heaven was watching, and the rest, well... call it water under the bridge. I didn't have the energy to float all that hatred anymore.

I hit the lime-colored button again and let the line die. There was no rush. God only knew when the authorities would get around to finding the rest of the bodies.

Through the door and down the hall the television was still rattling off local news, twenty-four hours a day—which, given the circumstances, wasn't so surprising. It was still that female anchor I didn't recognize, she was the one doing all the talking.

3:52 said the clock. A funny hour—either very late or very early, depending.

I wondered what time it was in North Carolina, and then I realized what a stupid thought that was, since we were both on Eastern Time. I dialed ten digits from memory and let the phone ring and ring and ring.

"This had better be important," the answerer slurred and growled.

"No caller ID? Or do I get special dispensation for shit like this?"

"Eden?"

"Hey, Dana."

She dropped the phone, or maybe adjusted it. I heard her shifting her body in bed, maybe sitting up or rolling over. "Holy shit, yeah. I called. I guess they gave you the message? Fuck the hour. Glad to hear from you."

"I haven't checked my messages, exactly. It's been a busy couple of days. But I'm here now, home. I'm back at Signal Mountain. But I wanted to call you. I think I need to talk to you."

"You okay? And I ask that from a relative standpoint, you know."

I smiled into the phone. She understood best; she always did. Better than Harry, even. "From a relative standpoint, I'm okay but not quite fine. I'm sorry, I know it's late. But there was no one else whose voice I really wanted to hear. It's been bad."

"I hear. What I hear, though—that wasn't a fraction of it, was it?"

"It'll take some time to tell. It might not all fit into a phone call."

"I understand," she said, because she did. "Maybe it's time for you to take a road trip. A little vacation."

"I might need more than a vacation," I confessed. "Things are different here now."

"Naw. You're just seeing things differently now."

"Whichever. Whatever. Same end result."

"Eden, sweetheart. Give yourself a few days to rest up, then come out here. Road trip. Vacation."

"No, I don't need a vacation. I actually feel pretty good for the first time in days. Something has been wrong for a while; you know that better than anyone. Ever since Avery died I've felt so much stronger, but every time I've used that strength it's taxed me. And now Malachi's dead, too, and I don't know how these curse things work—but maybe things will be better now, or different. And even if things get worse, I'm not going to learn how to fix them by staying here."

"But you've made plans there in Tennessee. What about school? What about getting your own place?"

"The place I planned to claim is underwater, and it will probably be condemned once it dries out. The school, hell. Half of that probably went underwater too. Everything's broken and shut down. If I stay, I'll just stay broken and shut down with it."

She breathed quietly for a few seconds before she responded. "It's going to take time to recover. It takes people time, and it'll take Chattanooga time. You could always make *that* your new direction, if you think you need a change in plans. You could stick around and become part of the recovery effort. It'll never get better if people don't work towards making it better. Even after what happened in New Orleans, the city's still alive, and it's coming back a little more every day."

"Ah," I smiled, but there wasn't any joy in it, "but this isn't New Orleans, and people here—they don't love this place, not the way natives of New Orleans love their home. Here, if people get out of town and find success, they keep their mouths shut about it. They don't tell anyone, and if they come home, they keep it short and sweet. There's a jinx on the place; there's this current that sucks everything down if you wade here long enough. This isn't New Orleans. No one wants to be from here. No one ever loves this place except for out-of-towners who move here, settle down, and mistake it for something it isn't."

A pause hung between us. "That's a little harsh," Dana finally said.

"No. I'm just tired of romanticizing the place. I never hated this town enough to want to destroy it; but it turns out I don't love it enough to try and save it, either." I stopped talking and snuggled back against the pillow, trying to think of something else to say. "Why do you think Benny left? Talk to him, if you think I'm overreacting. He's a prime example of what I mean. The moment you gave him a lifeline out of the valley, he hopped all over it. How's he doing, anyway? Is he okay?"

"He's good. He's living with one of the crew members here, another guy about his age. They've got a place together downtown. He'd probably love to see you, though. Friendly old faces. I don't work him that hard, don't worry. The station's commissioning a new miniseries on haunted places—we're doing haunted schools, hotels, and lighthouses to start."

"Lighthouses?"

"It happens more often than you'd think. If the ratings are good, I'm going to see about pitching ships and amusement parks next. People eat it up. But we're going to be busy—rich and busy. Can always use a few new hands up here, especially hands like yours, if you finally take me up on my offer. When can I expect you?" she asked, and then, before I had time to answer, "How long can I expect you to stay?"

I wasn't sure what to say, so I breathed into the receiver for a few seconds while I thought about it. I was about to start crying again, but I kicked it back long enough to respond… held it down long enough to answer her, and to convince myself that I meant it.

"How long will you have me?"

AUTHOR'S NOTE

This is a work of fiction, which probably dawned on you at some point before you met the homicidal zombies. Still, it's worth pointing out. You see, this book was sold and proposed before Hurricane Katrina ever happened—though much of it was written in that disaster's wake. It would be ridiculous for me to pretend that this is not a novel about a flood that overwhelms a southern city; and it would furthermore be ridiculous for the characters herein to pretend that their situation does not call to mind the hurricane and its aftermath.

So I gave a great deal of consideration to how I ought to approach this story, since the comparisons would be obvious and immediate. But let me be clear: *this* fictional story is not about *that* real-life story.

Chattanooga, Tennessee, and New Orleans, Louisiana, are two very different cities, having little in common except for a location south of the Mason-Dixon line. They have different landscapes, different people, different neighborhoods, different climates, different socio-economic problems, different tourist attractions, different perks, and different drawbacks. The residents of New Orleans do not see their hometown the same way residents of Chattanooga see theirs, and if the Tennessee River were to flood, most of the water would flood the tourist and business districts— not residential districts. An entirely different population would be affected.

These cities are about 500 miles apart.

I have fond memories of them both, but I would not be so arrogant as to equate the two, much less equate this novel's conflict with the events of August 2005.

So this is a book about ghosts, zombies, and a supernatural swelling of the Tennessee River that incapacitates the downtown Chattanooga, Tennessee, area. It's a scientifically inappropriate book in many respects: my imagined flooding does not necessarily follow a geologically likely course, my understanding of the TVA dam system is limited and, let's be honest—my zombies are improbable.

This having been established, in the interest of full disclosure, my citywide timeline is a little screwy. There has been a Starbucks on the first floor of the Read House for several years, the Clark's furniture building is well on its way to being converted to condos (or whatever), and there are a few other local glitches in continuity. You can write this, and probably a few other inconsistencies, off to the fact that I moved away from Chattanooga in March of 2006. The city has changed behind me, and I found it more convenient from a narrative standpoint to put my fingers in my ears and pretend I didn't know better.

I beg your indulgence in this matter.

However, a series of vintage KKK murals really *were* found in the old Clark's building, there really *is* a haunted room in the Read House (or so I am often assured), the Spanish Flu really *did* ravage the city in 1919, and the First Congregationalist Church really *was* one of the first of its kind in the area—openly welcoming both black and white members. I try to draw inspiration from real life when I can.

But at any rate, thanks so much for reading. It's been a privilege and a delight.

ACKNOWLEDGMENTS

Books never reach readers by one writer's hand alone—oh no. This one in particular would have never happened without the faith and guidance of my editor Liz Gorinsky, who deserves so much better than the drafts to which she is routinely subjected (by me). Likewise I must give thanks to my publicist Dot Lin, who arranges all the cool traveling and signing stuff; to my sister Becky Priest, who's always good for a surprise round of helpful proofreading; to John Scalzi, Bill Schafer, Jason Sizemore, and Jennifer Brozek, who are entirely too kind to me both online and in print; to Greg Wild-Smith, for keeping his cool every single time I've run to him saying, "GRAY-YUG, my Web page is doing something funny!"; and to Ian Goodman at Greyfriar's, for being so gracious about the fictional use of his real-life coffeehouse. And, of course, thanks to my husband, Aric—because with his support I was able to skip the nine-to-five grind for a few months while this book was being written. One of these days, I'll make it up to him.